PRINCE in Disguise

PRINCE in Disguise

STEPHANIE KATE STROHM

HYPERION
Los Angeles   New York

Copyright © 2017 by Stephanie Kate Strohm

All rights reserved. Published by Hyperion, an imprint of Disney Book Group. No part of this book may be reproduced or transmitted in any form or by any means, electronic or mechanical, including photocopying, recording, or by any information storage and retrieval system, without written permission from the publisher. For information address Hyperion, 125 West End Avenue, New York, New York 10023.

First Hardcover Edition, December 2017
First Paperback Edition, October 2018
10 9 8 7 6 5 4 3 2 1
FAC-025438-18250
Printed in the United States of America

This book is set in Bembo MT Pro, Avenir LT Pro/Monotype; Mrs. Eaves, Bjarne Handwriting/Fontspring
Designed by Marci Senders
Title lettering © 2018 by Andrew Brozyna

Library of Congress Control Number for Hardcover Edition: 2016042902
ISBN 978-1-4847-7567-7

Visit www.hyperionteens.com

SUSTAINABLE FORESTRY INITIATIVE
Certified Chain of Custody
Promoting Sustainable Forestry
www.sfiprogram.org
SFI-01054
The SFI label applies to the text stock

FOR MY SISTER

CHAPTER ONE

Tears coursed down my face as I tried to fight through the pain. There was no escape. I had gotten myself into this mess, and I could see no way out but through.

"You've only got sixty seconds, Dylan! And you've used up thirty of them crying."

My best friend, Heaven, kept her eyes glued to one of her dad's eight thousand stopwatches—perks of being a PE teacher's daughter, I guess—as I shoved the sixth and final cracker in my mouth. Who knew that the saltine, a cracker so innocuously bland it was only eaten by people with stomach viruses, could be transformed into a weapon of mass destruction?

"All the crumbs *must* be eaten, Dyl! *Wikipedia* was *very* clear on that count."

"Do you see any crumbs?" At least, I *thought* I said, "Do you see any crumbs?" But I could tell from Heaven's face that I said something that sounded a lot more like "Ooee sshmaprhh oompums?"

"Ten seconds, Dyl. And you've got to swallow it."

"I caaaaan't," I moaned through the most horrifically salty mouthful I'd ever encountered. I couldn't do it.

"Don't you dare touch that Snapple."

My hand had gravitated unconsciously toward the deliciously cold, fruity refreshment perched temptingly on the coffee table. I whimpered.

"Time, Dylan, that's time!" Heaven shook her head sadly. "I expected more from Little Miss Cast Iron Stomach. What happened to the Dylan Janis Leigh who got her picture on the wall at Pig in a Poke after she finished the Belly Buster in an almost record-breaking twenty-two minutes and forty-three seconds? Where's that girl?"

My Pig in a Poke glory days were behind me. I had officially failed the Saltine Challenge, but at this point, all I cared about was getting those saltines out of my mouth. I looked around for someplace to spit.

"Yoo-hoo!" Heaven and I turned as we heard the front door slam. "Mama? Dylan? Y'all home?"

My big sister, Dusty, sashayed into the room with the confidence of someone who'd been spray-tanned since birth. I'd hoped once her yearlong reign as Miss Mississippi ended she'd be less pageant prissy, but apparently she was branded a beauty queen for life. Thank God Dusty hadn't been crowned Miss America. I couldn't even begin to imagine how insufferable she'd be if she'd actually won the whole thing.

I froze. Dusty wasn't alone. She was being trailed by a cameraman, a guy holding a big fuzzy microphone, and a lady with a clipboard. That was one big camera. I felt like it was staring at me with its giant, eyelike lens.

"Whoa, Dylan," Heaven said quietly, tapping the back of my hand. "You okay? You just went super white. Like, whiter than usual."

"Dylan, what in the world is in your mouth?" Dusty had a special talent for making me feel like an idiot. Granted, at this exact moment in time I was being an idiot, but I swear, I could have been sitting in here doing my calc homework, and she still probably would have waltzed in and said, "Dylan, what in the world are you doing?"

"Saltines," I mumbled, transfixed by the camera's evil eye. Why wouldn't it stop staring at me? Was it on? Was it recording me right that instant? *Oh God.*

"The cameras will be gone soon, Dyl," Heaven whispered as she squeezed my hand. "You just have to deal with them a little bit longer."

I needed the cameras to be gone yesterday. Being sixteen was excruciating enough on its own without having to worry about avoiding cameramen who could preserve every awkward moment. Granted, they weren't there to film *me*, but they'd been dangerously close to getting my elbow in a shot one too many times. One of the many hazards of being six feet tall was limbs that seemed to go everywhere. And an inability to fade into the background. I envied five-foot-nothing Heaven her ability to hide, although my best friend, of course, was born to stand out. If Heaven were tall like me, I bet she would have been one of those girls who wore six-inch heels anyway and didn't mind people staring.

"Honestly, Dylan, I can't understand a thing you're saying," Dusty said with extreme exaggeration. Ever since *Prince in Disguise* and the Reality Channel had become a part of our lives, everything Dusty did, as long as the cameras were in the room, was with extreme exaggeration. "Unless you are regurgitatin' a meal to feed some baby birds, I would appreciate it if you swallowed. Now."

"She can't," Heaven supplied helpfully. "That's the whole problem. She failed the Saltine Challenge."

"Good Lord. Don't you two have anything better to do with your time?" Dusty popped the lid off her enormous fountain soda—she rarely functioned without a liter or two of Diet Coke coursing through her bloodstream—and held it expectantly in front of my face. I was torn, because I desperately wanted the saltines gone. But I also knew that if I spat out those saltines, there was a 100 percent chance that some choice footage of what would definitely look like me vomiting into an empty soda cup would end up edited into the *Prince in Disguise* finale. I had been so careful all summer long to be gone when the cameras were around, or, if Mom forced me to be in the room, to be boring. To not do anything that would ever, ever make the final cut and air on TV. But somehow, regurgitating saltines into Dusty's cup seemed like the lesser of two evils. I spat out all the cracker mush and feverishly gulped my Snapple.

"Dilly, where's Mama?" Dusty asked once I'd set the nearly empty bottle back down on the coffee table.

Every "Dilly" Dusty had ever uttered was like nails on a chalkboard. Which she was fully aware of, and exactly why she persisted in calling me Dilly.

"She's getting her teeth bleached," I muttered, looking at the carpet instead of the camera. Mom's endless pursuit of pearly whites was one of the side effects of being a cohost on *Good Morning, Mississippi!*

"Well, that's all right; I really came to talk to *you*, anyway." Dusty flashed her own recently bleached set of chompers. The two of them had probably single-handedly financed our dentist's boat. Dusty is practically Mom's clone. They're both blond former pageant queens who people describe as "leggy" instead of "gangly," which is usually what people call me. Before Dusty turned Princess Bride, she had even been planning on using her communications degree to follow Mom into a career in broadcast journalism. See? Total clones. And then there's me—even taller, not nearly as blond, and totally unsuited for a tiara. In every way possible.

"Why do you have to talk to *me*?" I mumbled through gritted teeth. "I mean, why are you here with . . . them?" I inclined my head vaguely in the direction of the camera.

"Oh, ignore them." Dusty waved her hands dismissively at the camera crew, silver Tiffany bracelets jangling on her long tan arms. "Just pretend they're not even here."

Right. Like that was possible.

"This isn't a good time," Heaven piped up bravely. "Dylan and I are very busy. She's helping me with a, uh, a science project."

It was a valiant attempt, but I knew Dusty well enough to know that nothing could deter her. She was just like all those stupid T-shirts she wore to the gym that said dumb things like "Southern girls are diamonds and buckshot!" or whatever. She looked pretty on the outside, but underneath, she was tough as the beef jerky they sold at the gas station.

I shot Heaven a grateful look and mouthed "Save yourself" as Dusty's manicured talons closed around my wrists.

"Come here, baby sister." Dusty hauled me onto the couch, where I landed with a fairly undignified thump.

"Is it on?" I whispered as Dusty sat down next to me, smoothing her skirt.

"Is what— Of course the camera's on, that's why it's *here*, dummy. Dylan, just *ignore* it!" A cloud of annoyance passed across Dusty's perma-grin. "Look at me. Me!" She snapped her fingers in my face, like I was a dog she was trying to train or something. I tore my gaze away from the carpet. Out of the corner of my eye, I caught Heaven snapping her own fingers, lips smushed into a duckface I recognized instantly as her "annoyed Dusty" impression. I stifled a giggle.

"That's better." Dusty sighed contentedly. "Now, just keep your focus right on over here." She waved her French manicure around her eyes. "Listen, Dilly—"

"Don't call me that," I muttered.

"Sorry," she huffed. "Dylan."

"Thank you." I was surprised she listened. But she probably still wanted everyone at the Reality Channel to see her as the world's greatest human-slash-sister.

"Listen, Dylan," she started again, suddenly all smiles, like the last fifteen seconds hadn't happened. Was it possible that reality TV was turning my sister into even more of a pageant-bot than she already was?

"I'm sorry, can we get the other one out of the shot?" the clipboard lady interrupted.

"The other one? Well, excuuuse me," Heaven said. "Dylan, I'll be in the kitchen if you need me. I believe there are some

Cheetos in there who would appreciate my presence." She stalked off.

"Heaven—" I protested meekly.

"Not staying where I'm not wanted!" she called as the kitchen door swung shut behind her. It was a dramatic exit, worthy of one of Tupelo High Show Choir's finest.

Now I was really on my own.

"All right, go ahead, Dusty."

"Dylan." Dusty smiled again, as if my best friend hadn't just been forcibly ejected from the living room. "You've been by my side my whole life. As my sister, as my friend, every step of the way."

I stared at her blankly. Why did she sound so scripted? I felt like I'd landed onstage in a play but didn't know any of the lines.

"Stop. Jiggling."

"Huh—what?"

"Your knee." She tapped it briskly. "Stop jiggling your damn knee. That won't read well."

I reddened and concentrated on gluing my knees together and sticking my socks to the floor. I never realized I was bouncing my knee up and down; it just kind of happened on its own. Despite Mom's best efforts to drill it out of me.

"You were there as I started to fall in love with Ronan. And now it's time for Ronan and me to start the journey of our lives together, as husband and wife. And it's time for me to begin that journey with a countdown to the crown."

"You're not getting a crown," I interrupted. "Ronan isn't a prince. He's a lord. You know you're not actually going to be a princess, right? Just a lady. Or is it the Right Honorable Dusty?"

"She's worse than I thought," the woman with the clipboard

muttered. "Dusty, keep going, honey," she added, louder. "We'll edit this all later."

"Sweet Lord Jesus in heaven, Dylan, are you trying to kill me?" Dusty hissed between clenched teeth. "Can you just go with this? For once? Try *not* to make my life more difficult?"

"I'm not trying to be difficult," I hissed back. "I just hate cameras. Which is why I told you clearly, explicitly, way back in the beginning, that I wanted no part in this."

"Believe me, I am well aware." Dusty grimaced. "You think I wanted you in this? Didn't I do my damn best to keep you out of all of *Prince in Disguise*? Trust me, Dylan, this has nothing to do with me, and everything to do with the network. I tried to warn them about what you were like."

About *what I was like*? What did that even mean? I didn't want to be part of the stupid show anyway, but I couldn't believe Dusty had wanted to keep me out so badly. It still stung, even though rationally I knew that didn't make any sense.

"Dusty, let's get going here," the clipboard lady called out.

"Absolutely, Pamela!" Dusty trilled. "Just havin' a little heart-to-heart with my baby sister."

"A sister is a special friend!" I trilled, imitating Dusty's saccharine tone. She elbowed me in the side.

"Ow!" I yelped.

"Don't make fun of me!"

"Keep your bony elbows to yourself!"

"Girls!" Pamela barked. Both of us sat up straight. "I'll cut right to the chase. As you know, *Prince in Disguise* has been a huge hit for the network."

Prince in Disguise. What a stupid idea for a show. A "prince"— who isn't a prince at all, just a lord, even though no one will listen to me no matter how many times I bring that up—comes to America and pretends to be *not* royal in order to find a good ol'-fashioned bride who loves him for what's on the inside. Foolproof. Especially because reality TV has the *best* track record for matchmaking. There's been, what, *one* successful *Bachelor* marriage in approximately four hundred seasons?

And unluckily for me, TRC sent Ronan Dougal Murray, Lord Dunleavy, to Tupelo, Mississippi, where he got one look at my sister making a very special Miss Mississippi appearance at Tupelo's All-America City Family Picnic in the Park, and promptly fell head over heels in love. Or whatever passes for love on reality TV. I had nothing against Ronan, per se—he'd always been perfectly nice—but I was skeptical. How could you fall in love with someone you'd only dated in front of cameras for a matter of weeks? It was insane.

"We couldn't be happier about how the series wrapped." Pamela smiled at Dusty in a way that conveyed very little actual human happiness.

Of course they were happy. On what was supposed to be the last day of filming *Prince in Disguise*, when I thought we were done with the Reality Channel forever, Ronan revealed he was secretly a lord, and then he dropped to one knee and proposed to my sister. See? Ronan seemed nice, but he was probably insane. You don't *marry* someone you just met. Did they not have *Frozen* in Scotland?

"To capitalize on *Prince in Disguise*'s success, TRC will be filming *Happily Ever After with Dusty and Ronan: A Scottish Royal Wedding*."

"My big sis, the tall blond Kardashian," I muttered. Dusty

glared at me. Probably because I'd just shared her secret life goal out loud.

"But Dusty and Ronan have proven so popular that we'd like to be able to share more than just their special day with their fans."

"You have fans?" I asked archly. Dusty ignored me. I knew she had fans. I just preferred to pretend that these fans didn't exist, that there were no Dusty and Ronan message boards or *Us Weekly*s with my sister's face splashed across the cover. It was too weird to think about total strangers somehow being invested in my sister's wedding. In her *life*. Way too weird.

"Which is why," Pamela continued, like I hadn't said anything, "we will also be filming *Countdown to the Crown*, showing the weeks of planning and prep we'll need leading up to the wedding. It will all be filmed at Ronan's family estate in the Highlands."

Countdown to the Crown. Seriously? No wonder Dusty thought she was getting a tiara. The entire network was in on this delusion.

"Sounds delightful. Thanks for the info. I'll be sure to circle it in my *TV Guide*. Have fun in Scotland, Dusty!" I brimmed with false cheer. "Why are you telling me this?"

"Because, Dylan, although you aren't exactly what we . . . expected"—Pamela looked at me like I was a flaming bag of poo on her doorstep—"the whole royal-wedding-sisters concept has tested very, very positively with our focus groups. Blame the Middletons. People want to see Dusty with her sister by her side. They want American Middletons. So even though . . . Well, the benefits outweigh the risks. That's what editing's for, right?"

"Benefits of what?" I asked suspiciously.

"You coming to Scotland with me," Dusty said bluntly. "For the show. Filmin' the whole *Countdown to the Crown*. Mama's coming, too, obviously."

"No," I gasped. "What? No. I will not be on the show. I cannot be a part of any *Countdown to the Crown*. Dusty, you know I hate cameras!" I pleaded. "This isn't what we talked about. I thought they were just filming the wedding. You said people just wanted to see you and Ronan and some impressive tablescapes. And you promised that there would only be blurry background shots of me bridesmaiding!"

I knew I sounded like an ungrateful troll who didn't want to be part of her big sister's wedding, but being a featured member of some random royal spin-off sounded like actual hell on earth. Of course I wanted to be at Dusty's wedding—I just didn't want anyone looking at me while I was there. And I certainly didn't want anyone *filming* me.

"Things change," Dusty said coolly.

"I am not reality TV material," I insisted. And I certainly wasn't any kind of American Middleton.

"No kidding."

"I can't do this. What about school? School's important," I babbled. "I can't miss that much school."

"We're on a pretty tight timeline here—*Countdown to the Crown*, wedding included, will wrap in three weeks. And we'll primarily be filming during your Christmas break, so you won't miss that much school."

Great. Not only was Dusty ruining Christmas—seriously, who else besides my insane sister would be selfish enough to have a Christmas Eve wedding?—but now she was also stealing my whole vacation. I could kiss my grand plans of sleeping until noon and spending all day watching TV in my pajamas good-bye.

"Plus, Scotland will be a real once-in-a-lifetime learning opportunity! You'll experience a new culture. See Europe!" Pamela continued, displaying more enthusiasm than I'd seen so far.

"Mama already signed off, Dylan. It's happening. She's not leaving a sixteen-year-old alone for almost a month. You're coming to Scotland."

"But—I—I—"

It's not like I had anything against going to Scotland. Of course not. I would have loved to go to Scotland. In a situation that in no way, shape, or form involved filming a television show.

"The network needs you, Dylan," Pamela said. Then she added, as an afterthought, "So does your sister."

"Get on board, little sis. Because you're coming if I have to handcuff you to the airplane seat."

I blanched. For all her sunny Southern-belle charm, Dusty was not above using brute force. She fought dirty. Like *biting* dirty. Oh God. I was trapped, wasn't I? Totally, completely trapped. Suddenly, I didn't feel so good.

"All right. The sister's on board. Just give us one for the cameras, Dusty," Pamela instructed.

"Dylan." Dusty clasped my hands in hers. Were those actual *tears* shining in her eyes? She took a deep breath. "Will you be the Pippa to my Kate?"

And it was a real good thing I hadn't swallowed those saltines, because otherwise, they would have come right back up.

CHAPTER TWO

Whoever thought Scotland in December would be romantic was probably deranged. Actually, considering that Dusty, clipboard Pamela, and whatever depraved minds ran TRC had cooked this spectacle up, they were *definitely* deranged.

I stamped my sneakers against the gravel of the parking lot, trying to get feeling back in my toes. I should have been enjoying my last few moments of precious freedom from the cameras, but I couldn't focus on anything besides the fact that I was slowly freezing to death. Well, not that slowly. Hugging my arms tighter around myself, I watched my breath puff white clouds in the crisp air. Forty minutes. It had been forty minutes.

I pulled the TRC travel itinerary out of my jeans pocket and unfolded it, checking one more time. Yup, there it was, in Times New Roman black and white—*Kit Kirby, groomsman, will pick Dylan up at the Dunkeld & Birnam train station.* Here

I was. At Dunkeld & Birnam. At the train station. And no Kit Kirby.

When I'd convinced Mom that she and Dusty should leave a few days before me so I could take my Spanish test, I thought I'd won the lottery. I mean, two extra days free from TRC? I'd take it. But now, I wasn't so sure. I was pretty confident that TRC wouldn't have left *Dusty* stranded at the Dunkeld & Birnam train station. Actually, "station" was a generous term. It was a platform in the middle of the woods. There was no actual station building I could wait inside to shelter myself against the elements—just a cement platform plonked down beside two solitary-looking train tracks in a copse of leafless trees, their barren brown branches scratching at the leaden sky.

"Shouldn't there be snow?" I muttered, more to watch my breath continue puffing white than for any other reason. I wasn't usually in the habit of talking to myself, but, well, it had been forty minutes. I was not the type of person who did well left alone with her thoughts.

"Not this year," a male voice cheerfully responded. "Not yet, at any rate."

"What the—" I whirled around, nearly toppling over my suitcase. How long had this apparition in a charcoal peacoat been standing behind me?

"No snow yet this year. It's a bit brown, wouldn't you say?" the apparition continued as I tried to regain my balance, spreading my arms out wide for leverage. "It'll look much better once the snow comes in. Less bleak. At the moment it's downright Brontë-esque. Brontë-ian?" He furrowed his brow, deciding. "Neither sounds right. Either way, it's bloody *Wuthering Heights: Even Farther North* up here."

"You scared me!"

"Sorry about that." His continued cheeriness was proving extremely annoying. "I thought you knew I was there, considering you were talking to me."

"I wasn't— I mean I was— I mean— Are you Kit Kirby?"

"No." He shook his head, then adjusted the striped scarf around his neck. "Sorry. Should I be?"

"Yes," I snapped. "And you should have been Kit Kirby an hour ago."

"Right. Terribly sorry about that." An amused smile tugged at the corners of his mouth. "Haven't quite mastered the art of identity theft as of yet. Or transfiguration. Sadly, never got my Hogwarts letter."

I frowned at him. Not even a Harry Potter ref could distract me from my frigid state, and my annoyance with the boy who was most assuredly *not* Kit Kirby. Not-Kit-Kirby was tall, taller than me even, with hair so dark it was almost black and surprisingly light blue eyes. He was so pale that if I was the kind of girl who thought vampires were hot, I might have found him attractive, but I'm not. So I didn't.

"I've been waiting here for almost an hour." I hopped back and forth, trying to keep my legs from going numb. That was sort of out of nowhere, yes, but I had a vested interest in turning this conversation toward how I could get inside.

"That's dreadful. Why didn't you ring someone?" His brow crinkled in confusion.

"My cell phone doesn't work over here."

"There's a pay phone, actually," he said kindly, as though he were explaining something to a small, confused child. I jerked my thumb at the handwritten Out of Order sign. "Ah. Right."

He nodded swiftly. "You were waiting for Kit Kirby, you say?"

"Mmm-hmm," I murmured, hugging myself again.

"Here for Ronan's wedding, then, are you?"

"Yeah." I was slightly taken aback. How did he know? "Are you Kit Kirby's replacement? Or does the whole country know about this spectacle?"

"A bit of both, really," he said. "Seems like all of Perth has been turned upside down."

"Tell me about it." I didn't know what Perth was, but I sure felt like everything had been turned upside down since TRC came into our lives.

"Although I have to admit, I didn't come specifically to fetch you. I was just taking a shortcut through the station when you addressed me. This is a bit of a happy coincidence."

"Lucky me," I muttered. "Assuming you're not a murderer, and since you seem to know who Ronan is, do you mind giving me a ride to his estate? Where's your car?"

"Not a murderer. Although, look at Raskolnikov. We don't really know what we're capable of, do we?"

"Car?" I repeated. What a weirdo. Now was not the time for Russian literature. Although honestly, was it *ever* the time for five hundred pages of suffering? One slog through *Crime and Punishment* had been more than enough for me.

"What car?"

"Your. Car," I enunciated clearly through clenched teeth. He seemed a bit on his own planet, one where he was hanging out with wizards and Russian ax murderers.

"Oh, I haven't got a car." He stuck his hands in his pocket and smiled. "I've got a fantastic bicycle, though. Left her at home, sadly."

"Her?"

"Mrs. Manson Mingott. She's a real lady."

"Oh-kay," I sighed. "You have no car. How are we—or how am I, at least—getting to the estate?"

"Oh, that's terribly far from here." He shook his head sadly.

"Of course it is," I muttered. "Can you at least point me in the direction of somewhere warm?"

"I'll do you one better." He reached toward me, and I stepped back to avoid contact as his fingers closed around the handle on my suitcase. "I'll take you there myself."

"In what? Your nonexistent car? The handlebars of your invisible Mrs. Maggleby Marjorine bike?"

"Mrs. Manson Mingott," he corrected me. "It's not a far walk. Not to somewhere warm, at any rate. Town's just down the hill there." He started rolling my suitcase through the gravel and out of the train station's parking lot. "You Americans." He chuckled. "Always driving everywhere."

"That's more of an LA thing, actually." I bristled. Not that I actually knew that, never having been to LA. But I read stuff. "We walk plenty in Mississippi."

"Mississippi? You're a friend of Dusty's, then?"

"I'm her sister."

"You *are*?" He whipped around to face me, mouth hanging open.

"Don't look *so* shocked. It's not completely impossible."

"No—no—of course not," he sputtered. "I didn't mean anything by it. You're just very . . ."

"Different," I supplied. "I know."

"Different is good," he said simply, and in spite of myself, I was weirdly pleased by it. Dusty tended to bring out the defensive side of me—it was hard being the little sister of the most beautiful girl in Tupelo, not to mention that she had been my high school's head cheerleader, class president, prom queen, and yearbook editor. Someday, I wanted to live in a place where I never heard "*You're* Dusty's sister?" ever again.

We turned out of the parking lot and onto the road, where the cobblestoned sidewalk was so narrow we had to walk single file, affording me a view of the back of his head and not much else. His dark hair was so close to black it glinted almost blue in the afternoon light. "I was mostly surprised because you sound nothing like Dusty. Are you sure you're related?"

"Pretty sure. Or I'm in for a very surprising revelation on this season of *Prince in Disguise.*"

He smiled. "Why don't you have an American accent?"

"I do. I just don't have a Southern accent."

"Well, why not?"

"I squelched it. Like a bug. Which, I see, with regards to your own accent, you have made no such effort to do."

"Why on earth would I want to?"

"You're practically unintelligible."

At that, he laughed out loud. Which was nice, I guess, since I was being kind of unfairly grumpy. It wasn't *his* fault that I'd been stuck outside for so long. I should have been grateful that he was taking me to town, and, presumably, somewhere warm.

"My English master at Eton would be very displeased to hear that."

I grunted in response, since I wasn't sure what Eton was. A school? Probably.

"What's your name, Dusty's mysterious sister?"

"Dylan."

"Dylan," he mused, like he was turning it over in his mouth. "That's a boy's name, isn't it?"

"*You're* a boy's name."

"Sorry?"

"Nothing," I mumbled.

"I didn't mean to offend you." He turned to face me, and his eyes were so blue they were really disconcerting. "Dylan is a terrific name. An absolutely top-notch poet. Oof, except for that horrid *Child's Christmas in Wales*. Can't stand it. Absolutely appalling. But aside from that, he's really not bad. You should be honored, truly."

"Oh. Thank you." No one had ever reacted to my name quite like that before. And I didn't have the heart to tell him that I was pretty sure I was named after Bob Dylan, not Dylan Thomas.

"They grow them big in the States, don't they?"

"Excuse me?"

"You and Dusty. And your mum. You're the tallest girls I've ever seen."

"Oh. Yeah. We're pretty tall."

I never knew what to say to that. I mean . . . I *knew* I was tall. It wasn't a surprise.

"It's a nice change of pace, to look a girl straight in the eyes. The women in my life seem to be positively Lilliputian. Real hobbits, all of them."

I couldn't get a read on this guy. Maybe it was some kind of British/American cultural divide. Historically, from my limited exposure to BBC programming, I didn't tend to get their sense of humor.

"I'm Jamie." He lifted the suitcase over a particularly large rift in the narrow cobblestoned sidewalk. "Since you didn't ask."

"Nice to meet you, Jamie. Sorry," I apologized. "I have terrible manners."

"As I expected. You are American, after all."

I glowered at him, but he turned around to flash me a grin. Kidding, then. I smiled back.

"This must be that famous British humor I've heard so much about."

"Ah, yes," he sighed. "The classic deadpan sarcasm of the Commonwealth. One of our greatest cultural legacies. Although I think the coming weeks will reveal themselves to be more of a satire."

"Not theater of the absurd?"

"Nice." He nodded. "A fairy-tale wedding, as envisioned by Ionesco. He'd be mad for reality TV, don't you think?"

I *mmm*ed noncommittally. Note to self: must stop referencing major artistic movements unless extremely well informed as to the particulars of said movements. This guy had already dropped more literary references in ten minutes than my English teacher had in the past three months.

"And here I'd thought America's only great cultural legacy was deep-frying everything."

"Hey now," I objected. "What about fish and chips? That's deep-fried. And it's, like, your national dish."

"That's classic. You deep-fry ghastly things."

The cobblestoned sidewalk narrowed even more as we moved onto a bridge. I sneaked a peek over the side to see a wide river flowing lazily downstream, bare branches reflected in its dark surface. Kind of pretty, in a spare sort of way.

"Ghastly?" I smiled. Not a word I'd heard in a long time.

"We deep-fry delicious things. You haven't *lived* 'til you've had a deep-fried Reese's."

"I don't think I've had any type of Reese's, and I'm quite happy with the amount I've lived, thank you very much."

"Really? Never had a chocolate peanut-butter cup?"

"Oh, peanut butter, bleagh." He made an odd sound low in his throat, like a cat with a hair ball. "Why are all you Americans so obsessed with peanut butter? It's bizarre."

"You've clearly been doing peanut butter wrong."

"There's a right way?"

"Yes. Forget the jelly. It's all about chocolate."

"I'll keep that in mind."

"And anyway, the deep-fried candy bar was invented in the UK. Deep-fried Mars bars. They originated at a chip shop in Scotland. So, that's on you, actually."

He stopped suddenly, about halfway over the bridge, and I narrowly avoided colliding with him.

"How on earth do you know that?"

"I watch a lot of Food Network," I muttered. God, I really needed to stop watching so much TV. Although that little tidbit had come in handy. So one point for TV, then.

"Fascinating," he murmured. "And welcome to Dunkeld," he added at a normal volume.

I followed the sweep of his arm to see a small town nestled at the bottom of a valley. Once I got over my initial embarrassment at how close the town was to the station—I could *easily* have found it if I'd ventured thirty yards from the train platform—I was somewhat caught off guard by its cuteness. The whole place was adorable. Small buildings with thatched roofs and wooden doors lined the narrow cobblestoned streets. Soft gray curls of smoke puffed out of squat, round chimneys into the pale blue sky.

"It's lovely," I said softly, in a voice that didn't sound anything like mine.

"It's really not bad. Rather nice place for the Dunleavy seat."

"Yeah, Ronan was lucky to grow up here," I said somewhat wistfully. Not that I had anything against downtown Tupelo. But it sure didn't look like this. "Are you from here, too?"

"Me? No, of course not," he scoffed. "I'm from Bakewell. It's about three hours north of London."

"So you're not Scottish?"

"No, English." He seemed surprised. "I thought you knew. The accent. And the fact that you said my national dish was fish and chips. Not haggis."

"Oh. Um, well, I knew you sounded different from Ronan. I just didn't really . . . think about it," I finished lamely. Since Jamie was involved with the wedding, I just sort of assumed they were from the same place. I mean, all of my friends were from Tupelo.

"Quite all right. I doubt I could discern a Mississippian from an Alabaman when push came to shove." He turned to face me. "Good Lord, your lips."

"My—my—what?!" I squeaked.

"Your lips." He leaned closer. Where was he going? I was frozen, and not because of the cold. "My God, they're positively blue."

"Oh . . . yeah. Well, I told you I was cold," I said defensively. Not that I thought he had just been captivated by my lips. Although maybe my lips *were* captivating. I'd never given them much thought before. But the fact that they had, as of yet, failed to captivate anyone, would lead me to conclude that they weren't.

"We need to get you inside, by the fire, preferably with tea, as soon as is humanly possible. To the Atholl Arms!" He took off running, somehow managing to drag my suitcase behind him.

"The *Atholl* Arms?" I blurted out in disbelief, spirits lifting as my lungs expanded and I broke into a run, all of my half-eaten plane snacks rattling in my backpack as it bounced. There was always something about those first few steps of a run, as my arms pumped and my feet left the pavement, that made it impossible not to smile.

"Yes, it sounds a bit like arsehole, doesn't it?" he yelled behind him as he thundered down the hill into town. I caught up with him easily but stayed a few paces behind to follow him. He didn't have the stride of a seasoned runner, but his legs were so long that he was covering quite a bit of ground rather quickly. Especially for someone in corduroys who was rolling a fairly large suitcase behind him. "No relation, I'm sure. Although I hear the first Duke of Atholl was a bit of a wanker."

Wanker. English over here was a whole different language.

In a matter of minutes, we arrived downtown. Fortunately, the Atholl Arms was the first building we encountered. Jamie flung open the rustic wooden door with dramatic flair and ducked inside. Ducking too, I followed.

Inside, everything was decidedly peachy. And floral. Directly in front of us was a large wooden front desk with rows of keys behind it and a curved staircase bedecked with evergreen boughs, big red bows, and twinkling Christmas lights. So the Atholl Arms was a hotel, then. To the left was a pub, the faint sounds of a televised sporting event humming softly in the background, and to the right a flickering fireplace and the overstuffed couches in the lobby beckoned temptingly.

"Your strongest pot of PG Tips, posthaste, Tilly!" Jamie bellowed, causing the woman behind the front desk to jump out of her seat and drop the thick paperback from her hands.

"I don't know what PG Tips is, but I probably don't like it," I mumbled, staring longingly at the plush maroon couch. My beverage preferences tended to fall pretty squarely in the Snapple family.

"Goodness, Jamie, she's nearly blue." The woman bustled out from behind the counter, revealing a festive cardigan and an ankle-length skirt that clashed merrily with her frosted blond hair and vibrant eye shadow.

"It was nothing of my doing, madam!" Idly, I wondered how they knew each other, if Jamie wasn't from here, but suddenly I felt like I was being drowned by waves of tiredness, sleepy in the warmth, and was more than happy to let them steer me toward the couch in front of the fire, narrowly avoiding a collision with a fat Christmas tree tucked into a corner of the lobby. "I was the gallant rescuer, I assure you," Jamie continued as they sat me down. "If it weren't for me, she'd most definitely be frozen solid."

"She is, nearly," Tilly clucked.

I sank into the couch. It was even plusher than it had looked. Really, it had surpassed plushy and gone right on to squashy. Bliss. "One pot of tea, then. Or maybe that isn't strong enough. Should I bring the brandy snifter?"

"I wouldn't, if I were you. She's American. They can be positively puritanical about spirits."

"American?" I could hear a smile in the soft burr of Tilly's accent. "Goodness, Jamie. Gotten yourself into a *Buccaneers* situation, have you?"

"Hardly, Tilly," he said. "Not all Americans have come crashing out of Edith Wharton novels."

As Tilly chuckled softly, my last thought, before my eyes closed, was that I wasn't nearly well-read enough for this kind of banter.

CHAPTER THREE

"Dylan, wake up."

"Just five more minutes, Mom."

"Seriously, Dylan, you've got to get up. Or you'll never be able to fall asleep tonight."

"Don't care." I burrowed deeper under the blankets. The sheets were soft, but something was scratching my cheek. I pushed it off. Where was Teddy? I felt around for him but came up empty.

"Dylan." Something shook me. "Get up. Now. Or the jet lag will ruin you from here to next Tuesday."

Jet lag . . . jet lag . . . Scotland! I wasn't at home in my bed at all, and Teddy was still packed. Whose bed was I in? I sat bolt upright as my eyes flew open.

"Good gravy, Dylan, you nearly knocked me unconscious!" Mom yelped as she sprang off the side of the bed.

"Thank goodness for those Piloxing reflexes." I drew the scratchy plaid blanket closer to my chin and snuggled back down into a horizontal position. It was decidedly chilly outside the bed's environs.

"If you're awake enough to mock core-based cardio fusion exercises, then you're plenty awake. Up, please."

Grumbling, I complied and hoisted myself up to my elbows. The effort was nearly Herculean.

"Where am I?" I looked around the room, past the glistening mahogany of the four-poster bed frame to see a matching wooden dressing table with a mirror and a giant armoire. The walls were deep green and covered in paintings of horses. Horses jumping, horses standing majestically, horses frolicking with hounds. This bedroom was designed for a My Little Pony fan with a penchant for plaid.

"This is Dunyvaig Castle. Ronan's family estate." Mom walked back toward the bed and smoothed the top blanket, her Pandora bracelets gently tinkling as they slid together. I looked out the small window, set between navy plaid curtains in a wall that was definitely stone, to see a foggy expanse of graying fields that instantly brought to mind the word "moors."

"But . . . the Atholl Arms . . ."

"TRC sent a van down to get you. One of the groomsmen called. They tried to wake you, but you wouldn't get up. They had to carry you into the van."

Huh. That sounded vaguely familiar, but the memory was so fuzzy it was almost like I'd watched it happen to someone else on TV. I was happy I had finally warmed up but disturbed that I was so easy to kidnap.

"What time is it?" I asked groggily. My view out the window wasn't giving me any clues. I certainly couldn't see the sun outside. The weather could only be described as "gray."

"Nine. You slept right through dinner."

"Oh. Huh. That's a first."

"I know." She smiled, her eyes crinkling in a way I knew she hated, but I loved. The faint lines around her eyes made her look more like Mom, and less like the Newscaster Barbie the rest of Tupelo saw every morning. "Luckily, you're still in time for breakfast. But you've only got half an hour."

"Then what are we waiting for?!" I leaped out of bed, nearly hissing in pain as my feet hit the ice-cold floor. I hopped toward my suitcase, ferreting around until I found my thickest pair of socks, which happened to be printed with penguins wearing scarves—an old Christmas present from Meemaw. "You'd think a prince would be able to splurge on the heating bill a little bit," I muttered as I pulled on the penguins.

"If you so much as whisper a hint that you are cold anywhere near Ronan's family—" Mom's tone had turned as icy as the floor.

"Jeez, Mom, I'm not *that* rude—"

"I will tell TRC you want your own spin-off," she finished. Sometimes it was easy to see where Dusty got her iron will from. Except Mom was way craftier than her eldest daughter. Dusty's threats all tended to be of the brute force variety, but Mom could come up with the kind of twisted things that would make a Disney villain shake in his animated boots. And even though I was pretty sure it was an idle threat, I could still feel cold sweat beading on my brow at the thought of it. "Swear to God, Dyl. You'll be locked into a reality series 'til you turn eighteen. This place probably costs a fortune to heat, and it is none of our concern."

"Mom, enough with the Machiavellian treatment! I'll suffer in silence! Swear."

"That's my girl. Now, are you going to change out of those grody jeans?"

And that's my mom. Always concerned with my wardrobe. I looked down and realized I was wearing my same outfit from yesterday, which I guess was less disturbing than if an unknown someone had changed me into pajamas. Even if I didn't smell particularly pleasant. I pulled a clean pair of jeans out of my suitcase.

"An equally grody pair of jeans. Perfect," Mom said under her breath. Ignoring her, I pulled out a long-sleeved tee and a hoodie. I promised I wouldn't *say* it was cold, not that I wouldn't *dress* for the cold. "Meet me outside when you're ready, Dyl. You'll never find the dining room on your own."

Jeez. How big was this place, anyway? Mom shut the door neatly, the engraved silver handle rattling slightly behind her.

What I had assumed was a closet turned out to be a private bathroom. At least this would be a plus for the next few weeks, I mused as I grabbed my toothbrush in an attempt to un-disgust myself. No sharing a bathroom. I could pee whenever I wanted. No more waiting while Dusty took forever doing her makeup and curling her hair and waxing her eyebrows and executing the rest of her endless beauty regime. Although I kept forgetting— Dusty didn't live with us anymore. Soon enough, she wouldn't even live in *America* anymore. So I guess her forty-minute-long showers weren't really any of my concern. Looking in the porthole-size gilt mirror hanging over the round porcelain sink—contrary to Mom's beliefs, I have *some* standards when it comes to personal appearance—I piled all my hair up into a weird bun thing and secured the front with a stretchy headband I found jammed inside my jeans pocket.

"You're ready? *This* is dressed for breakfast?" Mom asked skeptically as I joined her in the hallway, shutting my bedroom door behind me.

"It's not sweatpants."

"Really setting the bar high there, kiddo." Mom sighed. As always, she was impeccably turned out, even at nine in the morning. Although, since she usually had to be at the studio before dawn, nine was late for Mom. She smoothed her wrinkle-free slacks, her perfectly highlighted blond bob swinging against her collarbones.

"That's a punchy color." I eyed her sweater set as it burned my retinas.

"It's called coral, Dylan." She fiddled with the diamond stud in her ear. "A little color won't kill you."

Too late I realized I was wearing jeans, a navy hoodie, and a blue long-sleeved shirt. I probably looked like a sloppy Smurf. Oh well. It's not like I was trying to impress anyone here.

"Blue's a color," I said defensively.

"It's not the only color," she countered.

Mom abruptly started walking down the hallway. As I followed, I worried about ever finding my room again. Just like in a hotel, the hall was lined with identical doors. Every so often a painting of some imposing-looking dude in an old-fashioned suit or—surprise—more horses broke up the monotony of hunter-green walls and dark wooden doors. Eventually, we arrived at a wide, curving staircase and descended two flights, emerging into a grand entryway. But before I could really take in the floor-to-ceiling velvet curtains and the huge roaring fireplace, Mom barreled down the hall and hung a left into a formal dining room.

Ah, breakfast. The greatest meal of the day. Except snacks. Although, by definition, snacks are not meals. So breakfast it is.

Mom went to join a group of strangers sitting around the long dining table, leaving me to get my breakfast on. Eagerly, I approached the buffet set out on the sideboard, watching steam curl gently into the air off the silver chafing dishes. Was this just for the show? Or was a breakfast buffet standard prince operation every morning? Because if so, for the first time, I could kind of see the appeal.

I picked up a china plate, surprised at its warmth. Nice touch. From a wicker basket lined with linen, I selected two slices of perfectly square white bread and popped them into the gleaming toaster, making a face at my reflection. Warmed plate clutched in my hot little hand, it was time to get down to business. Eggs—yes. I scooped up two fried eggs, then two more, careful not to burst the fat yellow yolks. Sausage—why not? I was usually more of a bacon girl, but those links looked damn tasty. And then . . . it got weird. Mushrooms? Tomatoes? *Beans?* These weren't breakfast foods! And right at the end was the strangest thing of all, a little black hockey puck with weird bits in it. I poked at it experimentally with the tongs. No idea.

"Well, if it isn't the Little Match Girl."

"Excuse me?" Jamie. Of course. He of the endless literary allusions and the freakish blue eyes of a husky. I wondered if he'd been the one who carried me into the van. Probably not. He looked kind of twiggy. Although it was hard to tell with the enormous, ancient-looking Fair Isle sweater replete with moth holes he was sporting. The sole body part I could see was a large hand with narrow fingers holding a glass of orange juice. Clearly, I wasn't the only one who'd gotten the memo on bundling up.

The toaster dinged. Deftly, he scooped up the browned slices and deposited them onto my plate, adjacent to the eggs.

"Little Match Girl? Because you were frozen? The Hans Christian Andersen story?"

"Yeah, I got the reference." I returned to poking the puck. It was proving to be distressingly resistant to my attempts to pierce it. Like an actual hockey puck would be. "Not really my favorite story. Kind of a downer."

"Unlike that heartwarming, not-at-all-depressing Hans Christian Andersen classic, 'The Little Mermaid.'"

"It's heartwarming when it involves singing crabs. Say what you will about Walt Disney, that man knew how to jazz up a real bummer of a story."

"I feel quite confident that Walt Disney had long since shuffled off this mortal coil before the time Sebastian sang his first note."

"Yeah, well, they cryogenically froze him. So he probably still has storyboard input and stuff." Poke, poke, poke. What was this black disc? Animal? Vegetable? Mineral? I couldn't get any sense of its texture.

"That's black pudding, you know."

"It's *pudding*?!" Of all the things I had theorized the puck to be, *pudding* wasn't one of them. "How can it be pudding? It's not at all jiggly. It's just sitting there, completely retaining its shape without a cup. That's not natural. And what *flavor* is that? Please don't tell me it's dark chocolate."

Jamie choked on a sip of orange juice, spluttering madly. "Good God, woman, it's not a sweet pudding!" he exclaimed.

"Oh." Okay. So it was like a savory pudding. I'd seen chef-y stuff like that on Food Network. Like Parmesan puddings and snap-pea flans and other *Iron Chef* situations. "So what's it made out of, then?"

"Hmm . . . meat. Blood. Gristly bits."

"Blood?!"

"Yes, blood." He laughed. "You should see your face, Dylan. It's just another part of the animal, isn't it?" Fair point. "Black pudding isn't truly a pudding at all. It's a sausage. And besides, we need our blood. We're all vampires here," he added conspiratorially.

"That wouldn't surprise me in the slightest." I returned the tongs to the little plate they'd been sitting on. Definitely no black pudding for me. "We're in a castle, there's no sun in sight, and I have yet to see anyone with a tan. This is practically a vampire nest."

"Dilly!"

"Well, that's definitely not a vampire," I muttered as my orange Amazon of a sister charged into the room, camera crew following not so subtly behind her as she waved her arms in my direction.

"Don't be so sure," Jamie murmured in my ear. "I'm fairly certain that jaundiced glow had nothing whatsoever to do with the sun."

"She's usually better at toning it down," I muttered between clenched teeth, fake grin plastered to my face. Dusty was a sunless-tanning addict, but she usually had it down to a relatively natural-looking art form. She hadn't even been this orange for the Miss America pageant, and I'd thought that had been the zenith of fake everything. "Either she overdid it for the cameras, or you ghouls are just making her look darker in comparison."

Cameras. Or, in this case, *camera*. There it was, resting innocently atop some crew member's shoulder, its evil eye threatening to suck me into its black hole.

"Ignore it, ignore it," I whispered meditatively. Or attempted-meditatively. "Just pretend it's not there."

Jamie looked at me curiously. Right. Must remember to be more discreet when muttering to self like a complete nutjob. If I shifted slightly to the right, Dusty's well-volumized hair blocked the camera. Hmm. Heaven always insisted that Dusty's hair was actually a weave—maybe she was right after all. I didn't think a human head could naturally produce that much hair. Honestly, just looking at the massive effort Dusty put into her appearance exhausted me. What was the point of gluing and spraying yourself with all that fake stuff? Who had time for that?

Well, whatever. If I couldn't see the camera, I could pretend it didn't exist. I would do what I had to do to survive. And be able to reap the benefits of free breakfast buffets. Natch.

"There's my girl!" A masculine roar threatened to burst my eardrums.

Before Dusty could make her way to me, she was intercepted by a big bearded blur of a Scotsman. I hadn't even noticed Ronan sitting at the table. But when buffets are involved, I am easily distracted. Ronan tossed Dusty into the air, spun her around, and then dipped her low to the floor, kissing her loudly. No wonder TRC ate the two of them up. They were ridiculous.

"You missed breakfast, darling." He kissed her again. "Fancy a banger?"

"Ronan!" Dusty shrieked, swatting at him as she disentangled herself from his arms. "Naughty."

Jamie mime-retched neatly into his orange juice. Man, I was definitely not fortified enough to handle the two of them. I bit savagely into my toast. There was only so much ooey-gooey lovebirding one could take. Especially on an empty stomach.

"And look who's here, finally!" Ronan slapped me on the back so hard a halfway-masticated morsel of toast flew into the air. I prayed no one noticed. Oh God, did anyone notice? Maybe the lighting was dim enough in here to make half-chewed toast invisible to the naked eye. "Make it in all right, then, Dylan?"

"Yuppers." Did I really just say "yuppers"? Oh God. Yuppers, I did. They were definitely going to show that, too. What if it became my catchphrase? What if TRC sold mugs with "Yuppers" printed on them? Would I be known as the Yuppers girl, forever? Why did this camera have to be here, ruining everything? I missed the days when I could be an idiot in private, without my every blurt recorded for posterity and digitally transmitted into millions of homes across America. I heard a faint snicker. "Are you laughing back there?"

"Yuppers," Jamie replied. *Grrrrr.*

"Dylan," Ronan said, suddenly serious, "as well ye know, I'm an only child." Were we having some kind of serious family bonding moment here? I shuffled back and forth, feeling incredibly awkward. And then as the awkward cherry on top of the sundae, I banged my knee against the sideboard. I hissed in pain as Ronan kept talking. "I'd always thought, though, it would be fun to have a little sibling. And now, thanks to Dusty, I do!" He grinned. "Or I will, at any rate."

I tried to grin back. It was all very nice. But I really wished I didn't have quite so many eggs in front of me. And that my knee wasn't throbbing. Jamie, the coward, quietly sidled away, out of the camera's range.

"So, if ye would do me the honor . . . I got ye a little something." Ronan picked a pastel parcel off of a chair and handed it to me. Carefully, I set my plate down on the sideboard next to the black-pudding tray and tore off the wrapping paper.

Something turned out to be an enormous pale-pink T-shirt declaring "I'm the Wee Sister!" in pink glitter letters.

"Aren't you just the sweetest?!" Dusty squealed. "Oh, I could just *melt*! Dilly, I had no idea he was gonna do this, I swear!"

"You shouldn't have," I muttered, and really, he shouldn't have. But the look in Ronan's eyes was so sincere, like a hopeful little puppy, I felt compelled to try to say something nice. "It's really, um, great, Ronan, thank you. I'm . . . totally stoked to be your wee sister."

Ronan beamed like he'd just won the lottery.

"Put it on!" Dusty cheered. "Put it on! Put it on!"

"Definitely put it on!" someone male yelled. I had a feeling it was Jamie.

"Are you serious?"

"I'm wearing mine!" Ronan roared. He unzipped his sweater partway to reveal a baby-blue T-shirt with "I'm the Big Brother!" splashed across the chest.

"Now you *have* to put it on." Oh, Dusty was enjoying this. Damn her. If I didn't wear the shirt, I'd look like a total jerk. Sighing, I pulled it on over my hoodie. It fell to my knees.

"It's precious," Dusty cooed. "Just precious."

I shot her my least precious glare.

"It's just grand," Ronan murmured weepily. Ronan could be a real crier when he got worked up. Learned that from watching *Prince in Disguise*.

"Totally grand." I patted him awkwardly with my free hand, hoping to thwart any attempts at a hug. Ronan's hugs were of the bone-crunching, rib-cracking variety, and I was particularly attached to all of my ribs. I grabbed my plate and scuttled off to the table as Dusty fussed over him. Freedom. And food. Finally. I studiously ignored everyone at the table and started shoveling eggs in my mouth.

"Excuse me." Tap on the shoulder. Jamie slid into the chair next to mine. "So sorry to bother you, but I couldn't help but ask—are you, in fact, the wee sister?"

"Har-de-har-har."

"Do Americans as a people have trouble chewing? Or is this more specific to you?"

Dammit! Chew with your mouth closed, Dylan! I'd never had this many toast problems in Tupelo.

"Oh God. Sorry." I swallowed throatily. "It's a Dylan thing. I eat too fast. Always hungry. Although I don't usually choke on pieces of toast."

"Unless walloped by a Scots giant."

So he had seen. Which meant the camera had, too. Great. Choking out undigested toast, Yuppers, and a Wee Sister T-shirt. I was really off to a great start.

CHAPTER FOUR

"Are you done stuffin' your face, Dylan?" Dusty called.

"Give me a minute!" I growled back.

"She's finished." Mom somehow materialized and placed a warning hand on my back.

"Not finished."

"Yes, you are," she whispered, removing my plate. "You can go ahead and start the tour."

"A tour?" I swallowed carefully. Mission: Chew Successfully, accomplished. For once. "Is this mandatory?"

"Oh, don't be an old stick-in-the-mud, wee sister." I glared at Jamie but stood to join him. At least that somehow got Mom to back off. "Maybe we'll find a secret passage. A trapdoor. One of those bookcases that spins around to reveal a chamber."

"Do they really have that stuff here?"

"Only one way to find out, I suppose," Jamie said.

The rest of the group was massing together. I was still studiously ignoring the camera crew, so besides them, it was just me, Jamie, Mom, Dusty, and Ronan. Small group for such a big castle.

"How did everybody know there was a tour?" I asked.

"Did you not get an itinerary?"

"Oh. Yeah. It's in my other pants."

At the front of the group, Dusty performed a quick head count.

"Where's your mama, Ronan?" she asked.

"Mum's not—well, she's not, uh—she's not feeling well." Ronan flushed. Hmm. Weird. Well, maybe not *weird*, but the first time Ronan came over to our house, Mom practically threw him a parade. There were *balloons*. This fancy-pants Queen Mum couldn't even be bothered to show up for a tour of her own castle. And I certainly hadn't seen any balloons. Not that balloons were essential for my enjoyment of life or anything; they just add that certain je ne sais quoi to a festive occasion.

"Well, that's all right, I guess." Dusty frowned. "You gonna show us around, then, lovebug?"

"But of course, my bride!" And just like that, Ronan was back to his usual jovial self. Jamie and I shuffled into the back of the group.

"If I see anything that's even remotely mysterious," Jamie said in a low voice, "I intend to abandon the tour immediately. And I expect you to do the same."

"Naturally," I agreed. "At the first sign of suspicion. I'm planning to push on all the paintings, too. Just in case they spin open to reveal a shadowy passageway."

"Excellent thinking." He nodded decisively. "No one will suspect a thing as you randomly slide priceless works of art away from their appointed places."

"As ye may know, William the Conqueror tried to invade Scotland in the eleventh century, but he couldna do it." Up ahead, Ronan had started the tour, leading the group out of the dining room and down the hall. We were starting all the way back in the eleventh century? This was literally going to take forever.

"So how do you know Ronan, anyway?" I whispered to Jamie, so Ronan—or worse, Mom—wouldn't overhear me talking during the tour. "You've been here before, right?"

"Oh. Ah. Yes, I have. Although I haven't conducted a thorough secret-passage investigation as of yet."

"You guys must be pretty close if you're in the wedding."

"Aye, the days followin' the Norman Conquest were verra peaceful for the clans—or as peaceful as life in the Highlands ever was." I looked up to see Ronan thumping his chest.

"I think he's getting increasingly Scottish with age," Jamie whispered fondly, ducking his head down. "We're old family friends," he explained as we lingered in front of a painting of a foxhunt, letting the tour progress a bit down the hallway without us. "Our mums have known each other since they were in nappies. And they've been throwing us together since *we* were in nappies—or since I was in nappies, at any rate. I suspect it was because we're both only children," Jamie mused. "Mum wanted to make sure I didn't miss out on the fraternal experience. Ronan's quite a bit older than me, so we've never been fast friends. But friendly, certainly. It was a bit as I imagine it would have been like to have a much older brother who went off to university when I was still in school."

"Got it." We ambled down the long hallway, still keeping

our distance behind the group. "Must be nice, having a prince for a family friend."

"It certainly has its advantages." He smiled, like he was enjoying a private joke. Probably about polo ponies or something equally royal. "You know, of course, though, that Ronan's—"

"Not really a prince?" I finished for him. "Yes! Thank you! Finally! I'm not the only one!"

"But one can hardly blame TRC," Jamie said. "*Lord Dunleavy in Disguise* doesn't quite have the same ring to it."

"Fair enough."

"Which brings us, of course, to the Battle of Stirling Bridge, a grand day for us Scots—and Clan Murray," Ronan announced. The rest of the group was already in the next room. Jamie and I hurried to catch up.

We stepped over a wide threshold and into a large space with books lining the walls. There was even one of those rolling ladder things, just like in *Beauty and the Beast*! One wall of bookshelves was almost entirely eclipsed by an enormous Christmas tree bedecked with twinkling lights, tartan ribbon, and color-coordinated ornaments. I spotted none of the Popsicle-stick-and-pom-pom creations that usually adorned the Leigh family tree. This year, of course, we didn't have a tree, thanks to Dusty and the Wedding that Stole Christmas. Somehow, I was having a hard time imagining unwrapping presents underneath this professionally decorated balsam behemoth. Jamie and I quietly sidled into the back of the group as Ronan waxed rhapsodic about William Wallace.

"Hello, lovelies!" A very handsome hobbit strode into the room wearing a rumpled tux and a mischievous expression. He was unbelievably short, and a bit wide, but bore a striking resemblance to a goateed Prince Charming. "Hello, hello, hello!"

"Late for the tour, Kirby!" Ronan bellowed from the front of the line. "Ye wouldna think it was so hard to show up on time."

"Ooo, listen to himself. The laird is back in the castle!" The hobbit did a funny little jig with one arm thrown up in the air. "I dinna remember these dulcet Highland tones from our Cambridge days."

"Listen to yerself, Rob Roy, before you take the piss out of me." Ronan punched him on the shoulder, and the man staggered under the force of the blow. Sometimes I think Ronan forgot how big he was. "You're the one who always got more and more Scottish each train stop away from Eton."

"I couldna relax at school, with all those bloody toffs about, now could I?" He frowned with distaste. "Perfect Queen's English and all that load of cack."

"We invented the bloody language. Clearly, we know how one is supposed to speak it," Jamie piped in.

"Och, it's my favorite bloody toff!" The short man flew toward us and flung his arms around Jamie's middle. I made a mental note to figure out what the heck a "toff" was later. And a "laird." And a "cack." Actually, none of that conversation had made any sense.

"Have ye quite finished interruptin' the tour, then?" Ronan asked.

"Proceed!" The small man waved a hand grandly. "I willna hold you back from recountin' the glorious history of Clan Murray. I only wish to borrow wee Jamie for a minute. Och, stop growin', will ye?" he addressed Jamie. "Yer makin' the rest of us look bad."

"I canna control ye, Kirby. I never could." Ronan sighed. "Those of ye who'd like to see a pitchfork wielded in the rising of 'forty-five, follow me."

"Kirby? Kit Kirby?" I asked, finally putting two and two together as Ronan, Dusty, and Mom moved away toward the far corner of the room. Of all the ways I expected to finally meet the elusive Kit Kirby, I did not expect him to come waltzing by in a tux. Or to be the approximate height of my navel. "*This* is the man who left me to freeze at the Dunkeld and Birnam train station?"

"Not again!" Kit Kirby groaned, smacking his palm to his forehead.

"I was stuck there for— Wait, what? Again?" I asked.

"This happens all the time, unfortunately." Jamie shook his head sadly.

"Hardly!" Kit Kirby protested. "Last time it was an airplane hangar. Completely different."

"He has a propensity to abandon women at various modes of transport," Jamie explained.

"Never on purpose, mind you! Entirely and completely accidental. Punctuality is simply not my strong suit. We all have our own gifts, wee Jamie." Kind of ironic that Kit called him "wee Jamie," considering that Jamie was nearly twice his height.

"Gifts? You have gifts?" Jamie raised an eyebrow sardonically. Man, I wished I could do that. I experimented. Nope. Where one eyebrow went, the other would follow. "I was entirely unaware. Please, enlighten us."

"My charm, for one!" Kit stroked his neat goatee, eyes twinkling. "'S what makes me so popular with the ladies. Of all nations."

"Ah, yes, the ladies of all nations." Jamie sighed heavily. "It could have been far worse, Dylan. At least you weren't stranded in Azerbaijan without a passport. Or a wallet. Or a phone."

"That happened?" Nothing on his face betrayed that he was joking. "You're being serious right now?"

"Och, Sabina." Kit clasped his hands to his heart. "She was lovely. Eyes a man could drown in. If only I'd read the timetable correctly. Or owned a watch."

"What might have been . . ." Jamie agreed. "Anyway, Kit, meet your latest victim." Jamie indicated me. I waved. "You nearly killed her, you feckless bastard."

"I havena *killed* her! She's standin' here large as life!" Kit Kirby crowed triumphantly. "Snug and warm inside ol' drafty Dunyvaig. No harm, no foul, then?"

"Dylan," I supplied. "I'm Dusty's sister."

"*You're* Dusty's *sister*?!"

"Yup." Ugh.

"Kit Kirby, at your service, Dusty's sister." He bowed with the kind of flourish that made me think he was probably involved in community theater. "Terribly sorry about the business with the station. It willna happen again, I swear it. Well, probably shouldna swear it," he amended. "But. You know. I'll do my very best."

"I wouldn't count on that, Dylan."

"Why are you wearing a tux?" I asked curiously. He was wrinkled, sure, but awfully formal for the morning. It looked like he had slept in it. Or maybe not slept, if the blue circles beneath his eyes were any indication.

"Och, well, that's a long story." Kit Kirby's eyes twinkled. "But what could be better than a long story, a cold morning, and a roaring fire? It involves three Vegas showgirls, a deposed Saudi prince, and a horribly expensive bottle of champagne. . . ."

"Not one word more, Kirby," Ronan shouted. How on earth did he hear that? He was all the way across the room, waving the aforementioned pitchfork about. "Innocent ears," he continued. "Let's keep it clean in front of the wee sister."

"I'm not a baby," I muttered mulishly. I could handle it. I mean, I'd lived through Homecoming and the Tate Moseley Incident. Well, Heaven had lived through the Tate Moseley Incident, but I'd witnessed the whole thing. Nothing could shock me anymore.

"He's a bloody bat," Kit Kirby complained, once Ronan turned back to the tour and stopped waving his historical pitchfork menacingly. "Damned supersonic hearing. Worst prefect in the history of Eton."

"A prefect?! Those are real? Like Percy Weasley?!" I asked.

"Yes, Ronan distinguished himself admirably in his O.W.L.s," Jamie said seriously, only his eyes betraying that he was teasing. Stupid American me. Jamie must have felt like I did when Ronan came over for dinner and asked my mom if he should get a suit like Colonel Sanders's for formal American occasions.

"It's the N.E.W.T.s that really separate the men from the boys, Jamie." I sniffed in a dignified manner. The corners of his mouth twitched with a funny little *mmphmm* of laughter.

"Me and Ronan, we've been best mates since we were lads at Eton together. I can hardly believe it," Kit said mistily. "Ronan about to be married, wee Jamie following in my glorious foot-steps at Eton, and I'm just . . . old. Where does the time go, Dylan?" He clapped me on the shoulder, gazing unsteadily into my eyes. "Where. Does. The. Time. Go."

"So, uh, you guys went to Eton together? That's, what, like, a high school?" I gently removed Kit's hand from my shoulder, changing the subject.

"Yes, yes, like, totally, like, a high school," he Valley-girled at me. "I know your American lingo. I watch the films. That was way harsh, Tai," he added. "*Clueless.*"

Abandonment and near frostbite aside, someone who quoted *Clueless* couldn't be *all* bad.

"How they ever let you into Cambridge is simply beyond me." Jamie shook his head.

"It's my charm, is it no?" Kit Kirby's eyes twinkled. "Dinna worry, wee Jamie. I'm sure you can grace those hallowed halls, too, when you're old and distinguished like your uncle Kit."

"Not my uncle," Jamie mouthed.

"Ooo! Spirits!" Kit made a beeline for a cut-crystal decanter on a sideboard. He poured a healthy splash of something into a matching tumbler. Across the room, I could hear Mom asking something about window treatments. "Fancy a spot, Dylan?" Kit held his glass out to me, swirling the amber-colored liquid in the dim light.

"It's, like, nine thirty in the morning."

"Och, I'm in a different time zone." He shrugged. "Besides, the best man deserves a bit of tipple. It's the stress, is it no?" He downed the rest of his alcohol in one neat swallow. "All the responsibility. My poor nerves."

"You are shouldering the responsibility admirably." Jamie clapped him on the shoulder. "Brilliant job fetching Dylan from the train station."

"Ah, sod off, wee Jamie." Kit poured himself a second glass.

"We canna all be as prim and proper as His Royal Shyness, now can we?"

"Is that what you guys call Ronan?"

"Yes," Jamie said firmly. "Because he was a prefect."

"Right. A prefect," Kit said distractedly before taking another sip. "A bloody perfect prefect, more like."

"Precisely," Jamie confirmed.

"I, um, think the tour is moving on without us." I watched Dusty and Mom follow Ronan out of the room and disappear down the hallway. I definitely didn't want to get lost in a castle, particularly in the company of two insane people. Well, Kit Kirby was definitely insane. Jamie was just . . . quirky.

"Right you are, Dylan! Better to just take this lot along with us, eh?" Kit Kirby grabbed the decanter off the sideboard, tucked it under his arm, and started waddling toward the rest of the tour group.

"Unless I'm very much mistaken, that is Waterford crystal," Jamie said. "And the pattern appears to date from the mid-nineteenth century. Eighteen forty, if I had to hazard a guess."

"'If I had to hazard a guess,'" Kit mumbled. "What, you're a bloody antiquarian now? Violin wasna enough of a hobby for you, eh, Sherlock? Eeek, screeeek, screeeeeech."

I clapped my hands over my ears. If Jamie actually sounded anything like that on the violin, I prayed he wouldn't be playing at the wedding. Or anywhere in my vicinity.

"I'm simply reminding you that that thing is probably worth more than you are."

"Not bloody likely," Kit snorted. "I'm priceless, more like."

I easily matched Jamie's long-legged stride as we made our way into the hallway back toward the group, Kit scuttling along behind us. Up ahead, I saw Dusty turn and impatiently wave at us. I quickened my pace. "And I willna drop it. I've a very delicate touch. Hands of a baby angel. 'S what all the girls say."

"No offense, but I can't imagine anything I'd like to touch me *less* than the hands of a baby angel." I shuddered.

"Not even a giant squid?" Jamie asked.

"Hands of a baby angel is creepier. Why is the angel a baby? Why is it touching me? Am I dead? If the giant squid is touching me, I'd assume it was by accident. Like, I swam into its space."

"You'd have to be swimming awfully far out to swim into its space," Jamie said.

"You don't know how far I can swim."

"You're almost as strange as Jamie." Kit gawked at us.

"And once we're down this hallway we'll pass into the older part of the house." We were close enough to hear Ronan again. "Ye'll see much of the medieval architecture has been preserved, and we've a grand room for a snooker table."

"Come along, chickens." Kit had somehow moved ahead of us, almost caught up with everyone else. "There's snookeries to see."

"Christopher Clarence Kirby!"

He stopped dead in his tracks at the sound of a commanding female voice. "Unhand the Scotch this instant, or I will personally escort you to the dungeons."

And that was how I met Ronan's mom.

CHAPTER FIVE

"The gorgon has risen," Jamie whispered.

There was definitely something about Ronan's mother that suggested mythological beast, but I wouldn't have gone with gorgon. A head full of snakes would have looked way too untidy on top of that perfectly prim tweed skirt suit. Not a hair in her tasteful chignon was out of place. No, if she were any kind of creature, she'd be a dragon. A small dragon, as she was definitely several feet shorter than everyone in my family, but there was something reptilian in the coldness of her gaze and the high, sculpted arch of her cheekbones. Nothing in her profile would have looked amiss on a marble bust.

"Well, if it isna my favorite ladyship!" Kit walked down the hallway toward her, arms outstretched, with the decanter clutched in one hand. "A vision in tweed, as always. Positively younger every time I see you."

"Unhand the Scotch, Christopher." Ronan's mom neatly

sidestepped Kit's hug. Rebuffed, he placed the decanter down on a random side table, next to a wooden mallard.

"Mum!" Ronan took several long strides to join us, Dusty and Mom trailing slightly behind him. Looking at the two of them together, it seemed impossible that tiny Mrs. Dunleavy (was that what I was supposed to call her? I had no idea) had birthed a giant like Ronan. "Are you sure you should be up and about? I thought you weren't feeling well."

"I am *not* feeling well. But circumstances have changed, obviously. My home was no longer safe. The staff alerted me the minute Christopher arrived."

The staff? Oh my. Well, I obviously knew there was a staff. I had seen people in starched white shirts and gray slacks all around the place. And it would have been impossible for one person to keep something this big clean. But still, *staff.* It just sounded so . . . fancy.

"Och, Mrs. D.!" Kit groused. "Break one priceless family heirloom—"

"Or seven," Jamie cheerfully interjected.

"Or eat a wee bit of cake—"

"That was intended to serve two hundred and fifty people, including, but not limited to, the Duke of York," Jamie countered.

"Didna eat the whole thing now, did I?" Kit said defensively.

"No, just the middle."

Kit scoffed. "Middle's the best part, is it no?"

"You could have waited until it was time for pudding, like the rest of us, without scooping out the pastry's innards like an impatient barbarian," Jamie scolded.

"All I'm saying is," Kit insisted loudly, "make a few wee

mistakes, and a fellow feels like he's on bloody AMBER Alert forever. Hardly seems fair, does it? A few wee mistakes, weighed against the balance of a lifetime of friendship and devotion?"

"I think AMBER Alert is for missing children."

Everyone stared at me. Right. Apparently, I was not part of this conversation.

"Hmmmmmm." Despite being the shortest person in this awkwardly clustered group in the middle of a hallway, Ronan's mom somehow managed to look down her nose at all of us. Terrifying. Weirdly, though, her eyes lit up when they landed on Jamie. "You're looking well this morning, Jamie."

"Erm. Thanks." He reddened. Well, I guess we knew who Ronan's mom's favorite was. And it certainly wasn't Kit Kirby.

"Will your charming father be joining us soon? I had so hoped he would be able to arrive early. He is well aware, I trust, that Dunyvaig will always be a home to him."

"Very kind of you. But I think he's . . . busy."

"Of course, of course," Ronan's mom demurred. "I would expect nothing less from a man in his position."

His position? I shot Jamie a look, and he shrugged and mouthed something that looked like "business" in response.

"Well, I'm sure glad you're feeling good enough to be up and about!" Dusty said, the nerves audible in her voice through a veil of false cheer. Was Dusty *scared* of Ronan's mom? I had never seen Dusty less than 100 percent confident in a social situation. It was disconcerting.

"I most certainly am not." Mrs. Dunleavy turned the full force of her icy gaze on Dusty, who quailed in response, her smile faltering. God, I almost felt bad for my sister. Imagine having *that* as a mother-in-law.

"I feel simply horrid," Ronan's mother continued, wrapping a tartan shawl-like thing tighter around her shoulders, "but when one's home is in danger, one must rise to the occasion."

"In danger?!" Kit protested. "Danger?! Hardly. It's not as if I go round laying waste to civilizations!"

"*Kit Kirby: The Desolation of Smaug,*" Jamie whispered.

A snorty bark of a laugh escaped against my will. Everyone stared at me. Again. The camera was still rolling, and it hadn't missed a moment of my idiocy.

"Ah, yes." Ronan cleared his throat. "Ye havena met the rest of Dusty's family yet. Mum, this is Dusty's sister, Dylan."

Slowly, Mrs. Dunleavy extended a fine-boned hand. I shook it gently, feeling positively gargantuan in comparison. Was I supposed to curtsy? Oh well. Too late. A little bit of a How to Interact with the Nobility guide would have been really helpful, TRC. Although they were probably hoping we would all go full-on Ugly American and embarrass Ronan and his family.

"Dusty. Dylan. What . . . interesting names you girls have."

Oh, "interesting." I knew that "interesting." That was the exact same "interesting" Krystal Hooper used to describe Heaven's first-day-of-school outfit last year.

"When Ronan told me he was bringing home a girl called Dusty," she continued, "I thought, dear God, is it Cinderella?" Her laugh sounded like ice cubes tumbling into a glass. No one else joined in. I locked eyes with Dusty, who looked down, nervously fiddling with her hair.

"They're named after two of my favorite singers," Mom said gently, tactful as always. "Dusty Springfield and Bob Dylan."

"Not Dylan Thomas?! I've been deceived!" Jamie wailed, quietly enough that no one seemed to notice. We were getting good at having our own conversations outside of everyone else's.

"Named after singers? How . . . unusual." Ah, "unusual," the even less polite cousin of the bitchy "interesting." "Ronan is, of course, named after his late father." Ronan placed a comforting hand on his mom's shoulder. She patted it perfunctorily. "To have named your daughters after singers, I imagine you must have been something of a . . . oh, what is that term . . . groupie?"

"Mum!" Ronan gasped.

Rude! So rude! Mom was obviously not a groupie. Or old enough to be Bob Dylan's groupie.

Mom, to her credit, just laughed. "No, nothing like that. But much like Dusty Springfield, the only one who could ever reach me, was, in fact, the son of a preacher man."

"You are referring to the girls' father, I take it?" Ronan's mom sniffed. I stiffened, involuntarily, at the rare mention of my dad. Mom had obviously made this joke before, so the list of things I knew about him remained pretty much set at:

1. son of a preacher man (minister? pastor? unclear)

2. tall (obviously)

3. a complete and total jerk (again, obvious)

"And he is . . ."

"Not in the picture," Mom said firmly.

Not in the picture. Right. Mom's standard response. He'd been in the picture when Dusty was little, then disappeared shortly after I was born. So thanks for contributing to my birth, I guess, but otherwise, this man who was technically my father and allegedly existed had given me exactly one big fat load of nothing. And one not-so-little fear that I was the reason he'd left.

"Hmmmmm." I was beginning to dread that "hmmmmm,"

the way it whistled judgmentally through Ronan's mom's nose. So, maybe my mom hogged the bathroom and put way too much stock in personal appearance, but when you got right down to it, she was basically a baller. She'd somehow managed to keep me and Dusty from killing each other, gotten us through school, and, you know, clothed and fed us, all while being a picture-perfect cohost on Mississippi's number-one-rated morning talk show. *And* did all of that without the benefit of a *staff*. I stepped a little closer to her, protectively. Not that she really needed my help. Mom had never met an awkward social situation she couldn't sail through gracefully. Like I said, pretty much a baller.

"Tell me more about these divine window treatments, Florence," Mom said smoothly, changing the subject. Mrs. Dunleavy's nostrils quivered at the familiar use of "Florence," as I was sure Mom knew they would. She was a master of that prized Southern tradition of an insult so subtle you'd almost miss it. "Dear sweet Ronan couldn't recall where they'd come from, but I was sure you'd know."

Firmly, Mom steered Florence, as I would now think of her, away toward the windows. It seemed like the rest of the group let out a collective sigh of relief.

Something gurgled. I looked at Dusty. She'd turned completely green. Like a green I hadn't seen since the infamous Dollywood Barf-A-Thon the summer before her senior year.

"Excuse me, y'all, I just—I'm—going to find a bathroom." Dusty clapped a hand over her mouth and rushed out. Ronan hurried behind her, his brow furrowed in concern.

"Poor thing. Doesna stand a chance," Kit clucked sympathetically.

"What do you mean, she doesn't stand a chance?"

"No offense meant, Dylan, please! Nothing against your sister. Nothing at all. Lovely girl. And quite a looker."

"Yeah, yeah, I get it," I interrupted him. I'd heard quite enough on the subject of Dusty's looks to last me a lifetime. "Get to the point."

"I'm simply saying, that as divine as dear Dusty is, and as pure as her love for Ronan is, I'm sure, she isna exactly Lady Dunleavy's first choice of bride for her precious only son, is she?"

"Why not?"

Kit and Jamie exchanged a look. Okay, I wasn't dumb, I knew why not, but it was hard to imagine perfect Dusty not being good enough for anyone. I could have filled this castle with mamas in Mississippi who would die to have Dusty marry their sons.

"Let's see." Kit started ticking things off on his fingers. "She isna aristocratic, for one, and she's far too attractive, in that obvious, American way—"

"Nothing worse than being obviously attractive." Jamie shook his head. "It's so terribly vulgar."

"Ronan's mom doesn't like her because she's too pretty?"

"Much too pretty," Kit agreed.

"It would be better if she only looked attractive in dim lighting," Jamie added. "Whilst one was squinting."

"I can never tell if you're being serious."

"I'm hardly ever serious," Jamie said, with a completely straight face.

"I'm dead serious. Pardon me, lovey," Kit addressed the mallard on the table, moving it aside to rescue the Scotch decanter. "It's her bloody worst nightmare, is it no?" He started walking back toward the first room we'd been in, Jamie and I following. "Blond bimbo—no offense, mind—comes crashing in from the colonies to steal her only son. *And* brings along a tacky television crew. The horrors!"

"That's not Dusty's fault," I said stubbornly, no idea why I was defending her. I'd called her way worse than a bimbo. "Florence didn't have to let the camera crew in here. She had a choice."

Kit and Jamie exchanged a glance.

"It's not as if she *really* had a choice, though, did she?"

"Kit," Jamie warned.

"Common knowledge, is it no? Simply bringing the wee sister up to speed." He nodded at my monstrous T-shirt. "They needed the money," Kit said bluntly. "Takes an awful lot of dosh to keep an old pile of bricks like this going."

"So Ronan's family isn't rich?"

"Rich is a relative term, is it no?" Kit took a meditative swig straight from the decanter. Jamie winced. "Rich for regular folk, sure. But not quite enough to keep up with the crowned heads of Europe. Or turn the heat on, apparently."

"That's quite enough," Jamie said firmly.

"Ooo, sorry. I'm being vulgar, talking about money." Kit swayed slightly from side to side. "I've offended his delicate sensibilities."

"Why don't you take a seat, then, Kit?"

"Why don't you take a seat?" Kit muttered grumpily, but allowed Jamie to steer him back into the sitting room and toward an overstuffed love seat printed with cabbage roses that looked like it had come straight out of Meemaw's assisted-living facility. Guess not everything in a castle was classy. Kit slumped into a seated position, cradling the decanter like a baby. Gently, Jamie pulled a plaid throw off the arm of the love seat and tucked him in.

"Is he okay?"

"He's fine. He just needs a bit of a lie-in."

"Okay," I said skeptically. Passing out before noon seemed problematic to me. But what did I know?

"Come on." Jamie grabbed my hand. I was startled by the contact; he was surprisingly warm. "Fingers still frozen, Little Match Girl?"

"I'm in recovery. Someone abandoned me at a train station, remember?"

"I'm ignoring that slanderous insult!" Kit cracked one eye open. Not asleep after all. "You're in collusion, the two of you. That's what you're doing. Colluding. Trying to ruin my good name." He settled back in among the cabbage rose pillows, pulling the blanket up to nestle beneath his plump chin as his eyes fluttered closed.

"A bit like having a giant goateed baby, isn't it?" Jamie said fondly.

"A giant *drunk* goateed baby. You sure he's okay?"

"Positive. I honestly think he's more sleep-deprived than anything else. He's not usually awake quite this early."

"Fair enough. I'm certainly in no position to judge anyone who falls asleep on a couch."

"Absolutely not. You were positively comatose last evening."

The images that comment conjured up necessitated a brisk change of subject.

"So, what is he, your uncle?"

"Not at all. Ronan and Kit are childhood best friends. Making Kit another—"

"Old family friend?" I supplied.

"Precisely. They've always treated me a bit like an annoying younger brother. Never quite part of the gang enough to be included, but always part of the gang enough to be harassed."

"You don't have to explain being a harassed younger sibling to me. I could write a book about it. Okay. I think I've got it. How everybody knows one another, I mean. Finally." I nodded slowly. "They should have given us a family tree or something."

"That would have been far too helpful. And put them at cross-purposes. I imagine their aim all along will be to make us look foolish."

"My thoughts exactly," I agreed grimly. "So . . . what now?"

"What now . . ." Jamie repeated. "For starters, I think we've well and truly lost the tour."

"Yeah, if the tour is even happening anymore." I realized we'd also well and truly lost the camera. Things were looking up.

"We were never going to discover anything even remotely mysterious with that lot hanging about."

"Totally. Mom would murder me if I started randomly pulling books off of bookshelves to see if they swung open to reveal secret rooms. Way too messy. She's practically allergic to clutter."

"Bookshelves!" Jamie exclaimed delightedly. "You're a marvelous genius, of course. We've simply got to pull books until something reveals itself. Come on, then, Dylan!"

He grabbed my hand again and took off at a run, narrowly avoiding an end table holding a china shepherdess that was most likely priceless.

"Where are we going?" Were we holding hands? I mean, obviously, we were holding hands. But more in a grabbing-and-pulling way than in a walking-romantically way. So that probably didn't count as hand-holding. Not that it mattered or whatever.

"The library!"

"The library? But wasn't that the room we were in? With the shelves? And the *Beauty and the Beast* ladder?"

"No, no, of course not, that was the sitting room." Jamie led me through the halls at breakneck speed, twisting and turning suddenly, the slap of our sneakers muted by the plush carpet of the hall runner.

"Silly me. Just assumed the giant room with the endless bookshelves was a library."

"The nineteenth-century Dunleavys in particular were markedly bookish. I think rather a lot of them would have been scholars if they hadn't been required to run the estate. They amassed quite a collection. Unfortunately, most of it's botany. Terribly dull. Ah, here we are."

Simultaneously, Jamie pushed open a heavy wooden door and pulled me through it. A gasp of surprise escaped my lips.

CHAPTER SIX

It was like stepping into a jewel box. Tomes of every imaginable color climbed the walls, the gold leaf on their spines glinting in the firelight. The room was tiny, but so tall I wondered if it took up two stories. There was, of course, another rolling ladder, and the only wall space not filled with books was taken up by an enormous fireplace. Who the hell kept all these fires going? Oh, right, the staff.

Apart from several squashy leather chairs and one particularly squashy leather love seat, the only furniture in the room was a giant oak desk. I hopped up onto it, swinging my feet back and forth.

"Hmmm." Jamie stopped abruptly in the middle of the room. "I have . . . a feeling." He fell to his knees and began knocking on the floor, pressing one ear to the boards. "Sounds a bit . . . different . . . hollow, perhaps . . . could be something . . . right about . . . here!" He pulled up one corner of an Oriental rug with a flourish, revealing a trapdoor.

"You're joking." I slid off the desk. It was definitely a trapdoor. I'd never seen one in real life, but there was no mistaking it. There was even a little handle to pull it up by.

"Where trapdoors are concerned, I never joke. Well, hardly ever," he amended. "If I could think of a really brilliant pun involving trapdoors, I would simply have to succumb."

"You knew that was there the whole time!"

"How dare you malign my sleuthing abilities!" Jamie cried. "Madam, you have cut me to the quick! Perhaps I am simply preternaturally gifted at finding trapdoors. Did you consider that possibility?"

"I considered it. But I also considered the possibility that you're full of crap."

"A definite possibility." He grinned. "Shall we?"

"It feels less mysterious now that I know it was a premeditated trapdoor," I grumbled.

"The premeditated trapdoor," Jamie mused.

"That sounds like a bad Nancy Drew book."

"Oh, bother Nancy Drew. It's my title, not hers. I'd read a book called *The Premeditated Trapdoor*. Perhaps I should write one."

"First of all, I came up with that title. Technically. And second of all, I think the premeditated aspect takes all the mystery out of it. Doesn't sound like much of a page-turner to me."

"The door may be premeditated, but the destination is not." Jamie tapped the side of his nose. I'd heard the word "premeditated" so many times in the last couple minutes it had lost all meaning. He threaded his fingers through the small silver ring and pulled, lifting the wooden door aloft until it swung open to reveal the top of a flight of stairs.

"What are you waiting for?" I asked.

"Ladies first."

I peered down the hole, then looked back up at Jamie.

"Are you frightened?" he asked kindly.

"No!" All I'd seen were a couple stairs descending into black nothingness. What could possibly be frightening about that?

"Shall I go first? Check for monsters, bogeymen, that sort of thing?"

"I think I can handle a bogeyman." I repeated it back the way Jamie had said it, *bogey*man, not *boogey*man.

I took a deep breath and planted my foot firmly on the top step. Satisfyingly sturdy. All right, then.

"Deep into that darkness peering, long I stood there, wondering, fearing," Jamie recited.

"Is that part of *The Premeditated Trapdoor*?" Down another step. I still couldn't see the bottom of the stairs.

"Hardly. It's Poe. Move along, then, Dylan."

"Yeah, yeah, nevermore." Step. Step. "I'm going."

I reached a hand out into the darkness until I connected with the wall, trailing my fingers along it in the absence of a railing. Maybe lack of railing was standard trapdoor operating procedure, but I could have used one right about now. Carefully, I moved down, one foot in front of the other, until there were no more steps. The bottom. I inched forward, until suddenly the minimal light source was extinguished.

"Jamie!" I gasped. This was a kind of darkness I hadn't experienced since Heaven and I accidentally ended up in the basement during the church lock-in.

"Quite all right, Dylan?"

"No! Why did you close the door?"

"I didn't want to alert the others to the existence of the trapdoor."

"I'm sure if you know about it, the people who *actually* live here know about it," I grumbled. "What if we get trapped down here?"

"Impossible. We'll simply nip back up and push the door open. Easy."

"If we don't break our necks stumbling around in the dark first." I reached a hand out in front of me. "Exploring a black hole isn't really that exciting."

"If only we had a torch."

"A torch? What is this, *Frankenstein*?"

"Torches aren't merely for monsters, Dylan. . . . Just a moment . . ." I heard footsteps and the rustle of fabric. "Ah, here it is." A soft click, and a beam of artificial light pierced the gloom. "A torch."

"A flashlight," I responded. For the first time, I could see the low stone ceiling and narrow walls. It reminded me of when Hugh Jackman dragged that guy through a sewer in *Les Mis*, which was a mostly unremarkable movie, except for the fact that it inspired Heaven to cut all her hair off. Which I thought was totally bizarre, because who *wants* to look like a dead, toothless prostitute? Of course, Heaven ended up looking totally stunning, like Lupita Nyong'o. If I cut all my hair off, I would definitely look like a dead, toothless prostitute. Actually, I'd probably just look like a boy. "Did you stash that flashlight down here?"

"*The Premeditated Torch* is, naturally, the follow-up to the smash best seller *The Premeditated Trapdoor*."

"That is seriously the worst idea for a book series I've ever heard."

"Nonsense. Dashing British hero and his plucky American lady sidekick explore uncharted territory? It's brilliant."

"Plucky?" Eh, I'd been called worse. "And this territory has already been charted. By you."

"But it's uncharted for you, my plucky American lady sidekick." I turned to see him grinning at my side. "You can hold the torch, if you'd like."

"How benevolent of you." I grabbed the flashlight. "Guess that makes you the sidekick now."

"Lead on, then."

I pointed the beam of light straight ahead, seeing nothing but more Hugh Jackman sewer tunnel. It was crazy to think that we were wandering in this passage beneath the castle while everyone else just walked around oblivious above us. I wondered how many other people knew it existed. Probably everyone. But it was nice to at least pretend that I had found somewhere secret to hide from TRC. Even if that somewhere was a damp, airless tunnel. At the end of that hall, we came to a fork—the passageway seemed to continue endlessly in each direction.

"How long does this go on for?" I marveled.

"The tunnel system is quite extensive. I believe it goes beneath the entire main building, and may connect to some of the outer buildings. I'm honestly not certain."

"That's crazy." I shook my head. "Why all the secret passageways?"

"It's only a theory, but the bulk of the estate was built during a time of political upheaval. Perhaps it was an escape system."

"Huh. Which way?"

"Up to you."

I pointed the flashlight to the left, to the right, to the—

"Jamie," I whispered. "There's something glowing down there."

"Turn off the torch."

I did. In the darkness, it was easy to see a faint blue-white light to the left.

"Magic," I whispered.

"Sorry?"

"What? Um, nothing!" Obviously, it wasn't magic. *Obviously*. "We have to check that out, right?"

"I would expect nothing less from the intrepid heroes of *The Premeditated Trapdoor*!"

"You've gotta let that go," I groaned. I turned to the left, switching the flashlight back on and swinging it in front of me.

"Ow!"

"Dusty?" I asked curiously. The flashlight's beam illuminated my sister, squatting in front of a shoe box with her iPhone clutched in her hand.

"I said, ow! Honest, Dilly, you're shining that thing right in my eyes."

"Oh. Sorry." I pointed it at the ground. Dusty blinked, shaking her head. "What are you doing down here?"

"Facebook. For some reason my phone only connects to the Internet down here if I squat real low. Makes no damn sense."

Ah. Probably scrolling through her bazillion friends and admiring her selfie collection. Lest she forget even for, like, twenty minutes how popular she was.

"Why are you Facebooking in a dark tunnel?"

"I hid a phone down here. You know TRC doesn't want us to have any kind of contact with the outside world. Spoilers."

"Yeah, God forbid it leak on the Internet what your color scheme is." I rolled my eyes. "America would be devastated."

"I don't make the rules, Dylan." She dropped the phone back in the shoe box at her feet.

"No, you just break them."

"What do you want from me, Dyl?" Dusty jammed the lid back on the box with more force than was necessary, then rose to face me, eyes flashing. "I'm stupid if I go along with the show; now you're givin' me grief for goin' against it. Which is it? You can't have it both ways."

"I was just— God, Dusty, it was just a joke." Was she going to *cry*? It was kind of hard to tell in this light, but it looked like she was turning red like she did when she was going to *really* cry, not in the fake way she cried when her old boyfriend got the wrong flowers for prom, or when she was crowned Miss Mississippi. "Sorry, okay?"

"Whatever." She tapped her fingers briskly beneath her eyes, swiping away any eyeliner smudges. Because of course she couldn't look less than perfect for one single second. "I'm gettin' enough crap today, and I don't need any more from you."

"Are you feeling better, then?" Jamie asked solicitously. Oops. I kind of forgot he was there. Something about spending too much time with Dusty turned me into an obnoxious eight-year-old all over again.

"Oh. Yes, I'm all right. Just a bit of a tummy bug. It's the food y'all eat here. No offense, Jamie."

"None taken." He shrugged. "Britain's culinary foibles are a long-standing punch line."

"Not anymore," I argued. "Think of all the great British chefs. Jamie Oliver. Gordon Ramsay. Nigella Lawson."

"Thank you, Food Network," Dusty snapped. "The food's heavy. That's all I'm sayin'."

"Yeah, because we *never* eat butter. In Mississippi."

"Do you have to argue with every single little thing I say?" Dusty heaved a long-suffering sigh.

"Is Mississippi particularly known for its butter?" Jamie asked politely, ignoring the daggers I was glaring at Dusty.

"Um, no, not particularly," I admitted. "But the South is kind of notorious for drowning everything in butter. Buttered biscuits. Buttery grits. Butter, well, everything."

"Ah, I see. Like Britain's much-maligned culinary reputation. A sort of cultural joke that might not always be accurate."

"Exactly." Dusty jumped in. "Mama always cooked everything in Pam."

"Pam?" Jamie repeated curiously.

"It's a fat-free cooking spray," I explained. "Not important. Don't you have a tour to be getting back to?"

"Don't you?" Dusty replied pointedly. "I'm sorry. Were you two tryin' to be . . . alone? Together?"

"Dusty!" I shrieked. "Shut up!" I could feel my face getting hot. And then hotter still, as I realized I had just shrieked in what probably sounded like repulsion to Jamie, but was actually just embarrassment. Oh God, this day . . . just . . . had . . . to . . . end. At least I'd proved that it was scientifically impossible for a human being to spontaneously combust from mortification. Otherwise I would have been long dead.

"We were simply exploring the castle," Jamie said smoothly, as if my outburst hadn't happened. Dusty, on the other hand, was sporting an annoying expression of amusement. "Looking for trapdoors, secret passages, that sort of thing. As you can see, we succeeded admirably. As did you, apparently."

"Apparently." She shrugged. "Fine, let's get out of this cave. I think I can handle Her Royal Pain in the Ass again."

I snorted. Dusty was so much more fun when she wasn't pretending to be perfect.

"Walk, Dylan. You've got the flashlight."

Never mind. She was just bossy and annoying. Sighing, I turned back the way we'd come.

"So, Jamie, I don't know if she's told you, but Dilly's quite the track star." I looked behind me. Dusty had threaded her arm through Jamie's.

"It's cross-country," I muttered grumpily. "It's different. I'm a distance runner. I don't hop over things."

"Yes, she's quite sporty," Dusty cooed. "You could never tell it by the way she slouches and eats like a hog, but she's a real little athlete." There was nothing more annoying than Dusty in full-on Southern-belle mode. Also, what was her game here? I couldn't tell. Was she trying to sell him on me, or scare away the only friend I had in this godforsaken frozen chunk of rock?

Whatever it was, she was up to something, and I didn't like it.

CHAPTER SEVEN

My days at Dunyvaig took on a strange, dreamlike quality. Since I was deprived of the clock and calendar on my phone, everything felt timeless. With no TV, no phone, and nothing to do, I spent most days roaming aimlessly around the castle, eating as much free food as was humanly possible and having contests with Jamie to see who could throw more peanuts into Kit's open mouth when he passed out on the couch for his daily afternoon nap. I was shocked to discover a whole week had passed without me realizing it. All those peanut tosses had blurred together. Cabin—uh, castle—fever setting in after seven days of nothing, I laced up my sneakers, pushed open the heavy front doors, and set out for a run.

With each footfall on the ground, I could feel my head getting clearer. Everything was always better when my arms were pumping, my heart was beating quickly, and my breath was puffing white in short, sharp bursts. Well, my breath didn't normally puff white when I ran, but here, in the cool December air, I was using my winter gear for the first time since that freak cold snap sophomore year. And it felt good.

Even better, I had officially outrun the Reality Channel. The cameraman lasted for about seven minutes before concluding he had enough boring B-roll of me and then wheezing his way back toward the house. Finally, there was nothing staring at me with its giant, eyelike lens. Well, except for the quails. But they had two small beady eyes. And they didn't do anything except chortle at me grumpily as I ran past them. But really, it was their fault for sleeping in the road.

They were cute, though, all soft and brown, folded into little bundles like footballs nestling in the tire tracks. Every once in a while, I'd see the movement of a quail pecking its way through the forest that lined either side of the road. Quails. Kinda charming. Who knew?

I rounded a bend, coming out of the forested area into an open field filled with grazing sheep. In the distance sat three small cottages with thatched roofs, smoke puffing jovially out of their chimneys. Had I run off the grounds? Or was this all still part of the estate? If so, it was massive. Way bigger than I'd ever imagined.

Time to turn back. The last thing I wanted to do was get lost out here before it got super dark and I ended up roaming the moors all night long. With my luck, I'd run straight into the hound of the Baskervilles.

A roaring behind me assaulted my ears, sending my heart rate sky-high. The hound! I sped up, but turned to look behind me. Come on, Dylan. Obviously, it wasn't a hound. It was a green, muddy Range Rover that somehow appeared to be wider than the narrow dirt road it was traveling on. My foot caught on something and sent me sprawling forward. I landed heavily in the gravel and dirt, my knees and wrists throbbing with pain. I'd forgotten the number one rule of cross-country: Watch your feet—look where you're going. Don't turn around to check behind you for the hound of the Baskervilles. Well, I'd added that last part, but it definitely applied.

I'd landed squarely on my belly in a Dylan-size puddle. I rolled over and tried to pull my sodden sweatshirt away from my flesh, only to be rewarded by a sucking sound and the unpleasant heft of wet cotton.

The truck roared by, soaking me with a tsunami of brown water. With one chipper "Sorry, love!" in parting, my assailant disappeared. Gingerly, I pushed myself back up to standing, brushing a few bits of gravel off my shaking knees. I swiped the mud from my eyes and mouth with an equally muddy sleeve. It was time to head back to Dunyvaig and hope that today, the water in the ancient pipes was warmer than the air, because I was in desperate need of a shower.

Turning, I put one muddy sneaker in front of the other. After a few experimental jogs, I came to a stop—running in heavy, wet, dirty cotton was torture. This settled it—I was never doing one of those mud run things.

The wind whistled down the back of my neck, freezing me in my soggy sweatshirt. With each damp step my feet felt heavier, my limbs colder, and the castle farther and farther away. Why had I run so far? At this rate there was no way I'd make it back before it got dark out. And then I'd definitely get eaten by a hound.

Far too many agonizing minutes later, one of those thatch-roofed cottages appeared around a bend. There was no smoke coming out of this one's chimney, but maybe it was heated somehow. At this point I would have danced merrily into the flames of hell for a chance to warm up.

Very ungracefully, I clambered over the split-rail fence and landed with a thump in the open field behind it. A few sheep bleated noisily at me from their corner of the field but declined to come over and investigate what I was doing.

I fought my way through the tall grass until I finally made it to the front door. I sent up a silent wish that it was open and very, very warm.

"Hello?" I called, knocking at the door. No answer. I pounded harder on the weathered wooden doorframe, using both fists. "Hello? Hello?!"

Still no answer. I tried the door. The lock rattled but remained firmly locked. So much for warming up in the cottage. I couldn't believe I would have to walk all the way back to the castle.

A flash of color caught my eye. I turned the corner and discovered a little green Gator with bright yellow seats and rugged black tires parked right out back. I was shocked to see a familiar leaping deer on the front fender.

"John Deere," I muttered, bending down to examine the logo more closely. "Didn't think I'd see you over here." I patted the front of the Gator companionably, like it was an old dog sleeping in the last gasp of afternoon sunshine.

The keys were in the ignition, just waiting to be turned. Was it stealing, to drive this Gator back to the castle? Not if this was all part of the grounds, right? And especially not if I returned it. And it was the only thing standing between me and hypothermia.

Well, as Meemaw liked to say, God helps those who help themselves. So I jumped into the front seat and turned the key in the ignition. The Gator roared to life. Cautiously pressing the gas pedal, I rolled forward onto the road.

I relaxed my grip on the steering wheel as the Gator picked up steam, happy to see that the stiff breeze was drying me out. Somewhat. Even if it was freezing. Perhaps it was just my fate to never, ever be warm in Scotland. Or maybe it was my warm Mississippi blood. It had left me weak.

I must not have run as far as I'd thought. Before I knew it I was pulling up the long gravel driveway, then roaring around the circular part that led right up to the front of the house. Uh, castle. It seemed weird to just leave the Gator there, but I had no idea what else to do with it. If it didn't vanish of its own accord, I could always ask someone else where to put it later. Worst-case scenario, I could drive it back there myself. Once I was dry. And wearing a coat.

Up the steps to the front door I hopped over places where the ancient stone had cracked and split away. I pushed open the door and slipped inside. The foyer was deserted except for a tall dark-haired guy in a gray suit, hands in his pockets. I was surprised to see it was Jamie when he turned. He looked different, somehow, from the back. Like older or something. But then his hair fell in his eyes and he looked just the same as always. Even if he was wearing a tie.

"Hello there," Jamie greeted me cheerfully. "Are you a Swamp Thing?"

"No. I'm a Dylan Thing."

"Dylan!" he exclaimed. "I honestly didn't recognize you."

"Understandable." I tried to swipe some of the mud off my face and only succeeded in smearing it across my eyes.

"You seem to have encountered a bit of a situation. Was it the little lame balloonman?"

"What?" I stared at him.

"When the world is mud-luscious." I kept staring at him. "The little lame balloonman . . ." He trailed off and looked down at the floor, the tips of his ears turning pink. "It's, er, E. E. Cummings."

"Okay. Well. Clearly, E. E. Cummings never came to Scotland in December, because there is nothing luscious about this mud. I was running, and this truck blasted right on through a ginormous puddle in the middle of the road."

"Ah. I suppose that would account for . . ." He gestured to my appearance, but words seemed to fail him. "This," he settled on eventually.

"Yup. It was a drive-by mudding," I said grimly.

"You'd probably commit murder for a hot bath right now."

"Probably not, Raskolnikov." Oh. Was it weird that I referenced a conversation we'd had a week ago? Maybe? I watched him worriedly, but he didn't seem weirded out. "I may have committed grand theft auto, though."

He raised an eyebrow. Ugh. The jealousy continued. I wished I had better control of my eyebrow muscles. Was that the kind of thing you could train for? At, like, a face gym?

"I took a Gator and drove it over here. It was parked outside a little house. I didn't know if it was part of the estate, or what."

"I assume it must have been one of the groundskeepers' cabins. Unless you ran terribly far. There are several all over the estate. As well as barns and other outbuildings necessitated by the care and keeping of livestock."

"So all of this—all this land, these houses, the cows, everything—it all belongs to Ronan?"

Jamie nodded.

"That is *insane*," I marveled. "How could one person own all of that?"

"Well, the family owns it, technically, Ronan is simply the executor—"

"Still crazy," I interrupted. "It's as big as a town! You could fit, like, five hundred of my house in here. I can't even imagine what that would be like."

Jamie *mmm*ed noncommittally. I guess he was used to it, growing up with Ronan, but it seemed crazy to me. What must Dusty be thinking? What would it be like to marry someone whose idea of normal was a castle and grounds that were bigger than our whole neighborhood?

"So." I decided to change the subject, if all Jamie was going to contribute was an "mmm." "What are you doing here? Were you waiting for something?"

"I'm, simply . . . ahh . . . here." He gestured vaguely toward the hallway. *Huh. Weird.* Well, nothing about Jamie had been exactly normal so far. He'd probably wandered in while thinking about little lame balloonmen and gotten lost on the way to wherever it was he'd been going.

I realized with a start that there was a cameraman lurking in a dark corner next to an end table. Presumably he'd been there the whole time, although I had no idea *why*. This show was about Dusty and Ronan—why would they want any footage of *me*? And how did he even know someone would be coming through this door? Sometimes the camera crew appeared in the most random places. This one guy, who I'm pretty sure was named Mike, shot breakfast every single morning, even though it mostly consisted of people shoveling eggs and toast into their mouths in silence. How many shots did TRC really need of my mom pretending the coffee was strong enough?

Well, if I looked as disgusting as I felt, this clip would probably find a home right after the closing credits of an episode, while they played weird circus music in the background to make me look crazy. For a lot of *Prince in Disguise,* they edited Dusty's best friend, Anne Marie, to look like she was talking to a squirrel. Anne Marie may be kind of a nut, but she's not *that* nuts. And I had a feeling the Anne-Marie-crazy-circus-squirrel music was heading my way. Maybe there was enough mud on my face that no one would register that the mud creature was actually Dylan Leigh, unexceptional Tupelo High junior.

An elegant man in the pervasive white-shirt-gray-slacks staff uniform approached me and Jamie, flanked by another cameraman and a few other clipboard-toting production people. Great. The first cameraman must have been waiting for these guys. Or maybe he'd signaled them, somehow, that he'd gotten some prime crazy-circus-music footage? I didn't understand anything about the way this show worked, and I was starting to think that it might be better if I figured it out, fast.

"Pardon me." The staff man bowed as he came to a stop. "Dinner has already begun. If you'd be so kind . . ."

"If I'd be so kind as to what?" The man was inclining his head in the direction of the dining room, but there was no way I was going in there dressed like this.

"Allow me to escort you to the dining room."

"Yeah, thanks, I just need, like, a hot second to change."

"Madam." The butler from hell was right up in my face, his thin lips curling menacingly. The production people closed ranks around him, effectively blocking my way to the stairs. "Allow me."

The butler attached himself to my elbow and started firmly steering me toward the dining room. I looked behind me at Jamie, who seemed perplexed, which was gratifying but not particularly helpful. What would be more embarrassing— showing up to dinner like this, or attempting to tackle my way out of this situation and making a run for the stairs? Although I wasn't even sure the latter was an option. He had a surprisingly strong grip for an older guy.

As we entered the dining room, the gentle clinks of silverware and trickle of conversation died as a hush fell over the room.

"Jamie," I whispered in a panic as I involuntarily reached for his hand. He squeezed back. Everyone was dressed for dinner. Like, *dressed,* like they were going to church or a cocktail party or something.

"Did no one tell you to dress for dinner?" he asked quietly. Well, guess that explained the suit and tie. Selfishly, I wished I had a sloppy comrade-in-arms. Although unless Jamie took a quick detour to the kitchen for a swim through the gravy bowl there was no way he could be as sloppy as me.

"I didn't even know there *was* dinner." Everyone was still staring. Oh, why wouldn't they just look away? Not for the first time, I wished I were invisible.

I had never felt more conscious of the camera than when it panned up from my mud-encrusted sneakers to the totally goofy shorts-over-leggings combo and the pièce de résistance, a giant, grubby Tupelo High sweatshirt.

"Come on in, sweets, you're late for dinner!" Mom sounded just like honey, though the look in her eyes was anything but. "There's a space open for you right here between me and Dusty!"

Dusty. If anything, she looked even more uncomfortable than I did, poured into a hot-pink floor-length ball gown that displayed a vast expanse of tan cleavage. And to top it all off, she was wearing a tiara. A *tiara*. She looked ready to jet off to the Tupelo High Prom again. Shooting Jamie a baleful look, I marched over to meet my doom. My old enemy the butler reappeared in front of me, having procured a towel from God knows where. He laid the towel over my chair, just like Tate Moseley did before he let his dogs into his new truck. Feeling a little bit like Tate Moseley's dog—the less cute one—I slouched into my seat.

"What on God's green earth do you think you're wearing?" Mom whispered between clenched teeth, her face frozen into a smiling mask.

"I didn't know this was a formal dinner! I didn't even know there *was* a dinner! Shouldn't there be a schedule, or something? If they would just give me a schedule, I'd be on time for stuff like this! If I'd known there was going to be dinner, I never would have gone on a run! You know I always prioritize food over running!"

"You're late. And you look disgraceful."

"Thanks, Mom."

It *was* kind of weird, actually, now that I'd thought about it. They'd sent me an itinerary before I came, but it was just for travel. Did everyone else have a shooting schedule except for me? Were they trying to sabotage me or something? It sounded paranoid, maybe, but they were starting to make me feel paranoid.

A plate of pink mush appeared before me, deposited by a white-gloved hand.

"Well, at least not all is lost—thank goodness for a refreshing cold appetizer!" Mom laughed a dumb little tinkly laugh, just like Dusty's, and everyone returned to their regularly scheduled conversations. I poked halfheartedly at my pink mush with my silverware.

"It's fish," Dusty said. "Salmon rillettes."

"Gross." I dropped the fork.

"Call me a tacky American, but I would kill for a plate of chicken fingers with ranch dressing right now." Dusty leaned forward, resting her chin on her hand. On her left, Ronan chattered away obliviously with his mom, shoveling fish mush into his mouth as he reenacted what looked like a particularly violent rugby game. "Then again, I am a tacky American. I look like a goddamn Barbie."

"At least you're a Barbie with regard for personal hygiene. I look like Pig-Pen."

"I think you and I got very different memos on the dress

code," she whispered as she leaned over to adjust the strings on my hoodie, hiding her face from the camera with her hair.

"Ya think?" I whispered back, leaning over to adjust her necklace in return. We probably looked like monkeys grooming each other, but I didn't know any other way to try to hide from the cameras. "Why are they trying to make us look stupid? I thought America loved you and just wanted to share in your special times blah, blah, blah."

"Maybe that got boring," Dusty said ominously.

I jumped, noticing the camera hovering inches behind my shoulder. If anything it seemed more sinister than before. I always knew there was an element of fakery to reality TV—I wasn't an idiot—but actually being manipulated by the production team felt so much worse than I'd imagined it would. This dumb show was as fake as Dusty's tan. I realized with a thud that they were almost definitely setting me up to be the Anne Marie of *Countdown to the Crown*. Why else would they have insisted I attend a formal dinner in muddy running gear? I was going to be Dusty's dumb sister. The comic relief. The stupid American. Ugh. I didn't need any help looking like an idiot. Clearly, I could manage that perfectly fine on my own.

Suddenly, Dusty flashed her megawatt grin, quick as turning on a light switch. "My goodness, Dylan!" she exclaimed. "Looks like you got yourself into quite a mess!"

Typical Dusty—deflecting negative attention away from herself by making me look bad.

"Dylan saved me from a wild boar." I looked across the table and my eyes locked with Jamie's. "Unfortunately, her wardrobe was a casualty in her efforts to secure my safety." A smile tugged at the corners of my lips. "She was terribly valiant. Quite dashing, really."

"Jamie, how very silly." Ronan's mom laughed in a way that was probably supposed to be carefree, but just sounded slightly deranged. It was bizarre, how nice she was to Jamie. Well, I guess he was a lot more polite than Kit Kirby. When it came to choosing a groomsman for Florence to favor, it wasn't much of a contest. "Wild boar haven't roamed the lands at Dunyvaig since the time of Henry the Eighth."

"Girls can't be valiant." Kit waved his wineglass around, splashing Jamie with a few white drops. Well, look who was up and conscious. "Or dashing. It's a male adjective, is it no?"

"I can assure you, she was valiance personified." Jamie cut a neat square of fish mush. "What a particularly refreshing rillette."

And just like that, things didn't seem so bad.

"He likes you," Dusty said softly.

"What? He? Who? No. What? I mean, what? No."

"Yes, he does, you twitchy li'l owl. It's so obvious that even *you* must notice it, Miss Never-Had-a-Boyfriend."

"I've had a boyfriend," I said defiantly. It was already embarrassing enough being a sixteen-year-old who'd never been kissed. It was way worse being a sixteen-year-old who'd never been kissed when your big sister had never, ever been single. "Just because you've had, like, a thousand boyfriends—"

"I have not had a *thousand* boyfriends—"

"Doesn't mean you know everything and I know nothing. I've had a boyfriend." I grumpily spooned some fish mush into my mouth. Mistake.

"Dilly, if you're even thinkin' about mentionin' the name

Matty Van Meter right now, that's downright embarrassing. Y'all were in first grade."

"He was still my boyfriend."

"He's strange. But handsome. In a strange way. Jamie, I mean. Not Matty Van Meter. He was an unfortunate-lookin' child."

"He looked *fine*. And he had a lot of Playmobils."

"An admirable quality in a beau, I'm sure." She took a dainty sip of wine. Somehow not a single smudge of hot-pink lipstick or sticky gloss remained on the glass. It was things like that that made me wonder if Dusty was human. "Have you asked Jamie about his Playmobil collection?"

"Um, no." I snorted. "My priorities have shifted slightly since first grade."

"And what are they? These estimable man priorities?"

"I don't know, Dusty! God!" I gulped down some water. Bubbly. Wasn't expecting that. Dusty thumped me on the back as I coughed my way back to equilibrium. "What's with the third degree? I just want someone who's nice and smart and interesting and thinks I'm nice and smart and interesting. It's not brain surgery."

"No, it's not, is it?" she said softly. "When it's right, it's dead easy." I followed her gaze over to Ronan. The rest of this show may have been a farce, but she really did love him. Even I could see that. "Want some advice?"

"Advice? What kind of advice?"

"Man advice, dummy."

"From you?" I snorted. "No thank you."

"Excuse me? I am the ultimate source of man advice. In case you haven't noticed, I am *engaged* to a *very* handsome man. Obviously I know what I'm talkin' about."

"No, it's okay, I got it, thanks. I picked up a few tips in a lifetime of being your sister. 'Ooo, tee-hee-hee! Giggle, giggle! Oh my stars, aren't you a big strong man!'"

"I do not talk like that—"

"'Land sakes, your bicep is bigger than my teeny tiny waist! Ah bet you could bench-press me! Oh, whoopsy-daisy, look at that, Ah have exposed a vast array of cleavage!'"

"Oh, hush your mouth," Dusty muttered grumpily. "I was just tryin' to help you reel in that big weird fish." She indicated to Jamie across the table, who, thankfully, seemed wholly engrossed in trying to keep Kit from spilling his wine. "But he seems to like you as is anyway." She sniffed. "So I guess just keep doin' what you're doin'."

"That's the plan."

"So you admit you have a plan for reelin' him in?" Dusty pounced.

"What? No—"

"But that's exactly what you said—"

"What I *meant* was that the plan was to just keep doing what I was doing because I have absolutely no plans or designs or intentions on anything involving fish or boys or whatever!"

It was truly a testament to the cavernous acoustics of the dining room that no one appeared to have heard my outburst.

"The wee sister doth protest too much, methinks," Dusty drawled archly.

"Can it, Shakespeare," I snarled.

It was going to be a very long night.

CHAPTER EIGHT

I realize that eating a twelve-course dinner doesn't exactly qualify as a hardship. But eating a twelve-course dinner while encrusted with dried mud and slowly freezing to death under a particularly pernicious draft was not one of the highlights of my existence. I was much happier now that dinner was over and I was safely tucked up in bed. If TRC had expected either drama or hilarity to ensue by encouraging Dusty to dress up like a delusional Barbie and dragging me through the mud, they must have been sorely disappointed. The only moderately interesting incident at dinner had occurred when Kit Kirby reenacted parts of *Pippin* with a Cornish game hen. That strange, short man was headed straight for his very own spin-off series. *Keepin' It Kirby*, or something like that. Heaven would definitely DVR that one.

Heaven. Man, I wished Heaven were here. Jamie had turned out to be a surprisingly fun partner in crime, but I couldn't exactly talk to Jamie *about* Jamie, now could I? Because as much as I had protested to Dusty . . . I did want to talk about Jamie. Desperately. Just not with Dusty, who loved to tease me about my perpetually single state and had only ever dated football players and prom kings and, you know, a right honorable lord or whatever. She would never understand Jamie.

I wondered if Heaven would think he was weird. Probably. But there was good weird and bad weird, and Jamie was definitely good weird. I liked that I never knew what he was going to say next. I liked that he looked for trapdoors. I liked that he made me laugh over salmon rillettes. Hell, I just plain liked him. Which was not something I had said out loud to a boy since Andy Chan told me I was stinky and gross in fourth grade. I could barely even bring myself to *think* that I liked Jamie, totally alone with only Teddy for company.

Although . . . A horrifying thought drifted along. Did everyone know I liked him? Dusty did. Oh God. Did that mean *Jamie* knew I liked him? Too humiliating to contemplate.

I burrowed deeper under the blankets, willing myself to emanate more body heat. After a hot shower followed by a long soak in a deep porcelain tub with actual claw feet, I was thoroughly de-mudded, but cold once again, thanks to my still-wet hair. Normally I never bothered with a hair dryer, but I was sure wishing I had one right now. Not that I wanted one badly enough to go ask Dusty for hers. Firstly, I had no idea where in this maze of a castle she was staying; secondly, she would undoubtedly tease me for attempting uncharacteristically girly things with a hair dryer; and thirdly, I definitely did not want to interrupt any nocturnal activities that she and Ronan may or may not have been participating in.

Was Dusty right? Did Jamie like me? He certainly seemed

to like spending time with me. But the options here were somewhat limited. Ronan was on Planet Mush with Dusty, and Kit Kirby was a giant drunk baby with no concept of time. And if I was being honest with myself, I wasn't sure what was scarier: if Jamie didn't like me . . . or if he did.

Knock-knock-kna-knock-knock-knock.

"Hello?" I whispered, drawing the covers up to my neck. Who could possibly be at the door? As always, I had absolutely no idea what time it was, but it felt late. Like the middle of the night.

"Do you want to build a snowman?"

I slipped out of bed and nearly jumped in shock as my feet touched the icy floor. Somehow the cold managed to cut through my penguin socks. I slid closer to the door.

"Come on, let's go and play."

"Jamie?" I asked. Who else would it have been? I mean, I guess it could have been Ronan with a new phase in Operation: Wee Sister. Although I doubted Ronan could have gotten through any of "Do You Want to Build a Snowman?" without bursting into tears.

"I never see you anymore."

"You saw me at dinner." Definitely Jamie. Ronan would have had much more rumbly Scottish *R*s.

"Come out the door. It's like you've gone awaaaaay!"

I pulled the door open. Jamie's mouth was still opened in a wide "aaaay."

"Um, hi."

"Hello there." He grinned.

"This is a bit of a change from E. E. Cummings."

"Poetry comes in many forms, Dylan."

"Are you wearing a pajama suit?" I asked incredulously. He looked like he'd wandered straight out of *Peter Pan*. I didn't think people actually wore those things anymore.

"Naturally. I'm not an animal."

"This is, like, a whole matching . . . thing." Unless I was mistaken, the trim of his navy pajamas matched the tartan of his bathrobe. He was more coordinated for sleep than I usually was for a school day.

"If you're referring to my dressing gown, I can assure you, it is essential when navigating these drafty halls."

"You just look a little formal, that's all."

"The various elements of my ensemble are certainly no more ludicrous than those creatures cavorting about on your trousers."

"I'm actually wearing three different pairs of pants right now. And that creature is Tweety Bird. And these were a gift from my meemaw. And I would really prefer to go back to discussing *your* pajama situation."

"Or we could simply cease discussing pajamas altogether."

"Deal."

I stuck out my hand.

"The Pajama Amnesty Accord of Dunyvaig Castle is hereby consecrated."

We shook, Jamie gripping my fingers firmly, holding on just a bit longer than was normal—or was that just my imagination? Or was *I* the one who was holding on too long? Quickly, I dropped his hand like it had scalded me. Now that I had admitted to myself—and to Teddy—that I actually liked Jamie, I was insanely paranoid that he would discover it. How did anyone actually maneuver into becoming someone's girlfriend? It seemed impossible. The whole process was littered with minefields of mortification. I'd done nothing but shake his hand, and my cheeks were burning like I'd jumped his bones on top of the mixed-berry pavlovas during dessert.

"Do you want to build a snowman, then?" he asked.

"I'm sorry?"

"Put on your shoes," he commanded. "Quickly now."

"Um, okay." I retreated into my bedroom and grabbed a pair of half-destroyed Uggs that had once been Dusty's. "Why am I putting my shoes on?"

"Because although you have declined to answer my question as of yet, the fact that you are pulling on those shapeless brown lumps confirms that you are not disinclined to build a snowman."

"They're Uggs. And they're comfy," I said. "Wait, are you serious about a snowman?"

"As serious as I was about that trapdoor."

I caught a half smirk as Jamie turned and walked down the hallway, me following hot on his heels.

"Jamie. Wait. Jamie." I reached out and tugged on his hand, and he stopped. "A snowman? Is it snowing?"

A grin broke out across his face, and I swear I felt something crack and melt inside my chest, like it was gonna warm me all the way through.

"I think it's best if you see for yourself."

He kept my hand tucked in his as we flew down the long, wide staircase with its maroon carpet. We made our way into the grand entrance hall, and Jamie pushed one of the enormous doors open just wide enough that we could slip through, then shut it behind us.

Everything outside had been transformed. Before, there

had been nothing but gray and brown; now all I could see was sparkling white. The moon hung full and low in the sky, illuminating the grounds as they shimmered. In the distance I could barely make out the trees of the forest that comprised the edge of the estate; the lawn seemed limitless.

"I've never seen snow before," I whispered.

Jamie took my hand again and led me down the stone steps to the lawn, my feet sinking into the snow. Marveling, I held out my hand and watched the flakes land in my palm. When you looked closely, each one really did look like its own little star, more intricate than anything Heaven and I had cut out of construction paper in elementary school. I looked up, and all I saw was Jamie. A shock of dark hair falling into startlingly blue eyes framed by long, long lashes. He was so close, I could feel each puff of breath as he exhaled, a warm caress in the cold air. I tilted my head up to his, our noses nearly touching. I could hear his heart beat—or maybe it was mine—a gentle *thud*, *thud* in the otherwise silent night. Soft as a feather, he brushed his lips against mine, cold and cool, a whisper of a kiss.

"I've never been kissed before, either."

If he was surprised, he didn't show it. Although I could have killed myself for blurting that out.

"Good." He smiled. "That way you'll never know if I'm rubbish."

He wasn't rubbish. He was the opposite of rubbish. He kissed me again, more firmly this time, and it was like I melted into him. All the worries I'd had that when someone finally kissed me I wouldn't know what to do vanished in an instant. It was like I'd been born to kiss Jamie . . . Jamie . . . I realized suddenly that I didn't know his last name. Probably not a good thing. But did I care? Not in the slightest. Because Jamie was kissing me, his large hands pressed against my back like we were dancing, my hands somehow snaking around to feel the soft hairs at the back of his neck, and who knew that having someone else's tongue in your mouth—which sounded so weird in theory—would be so perfect in real life.

We broke apart, and I looked up at him, hardly able to believe this was really happening.

"You have snow in your eyelashes, Dylan," Jamie said matter-of-factly. He brushed a thumb against my cheek. "Suddenly I saw the cold and rook-delighting heaven."

"What now?"

"It's Yeats."

"Shut up and kiss me, Yeats."

He threw his head back and laughed. "I thought it was a moment for poetry!"

"Na-unh." I grabbed the lapels of his bathrobe. Now that Jamie had kissed me, it felt like there was nothing more to be embarrassed about. I could do anything, because I *knew* he liked me. I felt so fearless, like I was flying. Maybe you really could get high on life.

"I had always suspected you American women would be quite forward."

"Less talking, more kissing."

"So terribly forward."

"Are you complaining?"

"Most decidedly not."

Jamie crushed me into his chest as his lips found mine. He was definitely not complaining.

My eyes flicked open as a beam of light cut through the quiet darkness. I shut them again against the light, burying my face in Jamie's neck. *Mmm.*

"Good God, Dylan, you've transported me to a higher plane. Should we go into the light? Are we dead?"

I smacked his arm. *Light— Wait—*

"Jamie!" I stood upright. Now was not the time for casual neck smelling, even if someone smelled tantalizingly of cinnamon, like a manly Christmas cookie. "It's the show. Right? The camera crew. They must have followed us."

I knew no one at TRC was particularly interested in filming me. But I'd watched enough reality TV to know that making out was always worthy of airtime, no matter how weird and gangly the participants were. And that was the last thing I wanted.

"Perhaps they haven't found us quite yet," he said grimly. "Come on, then!"

He grabbed my hand and started running toward the woods, away from the light. I looked behind me, to see if I spotted any cameras, but there was nothing other than that blinding beam of light.

"I really hope they didn't see anything," I murmured as we broke out of the driveway and turned right onto the road.

"Embarrassed by me, are you?" he asked lightly.

"Don't be ridiculous," I scolded. "I would just really rather not have my first kiss broadcast on national television. That seems like a special circle of humiliation hell."

"It is somewhat inconceivable to me that two people who hold their privacy in such high regard have somehow ended up on a reality television program."

"You and me both, buddy."

For a moment there was no sound but the squeaky crunch of the snow beneath our feet. Not even so much as a chortle from a quail. The light that had startled me was long gone, too. If we'd outrun TRC, it didn't seem smart to be running into a forest in the middle of a snowstorm.

"Should we head back?" I asked, yet made no move to slow down.

"Never fear, we're almost there. Do you see the light?"

"What, from the show?" I looked back. "They can't still be following us."

"No, up ahead. From the barn. There. See?"

Blinking through the snow, I did, in fact, see a very faint light in the distance.

"Don't worry, it's closer than it appears," he assured me.

He wasn't wrong. Only a few minutes later, we turned off the road and plowed through the snow toward the light. I couldn't believe how quickly it was piling up—it felt like we'd only been outside for minutes and the snow was already well past my ankles. With a deafening creak, Jamie wrenched open one of the enormous barn doors. The wind buffeted us inside, leaving a snowdrift at our feet as Jamie pulled the door closed behind him. We were greeted by a blast of warm air and the overpowering scent of horse.

"Wow." I vigorously brushed snow off my arms and shook it out of my hair. "It's warm. I can't believe it."

"They've always taken better care of the horses than the people here at Dunyvaig."

Someone nickered softly in agreement from his stall.

"This is a huge barn." We stood at one end of a long alley of stalls, under an enormous cavern of rafters. Everything was made of blond wood and illuminated by the soft golden glow of silver lamps hanging above each stall. I wandered closer to the first stall, lured by a snort and an insistent stamp of hooves.

"Ronan's mum was quite the equestrienne in her day. She rode for Great Britain in the Olympics."

"What? No she didn't. That's insane."

"She did indeed. Didn't medal, but she rode. Of course, she went on to be very involved in the movement to grant Scotland its own Olympic team, so I'm not entirely sure of her feelings on the Olympics at the moment." Something settled onto my shoulders. Jamie had wrapped a plaid blanket around me. "Don't worry, it's clean."

"How do you know?"

"I smelled it."

"Very scientific. Thanks." I pulled it tightly around me, closing it with one hand. Between the blanket and the heated barn, this was by far the warmest I'd been since I'd left Mississippi.

"Hey, girl," I cooed softly at a large brown horse who'd leaned her head out of the stall to investigate us.

Jamie tapped a brass nameplate on the front of the stall door.

"Uh, boy," I corrected myself. "Hey, boy. Wenceslas. That's a hell of a name for a horse."

"Must be a hell of a horse."

"I love the way their noses feel." I reached out a hand to stroke his nose. "So soft. Like velvet." He nickered into my hand, blasting me with hot breath and probably just a little bit of horse snot. "Man, I wish I had an apple or some baby carrots or something. I love the way it feels when they pick food up out of your hand. It's amazing that something so big can be so gentle."

Jamie circled his arms around my waist, looking over my shoulder at the horse. I leaned back against him, watching Wenceslas blink his big brown eyes. Jamie pressed a soft kiss against the side of my neck, and my toes curled in my Uggs. Was this what it was like when you liked someone who liked you back? Was it really just this easy? That was what Dusty had said at dinner, after all. Maybe she had some idea of what she was talking about.

Honestly, though, it was hard to believe that any of this was real. The midnight knock on the door, the snow, the kiss. I had a sinking suspicion that I'd wake up and find out that none of it had happened. Or even worse, that I'd wake up and return to my horribly awkward self and be unable to make eye contact with Jamie, let alone enjoy toe-curling neck kisses while cuddled in a horse blanket.

"The snow's really coming down." There was a small window in Wenceslas's stall. Through it, I could see nothing but white.

"Erm, yes, I suppose it is," he agreed.

"Should we go back?"

"I'm not sure that would be wise." I looked up at him. A cute wrinkle sprang up between his eyebrows as he frowned. "I fear we'd strike out into the snow and be unable to find our way back to Dunyvaig."

"So we just . . . stay here?" Leaving his embrace, I turned to face him.

"For the moment, I suppose."

Stay here. For the moment. Totally alone. In a smelly yet somehow sort of romantic horse barn. Alone. With a boy. With Jamie. In the night.

"It wasn't a terribly well-thought-out plan," he continued,

oblivious to the mental roller coaster I was riding. "I must admit, I didn't think far beyond my attempt to rescue the beautiful girl from the clutches of the nefarious television producers."

Beautiful?

"I can assure you," he continued, "this wasn't some sort of premeditated horse-barn seduction."

"Follow-up to the international best sellers *The Premeditated Trapdoor* and *The Premeditated Torch*."

"Unfortunately for *The Premeditated Horse-Barn Seduction*, it didn't quite enjoy the critical success of its predecessors," Jamie said seriously, his eyes dancing. "The adult content ruffled quite a few feathers in the literary world. Naturally."

"Naturally," I agreed.

"Honestly, Dylan"—he swallowed loudly—"it was never my intention to abduct you."

"I know."

"I'm glad. Because I . . . I quite like you." He scratched the back of his neck self-consciously, looking up at the rafters, looking anywhere but at me. "And I'd like you to think well of me," he mumbled.

"I do." I reached out to touch his chin, and he turned the full force of those clear blue eyes on me. "And I quite like you, too," I added shyly.

"Glad that's settled, then." He smiled. "Would you like to see the hayloft? There are bigger windows up there. We can watch the snow fall."

"Sure." I pulled my blanket a little tighter around me. "Bye, Wenceslas." He snorted in response to my final nose pat.

We climbed up a metal ladder to the hayloft. There was

no floor in the center of the room, so we could see down to the stalls. Hay bales lined the walls on all four sides of the barn. Conveniently, there were a few stacked almost like risers beneath the large windows on the side. Jamie spread a blanket over the lower bales, and we settled in. I extended my corner to him, and he snuggled under, draping an arm around my shoulder as he wrapped us up in the blanket.

We sat in silence, watching the snow drift down outside the window. The flakes were so large and fluffy, they seemed suspended in the sky, almost motionless. There was no sound except for the gentle snorts and stamps of the horses in their stalls below. I could smell the sweetness of the hay and the warm, earthy scent of the horses, both so strong they were almost tangible. Everything was so still it was one of those moments where time no longer seemed to have shape or logic; we had fallen through a moment and all I wanted to do was stay there, drifting like the snowflakes outside the windows. I had thought romance was fireworks and dancing, bright lights and big noises. Now I knew that romance could be perfect stillness.

Because there was Jamie. His warmth. His long leg resting against mine. His cinnamon cookie smell. My knee bumping against his. And to just be with him, touching him seemingly accidentally although we both knew it wasn't—that was perfect.

"It sifts from Leaden Sieves," he quoted as we watched the snow fall. "It powders all the Wood."

"Hmm?"

"That's one of yours. Emily Dickinson."

"Ah." I nodded. "Amherst's most glamorous shut-in. Sorry." I covered my mouth as a yawn escaped.

"Not the time for poetry, then."

"No, I mean, if you can't handle a poem trapped in a barn during a midnight snowfall, when can you? Definitely the time for poetry. I'm just sleepy. A lunatic in a pajama suit woke me up in the middle of the night."

"According to the Pajama Amnesty Accord of Dunyvaig Castle, pajamas were no longer to be discussed."

"Sorry, sorry." I yawned again.

"Close your eyes, Dylan," he said softly.

"My mom'll kill us if we stay out all night." And yet somehow, my eyes fluttered closed, and my head drifted to rest on Jamie's shoulder.

"We'll be back before anyone wakes up," he said confidently.

"Jamie?"

"Mmm?"

"We were lucky this barn was so close. And warm."

"Yes, lucky indeed. Bit of a happy coincidence."

"*Happy Coincidence.*"

"Sorry?"

"*Happy Coincidence.* That's what you should call your book. Forget *The Premeditated Trapdoor.*"

"You never forget your first trapdoor, Dylan," he said seriously.

I knew I wouldn't.

CHAPTER NINE

Something was poking my back. No, a thousand somethings were poking my back. Little scratchy somethings. What was wrong with this bed? And there was something heavy on top of me, right across my middle. I shifted under its weight.

It was an arm. Oh my God, it was a human arm. I screamed and flung it off me.

"Argh!"

THUMP.

"Honestly, Dylan, are you trying to murder me?"

I leaned over and saw Jamie on the floor. The floor made of weathered wooden planks and covered in stray bits of straw. Definitely not my bedroom.

"I realize I may not be a particularly pleasant sight first thing in the morning, but I can't possibly be as horrible as all that."

"Sorry." I reached down and helped haul him back up onto

the hay bale. Hay bale. Barn. Snowstorm. Kiss. Everything from last night came rushing back to me. I was still in the barn—it definitely hadn't been a dream. It was *real*. Jamie had really kissed me. I could only hope I still looked okay in the light of day. In his rumpled pajamas, with bits of hay stuck in his dark hair, Jamie had never looked more adorable.

"Good morning to you, too, darling." He smirked, reaching one hand toward my face. I stiffened as he pulled a piece of straw out of my hair. "The rustic look suits you."

"I *am* a country girl, after all."

"Ah, yes, the belle of Mississippi. Where is it, again? That you're from?"

"Tupelo."

"Too-puh-lo," he enunciated carefully. "What a marvelous word. What does it mean?"

"Um, not sure. I think it's a kind of tree?"

"Fascinating."

"Wait . . . Jamie . . . what are we doing? We can't sit here talking about trees!"

"I admit perhaps dendrology is not the *most* gripping topic, but I do enjoy learning more about your origins—"

"No! Look!" I pointed out the window above the hay bales. Cheery golden beams of sun streaked through the glass—what a perfectly beautiful day to be murdered by my mother. "It's morning. We have to go, like, now."

"It was the nightingale, and not the lark, that pierced the fearful hollow of thine ear."

"What? Birds? You hear birds?"

"Believe me, love, it was the nightingale."

"Jamie, I seriously don't hear anything."

"It's Shakespeare, Dylan! Juliet!"

"Yeah, okay, Juliet, let's go." I started pushing him toward the ladder. "Chop-chop. Off the balcony. Let's move it."

"I worry you lack a poetic soul."

"Someone here has to be practical." I followed him down the ladder at lightning speed, the metal cold against my hands. "Now wouldn't it be convenient if there was a Gator stashed around back of this barn, too?"

"I don't think so." He furrowed his brow. "However, we are quite literally surrounded by alternate means of transportation."

"Meaning?"

"Horses, Dylan."

"Horses?"

"Yes, horses. You sit on them and they take you places. For hundreds of years they were the primary means of rapid transport."

"Sure, eons ago. There's a reason we moved on to cars. Cars aren't alive. They don't move around underneath you. They're not wily and tricky."

"Have you never been on a horse before?" He seemed confused.

"Yes." I lifted my chin defiantly. "Once. On a pony ride. At a county fair. And that was enough."

"But you're *American*."

"Yeah, so? Do you think I'm like a cowgirl or something, Jamie?"

"You're from Mississippi."

"That's not exactly rodeo country. Do *you* know how to ride a horse?"

"Of course," he answered, like it was the most natural thing in the world.

"Of course," I muttered. "Well, horseback riding wasn't covered in gym class, so I'm going to get walking, and I'll see you back at the castle."

"Don't be foolish, Dylan." He grabbed my arm, stopping me. "We'll return to the castle much earlier if we go by horseback. We can ride together."

"Together?" I parroted.

"Yes." He grabbed a metal-and-leather contraption off a peg on the wall and started walking to the first stall. "It's not an ideal situation for the horse, as it can cause kidney damage long term—"

"Well, if it damages the kidneys, then we probably shouldn't," I interrupted.

"But for a short period of time on a big enough horse it should be fine," he assured me. Except I wasn't exactly assured. "Hello again, Wenceslas." He opened the first stall and approached the big brown horse, fitting the reins over his head and plunking the metal piece right in his mouth. Somehow, Wenceslas seemed a lot bigger today than he had last night. "Besides, you like horses, don't you?"

"Yeah, I like horses. I like patting their noses and feeding them carrots. I don't like getting *on* them."

"I worry that you were taken to some horrific county fair that traumatized you for life. I promise you, it's perfectly safe. All of the horses here are impeccably trained. They're far better behaved than most of the humans."

He led Wenceslas out of his stall and into the aisle, right up to a wooden box-type thing that looked like a tiny set of stairs. Jamie hopped up onto the box, swung his leg over, and just like that he was on top of the horse, sitting like he was born to be there.

"Don't you need a saddle?" I asked in a shrill voice that sounded nothing like me. "Shouldn't there be a seat there? Doesn't that serve some kind of seat-belt function?"

"I'll be your seat belt. Come along. Up on the mounting block now."

Obediently, I took the first two steps up the mounting block. Much as I was nervous to get on the horse, I *really* wanted to get back to the castle. On the top step, I swung my leg over, until I was somehow sitting right behind Jamie.

"Now, that wasn't so bad, was it?" he said. "Hold on tight."

I wrapped my arms around his waist, reminded of Dusty's old boyfriend Dyron with the motorcycle. Except, unlike Dyron's motorcycle, Wenceslas had no flames painted on his sides. I could feel Jamie's warmth through his dressing gown. Resting my cheek against his soft flannel back, I relaxed into him.

"There we are," he said softly. "Ready?"

"Ready."

With no discernable "Hi-ya!" or "Tallyho!" or anything like that, Wenceslas started moving. I gripped Jamie even tighter. We trotted down the hallway, straight toward the barn doors. The very big, very solid, very closed barn doors.

"Jamie," I said suddenly, "the doors. How will we—"

"Hold on!" he shouted, but instead of slowing down, we went faster and faster. I closed my eyes, bracing for impact.

But no impact came. I felt the cold slap of the wind whistle past my cheeks. I cracked an eye open. We were outside. But how?

I turned around just in time to see the huge barn doors swing shut behind us.

"They're automatic?!" I exclaimed, laughing with relief.

"Motion sensor. I told you they spared no expense when it came to the horses!"

We moved into an even faster pace, less bumpy than before. The snow was so deep it covered most of Wenceslas's legs, but it didn't seem to be slowing him down at all. It was almost like he was swimming through snow. Now that it had stopped coming down, the castle was easily visible across the lawn. I narrowed my eyes against the blinding glare of sunlight reflecting off the drifts.

"Bracing, isn't it?" Jamie shouted. Something about being on horseback was making us both very loud. "I feel like an arctic explorer! On the way to the pole with Admiral Perry!"

"Glad you're having fun. I would be enjoying this a lot more if I knew my mom was still asleep."

"Where's your sense of adventure, Dylan? How often does one get stranded in a horse barn during a Scottish snowstorm?"

"Never."

"Precisely. I'm sure there is some sort of exception clause for wonderful adventures that precludes one from getting in trouble. The Narnia bylaws or some such."

"My mom makes her own laws." But honestly, now that we were rolling toward the castle, with my arms around Jamie, I felt a lot less scared of Mom. And also less scared of being on the horse. Turned out to be no big deal. Jamie hadn't kissed me again this morning, but at the very least, things weren't awkward. And he was still willing to make physical contact. "Where are your parents?"

"Working," he said vaguely. "They travel quite a bit. I'm on holiday from Eton at the moment, and I would much rather be here than in an empty house."

"Totally. Are they coming to the wedding?"

"Probably."

"If they want to celebrate Christmas with you, they don't really have much choice, do they? I still can't believe Dusty's getting married on Christmas Eve. She's insane. Does she just expect everyone to abandon their families and celebrate her instead? I hope the camera crew's getting paid overtime."

Jamie mumbled something that might have been "mmm" or "erm," but definitely wasn't a word.

"Florence was asking about your dad on the first day, right? Are they friends or something?"

"Somewhat, I suppose. Here we are!" he announced abruptly.

I got the sense that Jamie wasn't exactly keen to discuss his family. I understood, though. I hated when people asked me about my dad—knowing literally nothing about him, I had nothing to say. And the last thing I ever wanted to hear was any sweet "Bless your heart" of pity. Mom and Dusty and I had done just fine without him.

Well, Wenceslas really did get us there quickly. I guess horses had something to recommend them as a mode of transportation after all. Jamie hopped off first, then helped me down, his hands on my waist. Somehow my sweatshirt rode up and his hands ended up on my bare skin. Blushing, I quickly pulled my shirt back down and decided to pretend it hadn't happened.

"Please let everyone be asleep," I prayed fervently as Jamie pushed one of the enormous castle doors open.

As per usual, my prayers went unanswered.

"Well, well, well."

Dusty stood in the doorway with her arms crossed, wearing nothing but a minuscule hot-pink silk bathrobe, hair up in jumbo rollers on her head. Before this moment, I felt like I'd never really understood the phrase "the cat who got the canary." Now I'd seen the textbook definition. Dusty was smiling like a tabby who'd just caught the biggest, fattest canary the world had ever seen.

"Good morning, Dusty!" Jamie said cheerfully. "Beautiful day, isn't it? Perfect for a constitutional! Dylan and I decided to take an early morning turn about the grounds."

"So that's how you're gonna play it?" One of Dusty's eyebrows rose dramatically. God, could everyone do that except for me? "The early-morning-walk routine? That's real amateur-hour stuff, children. Especially as y'all are still in your pajamas. And what pajamas they are." She shook her head. "Real sexy, Dylan."

"These were a gift from Meemaw! And I wasn't trying to be sexy!"

"She doesn't have to try. It's effortless," Jamie said loyally, although that was of course the exact wrong thing to say, as Dusty's smile curved up into Cheshire cat proportions.

"This is an extraordinarily interesting turn of events for a Sunday morning," she drawled delightedly.

"Is Mom up?"

"Could be. Couldn't be. All I know is she hasn't come out of her room yet, so y'all appear to be in the clear. For now."

The relief that washed over me was palpable, like I was planted in the icy-cool wave pool at Geyser Falls on the hottest day in July. I exhaled so loudly it startled Jamie.

"Thing is, I haven't decided if I'm gonna tell her 'bout all y'all's midnight adventures yet."

"Dusty!" I exclaimed. "How could you?"

"I am simply looking out for the virtue of my baby sister," she said, placing an arm protectively around my shoulders. "It is my sisterly duty to inform Mama if y'all have stepped outta line. For your own good."

"I can assure you, her virtue is perfectly intact," Jamie piped up.

"Please don't use the word 'intact' when discussing my virtue." I shuddered. "I'm not Tess of the d'Urbervilles."

"Was she in your grade?" Dusty cocked her head, thinking. "That trashy blond who worked at the Dairy Kream?"

"Tess of the d'Urbervilles is the protagonist of a Thomas Hardy novel," Jamie said. "Ran into a bit of an unfortunate situation after falling asleep on a coat."

"Well. Maybe I should tell Mama so y'all don't end up like Tess of the d'Urbervilles."

"She was a victim of her times!" I protested.

"Or Tess of the Dairy Kream," Dusty added ominously. "Maybe I should tell."

"You wouldn't." I narrowed my eyes.

She raised an eyebrow again, as if to say, *Try me.*

"After all I've done for you?" Okay, now I was seriously pissed. "I hid all those empty bottles of Southern Comfort under my bed for you after your junior prom. I was *ten*. That was messed up, Dusty. You shouldn't have asked me to do that."

"Shut it." Her eyes nervously darted to the left.

"What are you looking at? I . . . Oh." I couldn't believe I hadn't noticed. I couldn't believe I had let myself relax for one moment, and forgotten, and somehow thought I could have a private conversation. There was a cameraman in the doorway, partially obscured so I hadn't seen him right away, but there. He'd clearly caught the entire conversation. "I guess it doesn't matter anymore," I said dully.

"What doesn't matter?" Dusty asked.

"You telling Mom. She'll see it on TV in, like, however many months." I gestured to the camera.

"Don't look at it," Dusty hissed sharply between clenched teeth. "Pretend it's not there."

"How can I pretend it's not there? More importantly, how can *you* pretend it's not there? How can you be so *fake*, just like this stupid fake show?" I gulped some air in, trying to calm down, and failing. "I'm not okay with all my private moments being broadcast for the world to see! I can't live my life in front of the cameras like you can! It's weird, Dusty! It's not natural." I hated how emotional I sounded. I hated that I could hear the catch of tears in my throat. "I just wanted this one thing to myself. I just wanted this me-and-Jamie . . . thing . . . whatever it is . . . just to be between me and Jamie. Not TRC. You know?"

Jamie squeezed my hand. Hurriedly, I brushed a tear off my face. I couldn't have been more embarrassed if I'd peed on the rug.

"That's not what you signed up for, Dylan." Clipboard Pamela slid past the cameraman and into the room with the silent tread and menacing air of a dementor. "Or what your family signed up for. For the next couple weeks, everything that happens, happens in front of us. Just keep living your life normally. We'll simply be here to record it."

"There's nothing normal about this," I muttered. "Are we done?"

"Please, return to your conversation." Pamela smiled graciously. "Just pretend we're not even here."

Pamela slid out of the room as silently as she'd come.

"Is that how you knew where we were?" I asked Dusty. She was having trouble meeting my eyes. "Did Pamela tell you? Did she march into your room and wake you up? Just to manufacture a bit of drama for TRC?"

"Drop it, Dylan," Dusty warned.

"Fine. Sure. We can keep it all fake. I'm going back to my room before Mom gets up. All things considered, I'd prefer to be murdered when I'm back on American soil. And not on camera."

I pushed past her to march up the stairs. With my luck I'd run straight into Mom on my way back to my room.

"Are you all right?"

Oh God. Jamie.

"Jamie, I'm so sorry." I rushed to apologize as we stepped into the upstairs hallway. "I know I turn into a giant baby around Dusty. She just drives me insane."

"Please, no need to apologize. Although I don't have any siblings, I can imagine that must be a charged dynamic. And these are certainly unusual circumstances we've all been thrust into."

"I know. . . . I'd just rather you see my good side."

"I quite like all of your sides." He grinned.

"Well. Um. Thank you," I said. I was not used to being complimented this much. It was nice, but it was so weird. This was the kind of thing that happened to people in movies. Or to girls like Dusty. Not me.

"Here is where I leave you," he announced. We'd somehow

ended up back at my room, no Mom in sight. Maybe small miracles were possible.

"Where's your room, anyway?"

"In an entirely different wing altogether."

An entirely different wing? A *forbidden* wing?

"I warned you never to come here!" I roared.

"Sorry?"

"It's, um, it's from *Beauty and the Beast*. There's a, um, wing. In that. Also." Such a weirdo. Why was I such. A. Weirdo. "I should probably get out of this hallway."

"Probably." Jamie seemed on the verge of laughter, but he was repressing it valiantly. "Good morning, then, Dylan," he murmured.

"Good morning."

He leaned in and kissed me once, softly, on the lips. And then he was gone.

As soon as I'd shut the door behind me, I permitted myself a brief happy dance and a few gleeful squeaks. Jamie had kissed me. He'd kissed me! In a snowstorm, in a barn, and then in the light of day, which meant it was *real*. This was no Tate Moseley Incident. Something was happening here.

I raced to the shower, eager to make it to breakfast before the buffet closed. I had been kissed. Finally. *Finally!* And by someone I actually liked.

A short while later, I hummed "Do You Want to Build a Snowman?" as I toweled my hair dry, pulled on some cleanish clothes, and began my skip along the hall and down the stairs to breakfast.

Something even better than bacon awaited me at the dining room table.

"Heaven?!"

"I knew you'd show up in time for breakfast!"

She bounded out of her chair. I hugged her so tightly I may have lifted her a few inches off the ground.

"Easy, Dylan!" She laughed as she made her way back to the table. "Guess you missed me."

"You have no idea," I said fervently as I sank into the seat next to her. "What are you doing here?" I exclaimed.

"Y'all are too white." Heaven slurped her cereal milk delicately.

"I'm sorry, what now?"

"You heard me. Network wanted some diversity. If y'all think I'm going to sit around spouting some nonthreatening sassy-best-friend crap, y'all have another think coming." Someone cleared his throat. I looked—the only other person in the room was a cameraman in the corner. Of course. "Oh, just edit around it, camera monkey." She waved her spoon menacingly at him. "He's been following me around waiting for an 'Mmm-hmmm' or a 'No he didn't!' all morning."

"I'm so glad you're here. I am in desperate need of some best-friend crap. No need to be sassy."

"What is it?" She put down her spoon and squinted at me. "You look like you have to pee."

"I don't have to pee! I'm bursting with *information*."

"Ooo, if you look like you have to pee, this'll definitely be good. Spill."

How perfect was this timing? I had finally, finally been kissed, and boom! My best friend appeared to discuss it! Although . . . on second thought . . . maybe this timing was a little *too* perfect. Suspiciously perfect. Did TRC fly Heaven out here *because* I'd kissed Jamie? So we could discuss it? No. Logistically, that made no sense. It wasn't even physically possible, and TRC certainly didn't care enough about me and whatever I did or didn't do in horse barns to fly Heaven out because of that. All that America cared about was my perfect sister and her perfect wedding to her perfect not-really-a-prince, and so that was exactly what TRC was going to give them. They'd probably just rewatched the footage from back home in Tupelo and realized Heaven could, in fact, liven up the proceedings. I was downright boring, honestly, and Heaven had a knack for saying the kinds of things that ended up being other people's Facebook statuses.

"Hello? Earth to Dylan?"

"Huh?"

"Aw, man." She scooped up a few cornflakes. "You lost your pee look. Did you forget?"

"No, I didn't *forget*. I'll just have to tell you . . . later."

"Ohhh." She nodded in the direction of the camera. "I wouldn't bother, Dyl. Haven't you learned anything from reality TV? You can't hide from those cameras. There are no secrets here. Might as well spit it out." The cameraman coughed again. "I'm sorry. Do you have something in your throat?"

He shook his head, almost imperceptibly.

"I don't think you're supposed to talk to them," I muttered.

"I'll talk to whoever I damn well please," she sniffed. "What's your name?"

"He's not gonna answer." I shrugged. "But I'm pretty sure it's Mike."

He didn't answer. But I was almost positive I'd heard Pamela call him Mike once. Or maybe she was talking about a microphone.

"Just edit around it, all right, Mike? This one must be new to the biz." She jerked her thumb at him, rolling her eyes.

First Dusty, now Heaven. Why was it so easy for everyone else to resign themselves to the inevitability of the all-pervasiveness of the cameras except for me?

"If it's all the same to you, I'd rather just . . . wait."

"Suit yourself." *Crunch, crunch, crunch.* "It'll end up on TV no matter what. And I'm not waiting 'til we get back to Mississippi to hear what's giving you that gots-to-pee look."

"Yeah, I can't wait, either," I said glumly. But was that my only option? Talk about how mushy Jamie made me feel, knowing full well that he'd be able to watch it on TV, along with everyone I went to school with? The only thing I could imagine that was more horrible than that eventuality was not being able to discuss it at all. God, it was like the Sophie's Choice of gossiping.

"So, what's up with this dance class?" Heaven asked. "Did you volunteer for this? Or are they making you? I was shocked when I saw it on the schedule."

"*You* have a schedule? Seriously?! Does *everyone* have a schedule except for me?"

Heaven stared at me blankly. Obviously, she had no idea who did or didn't have a schedule.

"Dance class?" I asked.

"Uh-huh." Heaven pulled a piece of paper out of her pocket and tapped a neat line of black Times New Roman type. *Dance class.* And there was my name. And Jamie's.

Guess Heaven and I would be having that talk sooner than I anticipated.

CHAPTER TEN

Just a few hours later, I was hunched over in a closet, trying to keep my head from banging into the ceiling. Every time I took a particularly enthusiastic breath, one of my elbows collided with a paint can. This closet was not built for the tall.

Hearing footsteps in the hallway, I peeked out of the door. *Jackpot.* I pulled Heaven inside with one arm and shut the door behind us with the other.

"Listen, buster, I have a black belt in karate—" was all she got out before I clapped a hand over her mouth.

"You *own* a black belt, maybe." I snorted. "That's not quite the same thing."

"Dylan?" she mumbled.

I dropped my hand from her mouth and reached up to tug on the chain over my head. A single bulb flickered on, illuminating me, Heaven, and a whole bunch of neatly ordered cleaning supplies.

"You damn near gave me a heart attack!" She angrily balled her hands into fists at her hips.

"Careful, don't step in the mop bucket," I cautioned.

"Were you trying to kill me? I thought I was being abducted!"

"I just wanted to talk to you in a place with no cameras."

"Well, mission accomplished. Couldn't you have wanted to talk to me in a place with no spiders?" She shuddered. "I see, like, two spiders. Already. And that's just the ones I can see."

"I kissed someone," I blurted out.

Heaven's eyes grew big as saucers and her mouth formed a perfectly round O.

"Or someone kissed me," I hurried on. "Doesn't matter. There was kissing going on."

"Like, plural kissing? Like, more than once?"

"Uh-huh."

"No way!" Heaven hugged me tightly around the middle. "I never thought this day would come!"

"Hey!" I extricated myself from the hug. "I'm not *that* tragic."

"No, no, of course you're not tragic. This is so exciting!" She reached her hands up to smoosh my face. "My big little Dylan is all grown-up! And check you out—talk about romantic circumstances. Who locks down their first kiss in a castle? Sure beats Tate Moseley's garage," she finished glumly.

"Hey now," I said sternly. "Stop it right there. Tate Moseley doesn't deserve any of your brain space."

"Right, right." She flapped her hands near her face, like she was waving away any thoughts of the Tate Moseley Incident. "This isn't about Tate. Or me. This is about you! And your new man! Damn, I can't believe you kissed someone, and I don't even know who he is!"

"The advantages of leaving Tupelo," I said drily.

"What's his name?"

"Jamie."

"Jamie," she breathed. "Don't tell me he's Scottish."

"No. English."

"Even better!" she squealed, grabbing my hands with delight. "Man, Krystal Hooper would poop her pants if she knew you were over here making out with some English dude."

"I know." I grinned.

"Well. How did this happen? Tell me everything!"

I launched into the speedy recap version of my adventures with Jamie, from our meeting at the train station, to the trapdoor, and, of course, the snowfall and the kiss and the night in the horse barn.

Although instead of looking swoony, as I expected, Heaven mostly looked . . . skeptical.

"Dylan, I love you dearly, but I'm pretty sure you just recounted the plot of a Lifetime Original Movie."

"No, it wasn't a movie! It was real!"

"Although I think the girl got murdered in that one. *Murder in a Horse Barn*? No, that's not it. *Snowstorm Murder*?" she guessed. "*The Scottish Murder*?"

"Well, I'm not murdered. Obviously. See? It was real."

"Really? Damn." She shook her head. "When you do a first kiss, you do it *right*."

I giggled.

"Was that a giggle?" Heaven's jaw dropped. "You are in serious, serious trouble. Permission to leave the closet now?"

"I guess." I fiddled with the pin on my shoulder, which was keeping my tartan sash in place. "I'm not ready to dance."

"You're never ready to dance. That's why you have me."

Unceremoniously, she pushed me out of the closet. I scanned the hallway—not a camera in sight. We appeared to have gone undiscovered. Heaven shut the door firmly behind her.

"Ya look good, Dyl." She assessed me critically. "This suits you, somehow, this old-fashioned thing. You have a regal neck."

"Um, thanks." I rubbed my neck self-consciously. I could not imagine how it was possible that a white puffy-sleeved dress with a tea-length tulle skirt could possibly suit me. This was some weird, ancient ballerina thing.

"You know *La Sylphide*?" Heaven asked.

"La what?"

"It's a ballet," she explained as she lifted one black slipper–clad foot and pointed it gracefully. "This Scottish guy is all set to marry a nice girl named Effie, but then he falls in love with this fairy chick in the woods and messes it all up."

"Like you do."

"Anyway, that's what these outfits remind me of. The old-fashioned tutus from *La Sylphide*. Especially with these tartan things pinned up at our shoulders." She tugged on the blue-and-green plaid swatch hanging down my back.

"You don't think we have to do, like, ballet . . . do you?" I asked nervously.

"Who knows?!" Heaven did a grand jeté down the hall, her white skirt flying as she leaped through the air. "I just hope we get to keep these outfits."

"You can have mine, too," I muttered.

Heaven led me down the hall, dancing a few feet ahead, just like I imagined that Sylphide fairy thing must have led the ballet guy into the woods.

"Heaven, what happens at the end of *La Sylphide*?"

"Oh, I think everybody dies," she replied nonchalantly. "Wow." She stopped suddenly in front of an enormous open doorway.

"Whoa." I nearly bumped into her as I stopped at her shoulder. The rest of Dunyvaig Castle was grand, of course, but nothing had prepared me for the ballroom. The white walls were trimmed with gold, sparkling nearly as much as the candelabras set all along the walls. I looked up to see an enormous mural of stags covering the high ceiling. Three large crystal chandeliers hung down, dominating the room. I had never seen anything like it.

"Now, when somebody said 'castle,' *this* is what I was expecting," Heaven murmured appreciatively. "Is this where the reception is going to be?"

"No idea. You think Dusty shares her wedding plans with me?" I snorted.

"Come on in, y'all!" Dusty called from across the ballroom, waving one hand as she leaned into Ronan, his arm around her waist.

It still surprised me, sometimes, how beautiful Dusty was. Almost like I'd forget, then turn around, and be taken aback by it all over again. As we made our way over to her, I wondered, not for the first time, what it would be like to be that beautiful. If everything would be easier. If I would like to have people look at me, instead of cringing anytime someone noticed me.

"Heaven." Dusty reached out a hand and clasped one of Heaven's perilously close to her prominent bosom. "Thank you so much for comin' over here to join us. It'll be so much easier to do all the rehearsin' with you standin' in for Anne Marie."

"Dusty invited you?"

"Uh-huh." Heaven smirked at me. Okay, so TRC had actually invited her, but for the sake of the show, Dusty had invited her. It was too confusing, these parallel lines of what was reality and what was reality TV. Why did we have to play along with the fake plot? It was all so dumb. "Thank you so much for asking me, Dusty. I've always wanted to see Europe! This is so cool."

"We're glad to have you." Dusty smiled.

"Where's Anne Marie?" I asked.

"Some med school somethin'." Dusty waved her hand dismissively. "That girl's schedule is crazypants."

"Anne Marie is in med school?" I asked in disbelief. "Your best friend–slash–future bridesmaid. Anne Marie. Is in med school?"

I couldn't have been more shocked if Anne Marie had landed on the moon. My earliest memory of Dusty's oldest friend was watching her eat a crayon in our living room. If this was the future of medicine, I feared for the human race.

"Please try not to act so surprised when she gets here, Dylan," Dusty sniffed. "It's insultin'."

"Hey there, Ronan." Heaven interrupted us before I could stick my foot any further into my mouth. "Looking good. Nice to see you again."

"I'm verra sorry." He frowned as she shook his hand vigorously. "Have we met?"

"Technically? Not really. But my elbow was at y'all's engagement party. I mean, I was there, too," she clarified, "like, in the same room with y'all. But all you could see on TV was my elbow."

"I'm sure you have grand elbows," he said gallantly.

"Dude, the prince likes my elbows!" Heaven squeaked.

"Not a prince," I whispered back.

Something—or someone—bumped gently into my side. I turned and came face-to-face with Jamie's clear blue eyes.

"I'm wearing a kilt," he announced proudly.

"That you are." On top he wore a plain white button-down shirt with a black tuxedo jacket, but below it was a blue tartan kilt with fancy knee socks. Come to think of it, Ronan was wearing a kilt, too, albeit in a different color; it just didn't look unusual on him. Ronan had worn a kilt the first time he came over to our house for dinner. Although I think TRC may have had a hand in that. "Why is Ronan's kilt greener than yours?" I asked. "Do the plaids mean something?"

"It's a family tartan," Jamie said hastily, then coughed. "I've always suspected my calves were my best feature. It's a shame they've been imprisoned in my trousers for the past sixteen years."

"Did someone say 'imprisoned in my trousers'?" Heaven turned toward us as Dusty and Ronan resumed their regularly scheduled activities of nonstop cuddling and making kissy faces.

"Hello there." Jamie stuck out his hand. "Pleasure to meet you. I'm Jamie."

"Jamie?" Heaven's eyes lit up. "*The* Jamie?! Well, well, well." She took his hand and shook it slowly as she looked him up and down. "He's certainly tall enough."

"Tall enough for what, may I ask?" Jamie inquired politely.

"You know," Heaven said meaningfully.

Oh brother.

"Jamie, this is my best friend, Heaven."

"*Very* best friend," she added. "I know everything," she whispered, leaning in close.

"Then I'll do my utmost to ensure Dylan only provides you with exemplary reports in areas where I am concerned."

"I like this one." She squinted at him critically. Then she snorted. "This one. Not like there's been a bunch. Jamie, you are the first guy Dylan's ever—"

"Great!" I interrupted them briskly. "Great introductions, just great stuff all around."

They both stared at me.

"Should we get some dancing going?" I asked, pulling at the neckline of my dress. How was it suddenly so hot in here? "Like, we've got these stupid shoes on, might as well dance, right?"

"I couldn't agree more!"

Kit Kirby leaped into the room with a grand jeté even higher than Heaven's had been, his short legs sticking out from beneath his kilt in a perfectly perpendicular line to his round torso. He landed in a plié, bringing his arms above his head with a dramatic flourish.

"The dance!" Kit declaimed grandly, stepping toward us with outstretched arms and pointed feet. "Poetry in motion! Och, Scottish country dancing, the finest jewel in the artistic crown of the British empire! You American ladies are in for a treat! It's your first ceilidh, int'it?"

"Cay-what?" I asked.

"Ceilidh," Ronan answered in his rumbly Scottish burr. "A ceilidh's a Scots party of sorts with music and dancing. And you can bet your arse our wedding will be the biggest damn party the Highlands have ever seen!"

I legit could never keep a straight face when Ronan started waxing lyrical about Scottish traditions or even mentioned the word "Highlands." I knew the Highlands were, like, an actual geographical location, but whenever Ronan said it he sounded one step away from painting his face blue.

"Hear, hear," Kit Kirby cheered. "I plan on dancing 'til dawn and waking up either engaged or imprisoned. Or both."

"Ooo, that'd be a real fairy-tale ending, Cinderella." Ronan laughed.

"You're not the only one who deserves a happily ever after, yer lairdship," Kit retorted. "Now, everyone," he addressed the five of us, suddenly all business. "When we begin to dance, please, dinna be intimidated."

"Intimidated?" Heaven crossed her arms. "By you?"

Heaven wasn't just in show choir. She was also on the dance team, and anytime she began to move, a dance circle magically formed around her. Going to a school dance with Heaven was like being an awkward extra on the set of a music video. You just had to get out of her way or prepare to be demolished by a tornado of rhythm.

"Is that a challenge, you wee slip of a thing?" Kit stepped up to her, belly first.

"Could be." She posed, one hand on her hip. "You looking for a dance battle?"

"Jazz shoes at dawn!" he cried.

"Can we please begin?"

I hadn't even noticed Ronan's mom come into the room. Or the violinist behind her. But as soon as I heard her crisp tones, it was like the temperature in the room dropped five degrees. Unlike the rest of us cotton balls, Florence was wearing a black velvet blazer and a calf-length tartan skirt. I swear, that woman owned more blazers than Hillary Clinton.

"Two lines. Ladies and gentlemen facing," she commanded. "Jamie, your posture is, as always, impeccable."

I rolled my eyes at Jamie as I walked into the girls' line. His posture was, as always, unremarkable. He must have written Florence some really choice thank-you notes in his childhood or something.

"This isn't over," Heaven mouthed at Kit Kirby as she stalked across from him to the head of the line.

"The first dance at the reception will be the Scottish Grand March," Florence announced.

"Our first dance?" Dusty's brow wrinkled as we all turned to look at her. "But that's not our song."

"I'm sorry?" Florence asked frostily.

"Our song is 'It's Your Love.' Tim McGraw and Faith Hill?" Florence remained stone-faced as Dusty kept talking. "It was playing at the bar the night we first kissed. Remember, boo?"

Ronan leaned across the line and squeezed her hand.

"It's tradition," Florence sniffed. "The bride and groom always enter the reception hall to the Scottish Grand March, followed by the wedding party. I suppose you may have your American first dance afterward."

"Well . . . all right, then," Dusty said in a watery voice. "I mean, that's great!" she added brightly, smiling desperately at Florence. "I'm so honored to do the Scottish Grand March. Thank you so much, Lady Dunleavy."

"Um, excuse me?" I raised my hand, like I was in school. "Followed by the wedding party? Do we have to do a dance? Like all of us?"

"Yes."

"Dancing's not really my thing," I said lamely.

"You'll be fine, wee sister," Ronan said kindly. "It's mostly marching around in a circle."

"Precisely. No challenge at all for a dancer of any merit," Kit added.

"We'll see who's got merits once we start this march," Heaven said.

"The march will be merely the beginning. We will of course have a traditional ceilidh band playing traditional Scottish music throughout the reception," Florence continued.

That was a lot of traditional.

"Will they know any Tim McGraw?" Dusty asked worriedly.

"I'll make sure they do, darlin'," Ronan promised.

"While I cannot promise any Tim McGraw"—Ronan's mom spoke over her son—"I can assure you they will be playing 'The Duke of Atholl's Reel,' and you will all be dancing it."

A snort escaped. I hastily tried to cover it up as a cough.

"Atholl?" Jamie mouthed across the line.

"Yup," I mouthed back.

He nodded sympathetically.

"The Duke of Atholl's Reel is Dunleavy tradition!" Florence said shrilly. "And I expect perfection in its execution."

"Perfection is guaranteed," Kit Kirby declared.

"From some of us," Heaven countered, apparently having forgotten that Anne Marie, not her, would be doing these dances on the big day.

Ronan's mom began walking us through the steps of the dance. There was a lot of pacing back and forth and hopping and skipping from side to side. I wasn't really getting any of it.

But the beautiful thing about dancing in a line was that if the people around you knew what they were doing, they could just push you along. And that's exactly what they did.

After several dry runs, Florence cued the fiddler, and we began walking toward each other and skipping back and forth.

"Dylan," Jamie whispered as we circled with our arms around each other's waists. "I want to take you on a date."

"A date?"

"Yes, a date," he repeated as we spun the other way. "A proper date. One that doesn't involve horse blankets. Something outside the grounds of Dunyvaig Castle."

We backed away into our respective lines. Hop, skippity, skip. Skip, skip, skip. First Dusty and Ronan passed, then Heaven and Kit; then we joined hands and skipped together down the aisle of dancers.

"What, like, dinner and a movie?"

"Something like that," he answered, an amused smile playing about his lips. "Will you go out on a date with me?"

"Um. Sure." As I realized suddenly that I didn't sound particularly enthusiastic, I continued, "Yes. Yes I will."

"Good."

He deposited me at the end of the line, and we clapped in time with the music as Ronan spun Dusty through the dancers and around the room.

"Friday. That's the traditional date night, yes? I'll pick you up at eight," he said, clapping away merrily.

"What exactly is Mr. Darcy blabbering on about over there?" Heaven asked, leaning into my ear so I could hear her above the music.

"Dinner at eight."

"What?"

"A date," I marveled. "I'm going on a date."

"This really is a castle of miracles," Heaven marveled right back.

"Shut it," I whispered.

But even though I'd never admit it, I agreed.

CHAPTER ELEVEN

Somehow, I survived five days of torturous anticipation, during which I managed to remain relatively normal around Jamie and committed myself to attacking any and all chocolate-covered biscuits with gusto. As I walked into my bedroom on Friday afternoon, I stiffened involuntarily, the hairs on my neck rising. Something was off. There was a dress waiting on my bed, and it wasn't mine.

I walked toward it suspiciously, just in case it decided to fly up and try to smother me. But it remained stationary.

"What's up with all these white dresses?" I muttered as, almost of its own accord, my hand reached out to touch it. "I'm not the one getting married."

The dress had long sheer lace sleeves and a short ruffled skirt below the dropped waist. The ivory lace was made up of cascading flowers and vines, but not in a way that looked cheesy or tacky. It was like a modern princess dress. It looked like a dress that belonged in this castle.

I noticed a shoe box to the right of the dress with an envelope propped up on top. Curious, I opened it.

Production thought you might not have brought anything suitable. Enjoy your date!

~ Pamela

A chill ran down my spine as I sank onto the bed. Of course they knew. Of course. How could I be so stupid to think that leaving Dunyvaig meant leaving TRC behind? Part of me wanted to stuff that dress in the bathtub and drown it out of spite, but it was too beautiful to destroy. And what if Jamie was wearing a suit and I showed up in jeans and a T-shirt? I'd look like an idiot. Maybe it was better to take the dress from the devil and save face. Hell, this was actually *nice* of them, in a strange, interfering way. It would have been way worse if they'd sent me out on a date in my gym shorts or something. Maybe Pamela wasn't conspiring with the network to make me look like a total idiot after all.

Honestly, though, I had a hard time believing Pamela wanted me to look like anything. I couldn't imagine that anyone at TRC could possibly be interested in the dating misadventures of Scotland's two most socially awkward tourists. They must have been really starved for footage if they thought sending cameras to downtown Dunkeld with me and Jamie was a worthwhile use of their time. This dress seemed like a useless expense for something that would inevitably end up on the cutting room floor. Or whatever the digital equivalent of that was.

A knock at the door. Was that Jamie? No! Impossible! It wasn't anywhere near eight, and I wasn't anywhere near ready!

"Dilly?"

Definitely not Jamie.

"Dilly, it's Dusty. Let me in!"

I swung the door open. She looked good even in yoga pants and an absolutely enormous Cambridge rugby shirt that must have been Ronan's. Annoying. Although why anyone required a full face of makeup when roaming around in a sweat suit was beyond me. The world wasn't going to end if Dusty didn't wear eye shadow 24/7. I wondered if Ronan had ever actually seen her real face.

"Are you moving in?" I pointed to the rolling suitcase at her feet.

"Naw, that's hair and makeup stuff." She strolled right past me into the room as I shut the door behind her. "I thought I could help you get ready for your date!"

"Oh Lord," I moaned. "Did they broadcast this on the news? Is there an unofficial Dunyvaig Castle newsletter I haven't been getting? How does everyone know about this?"

"There are no secrets in this place," Dusty said darkly as she unzipped her suitcase. "You should just be happy the camera isn't here now."

"Yeah. How exactly did you manage that?"

"I sold them on a movie-makeover-type transformation, but they want it to be magic. They don't want to, like, see the process."

"I don't understand why you had to sell them on anything," I said. "This show isn't about me. It's about you. Why do they want to film this at all?"

"They film *everything*, Dylan. That includes Mama doing her crossword puzzles. That includes Ronan flossing after breakfast. That includes you. Get used to it."

Get used to it? Never. I snorted at her, but she ignored it.

"Besides, everybody loves a makeover, but nobody wants to see the foundation go on." Dusty busied herself unpacking various potions and bottles and setting them up on my desk. "TRC wants the audience to think you waltzed up here all . . . *you* . . . and waltzed right back on down all Princess Barbie."

"Like Hermione at the Yule Ball."

"Yes, nerd." She rolled her eyes.

"Harry Potter is not nerdy!" I cried. "He is a universally beloved boy wizard!"

"You're not helpin' your case, Dilly."

"Well, you can pack right on back up and take your Harry Potter hatred out of here. I don't need that attitude. I don't need your help getting ready for my date. And I definitely don't need a makeover."

"Come on, dummy." She kept unpacking, ignoring me completely. "Jamie likes you just as you are, and that's great, but everyone can use a little bit of enhancement."

"I really don't want to be enhanced." I folded my arms across my chest protectively.

"Dylan." She finally stopped unpacking, sat back on her heels, and looked up at me. "Do you remember what your favorite movie was when you were little?"

"Um, abrupt change of subject, weirdo."

"Answer the question."

"*The Little Mermaid.*"

"That's right." She smiled fondly. "You made me watch that thing so many damn times. I considered doing serious damage to that DVD to free myself from a lifetime of listenin' to 'Under the Sea' fourteen times a day. And do you remember what your favorite part was?"

"The crab?"

"No, it was not the crab," she scoffed. "It was the part when Ariel comes into the dining room wearing the pink dress, and Prince Eric sees her, and his li'l cartoon eyes light up because she is just so damn beautiful. You made me rewind it over, and over, and over again. You *loved* that part. Sometimes that was the only bit you watched all day."

"Okay . . ."

"And when you walk down the stairs tonight," she continued, "and Jamie is waitin' there to take you out, don't you want his eyes to light up just like he's Prince Eric in the ballroom? This is your pink-dress-Ariel moment," she said seriously. "Live the fantasy a little."

I looked at her in silence. She looked back at me, steely eyed.

"Fine," I said in the quietest voice imaginable.

"I'm sorry, what was that?"

"Fine," I repeated, louder. "Fine, okay, fine! Do whatever! Just don't be annoying about it!"

"Oh, Dilly!" she squealed, leaping to her feet and squeezing me into a tight hug. "This is going to be so much fun! You won't regret it, I swear! And I won't be annoying at all!"

"Too late," I murmured through the muffled strangulation of her hug.

I had no idea why I was doing this. No, that was a lie—I knew exactly why. I hated myself for admitting it, but I wanted Jamie's eyes to light up like he was a cartoon and I was a mermaid. And also a cartoon.

"All right, now, first things first." She released me from

the hug and leaped back to the suitcase, which she began rummaging through like a rabid badger. "Aha!" She sprang up, triumphantly holding a small box aloft.

"Dusty, no," I commanded. "Put the Clairol down."

"But you said—"

"I'm not going blond."

"But you're already blond!" she protested. "It's just sort of . . . dirty . . . and ashy . . . and sad."

"Thanks," I said sarcastically. "I'm not going blond like you and Mom."

"No, not like me and Mom. Go blond like *you*. See?" She held the box up to the side of my head. "It's your color, just a little brighter. A real natural, soft, honey blond. Just trust me, Dilly. Please. Can you trust me?"

She'd asked me to trust her before. And I'd ended up drinking salad dressing because she'd sworn it was lemonade. Somehow, I still hadn't learned.

"Fine." I capitulated. "Fine. If we're gonna do this, let's just do this."

"No more fighting me?"

"As long as there's no blue eye shadow."

She grinned. "Deal. Now get in the bathroom, girl, we've gotta get you ready!"

What felt like hours of plucking and primping and curling later, I stood in front of the bathroom mirror, touching my face in disbelief. Who was this stranger with soft gray-blue eyes framed by long dark lashes? Whose plump peachy lips were those? They sure weren't mine. Hell, even my nose looked straighter, somehow, and I'm pretty sure Dusty hadn't engaged in any clandestine rhinoplasty while I wasn't paying attention.

As much as I hated to admit it, she was right about the hair. Brightening it up a little bit made my whole face glow. Or maybe I was just excited to see Jamie.

"Do I look okay?" I asked nervously as I crossed out of the bathroom, tugging on the hem of my dress. "Is this dress too short?"

"No!" Dusty yelled. "It's perfect. As long as you stop playing with your skirt like a toddler."

Suddenly, Dusty clamped her lips together and bolted for the bathroom. She didn't even have time to shut the door behind her before I heard the unmistakable splatter of vomit.

"Jeez, overreact much? I thought you said I looked okay!" I followed her to the bathroom, leaning against the open doorjamb. "What the heck is going on with you, Barfy? Are you pregnant?"

Blearily, Dusty looked up from the toilet bowl. But the expression that flitted across her face wasn't nausea—it was panic.

CHAPTER TWELVE

"Oh my God," I whispered, realizing that my joke wasn't actually a joke at all. "You are. You're pregnant."

"Not everyone who barfs is pregnant." She wiped a hand across the back of her mouth and rose to her feet, flushing the toilet.

"No, but *you* are." I watched as she neatly rinsed her mouth out with water from my sink, hardly able to believe what I knew, somehow, was true. I prided myself on being able to see pregnancy plot twists a mile away on TV; how could I not have figured this out earlier? Maybe because it seemed impossible that perfect Dusty could be pregnant and not yet married. "You've barfed at least twice since we got here. Highly unusual behavior. *And* you've been looking particularly busty."

"Don't look at my bust, weirdo."

"I can't help it; they're just out there!" I pointed at the large boob-shaped lumps discernible even under her oversize rugby shirt. She crossed her arms over her chest. "Admit it! You're pregnant!"

"There is nothing to admit! I'm just havin' some tummy troubles, and that is *all*."

Dusty and I stared at each other, neither willing to look away. Or blink. And then, a really, truly horrible thought occurred to me. I didn't want to think that Dusty would do something so life altering for such a stupid reason, and yet . . . she'd gone so far down the reality TV rabbit hole already. . . .

"Did Pamela put you up to this?" I asked, trying to find some semblance of the truth in her eyes. "To create more drama for the show? Is this all a plot twist? Did Pamela impregnate you?!"

"Of course she didn't, you wackadoodle!" Dusty sighed, exasperated, balling her hands on her hips.

"Dusty!" I cried. "You can't have a baby for ratings!"

"I'm not havin' a ratings baby!"

"Do you even know where the line is anymore? Between reality and reality TV? Is any of this real, Dusty? Are you real anymore?" I pinched her.

"Ow!" she shrieked. "Did you just *pinch* me?" She rubbed her arm exaggeratedly. "Of course I'm real, dummy."

"Are you? What about all of this? You don't even have real eyelashes, Dusty." I waved my hand in front of her face. "This show is so fake. And it seems like you're being fake right along with it."

"Ouch, Dylan. Why don't you tell me how you really feel?"

"I'm sorry, I just . . . I just don't understand any of this. It's so dumb, the way we have to pretend things are real when we know they're not. How are you so okay with all of it?"

"Because it's not real life. It's just a show. So it doesn't matter.

Goin' along with what they want, givin' Pamela what she wants to see, none of that stuff matters. What matters is me and Ronan. That's real."

"And the baby's real?"

"I—" Dusty hesitated, emotions flitting across her face so fast I couldn't read any of them. "Goddamn it, Dylan, Ronan and I promised nobody would know but us. I just wanted this one thing to myself, you know? This one big special thing just for us." She placed a protective hand over her belly.

"I'm sorry, Dusty, I wasn't trying to make you— I mean, I'm not—"

"The baby's real," she confirmed quietly, looking down at her stomach, almost like she couldn't quite believe it either.

"Wow. I just— Wow." I couldn't believe Dusty was really pregnant. That she was going to have a baby. That there was going to be a brand-new addition to our family, which had been such a small, self-contained unit of three for so long. "How did this happen?"

"Sometimes accidents—beautiful accidents—happen between two consenting adults who are madly in love—"

"La-la-la-la-la!" I covered my ears with my hands. "Never mind. Don't know why I asked that. I don't want to hear it."

"Dilly." She lifted my hands off my ears, a pleading look in her eyes. "You can't tell anybody. Not a soul. Nobody knows."

"Not even Mom?"

"Not even Mom. Just me and Ronan. And I can't have his mama findin' out before the wedding. She ain't exactly my biggest fan."

"I won't tell. I promise." My hand reached out involuntarily toward Dusty's stomach. I pulled it back before making contact.

It seemed impossible that there was a future niece or nephew in there. I was going to be somebody's Aunt Dylan! "Maybe Florence will be happy about the baby."

"Happy?" Dusty asked incredulously. *"Happy?"*

"Um, yeah. Babies usually make people happy. 'Cause they're like cute and small and stuff. . . ." Catching sight of Dusty's expression of disbelief, I trailed off into silence. "She's gonna be a grandma?"

"No, Florence is not gonna be happy about the baby. She's gonna think I'm a slut who can't keep my damn legs closed."

My jaw dropped open. That was the kind of language that caused people to lose their Miss America titles.

"Or worse, that I tricked Ronan into marryin' me. That he's only marryin' me 'cause of the baby. And I'm exactly the worst kind of social-climbin' manipulative gold digger everyone thinks I am. Gold digger," she snorted. "Ain't that ironic. There's nothin' here to dig. What's left of Ronan's family money is tied up in keepin' this stately pile from tumblin' down around us."

Apparently, Kit had been right on the first day I'd met him. Well, it made sense, really—Ronan didn't seem like the kind of guy who would pursue reality TV fame without a reason. And certainly Florence would *never* have let cameras in here without a *really* good reason. But it was obvious how much Ronan loved his home, and how proud he was of its history. Even I could understand sacrificing your privacy for something you loved that much.

"Then talk about that," I encouraged her. "In your confessional. Show Florence and everyone else that you're not interested in Ronan for his money. Because he doesn't have any."

"Nah, that won't play well. They'd never air it. It's not part of the fantasy. Cinderella isn't supposed to move into a castle with extensive water damage, a cracked foundation, and lead pipes."

Lead pipes? I did a mental tally of the amount of tap water I'd consumed in the past couple weeks, and I didn't like my odds.

"But a baby? That's great television." She sighed. "Can't wait to see what Twitter has to say about this one."

"Maybe it's not that big of a deal, Dusty," I said tentatively. "I mean, you guys love each other. And you're getting married. And you were gonna get married anyway. Uh, right?"

"Of course we were," Dusty said angrily. "We didn't find out about the baby until after we got engaged."

"So maybe—"

"Maybe nothin'. Florence can't find out about this baby. I need you to swear you won't tell a soul. Not Heaven. Not Mom. Not Jamie. Nobody."

"I swear, Dusty. I won't tell anyone. Promise."

I held out my pinky, like I had so many times when I was little. She hooked hers in mine, and we shook.

"It almost feels good, to tell somebody else," she said with a sad smile. "Of course, I'll be pissin' myself for the next week, worryin' you'll let somethin' slip—"

"I won't! You can trust me, I—"

"But it still feels kinda good. To tell my sister. And nobody else. I don't need all of America's opinions on the peanut right now."

"Can I seeeee?" Someone who sounded like Heaven was banging on the door. Dusty and I both jumped, then stared at each other.

"Should we let her in?" I whispered.

"No, let's be super suspicious and lock the door. She wants to see your makeover."

"My what?"

"Makeover. For your date. Honestly, Dilly, sometimes I think everybody got it wrong and *you're* the dumb one."

"Dumb one? Who thinks you're the dumb one?"

Dusty flapped her hands at me as she went to open the door. First I find out the magnificent Dusty is premaritally pregnant, then that she worries people think she's dumb? I needed to sit down.

"DYLAN!" Heaven shrieked, practically rattling the pictures on the wall as she plowed into my room. "HOLY HECK, YOU LOOK LIKE A COMPLETELY DIFFERENT PERSON!"

"It's not a big deal," I muttered. The big deal was sitting in utero two feet to my left.

"It is a *huge* deal." Heaven placed her hands on her hips. "You look amazing! And it's your first date! At the advanced age of sixteen!"

"Sixteen is not that old—"

"Why don't you just put your damn heels on?" Dusty suggested. "Don't want to keep him waiting too long."

"Is he waiting? Am I late? Oh my God, am I late?" I reached for the shoes, tripped, landed on the rug, and sent the shoe box flying across the room, where it smacked into the door and fell to the ground.

"Oh, girl." Heaven hauled me up to my feet as Dusty bent down to retrieve the shoes. "Try to keep it together, 'kay?"

"This *is* me keeping it together."

I sat down on the bed and took the shoes from Dusty, slipping them on one at a time. I hadn't worn heels since . . . ever? The last thing I needed was to look *taller*. This was going to be interesting.

"I really hope this date doesn't involve a lot of walking," I prayed fervently as I rose to stand, testing my weight on uneven footing. I must have been nearly six foot five now. Someone should warn the villagers. I didn't want to accidentally kick off some kind of *Attack of the 50 Foot Woman* mass panic.

Another knock at the door. All three of our heads swiveled toward it.

"Is that Jamie?" I asked, my voice almost unrecognizably squeaky. "I'm not ready! I mean, I am ready, but I'm not ready. Oh God."

"Sweets, are you ready?" Definitely not Jamie. Mom. Dusty flung the door open, and Mom walked in, holding a very old-looking camera.

"Oh God, Mom, no," I groaned. "No pictures. Please."

"Do you know how hard this was for me to track down?" Mom ignored me completely and started snapping away, the flash making tiny explosions in the dim lighting. I did my best to blink in every shot so they'd all be unusable. "TRC may have taken my phone, but I am not letting my baby leave for her first date without photographic evidence."

"You got your evidence, okay? Now can you stop?" I pleaded. "I am well and truly mortified. Mission accomplished, Mom."

"Go take one with your sister. Heaven, you get in there, too."

Dutifully, I stood between Heaven and Dusty and grimaced as they posed. Surely royal ships had been launched with less fanfare.

"Are we done now?" I knew I sounded whiny. But I *felt* whiny.

"This one's going straight on the fridge. And maybe in the Christmas card, too," Mom said happily.

"Great." With my luck, Mom would probably add in a lovely handwritten note that read, *Season's Greetings from the Leighs—can you believe someone finally asked Dylan out?! We all thought that would never happen!* or something equally terrible. "Time to go. Heaven, can you grab my sweatshirt?"

"Your sweatshirt?" Mom yelped. "Dylan. Honestly. You are not tossing a *sweatshirt* on over this gorgeous dress."

"You can borrow my nice coat," Dusty offered. "And you can borrow as much of my clothing as you like the rest of the time you're here. Maybe that'll get you to stop dressing like a tween skater boy."

Mom and Dusty shared an extremely annoying amused glance.

"Is it really time to go?" Mom asked, checking the delicate gold watch on her wrist. "I don't want her to get there too early. Nothing wrong with keeping him waiting a little." She winked. I blinked back at her stonily.

"Jamie might be able to wait, but production can't. Heaven, get her to the stairs," Dusty ordered. "I'll meet y'all down there with the coat. But make sure she walks down 'em alone. You can't be in the shot. You neither, Mama."

"Yeah, yeah, got it." Heaven took my arm and led me down the hall, like she was helping an old lady cross the street. "'Stay out of the shot, Heaven. Don't get in the frame, Heaven.'"

"Reality TV not all it's cracked up to be, eh?" I teased.

"So it's not as glamorous as I hoped. Doesn't matter. I'm still plannin' on being the Bachelorette in about a decade or so."

"Good luck with that." We'd reached the end of the hallway. The staircase loomed below me, curving down into oblivion. And Jamie. "This is weird, Heaven," I whispered, clutching her arm tightly. "This is too much."

"Too much?"

"There's too much going on."

"With the date?"

"Um. Yeah. With the date." I sternly squelched all baby-shaped thoughts from my mind. To be fair, even if Dusty's news hadn't thrown me for a loop, I would have been freaking out about the date anyway. "It's way too much. Like, too much pressure. Too fancy. I know this is beautiful and magical, and we're in a castle, and I've sure never looked better, but I feel like I'm going to prom. Right now I almost wish I'd met Jamie in Tupelo," I said wistfully. "And we were just, like, going to watch a movie in his mom's basement."

"With the door open, of course." Heaven grinned.

"Of course." I grinned back.

"Dylan, all this extra shizz"—she gently untangled a few strands of my hair from a dangly earring—"it's just frosting. Icing on the cake. You're just going to hang out with a boy you like. That's all it is."

"Then why am I so nervous?" I whispered.

"'Cause you like him, stupid." She rolled her eyes. "I threw up in a trash can in the girls' bathroom at the Cineplex when Tate took me to the movies for the first time."

"You did not."

"Did too. Just never told you 'cause I was embarrassed."

"I am appalled that you would keep something like that from me." I feigned outrage.

She shrugged. "I'm tellin' you now. Now quit stallin' and get down there."

"Okay, okay." I exhaled slowly. "I can do this."

"You were born to do this, baby," Heaven said encouragingly. "Float like a butterfly, sting like a bee."

"Sting?"

"So maybe Dad's advice doesn't work in every situation." She shrugged. Heaven's dad coached football at our school, and whenever I was in need of motivation she tended to channel him. "Just get down there, all right?"

"All right."

And there it was—the camera, resting on the shoulder of a skinny guy in a dark blue sweatshirt. He was waiting for me at the top of the stairs, the lens only inches from my face. I took a shaky breath, conscious of the camera's eye on my sweating forehead, my nervously fluttering hands, my too-fast heartbeat that thudded so loud I was sure the camera could hear it. He was close, too close. I felt like I was suffocating. Breathe, Dylan. I had to remember to breathe.

I placed one heel on the top steps. For balance, I rested one freshly manicured hand on the wooden banister and began my slow descent, the cameraman mere inches behind me, slightly off to my side. This would be fine. Everything would be fine. I'd walked down a hundred thousand staircases in my lifetime. Sure, I'd never had a cameraman following me before, but I'd try my best not to let him see how badly he'd rattled me.

And then Jamie appeared, waiting at the bottom of the stairs, almost painfully handsome in a dark gray suit with a simple striped tie. He'd done something with his hair so it fell in a soft dark curl across his forehead. Pamela may have been the devil, but I thanked her from the bottom of my heart for getting me this dress. Because Jamie's jaw had dropped, and he was looking at me with the kind of light in his eyes that I'd only ever seen in movies, and I never thought I'd see when someone looked at me.

Jamie took a few steps toward me, his own cameraman trailing behind him, almost like he was being pulled by an invisible string, until he arrived at the foot of the stairs. He reached a hand out, and I took it, landing beside him on the ground with only the barest hint of a wobble. I knew there was a camera behind him, and another that still hadn't left my side, but for the first time, I didn't care. It was only me and Jamie.

"Dylan," he said, "I . . . There are no words." He shook his head. "For the first time in my life, language has failed me. Utterly."

"No poetry, then?"

"You are poetry," he said simply. "I'm sorry." He rubbed his brow, wincing. "Was that naff? No, don't answer that—it was terribly naff."

"I don't even know what 'naff' means."

"Erm, cheesy."

"It was very cheesy. But I liked it anyway."

And then we just stood there grinning gooily at each other for a couple minutes.

"Eh-hem."

I turned. Dusty stood behind me, holding a thick emerald-green wool coat open. Mom hovered just behind her shoulder, smiling her real smile—the one she saved for me and Dusty—the one that never made it on the air at *Good Morning, Mississippi!* I was seized by a desire to run over and hug her as tightly as I could, but I didn't want to look like a baby. I was going on a date, not leaving for college.

"Have fun, Dylan," Mom mouthed at me, silent so the mic couldn't pick it up. "Have *fun*."

I nodded at her, almost imperceptibly. Her smile widened.

"Don't want you to freeze that flat butt of yours off, baby sister," Dusty said as she helped me into her coat.

"Thanks." I pulled the coat closed and fastened the top button. It swung out around me in a bell shape. "You're, um, you're okay?" I asked quietly.

"I'm *fine*, Dylan." She narrowed her eyes at me, but not in a mean way. "Don't think about me, all right? Just have fun on your date. It took you long enough to get one. Might as well enjoy it."

"Shall we?" Jamie asked before I could come up with a crushing retort. He held out his arm. It felt weird to take it, like I was a character in a play, but I honestly wasn't sure I could walk down the front steps without holding on to someone.

A uniformed member of the staff swung open the door. Outside, it looked like the front of a Christmas card was waiting for me. Big, fat, fluffy flakes of snow fell softly onto a deep-crimson sleigh and two dappled gray horses. A driver in the front tipped his top hat. The cameraman next to him tipped nothing, just kept the camera trained impassively upon us. It was Mike, from breakfast. Guess he'd finally been taken off the breakfast shift. Or maybe he was relegated only to shooting the most boring, unusable footage. Maybe he was on the Dylan beat, for when TRC was desperate for a couple minutes of filler before the next commercial break.

"Is this for us?" I squeaked.

"You know I don't have a car." Jamie led me toward the sleigh. "And I know you like horses. Especially when you don't actually have to ride them."

"That is true." Jamie helped me into the sleigh, and I slid under a thick fur blanket. *Mmm, soft.* "But this is like a whole big deal."

"Well, you're, like, a whole big deal, Dylan." He settled in beside me and bent down, scrambling around by our feet. "Hot chocolate?" He popped back up with a thermos.

"Sure." I took it and unscrewed the lid. Jamie put his arm around me, and I snuggled in as I took the first hot, creamy sip. I had never tasted anything so good.

"Ready, sir?" the driver asked.

"Ready," Jamie replied.

The driver clicked his tongue, and, I swear to God, with a jingle of actual sleigh bells, we took off into the night.

CHAPTER THIRTEEN

"A re you terribly hungry?" Jamie asked solicitously as we whizzed down the lane.

"I mean, I'm not starving, but I thought there was dinner involved on this date . . . thing."

It was a date. Not a date *thing*. Why couldn't I just call it a date?

"Naturally. I was simply hoping we might make a detour before dinner, if that's all right with you." Jamie seemed different, somehow. Stiff, almost. He was nervous, I realized as I watched him swallow a few times, his Adam's apple bobbing. The camera certainly wasn't helping anything. Jamie kept glancing over at it. I guess it could have been worse—Cameraman Mike could have been sitting in the back with us—but the lens of the camera still felt awfully close.

"Yeah, that's fine. I'll survive."

"Survival is insufficient. Shortbread?"

He pulled a basket up from under his feet and pulled back the linen napkin on top, exposing golden rounds of shortbread dusted with sugar crystals.

"Thanks." I took one and nibbled it nervously, trying not to think about Dusty's baby bombshell. Now was not the time for babies on the brain. I would end up blurting something out, or act like a complete space cadet the whole night. Now was the time for compartmentalizing. And my awesome powers of denial. They had helped me attempt to tune out the cameras so far; I knew they'd help me here. "What else do you have under there? A chess set? Flare guns?"

"Nothing excessive. I simply wanted to be prepared."

"You're definitely prepared. You could give a Girl Scout a run for her money."

I took a second round of shortbread while Jamie grabbed his own before placing the basket back down at his feet. He lifted up his arm and I snuggled in, deeper under the blanket and closer to Jamie. Was this really happening? How could this possibly be real life?

The cameraman in front of us shifted his weight as the sleigh rounded a bend rather quickly. Oh, right. It wasn't real. Not really. None of this was. I was seized by a sudden urge to ask Cameraman Mike why, exactly, he was here. *Countdown to the Crown* was about Dusty's wedding—not Dylan's first date. I could imagine Krystal Hooper and everyone else back home feverishly fast-forwarding over anything involving me until TRC got back to the good stuff. Even with the admittedly impressive sleigh, I couldn't comprehend why anyone would want to watch this. But Pamela had explained in no uncertain terms that we were never, under any circumstances, to address the camera crew directly. And the idea of crossing Pamela scared me more than I wanted to admit.

"Look at the stars, Dylan." Jamie pointed to the sky. "How countlessly they congregate o'er our tumultuous snow," he recited.

"Who was that?" I asked.

"Robert Frost," he answered. "*Stars*. Look up, Dylan."

I looked. There were more stars than I'd ever seen in my life, twinkling above us in the velvet black sky. None of those stars were moving, but I made a wish anyway. Then another one—one for me and Jamie, and one for Dusty and the baby.

"Twinkle, twinkle, little star," I proclaimed solemnly. "How I wonder what you are."

"Beautiful, Dylan," he complimented me. "Really makes you ponder the mysteries of the universe."

"That's what I was going for. You should hear me do 'I'm a Little Teapot.' It'll make you reconsider your entire notion of what humanity is."

"Aren't we all just little teapots?"

"Just waiting to be tipped over and poured out?"

He grinned. "I had always thought it was impossible to talk to girls," he mused. "But with you, everything is so easy."

"I feel the same way with you." I was too shy, in that moment, to make eye contact, but I squeezed his hand, and he squeezed back, like we were playing a two-person version of that pass-the-pulse game we did before the spring musical. That was pretty much the only thing I remembered from my brief flirtation with running a light board.

"I hadn't thought it was possible to instantly feel so at ease with someone. It almost makes me reconsider my opinions on soul mates. Or love at first sight. Not that I think we're soul mates. Or in love. Yet. Ha-ha." Jamie emitted a strangled little laugh as he turned tomato red. "Erm, yes, more hot chocolate?"

"Dude, relax. It's kind of nice to see you get flustered." I sighed as I accepted the thermos of hot chocolate. "I feel like I'm always saying awkward stuff, and you've got it so together."

"I can assure you, Dylan, I am the opposite of together. It's simply the accent. For whatever reason it fools Americans into thinking we Brits are far more intelligent and self-assured than we actually are."

"You may have a point there."

The carriage started to slow, and even in the dark, I knew instantly where we were. You spend forty-five minutes freezing your toes off in front of an abandoned platform, and it has a way of staying in your brain.

"We're going to the train station?" I asked. "Are we leaving Dunkeld?"

Maybe this was going to be some *Bachelor*-style fantasy date. Was it an overnight? I hadn't brought pajamas. Or a toothbrush.

"Not exactly," he answered, and as we pulled into the driveway, I knew why.

Just beyond where the sleigh came to a halt, the gravel driveway had been flooded and frozen over. All around the impromptu skating rink, streetlamps wrapped in greenery with big red bows cast a golden glow.

"Let me guess—you've also got ice skates hidden down there."

Jamie pulled up a pair of large white ladies' skates. "How on earth did you guess?" He handed me the skates and grinned. "I wanted to go back to where we first met," he explained as he hopped down from the sleigh and made his way over to my side. "But I thought this would be vastly preferable to freezing in silence for forty-five minutes."

I melted a little bit—some incredible thought and care had gone into this date. But then I sort of immediately froze up again at how straight-up *Bachelor* the whole scenario was. The winter wonderland date, usually complete with fake snow and snuggly ice castle, happened almost every season. If Jamie's next words were "Scotland is the perfect place to fall in love," then I was out of there.

An awful feeling settled deep into the pit of my stomach. Had Jamie planned this date? Or had it all been cooked up by TRC? Maybe this was how they were going to make me and Jamie interesting—by throwing us into some over-the-top romantic scenario that their production team had created so that single ladies across America would swoon. I was constantly scoffing at how stupid all the girls on *The Bachelor* were, to think their date had actually planned every rock-climbing/ private-concert/hot-air-balloon escapade that had obviously been engineered by ABC. Was I just as stupid? I certainly didn't want to be on a dumb magical Christmas date if Pamela had planned all of it.

"May I?"

Jamie was kneeling down by my feet in an entirely too Prince Charming fashion. I awkwardly stuck a foot out, and he slipped off one of my heels, placing it carefully on the floor of the sleigh. He loosed the laces on the ice skate and brought it up to my toes.

"I've, um, got it." I abruptly grabbed the skate out of his hands. "I can do the laces. I know how to tie a shoe."

"As you wish," he responded simply before disappearing around the other side of the sleigh.

Damn that *Princess Bride*-ing mofo! Chivalry was wasted on me. I knew I was supposed to be swooning. I was on a fantasy ice skating date created out of nothing at the less-than-romantic spot of our first meeting. Jamie was pulling a Cinderella on my abnormally large and not at all lovely feet. He looked so handsome in the moonlight it made my heart hurt. And yet I couldn't quite enjoy it. I couldn't shake my suspicions that the whole thing had been set up by TRC. Or even worse—what if *Jamie* had been set up by TRC? Maybe Pamela had encouraged him to take pity on Dusty's weird sister, to play along with this date for the sake of engineering a halfway usable story line for the show. But then Jamie's mouth twisted into a sweetly lop-sided grin, and I hated myself for thinking that. He was real. He had to be.

I gingerly placed one foot out of the sleigh, wobbling as it came down onto the slick ice. Holding on to the sides of the sleigh for dear life, I brought the other foot down to meet it. This was probably the time to mention that I'd never success-fully skated without holding on to something before.

"Going all right there?"

Somehow Jamie was already on the ice.

"Yuppers."

Yuppers. Somehow, it didn't sound quite so bad anymore. I took a big wobbly step toward him, holding out my arms for balance like an ungraceful ostrich as I struggled to remain upright.

"Goodness!" Jamie exclaimed as he skated toward me and wrapped his arms around my waist, finally steadying me.

"Goodness?" I repeated.

"I have a tendency to assume the vocabulary of someone's rather dotty great-aunt when startled. Have you skated before?"

"Sure. But not in any kind of capacity that didn't involve holding on to walls."

"I shall be your wall, then," he said gallantly.

"Thanks, courteous wall."

"Dylan!" he exclaimed with delight.

"You're not the only one who can quote poetry. Or a play, technically."

Jamie began skating backward, hands around my waist, as he towed me away from the sleigh.

"Jamie!" I shrieked as I clapped my hands around his. "We're moving!"

"That is the idea." How the hell did he make this look so easy? "Keep your knees bent. It's much easier to balance that way."

Obediently, I bent my knees.

"How did you come to know so much about Shakespeare's walls? Look up," he commanded. "Not down at your feet."

"Oh. Right." I looked up into his clear blue eyes. A shock of dark hair had already come loose from whatever hairstyle he had attempted, falling temptingly along his brow. "We had to do scenes from *A Midsummer Night's Dream* in eighth grade. I played the wall."

"O wall, O sweet, O lovely wall."

"I can promise you there was nothing sweet or lovely about middle-school Dylan. I had braces and awful bangs and a somewhat tenuous relationship with personal hygiene. Also I was a practicing Wiccan."

"How exotic! Did you have black nail polish and pentagram necklaces?"

"Of course. And I listened to satanic rock and tried to cast curses on the popular girls."

"Did it work?"

"Never. But Heaven says it's because she was counteracting all of my dark magic with light."

"How lucky for those popular girls Heaven was there to protect them."

"Lucky for me, really, that I was such a weirdo and still had someone to sit with at lunch."

"Terribly lucky," Jamie said wistfully. "Here. Let's try you a bit more on your own, then."

"Don't let go!"

"Never," he promised.

He released my waist but kept one of my hands tucked tightly in his as we skated side by side. Well, as Jamie skated and I concentrated on bending my knees and not falling over.

"How are you so good at everything?" I asked.

"Sorry?"

"You ride horses like a knight or something, you skate flaw-lessly . . . How are you so good at all these things?"

"I am passable at two activities," he said, brushing off my praise. "That's hardly excellence in all forms. I'm rubbish at most sports."

"You say that now, but you're probably, like, a champion fencer and a nationally ranked tennis player and a chess prodigy."

"If only," he said lightly. But I had a feeling he was all three of those things and just didn't want to say it.

A particularly strong stab of ankle pain distracted me from

my thoughts. How did Jamie make this look so effortless?

"I didn't realize I had such weak ankles," I mused. "I guess they have to hold up a lot of tall person, but you'd think they'd be used to it by now."

"Are they bothering you?"

"They're, like . . . throbbing. Can I do something for this? Can you strength-train your ankles?"

"I haven't the slightest idea. You're the athlete, not me. This is the most physical activity I've had in ages."

"Sure. Secret fencer-slash–tennis champion," I muttered.

"Sorry?"

"What about your bike?" I asked at a normal volume as he towed me back over to the sleigh.

"That's a means of transportation. I'm not one of those ghastly cyclists decked out in spandex who subsist on sports gels."

"Does your bike have one of those little baskets on the front?"

"It most assuredly does not. Nor does it have streamers on the handles or a bell shaped like a ladybug."

"You literally just described my childhood bike."

I sank down to sit on the footboard of the sleigh. My ankles nearly sang with relief as I loosened the laces.

"Ready for dinner, then?" Jamie asked once we were freed from our skates and sitting back in the cushy seat again.

"Always ready for food."

I half fell onto Jamie as the sleigh began moving, knocking me off-balance.

"Have you guessed where we're going?"

"Hmm . . ." As we rose over the bridge, the lights and puffing chimneys of downtown Dunkeld came into view, like something that should be inside of a snow globe. "If we started at the train station, then we must be headed to the Atholl Arms?"

"Correct," he said, pleased.

"I promise I won't fall asleep on you this time."

"Even if you do, it certainly won't be any trouble to carry you home again."

"You carried me into the van? Oh God. We'd just met. That's mortifying."

"Well, I'm relieved to know the thought of me carrying your unconscious body is no longer mortifying now that we've become better acquainted."

"I'm sure I did something embarrassing while I was sleeping," I said glumly.

"Not at all. You slept with your head on my shoulder. It was rather charming."

We sat in silence for a moment, contemplating that. I was pretty confident that I'd drooled on him and he was just too much of a gentleman to say so.

"This is really nice, Jamie. This . . . this whole . . . every-thing . . . it's really nice," I finished lamely. And because that seemed wholly insufficient, shyly, I leaned over and kissed him on the cheek.

"You missed, Dylan."

"What?"

"You missed," he said again, softly, as he leaned closer. The last thing I saw was his dark eyelashes fluttering closed before he captured my mouth with his. And then everything faded away except for me and Jamie, and I felt like I could never be cold again.

CHAPTER FOURTEEN

"Jamie! My goodness!"

At the sound of a shrill female voice, I opened my eyes to see a scandalized Tilly standing on the front steps of the Atholl Arms.

"You are the last young man I expected to see ravishing a lady in a carriage!"

"He wasn't," I hastened to explain. "I mean, it was a consensual ravishing."

"*The Consensual Ravishing*," Jamie said, as I knew he would the minute that idiotic sentence left my mouth.

As the cameraman hopped off the front of the sleigh, I realized I'd been making out with Jamie literally in front of the camera. Oh my God. I sank deeper into my seat, burning with mortification. How could I possibly have let my guard down? I had played right into TRC's manipulative hands. I hated to admit it, but maybe Dusty had been right, and you *did* adjust to the camera eventually—because the minute I closed my eyes and started kissing Jamie, I had totally, completely forgotten it existed. And now Dusty and Mom and all the randos from the back of my calculus class were going to see it.

"At least you're still all buttoned up, poor duck," Tilly clucked as she bustled me out of the sleigh and into the warmth of the inn. "Loose hands of an aristocratic roué and all."

"Aristocratic roué?" I mouthed at Jamie.

He shrugged wildly and mouthed back something that looked like "Romance novels."

"I expected more." Tilly waggled her finger at Jamie.

"Blame it on the moonlight, Tilly. I suppose we got a bit carried away."

"Hmph. Moonlight," she snorted. "Give me your coats, then, and off to dinner with ye."

Jamie helped me out of my coat and handed it to her. We followed Tilly's stiff back as she marched down the hall. The Christmas decorations at the Atholl Arms appeared to have multiplied since the last time we'd been there. At the end of the hall, just past a mounted deer head wearing a Santa hat, she pushed open the door to a private dining room. The walls were decked out with glowing candles and green garlands. In the middle of the room an elaborate table was set for two. And, in the corner, I kid you not, there was a string quartet. In tuxedos. As we entered the room, they raised their bows and began playing a sweet melody.

A wave of something that felt disconcertingly like nausea rocked me.

"Excuse me," I said abruptly as I began backing out of the room past a very confused Tilly. "I have to go."

"Dylan, are you quite all right?" Jamie asked with concern.

"Yeah, yeah." I waved him away as he reached out for me. "I'll just, um, be a minute."

And just like Heaven had at the Cineplex on her first date with Tate Moseley, I bolted for the girls' bathroom.

The cameraman followed me for a bit, but I shut the bathroom door in his face when it blessedly appeared right off the lobby. Let him go film Tilly and Jamie and the string quartet. I just needed a minute. By myself. With no one looking at me.

Myself. Ha. I caught a glimpse of a girl in the mirror above the sink. I had no idea who she was. I rubbed at my eye, watching my makeup smear.

I sank to the floor, relishing the cool tile at my back. Despite the cloying scent of the potpourri, I felt like I could breathe a little easier in here, with no one's eyes on me.

A knock at the door.

"Go away!" I yelled.

A knock again.

"You can't film me in the bathroom! I'm pretty sure that's illegal!"

"I'm not trying to film you." Jamie. "May I come in?"

"Um. Sure."

He slid into the small bathroom, shutting the door quickly behind him, keeping it closed with his back. The cameraman was probably hot on his heels out there.

"What on earth are you doing down there?"

"Just, um, taking a minute," I answered.

"May I join you?"

I nodded as he slid down the wall next to me and pulled his knees into his chest.

"So this is the ladies' room," he observed. "Pinker, on the

whole. Equally floral." He inhaled deeply. "Smells about the same, shockingly."

"I think that's the potpourri." I pointed to a basket of what looked like wood chips resting on the counter.

"Keenly observed, as per usual, Dylan." He cleared his throat. "While we are on the subject of observation, I may not be a dating expert, but I imagine that one's date hiding in the loo is generally not a favorable sign."

"Sorry," I whispered.

"Did I do something wrong?"

"No. No!" I rushed to explain. When I looked up I hated myself for causing that wrinkle of concern to furrow between his brows. "You did everything right. Maybe too right?"

"Too right?" he repeated.

"This is all so nice but it's all just . . . a little much."

"I see," he said stiffly.

"It's not bad, Jamie! It's perfect. But I'm not a princess."

"Not yet, at any rate. Shall we see how the next season of *Prince in Disguise* proceeds?"

"Hilarious." I knocked my shoulder against his. "But you know what I mean."

"I'm not sure I do."

"This just felt like too much . . . pressure."

"Pressure?"

"To be perfect. For me to be perfect," I explained. "Because this date is perfect. And I am so not. It just felt like too much."

"Dylan," he said after a pause, "why do you think I have so many poems memorized?"

"Because you're really smart," I answered immediately even though I had no idea where he was going with this.

"Oh. Erm, thank you." He blushed. "But I can assure you I am of most decidedly average intelligence. That's certainly not why I know so many poems."

"Then why?"

"I've spent rather a lot of time in libraries. I never made friends easily, in school. Still don't, as a matter of fact."

"Me neither," I said. "I'm so lucky Heaven sat down next to me on the first day of kindergarten and decided we were going to be best friends."

"I would have been exceedingly grateful for a Heaven of my own," he said fervently. "But as it was, I quickly found I preferred to spend my time in the library. Fictional friends never found me strange."

"I get that."

"I have no experience with real-life romance, Dylan, but quite a bit with love stories. You are the first girl I've ever asked out," he admitted shyly. "And I wanted it to be perfect. I wanted Jane Austen to wet herself at the romance of it."

"Jane Austen would have peed all over this date."

"That is a truly horrifying mental image."

"Sorry." I hid my face in my hands. "I'm not good with romance."

"I suppose I overdid it a bit."

"No!" I popped my head back up. "You didn't! The problem isn't you, it's me. This date was completely perfect. For a normal girl. Not a weirdo freak like me. You deserve someone who loves this stuff, who'll get swept up in the romance right along with you. Someone who wants all kinds of attention. Not someone who'd rather be invisible."

"I want *you*, Dylan."

He tilted my chin up with his hand.

"And you could never be invisible." He leaned in, and before I knew it, we were kissing. On the bathroom floor. Which was horribly unhygienic and probably disgusting, but was also somehow . . . perfect.

Knock, knock, knock.

"Just a minute!" we shouted in unison, then grinned at each other.

"If you're not peeing, you have to let me in or get out of the bathroom."

"He speaks!" Jamie whispered in amazement.

"I thought they'd taken a vow of silence," I whispered back.

"Seriously, guys," the cameraman continued, banging on the door. "Come out."

"We're coming!" I trilled. "Come on."

I sprang up to my feet—weak ankles be damned—and pulled Jamie up with me. We swung open the bathroom door and the cameraman leaped out of the way.

"So if we were at home in Tupelo," Jamie asked as we walked into the lobby, "where would we have gone on a date?"

"Well, we probably would have just, like, hung out in a big group in someone's basement a couple times first."

"Naturally. Terribly romantic, basements."

"Then maybe we would have gone to the movies." I was basing all of my Tupelo dating knowledge on Heaven and Tate Moseley. "Or gotten a burger or something."

"The movie I cannot do, but would you like a burger?"

"I would *always* like a burger."

"Then burgers we shall have."

He started walking confidently toward the bar at the end of the lobby.

"I'm sorry, Jamie." I pulled him to a stop.

"No, no, Dylan, please. I'm sorry. I suppose it was a bit much."

"It was nice, I swear. It was just that pressure . . ."

"To be perfect. I know," he said ruefully. "Well, then you understand perfectly how I felt as I attempted to plan our first date."

"So you planned this? Not TRC?"

"Oh, no, this was all me." He led me into the pub. We passed empty wooden tables and corner booths on our way up to the bar. "Actually, TRC had to rein me in quite a bit."

"Thank you." I squeezed his hand. "This is the nicest thing anyone has ever done for me."

"Even if you hated it."

"I didn't hate it!" I protested as he pulled a barstool out for me. I swung myself up onto the stool, resting my elbows on the bar. "It was awesome. I swear. I just—I don't like being in the spotlight."

He looked at me quizzically.

"I mean I don't like people looking at me."

"Who's looking at you?" He looked around the pub, confused. The few people in there were ignoring us completely.

"You are," I said in a quiet voice. And the camera was, too.

"Well, that, unfortunately, I suppose you'll have to get used to. For I've found I can't look away." That was the kind of thing that would have made me roll my eyes if I heard it on TV, but hearing it from Jamie, so sincere, made me feel like maybe there was something here to believe in. Not something to be scared of. "Two cheeseburgers with chips, please," he instructed the surly bald barman, who nodded once, then returned to wiping out glasses.

One song faded out as another started—something cheesy and eighties. The kind of thing Mom liked to listen to when she got ready in the morning.

"Will you dance with me, Dylan?"

"Dance with you?" I looked around. There certainly wasn't anything that even remotely resembled a dance floor. "Here?"

"It's hardly romantic. The cigarette butts and the low drone of the telly. Surely you can't object."

He was wrong—it was incredibly romantic. No one had ever asked me to dance at an actual dance, let alone created a dance floor where none existed for the sole purpose of dancing with me. But I let him pull me to his chest anyway, and we swayed back and forth, my heels making little sucking noises each time they pulled up from the sticky floor.

"I want to know what love is," Jamie warbled along, off-key.

"Sometimes it's okay to be quiet," I whispered in his ear.

"Let's be quiet, then," he agreed as he held me in his arms. And we were.

CHAPTER FIFTEEN

After a pretty sleepy Saturday at Dunyvaig, during which everyone napped so aggressively it seemed like they were trying to outdo one another, TRC had clearly decided to amp up the production values with whatever this event was that we'd all been forced to attend.

"So what is this again?" I whispered, attempting to hide from the camera behind my mug.

"Punch. Unless you got into the mulled wine," Jamie whispered back.

"No, not the drink. This event. I know it's not Christmas yet."

"Not Christmas. It's Burns Night. Although, in fact, it's technically not Burns Night at all, as that occurs in January. And it is most decidedly December."

"So then this is . . ."

"Whatever mishmash of Scottish traditions TRC could cram

into a winter evening. Fortunately, it is far too cold for any sort of Highland Games."

"Is that the thing where people throw huge-ass tree trunks?"

"That it is," Jamie confirmed. "If you're referring to the caber toss."

"Now *that* I would have liked to see," I said wistfully. "I bet Ronan could destroy a caber."

"He certainly has in the past. Although a Kit Kirby caber toss is by far the more entertaining event. One year it fell completely sideways and crushed the refreshment stand."

"That little man couldn't lift a caper, let alone a caber," Heaven announced through a mouthful of canapés.

"Heaven!" I jumped. "You know I hate it when you sneak up on me like that."

"Can't help it that I've got a silent tread." She popped another pastry puff into her mouth. "Y'all get one of these little things yet? I don't know what they are"—she licked her fingers delicately—"but they're delicious."

"Um, no," I said decidedly, at the same time Jamie answered, "It's a haggis puff."

"A what?" Heaven paused mid-chew.

"Haggis puff," Jamie said again.

"What's haggis?" she asked.

"It's a pudding of sorts made up of all the leftover bits of sheep—heart, liver, lungs, what have you—mixed with mash. Here it's been cleverly wrapped in a bit of puff pastry. Haggis is the traditional main course of a Burns supper as well, so I'm sure there's loads more to come."

"Blergh." Heaven let out a strangled little choking noise

as she delicately spat the remains of her haggis puff into an emerald-green cocktail napkin. "Excuse me, won't you?"

Heaven shuffled out of the room, rapidly turning the same color as her napkin.

"Where were we, then?" Jamie asked.

"Burns Night."

"Ah. Yes. Right. You really should be asking Ronan." Jamie looked around the room, where the man in question was holding court in front of the roaring fireplace, Dusty tucked adoringly under his arm. "It feels inappropriate for a non-Scot to be explaining it. I'm sure a tribe of tartan-clad clansmen will muster me right back to Heathrow on grounds of cultural infringement."

"I'll fight off any patriotic Scotsmen, I swear. I'm not leaving this corner to go talk to Ronan. We're in bad lighting, sort of muffled by whatever sound system is producing this fiddle music, and being boring. We're reality-TV repellent."

"Ah, but you're forgetting that I'm back in a kilt once again. These calves are camera magnets."

"Yeah, they're really something." I rolled my eyes good-naturedly.

"They seduced you, didn't they?" he asked, a legit twinkle in his eye.

"Jamie." I shushed him furtively, darting glances into the nearest ceiling corner. "Who knows if there's hidden cameras around here?"

"I think they know, Dylan. They went on a date with us."

"Oh. Right." I swallowed uncomfortably, remembering the fact that I had full-on made out with Jamie literally in front of the camera. "Even when you forget for a minute, it's still hard to get used to. That feeling that you're being watched."

"I don't think you ever get used to it. Not really," he said quietly, more like he was talking to himself than to me. He took a sip of his drink. "You had a question?"

"Oh. Right." I shook my head, trying to remember. "This party. What the hell is it? By the time you explain it to me, it'll be over."

"Sorry, sorry! Burns Night celebrates Robert Burns."

"Who is . . ." I prompted.

"Scotland's premier poet. He was born the twenty-fifth of January, 1759, so now the twenty-fifth of January is Burns Night."

"And what does one do on Burns Night?"

"Drinks Scotch. Eats a haggis. Recites the 'Address to a Haggis.'"

"The 'Address to a Haggis,'" I repeated. "You just made that up."

"I most assuredly did not. I would bet you ten quid that Kit Kirby will recite an 'Address to a Haggis' that will move you to tears, but it would be unsportsmanlike of me to take your money like that."

"Well, I'm certainly looking forward to that. Although I have to warn you, I haven't cried in public since the first time I saw *The Lion King,* so I wouldn't hold your breath. And that's it? That's the whole night?"

"People will continue to recite Burns songs and poems. And by people, I mean Kit Kirby. I have yet to attend a Burns Night where he let anyone else get a word in edgewise."

"So we're in for an evening of eating sheep lungs and listening to Kit Kirby recite poetry," I said grimly. "That's barely a step up from being in school. Hell, that might be a step back. Worse than cafeteria food and English class. I should have stayed home."

"I'm glad you didn't. Facing all these lunatics alone would have been dire. And I can assure you that Kit's recitation will be most educational. You probably shouldn't go back to school at all," he added lightly.

A leaden weight dropped into my stomach like I'd just eaten a whole tray of haggis puffs. I would have to go home. I knew, of course, that I would have to go home—this wasn't really my life—but I hadn't thought about it. About leaving Scotland. About leaving Jamie. About the expiration date stamped on our foreheads like we were grocery-store cold cuts. What happened when you met the person who you thought might just possibly be *the* person—*your* person—when you were only sixteen? And lived halfway across the world? It's not like we were going to get married and ride off into the sunset on Wenceslas. Jamie would live on forever as the story of my first kiss, but he'd cease to be a real person and become only a story. And that thought was almost unbearable.

"Y'all, those haggis puffs are deadly," Heaven announced as she returned to the room, clutching a small bottle of ginger ale. "I ran into Dusty in the bathroom barfing her guts out, too. These things are taking people *down*."

"It was the haggis!" I said loudly. Too loudly.

"Yeah, that's what I said." Heaven and Jamie were both looking at me like I was crazy.

"So, uh, is there gonna be other food at this thing?" I asked hurriedly, trying to distract them from my stupid blurt. "Or is it all haggis all the time?"

"There's traditionally a soup course," Jamie said. "Maybe cheese and pudding as well. And the haggis is always served alongside neeps and tatties."

"Neeps and tatties? That's not a food." Heaven shook her head.

"Food of the gods!" Kit Kirby boomed, arriving in our darkened corner of the party with a camera crew at his heels.

"People have *got* to stop sneaking up on us like this," I whispered to Jamie.

"Next party we're hiding behind a couch," Jamie whispered back.

"Was this a costume party?" Heaven asked archly. "Who are you supposed to be? Bob Cratchit?"

"I'm Robert Burns!" Kit protested, outraged, tugging at his white cravat. "Scotland's favorite son! The Ploughman Poet! The Bard of Ayrshire!"

"He could have gone up a size in the breeches," Heaven whispered dramatically behind her hand. "They look like tan jeggings."

"So, what's tatties and neeps?" I said desperately, hoping Kit hadn't heard the jeggings comment.

"Simple fare for simple folk like me!" Kit declaimed. "The Ploughman Poet!"

"Mashed potatoes and mashed turnips," Jamie explained.

"Thank you, Jamie," Heaven said pointedly. "I was just looking for a simple explanation, not a piece of performance art."

"The costume is a new feature," Jamie said politely. "Really adds something special to the evening."

"Stepping it up this year." Kit brushed some invisible dust off the lapels of his jacket. "Have to show the Americans what's what, eh?"

More like have to show TRC why he needs his own spin-off, I thought cynically. Then again, from the little I knew of Kit Kirby, this seemed pretty in character. Maybe some people just had the kind of personalities that were made for reality TV.

"Shall we get out of this dank corner, then?" Kit began steering us all out of our hidey-hole. No more comfortably hugging the wall for me. "The lighting is dreadful!"

"Can you believe this guy?" Heaven muttered as Kit strode grandly right into the center of the room. "What a show-off."

Privately, I thought Heaven's issues with Kit may have had more to do with the fact that she was worried there was only room for one breakout star from *Dusty and Ronan's Happily Ever After Royal Jamboree* or whatever this nightmare was called.

"I think maybe he just likes costumes?" I suggested.

"Yeah. I like costumes, too. But I'm not parading around here dressed like a slutty ladybug."

"Did you bring a slutty ladybug—"

"No, I did not," she interrupted me. We both looked at Jamie and Kit, deep into a discussion of how to tie cravats, and sank, almost in unison, into a deep, overstuffed floral couch.

"Mmm." Heaven closed her eyes. "This is nice. Cozy couch, warm fire, no one talking to us about cravats . . . Think anyone would notice if I took a nap?"

"Heaven," I began, not sure how to say what I wanted to. "We have to go home."

"What, now?" She cracked an eye open.

"No, not now. But we have to go home. Eventually. After the wedding."

"Um, yeah." Both eyes were fully open now. She struggled to sit up straight, sinking into the couch. "You just figuring that out now?"

"No, I knew that, I just sort of . . . forgot."

She looked at me with confusion, then followed my gaze over to Jamie.

"Ohhh. But, Dyl, this was always just, like, a fling. Not, like, a *thing*. You know?"

"But what if I want it to be a thing?" I whispered.

"Well, damn," she said flatly. "I thought this was just a 'Hey, I had my first kiss in a castle' kind of situation."

"I think we've evolved past that."

"But how can this evolve, Dylan?" she said seriously. "I don't want to burst any bubbles here, but you have to go home. And he has to go back to school. What then? You gonna be long distance across two continents? At sixteen?"

"I thought you were going to be all hopeless romantic with me here!" I complained. "You know, love can conquer all the odds?"

"LOVE?!"

Heaven was so loud conversation died down, and everyone turned to look at us, including all the camera and production people.

"I LOVE HAGGIS!" Heaven bellowed, and shot Ronan a thumbs-up, which he duly returned, accompanied by a huge grin.

"Good save," I muttered, attempting to sink into the couch and disappear forever. "I hope you're committed to eating a ton of haggis at dinner now."

"Are. You. Nuts?" she hissed between clenched teeth.

Luckily everyone else turned back to whatever it was they were doing before she started shouting like a crazy person. *"Love?"*

"I didn't say I loved him! I just—"

"But you thought it," she interrupted. "You thought you might. Or you could."

"Maybe."

"Dylan." She fixed me with a stare. It was hard to meet her brown eyes, usually so warm. "This is not going to end well. You are going to get hurt. I know you want me to sell you on the fairy tale, but I can't. Because this *isn't* a fairy tale. In a week, we're all going to turn back into pumpkins and go home to Mississippi. And this, whatever it was, will be over. You might be Facebook friends, you might e-mail or whatever, but it won't be what it was. And gradually it'll just fade away."

I heard her, but I didn't want to. Nothing she was saying was wrong, but it *felt* wrong.

"Damn." She chuckled softly, breaking the moment. "Who would have thought I'd be the one trying to convince you to be more cynical, huh?"

Neither of us said his name, but we both knew why. Tate Moseley was as much a part of this conversation as if he were wedged in between us on this hideous floral couch.

"Just try to live in the moment, maybe, right?" she said more gently. "Just appreciate it for what it is, you know?"

"Yeah."

"Are we cool?" she asked, concerned.

"We're cool." And we were. I certainly wasn't mad at Heaven; she'd said nothing but the truth—but that didn't mean I enjoyed hearing it. We only had a week left in Scotland, and that seemed like an impossibly short amount of time. I wasn't nearly ready to say good-bye to Jamie. And I was worried I never would be.

BONG!!!!!!

Of all things, a loud clang of a gong broke our moment. I turned to see a butler type in a tuxedo standing next to a still-reverberating golden gong, mallet in his white-gloved hand. I swear there hadn't been a gong in here before.

"Dinner," he announced, "is served."

"Well, then." Heaven pushed herself off of the couch. "Think I might need one of those at my house. Might inspire my brothers to shut up and get their asses to the dinner table in a timely fashion, huh?"

I nodded and smiled at her, but my thoughts were still lingering on Jamie and the future. We followed the swarm of people trooping into the dining room, falling into line like a herd of cattle.

The table was set formally as always, but the floral arrangements were composed almost entirely of thistles. The fat votive candles were wrapped in tartan bows, and even the plates were plaid. I found my name on a vellum place card embossed with a printed thistle, luckily right next to Heaven. A servant materialized out of nowhere to pull out my seat. To no one's surprise, the seat cushion was plaid, too.

At the first few notes of a low, droning bagpipe, we stood. A chef dressed in whites followed the bagpiper into the room, holding an enormous white serving dish containing a huge brown lump and a knife. Guess that was the haggis.

The bagpiper continued playing as the chef placed the haggis in front of Ronan. Ronan gestured to Kit, who strode grandly over to join him at the head of the table. As the song faded to a close, Kit raised his hands above his head, like he was about to address the heavens.

"Far fa' your honest, sonsie face," he began, hands still above his head. Who knew what the heck "sonsie" meant? "Great chieftan o' the puddin'-race!"

I snorted. Loudly. Mom and Dusty shot me identical *I will murder you* looks.

"Puddin'-race?" Jamie mouthed sympathetically.

At least somebody got it.

"The groaning trencher there ye fill," Kit shouted, pointing dramatically at the haggis, desperate to reclaim his audience. I tried to fix a rapt, attention-paying kind of look on my face. The more boring I was, the less the camera would look at me.

"His knife see rustic Labour dight," Kit intoned, like he was Macbeth, grabbing the knife off the plate and raising it solemnly aloft. With a lusty "an' cut ye up wi' ready sleight," Kit plunged the knife into the belly of the haggis and split it from end to end. I couldn't see entrails spilling out, even if the next line was something about trenching your gushing entrails. The haggis just kinda sat there quivering, but Heaven looked a little green anyway. She pulled her tiny bottle of ginger ale out from under the table and took a desperate gulp.

"Five more stanzas," Jamie mouthed, holding up five fingers.

I smacked my head with my palm. Probably a little too loudly. Whoops.

And so Kit continued on, hopping about the room like a demonic haggis elf. Finally, he strode back to the haggis with weighty, measured steps. Did this moment of gravitas mean we were nearing the end?

"But, if ye wish her gratefu' prayer," Kit said quietly, almost in a whisper. Pause. Pause. Dramatic pause. Longest dramatic pause in the history of mankind. "Gie. Her. A. HAGGIS!"

He roared the last line, raised his hands to the sky, then bowed low, his hair flopping madly. He rose back up to thunderous applause, face red and shiny from the exertion. I made eye contact with Jamie and mimed wiping away a few tears. Maybe I hadn't cried. But I was certainly entertained.

"All righ', then." Ronan clapped Kit on the back. "Couldna ha' said it better myself. Now, my new American family, ye may not know much about Burns Night. I'm wagerin' this is yer very first Burns Supper. They've got an order, usually, and a tradition to it."

"Tradition is the hallmark of Burns Night," Florence sniffed.

"Forgive me, Mum, for I'm goin' to break tradition for a moment here," Ronan continued. "Do somethin' new because I'm about to make a new start—and make a brand-new family." He squeezed Dusty's shoulder. Brand-new family? Was he *trying* to tip everyone off about the baby?! I looked wildly around the room, but everyone was smiling blandly, not in the least bit suspicious. "Usually, the Toast to the Lassies happens after dinner. But I canna wait that long. Because there's one lassie in particular I need to toast this evenin'." White-gloved waiters appeared out of nowhere, circulating with champagne glasses.

"Oh, Ronan!" Dusty giggled, hiding behind her hair. She couldn't drink that champagne! Wouldn't everyone get suspicious if she didn't drink as part of her own toast? God, this baby was already giving me an ulcer, and it wasn't even born yet.

"Can we all git to our feet?" Ronan asked, and with much scraping and bumping, we rose.

"Here's to Dusty," he said. "My bonny bride. The girl who

changed my life for the better in every way, when I didna even know it needed changin'."

"Are we toasting the bride?" a confident American voice drawled. I turned to see an older, blondish guy with very white teeth leaning against the doorway. He watched us all with amusement, the corners of his eyes crinkling in his suntanned face. "Isn't that usually her dad's job?"

The champagne flute slipped from Mom's hand and shattered into a cloud of broken glass.

"Daddy?" Dusty whispered.

CHAPTER SIXTEEN

"I know I'm a little early," he continued, oblivious to the chaos he'd created. Everything seemed fine on the surface, but I could feel something invisible moving through the room, like shock waves from an underwater explosion. "Rehearsal dinner's not for a few days yet, right, puddin'?"

"Right," Dusty said shakily, pale under her spray tan.

"Wanted to make sure I was nice and rested up for the big day." He grinned. I couldn't stop staring at him. "Lookin' good, Laurie."

He nodded at Mom. She nodded back, her hands fluttering like she was still trying to hold on to that shattered champagne glass. But the staff had already swept the shards up into a neat little dustpan.

"Dude," Heaven whispered. "Is that your dad?"

I shrugged, wildly. Was that my dad? Was this tall blond stranger in a gray suit my dad?

Jamie caught my eye across the table and raised his eyebrows questioningly. I shook my head.

Heaven's hand found mine and held it under the table. I couldn't believe this was happening. I hadn't seen so much as a picture of this man, and here he was. Out of nowhere. It seemed impossible that he could exist, an actual three-dimensional person, who had been living a life concurrent with, but completely separate from, mine.

"Who are you?" Florence asked imperiously, commanding the attention of the room. Even with the father-shaped bomb that had been dropped into the middle of it, ready to detonate at any moment.

"I'm the father of the bride. Cash Keller," he said. "Pleased to meet you, ma'am."

Cash Keller. It sounded like a fake name. Like a character in a bad made-for-TV movie. Like someone you thought was a nice guy until he married the heroine and attempted to murder her as part of some elaborate financial scheme.

"I know him," Heaven murmured curiously. "Cash Keller. I know him."

"Well, that makes one of us."

"He's familiar."

"He looks familiar?" I asked, squinting at him. He didn't look familiar to me.

"Naw, I mean he looks kind of like Brad Pitt, but that's not it. He seems familiar." Heaven closed her eyes. "No, he *sounds* familiar."

"Quite a place you got here." Cash—my dad—whoever he was—whistled. "Yep, this is quite the pile of bricks. You did all right for yourself, here, puddin'."

"Daddy!" Dusty exclaimed, scandalized, as a faint blush crept up her neck.

"Well, just look at you, sweetheart. So beautiful." He walked over to Dusty and held out one of her arms, like he was examining her. I half expected her to twirl. "Can't believe how grown-up you are. You're the spittin' image of your mama, I swear."

I guess it would be hard to believe how much someone had grown up in sixteen years. If you hadn't even bothered to see them once.

Much to my surprise, Dusty let him pull her into a hug. If she wanted to pretend this was some happy reunion, that was fine, but I wasn't going to play along. I looked over at Mom, pale and shell-shocked. What did you do, when suddenly faced with the father you'd never met? Mostly I just felt hollow and nauseated, like my stomach had dropped right out from under me. Like that weird feeling you get in an elevator sometimes.

I wished he hadn't come. I'd been curious about him, sure, but I would have preferred a photograph. I didn't want an actual flesh-and-blood human being to contend with.

"Cash Keller. 96.5, Scores Sports Radio." Heaven's eyes fluttered open. "That's how I know him! Cash Keller, 96.5!"

"Did someone say Scores Sports Radio?" Cash turned his blinding artificially white smile toward us, and I froze like a deer in headlights. "Is the little lady over here a fan?"

Cash walked right up to Heaven, turning the full force of his personality on her like he was switching on a lamp. I swear, it was like he was shining through his tan. He seemed like the kind of guy who was used to people liking him. Used to getting his way. He seemed like . . . well, like Dusty.

"Do you listen to 96.5 with Cash Keller in the mornings, sweetheart?" he prompted, nodding encouragingly at Heaven.

"Um, yeah—yeah," she stammered, looking wildly back and forth from Cash to me to my mom, clearly unsure of what the social etiquette was in this situation. "We listen to you every morning on the way to school. My dad loves you."

"Your daddy's a sports fan?"

"He's a football coach."

"My kind of man!" He rubbed his hands together gleefully. "Where does he coach?"

"Just at my school. Tupelo High."

"Hey!" Cash snapped his fingers together in recognition. "Dusty, that must be where you went! I'm sure you broke a hell of a lot of hearts on that football team." He chuckled.

It was at that moment I reached the horrifying conclusion that my dad had absolutely no idea who I was. He sure didn't recognize me, although there was also a distinct possibility that he had no idea I existed. I had thought he'd left *after* I'd been born, but I didn't really know. In all the pictures of me as a baby, it was only me and Mom and Dusty.

What was I supposed to do, walk up to him and formally introduce myself? "Hi, Cash Keller? I'm Dylan Leigh, the daughter you abandoned. Great to meet you. Crazy weather we're having, huh?"

I emitted an involuntary squeak of distress. Cash looked over and smiled blandly. He didn't know. He really had no idea who I was.

Run. I could hear it as clearly as if someone had spoken it in my ear. I had no idea what to do with Cash, or what to say to Mom, or even how I was supposed to feel. The only thing

I *did* know was I had to get out of there. I pushed back my chair and bolted from the room.

The stillness erupted into chaos behind me. I could hear shouting and chairs scraping and the jarring sounds of rattling silverware. The only voice I could make out was Jamie's, calling my name over and over again. Rounding the corner into the entrance hall, I pushed open the heavy doors to the castle and sprinted off into the night.

Eventually, the footsteps behind me faded. I knew it would be easy to outrun the camera crew, weighed down with heavy equipment. Hell, I could outrun everyone in that stupid castle. Especially if they bothered to stop for coats. I'd be long gone by the time they made it out here.

My lungs burned from the cold weather and the exertion. I hadn't been running here as much as I did at home, and I still wasn't used to the sting of the cold. But I ran anyway, almost reveling in the burn, as far and as fast as I could go.

Each footfall was like a slap through the thin ballet flats Dusty had lent me. I could feel each twig and rock articulated beneath the frost. Luckily, someone had plowed the road clean or I would never have gotten anywhere. Running through knee-deep snow was not something my cross-country coach had covered.

The moon reflecting off the snow was so bright it almost looked like daytime. I turned away from the fields with the sheep and the tiny cottages and the horse barn. A set of tire tracks led deeper into the woods. I was starting to lose steam from running flat-out, and the last thing I wanted to be in right now was an open field. Too visible. I pushed into the woods down the tire tracks, swatting branches out of my way as I went, my only impulse to disappear. To hide. I let the woods swallow me and ran until I couldn't see so much as a spire of Dunyvaig in the distance.

Panting, I half collapsed against a tree, sliding down until I sat in the snow. I guess there were limits to how far even I could run. So mission accomplished—I'd gotten away. But now I was outside, alone, in the cold darkness of December, wearing only a cranberry-colored dress and ballet flats. I shivered, rubbing my arms for warmth. As my heart rate started to slow and my flush fade, I was left drenched in cold sweat.

"I should've run away to a McDonald's," I muttered to myself. Then I would have been warm. And had french fries.

This was all too much. Way too much. I could compartmentalize Dusty's secret pregnancy, and ignore the cameras and the fact that I was days away from saying good-bye to Jamie, probably forever. But the completely unexpected reappearance of the dad I never thought I'd see again was beyond even my powers of denial. There was too much to feel, and the only option was to go numb, to feel nothing because I couldn't feel everything. Or maybe that was the cold setting in. I had no idea how long I'd been out here. My legs weren't stinging anymore; the stabbing pain of the cold had faded into a dull numbness. I hugged my knees tighter to my chest as my body shivered violently. It felt like I was coming apart at the seams, each shiver a spasm that rocked me to the core. I shut my eyes and buried my head in my knees, curling into as tight a ball as possible, scared to stay out here much longer, but too scared to go back.

The moon went behind a cloud, casting the woods deeper into darkness. I tried to wiggle my toes experimentally, but

I couldn't feel them at all. This was so, so much worse than being stranded at the Dunkeld & Birnam train station. I hadn't known it was possible to be so cold it was painful. I tried to think of August in Tupelo, of the kind of heat that shimmered on sidewalks and melted ice-cream cones before you could eat them. But all I could see was darkness and all I could feel was cold. I braced myself against another round of shivers, listening to the jarring sound of my teeth chattering.

The first thing I heard was the hoofbeats. The second was my name being shouted. The third thing was a lot of snorting, and then an absolutely enormous black stallion appeared in front of me, air bursting from his nostrils in white clouds.

"Dylan!" Jamie cried, pulling on the reins to bring the horse to a stop, the large hooves skidding in the dirt before my feet. Jamie did look rather dashing riding bareback, his dark hair shining in the moonlight, his kilt flapping in the breeze, but I was not in the mood for dashing. Or for a kilt, for that matter. I'd seen enough tartan in the past couple of weeks to last me a lifetime.

This was ridiculous. This was not real life. I blinked a few times, but Jamie and the horse remained firmly in place.

"I'm not Jane Eyre!" I shouted.

"Sorry?" He blinked somewhat owlishly a few times.

"I'm not Jane Eyre!" I repeated. "You can't Mr. Rochester your way out of everything!"

"Prior to this moment, I have never attempted to Mr. Rochester my way out of anything," he said, baffled. "I have neither dressed up as a fortune-teller to ascertain your intentions nor blinded myself in a fire. This very incident hardly qualifies as Mr. Rochester-ing, since I am still firmly atop my horse. And I'm not entirely sure that gentleman's name can be used as a verb."

"In America you can use anything as a verb!" I retorted shrilly, scrambling to my feet. "You can verb whatever you want! Thank the goddamn Smurfs for that!"

"I believe the Smurfs are Belgian, originally."

"*You're* Belgian! Originally!" I was aware that I had long since bypassed the realm of the rational, but I really didn't care. My legs were practically buckling underneath me, knees knocking with each fresh wave of shivers.

"Distantly, on my mother's side, as a matter of fact. But not since the fourteenth century. I believe it was called the Burgundian Netherlands in those days, however."

I raised my hands heavenward in the kind of epic shrug any mention of the Burgundian Netherlands justly deserved.

Jamie slid gracefully from the back of the horse.

"Just go." I backed away from him, closer to the tree. "Go back to the castle, okay? I'm fine."

He walked toward me. The horse, for his part, started snuffling about in the snow, presumably looking for some probably long-dead grass.

"You're not fine."

My bottom lip wobbled dangerously. Or maybe it was just disturbed by the force of my teeth chattering. I looked away, focusing on a whorl in a nearby tree trunk.

"Let me take you back to Dunyvaig, Dylan." He reached out a hand, slowly, gently, like I was a wild animal he was scared of spooking. "It's freezing out here. You can't stay out long. It isn't safe. You're shivering uncontrollably."

"Is saving people from hypothermia some kind of, like, life goal you have? You seem to do this a lot."

"Just with you, really."

His hand touched my cheek tentatively. I closed my eyes and leaned into it, the warmth of his palm cradling my face. It burned, almost, against the bitter cold of my skin.

"I don't want to go back," I whispered.

"I know. But unfortunately staying here isn't an option. You'll freeze to death. Better to be alive and in a socially awkward situation than dead and free."

"That's really inspirational. And seems very British. Is that how you guys tried to deal with George Washington?"

"I'm not entirely sure whether or not I should be offended. That seemed like a slight to the crown." He slid his tartan sash thing off, unpinning the heavy silver buckle that held it together, and shook it out. It was bigger than I expected. He wrapped it around my shoulders, bundling me up like a burrito. I was still shivering but felt much better wrapped up.

"Can we go hide in the horse barn?" I pleaded. "Just hide in there and bar the doors?"

"They'd find us eventually."

"Eventually is better than right now."

Headlights broke through the darkness. I buried my face in the tartan, seeing spots. The horse whinnied in alarm. Jamie grabbed his bridle, making soothing noises as the horse stamped the frosty ground warily. The horn blared, and the horse tossed his head in response. Jamie grabbed his muzzle and blew onto his nose, stroking the sides of his face.

My eyes adjusted to the light in time to see a shiny vintage convertible roll to a stop, a fur-covered lump in the driver's seat barely visible.

"Dylan!" Heaven. I recognized her voice at once. "The cavalry is here!"

"Why does everyone think I need to be rescued by means of some completely impractical mode of transportation?" I asked no one in particular. The horse nickered in response. He got it.

Heaven left the car running, headlights still on, and hopped out. She was wearing a thick fur coat that fell all the way down to her ankles.

"Why are you driving a convertible in December?" It wasn't the only question I had. But it was the first one that came to mind.

"I couldn't figure out how to get the top up on this stupid thing! It's from like the Paleolithic Period!"

"It's from 1966," Jamie answered.

"Is it *yours*?" I asked, boggling.

"Heavens, no. Look at the personalized registration."

I looked, attempting to shield my eyes from the glare of the headlights. The plate read KIRBY1.

"You stole Kit Kirby's car?" I asked incredulously.

"I didn't steal it on purpose. It was around back, and the keys were in it. I had to make sure you were okay. And there was no way I was running out here. I could never catch you."

There was something special about a friend who would steal a car for you.

"And the fur coat . . ." I prompted.

"Pulled it out of a coat closet. In case you didn't notice, it's *December*." She looked pointedly at my bare knees. "Heat's running, but it's not doing much. So let's jump in and get back to Dunyvaig before we all freeze our butts off, 'kay?"

I looked back and forth between the two of them, the friends who had ridden to my rescue. Who had come to find me in a dark forest and weren't pressuring me to talk about my dad or why I had run or anything. They just wanted me to be warm and safe. And maybe this was part of the mental confusion of early-onset hypothermia, but I had never felt so lucky. Who cared if my dad didn't recognize me? I had family. And friends. They knew who I was—and so did I.

Another set of headlights cut through the darkness as a white van barreled into the clearing. Once again, Jamie restrained the horse as he shied and whinnied in displeasure.

"Stop! Thief!" An incredibly angry Kit Kirby burst out of the van, coat flapping behind him like the wings of the angel of death. "Unhand the keys, you madwoman!"

It wasn't Kit Kirby who scared me, however. It was Pamela behind him, her hands clutching the clipboard as she watched the cameraman advance toward us, a grin on her face so wide I thought her face might split in two.

CHAPTER SEVENTEEN

The following afternoon, I had stopped shivering but couldn't seem to shake the cold feeling. Or maybe that was just because I was trapped in a room with Pamela. Balanced precariously on my knees, a teacup rattled in its saucer.

"So." Pamela took a loud, surprisingly slurpy sip, then set her cup decisively back in its saucer. "Here we are. All alone. Just you and me."

I narrowed my eyes and attempted to sip some tea. Hot. Too hot. A bit of scalding liquid sloshed over the side as I set the whole dangerous business down on the coffee table.

"I must admit, I was pretty surprised when I heard you wanted to have a little chat."

I looked at her. Yes, sitting down with Pamela had been my idea, but that didn't make being here any easier. The way I saw it, I didn't have much of a choice. Pamela needed to be kept distracted and as far away from my sister's burgeoning belly as humanly possible. And if that distraction was me, well, fine.

"Let's just clear up a few things before you film your first confessional."

"Confessional?" I spat.

"Do you know what that is?"

"Yeah, I know what that is," I snarled. "I watch a lot of TV. I just don't know why you'd want to film me talking to the camera."

"Everyone else has filmed a confessional. Most people have already filmed several. Dusty and Ronan do at least one a day, usually more."

"Makes sense. It's their show, right? No one is watching this thing to see me."

She fixed me with a stare.

Then Pamela sighed heavily, breaking the silence. "You know, Dylan, I've given you a lot of leeway. A lot."

"Oh, *have* you?" I asked sarcastically.

"Yes. I have, actually," she replied. "You made it very clear that you didn't wish to be a large part of this show. I respected that. I haven't asked you to film any confessionals prior to this. I've kept the camera crews as unobtrusive as possible."

I snorted. *That* was unobtrusive? Please.

"We have a problem, Dylan."

"We? There is no we. *I* don't have a problem." I crossed my arms defensively.

"Fine. I have a problem. And my problem is you."

I tried to fix her with my coldest stare. It made zero impact.

"You need to stop running away, Dylan."

"I haven't run away," I shot back. "I'm on the cross-country team. I run. It's something I like to do. Exercise."

The look she gave me informed me very clearly that she was buying none of my bullshit.

"Last night had nothing to do with aerobic activity. You can't run away from the cameras. You can't hide from the cameras. You can't lock yourself in the bathroom and shut out the cameras."

"Don't I get any privacy? It's a *bathroom*."

"If you're doing your business, sure. If you're in there with someone else having a conversation, then no. I thought you'd appreciate the fact that I only sent one crew member along on your date. You know what? We've gotten off on the wrong foot here." She waved her hands like she was trying to erase the last few minutes. "I'm sorry."

"Sorry?" I parroted in disbelief.

"Yes, sorry. Really, Dylan, I should be thanking you."

"For what?" I asked suspiciously.

"For Jamie, Dylan! Obviously." She laughed. "That was a really nice, very unexpected development. I honestly had no idea that would happen." She looked off into the distance, like she was visualizing something just out of sight. "That's going to be some excellent television. I expected absolutely nothing from you, and you've given us a great B story line."

I scuffed my sneaker on the carpet. Of course I was happy that I'd met Jamie, and that he'd kissed me, but I wished I hadn't given Pamela anything. My whole body recoiled at the idea of everyone watching me and Jamie on TV. I'd have to go on some kind of TV-smashing campaign all over Tupelo. And never look at the Internet ever again.

"Of course, single teenage boy, single teenage girl . . . I probably should have expected something to happen, hmm?"

She narrowed her eyes. "It's just that the way Dusty described you, I didn't think romance was a possibility."

Ouch. Well, she wanted me to talk about Dusty, did she? I clamped my lips together firmly.

"It must be hard, having a sister who is just so beautiful." She tilted her head to the side sympathetically, adopting what looked like a well-practiced *I'm listening* face. "Can't have been easy, growing up the younger sister of the most beautiful girl in Mississippi."

I looked over her shoulder. A cameraman had entered the small sitting room, closing the door quietly behind him.

"So I guess private time is over then?" I asked archly.

"I think so," she said. "We understand each other, don't we? Run away again and I'll slap your mother with a contract-violation lawsuit so crippling she'll have to mortgage your home just to pay the lawyer's retainer."

"What— You can't—"

"Of course I can. You'd know that if you'd bothered to read any of the contracts." She tsked. "So. Let's play nice, shall we? I got you a boyfriend—you're welcome—and you got me a B line—thank you—so it looks to me like we're even. Stay where the cameras can see you for the rest of your time at Dunyvaig. It's not so much longer to go. Shouldn't be hard. Okay?"

"Okay," I said through gritted teeth. I didn't know nearly enough about contract law to call her bluff. If this was a bluff.

"Now, isn't it better when we're all friendly?"

I bared my teeth in a ghoulish approximation of a smile.

"There you go. We needed this B line, honestly," she said, almost absentmindedly. "There's only so much mileage you can get out of the American bride who keeps puking up her

Scots fiancé's haggis. It was funny the first time, but she's going to have to keep it down at the wedding."

Puking up the haggis. My eyes snapped over to Pamela. Was she baiting me? She seemed unconcerned as she took another sip of her tea. It was possible she hadn't figured anything out yet . . . but if she hadn't, she was very, very close. I had to do something—throw her off the scent—anything. Otherwise Dusty's marriage, her life, her future, the baby—all of it— was toast.

"What if I wanted to be more than the B line?"

"Excuse me?"

I couldn't tell who was more shocked that I'd just said that— me or Pamela.

"I want to be more than the B line," I repeated, trying to sound like I meant it. "Me—me and Jamie, I mean. You can film us anywhere. All our dates. And I'll do the confessionals. I'll do one right now."

"This is a rather abrupt change of heart." She set her cup back in the saucer and eyed me warily.

"You—you were right before." The more time the cameras spent with me and Jamie, the less Pamela would be poking around in Dusty's business. I just had to make her believe this was what I really wanted. "About how hard it is, being Dusty's younger sister. How no one ever thinks I'm beautiful. How when Dusty's in the room, I'm invisible."

"Yes," Pamela purred, "that must be hard."

"So I want my own story line. One that's just about me. Not Dusty *at all*. Okay?" It seemed like she was kind of buying it. Or maybe my motivation didn't matter to her, as long as she got her footage. After all, I was giving her exactly what she wanted.

"Okay, Dylan. I'm glad we finally understand each other."
I hated when Pamela smiled at me. It freaked me out. "Mike
will check in with you later to film confessional stuff about
Jamie and we can add it in post. If you want this story line to
go anywhere, you cannot hold back on the romance. Please
spare no details. Understood?"

I nodded. The idea of having to recount, in detail, every
experience I'd had with Jamie made me want to hide in a cave
for the rest of my life, but for Dusty and the baby, I could do
it. I had to.

"But there's a few questions I'd like to ask you myself. The
sudden reappearance of your father last night must have been
quite a shock."

I wanted to play along with Pamela, for Dusty's sake, but I
didn't want to think about him. I didn't want to talk about him.
I wanted to pretend he didn't exist. That he'd never walked
into Dunyvaig at all.

"How did that make you *feel*, Dylan?" Pamela prompted.

"Nothing," I whispered.

"I'm sorry, what was that?"

"Nothing," I repeated. "I felt nothing."

Pamela narrowed her eyes at me. I knew I wasn't giving her
what she wanted. But I wasn't lying, exactly. I felt a hollowness
that I couldn't put into words. "Nothing" was the only word
I could think of to describe it.

"You must have been surprised."

"Obviously I was *surprised*," I snapped. "Exactly what you
wanted, right? The dramatic return of the absent father. That
must have been a real find for you. How long did it take you
to track him down?"

Play along, Dylan. You're supposed to be playing along. Why was that so hard?

"And why, exactly, was us finding Cash a problem?" She paused as I tried to think of an answer to her question that wasn't combative. "I don't understand why you think us bringing him to Scotland was some sort of plot. Typically girls want their fathers at their weddings."

Yeah, right. Bringing Cash in had everything to do with shock value and ratings and nothing whatsoever to do with Dusty's wedding.

"You know how much this means to your sister. Surely, Dylan, you *must* have seen the episode where Dusty told Ronan about your dad."

I had, in fact. It was the fourth episode that aired, and the first one where Dusty and Ronan got "real," or whatever passes for real on reality TV. Dusty had pulled out a picture of herself, tiny with a pouf of white-blond hair blowing in the wind, holding the hand of a tall blond guy in jeans—a picture *I* hadn't even known she'd had. She cried, then Ronan cried, and they bonded over the fact that they'd both grown up without fathers. Later, Ronan told Jimmy Kimmel that this had been the moment he knew he was falling in love with her. #FindDustysDad had even been trending on Twitter for a while. Odd that Cash hadn't outed himself then. Maybe he'd been waiting for a free plane ticket to Europe.

"Even after Ronan proposed, Dylan, don't you remember? 'Of course I always dreamed about my daddy walkin' me down the aisle, ever since I was a little girl. But I guess that's my one dream that can't come true.'" Pamela's impression of Dusty was pretty accurate, if somewhat cruel. I goggled at her, unable to believe she'd actually just done that.

Screw playing nice. Dusty didn't deserve that, and certainly not from Pamela, of all people. Dusty had given the network *everything* they could have possibly wanted, and Pamela couldn't even treat her with respect. What I wouldn't give to tell Pamela *exactly* what I thought of her and her whole stupid show.

"Dylan!" Jamie burst through the door, breathless. "You've got to help me! Kit Kirby's challenged Heaven to a duel!"

"A duel?!" I scrambled up to my feet, nearly knocking over my teacup in the process. "What, because of the car?"

"Yes, of course because of the car! He's absolutely livid! He's somehow located two rapiers, a broadsword, a mace, and a pair of dueling pistols that may have belonged to Sir Arthur Conan Doyle!"

"Seriously? The Sherlock Holmes guy?"

"There's no time to authenticate the pistols now; we have to stop the duel!"

"Don't stop it too fast." Pamela was already hustling the camera guy out of the room. "Find Kirby, before he gets to Heaven. We'll come back to this, Dylan."

And with that she was gone.

CHAPTER EIGHTEEN

"He's not really going to shoot her, right?" I asked anxiously, attempting to push my way past Jamie to rescue Heaven.

"Of course not. Particularly since there is no duel," Jamie said mischievously, a raffish look in his eyes.

"What now?" I stopped dead in my tracks, right in front of Sir Smirks-A-Lot.

"I've been pulled into this torture chamber often enough to know what was going on. I simply created a diversion to facilitate your escape."

"Well. Thank you. That was a hell of a diversion."

"In the words of Sir Arthur Conan Doyle, go big or go home."

"I really feel like you're feeding me a lot of misinformation about Sir Arthur Conan Doyle today."

"Perhaps." One side of his mouth quirked up into a funny half smile. "He was Scottish, you know."

"Really?"

"Yes, that much is true. Now perhaps we should go somewhere else before the crew of ghouls returns."

"Yes, please. Just—not too far," I amended, Pamela's warning about not running out of the camera's range ringing in my ears. At least if Pamela was busy hunting for Heaven and Kit, she probably wasn't overly concerned with trailing Dusty.

"How about the library? Would that distance trouble you?"

"I think I can make it."

We passed out of the small sitting room, Jamie shutting the door quietly but firmly behind us. Still unable to navigate anywhere at Dunyvaig, I let Jamie lead me down the hall to the library. I walked quickly, hoping we wouldn't bump into any cameras or the one person at Dunyvaig I wanted to see even less than Pamela—Cash Keller.

"So if Heaven and Kit Kirby aren't trying to kill each other, what are they doing?" I asked.

"They may still be trying to kill each other. They were being very coy about having to practice something for the wedding."

"Huh," I said meditatively as we walked into the library. I shut the door—I didn't think that counted as hiding from the camera. It's not like I'd locked it. "If they're attempting to do something together they've definitely killed each other. We probably should have just given them the dueling pistols and gotten it over with."

"Probably," Jamie agreed.

Inside the library, a fire crackled in the hearth. Someone had hung two red stockings on the mantel. A tartan blanket draped invitingly over the plump leather sofa. I practically dive-bombed it, snuggling up under the blanket.

Jamie joined me on the couch. He kissed me once—slowly,

sweetly. It was a happily-ever-after kiss, the kind the prince would use to wake up Sleeping Beauty.

"Are you all right, then, Dylan?" he asked quietly.

"No," I whispered. "But I don't really want to talk about him—it—anything. Ugh, I'm sorry." I sighed. "This is not the kind of thing you should be dealing with."

"What kind of thing should I be dealing with, then?"

"We just started, um, we just started, uh—"

"Dating, Dylan, I think you can say we're dating. We did go on a date." He smiled.

"Right. That we did. Okay, well, then, we just started dating. And you shouldn't have to deal with any of my runaway dad stuff."

"I want to deal with all of your stuff, Dylan."

"How does your dumb accent make even 'stuff' sound good?" I marveled, shaking my head. "This is a land of sorcerers."

"I think the fault lies in your American brain chemistry."

"Oh yeah?" I swung my legs up and plopped them into his lap, leaning back against the arm of the couch.

"Yes, yes, something about the way American brain waves receive a British accent. It scrambles the brain."

"Scrambles the brain?" I laughed.

"I must have scrambled your brain. It's the only reason I can think of that you seem to enjoy spending time with me. That you want to kiss me. That you *like* me."

"If anything, I scrambled your brain," I said, blushing.

"Perhaps that's what happens when you meet someone you really quite like," Jamie said thoughtfully. "You both feel a bit as though you've tricked the other person into liking you."

So many questions were poised on the tip of my tongue. *What happens after the wedding? Will I ever see you again? Does this feel as real to you as it feels to me?*

But I didn't ask any of them, because all of the answers I wanted seemed impossible. So instead, I leaned in, and I kissed him.

I scooted closer, almost in his lap, my arms around his neck. The fire was roaring, but it was no match for the warmth of Jamie's hands pressed against my lower back. It almost made me feel small, which was something I didn't think was possible. He pulled away for a moment, still with his arms around me.

"I think I could kiss you forever," Jamie murmured dreamily.

"I have absolutely no objection to that."

I leaned in again, but he stopped me, searching my eyes.

"For the life of me, Dylan, I cannot figure out why you like me." He shook his head. "Several weeks ago I could not have imagined having a conversation with a girl for this long, let alone kissing one. This all seems completely impossible."

"It *is* kind of impossible. And unreal. This whole situation is. But isn't this the moment where you bust out some poem about kissing and rook-delighting heavens and when it's right it's just right and all that?"

"Ah yes, 'When It's Right, It's Right'—one of Tennyson's lesser-known works." He nodded sagely. "I keep wanting to pinch you to make sure you're real. Or pinch myself to make sure it isn't a dream."

"Maybe it is." I ran a hand through his hair absentmindedly. It slid through my fingers like silk. "Nothing has felt real since

I got to Scotland. And I don't care. I don't want to wake up back in Tupelo. I want to stay in this dream a little longer."

"Hold fast to dreams," he said, "for when dreams go, life is a barren field, frozen with snow."

"Do you think Langston Hughes wrote that end part about Dunyvaig?" I asked.

"Yes, absolutely nowhere in America has barren fields frozen with snow."

"Shut up," I said eloquently.

He pulled me closer, until I was practically on top of him, capturing my mouth with his. For two people who had never been kissed until a week ago, we seemed to be naturals.

The library door slammed open with a bang, revealing Cash and a camera crew. Jamie and I jumped apart. I drew the tartan up to my neck, like I was a Victorian maiden who'd been surprised in her bedchamber. I don't know what the impulse was that had prompted me to cover up my not-at-all-revealing sweatshirt, but people do weird things when they're startled. Then I remembered that I was supposed to be dialing up the romance for the camera crew, so I patted the side of Jamie's face in what I hoped was a sensual manner. He looked at me strangely. Not romantic, then.

"Oh gosh!" Cash reddened and started to back up, but the camera crew prevented it. "Sorry, kids, I didn't—well, I, uh . . . didn't."

Words seemed to fail him. Barred from leaving by the camera crew, or maybe of his own volition—who could tell?—he stepped into the library.

"Isn't this the moment when you're supposed to yell, 'Dad, get out of my room!'?" he joked.

"This isn't my room." I bit back the "and you're not my dad" that lingered on my tongue, but I think he heard it even though it went unsaid.

"Real, uh, classic father-daughter bonding moment here, huh?" He laughed awkwardly.

"I wouldn't know," I said coldly.

"So this must be your young man, then!" Cash approached Jamie with his hand outstretched. Jamie scrambled off the couch and up to his feet. "Got to make sure you're good enough for my little girl, huh? Well, not so little anymore!"

"Yeah, you missed the little part," I muttered.

"I'm Jamie. It's a pleasure to meet you, sir." Jamie took Cash's hand. Cash shook it so vigorously I thought Jamie's arm might pop out of its socket.

"You don't owe him your politeness." I sprang up from the couch, ready to remove Jamie from that handshake by physical force if necessary. This was beyond bizarre. *I* hadn't even met my father yet. Shouldn't I meet him before *Jamie* did?

"I'm British! No matter what I say, it comes out polite," Jamie said helplessly.

Jamie eventually extricated himself and stood awkwardly to the side, as Cash and I stared at each other. He was tall, like I'd always thought he'd be, and blondish, like we all were. I searched the planes of his face for something, looking for a jolt of recognition—of sameness, somehow, but I couldn't see myself in him. His eyes were more blue, like Dusty's, less gray, like mine, but there was nothing in there that I connected to.

"Dylan," he said simply. Maybe he was looking for something in me, too.

"So you know who I am, then?" I folded my arms across my chest. "Did the PAs finally alert you to the fact that you had a second daughter?"

"Of course, I knew, I just didn't— Hell, Dylan, you were a baby last time I saw you! I could practically hold you in one hand. You're so grown-up now. It's no wonder I didn't recognize you."

"I fail to see how that's my problem."

"It's not, baby girl, it's not—"

"Don't call me that," I snapped.

"It's not your problem, Dylan," he said carefully. "It's mine. I realize I've been no kind of father to you girls, but I'm here now. That's all I can do—say I'm sorry, and be here for you now."

"Seriously?!" I laughed. "*That's* all you can do? Say you're here now? Well, yeah, of course you're here now. Awfully convenient that you decided to show up right when family bonding time was being televised."

"I didn't— That's not—"

"Hoping to get a couple nice mentions for your stupid radio show? Maybe parlay this whole thing into an on-camera position at ESPN?"

"Dylan, it's not about that." The tone in his voice was so after-school special it made me want to murder him. "I just wanted to be here for Dusty's big day."

"This is so transparent, it's embarrassing," I said, venom dripping from every word. In that moment, I hated him, hated everything about him, right on down to the Scores Sports Radio 96.5 insignia on his polo shirt. "You just wanted to be here for Dusty's big day?" I asked sarcastically. "Well, where were you for her high school graduation? Her college graduation? Believe me, she put in a hell of a lot more work to make it to those big days."

"I know I missed a lot, Dylan." He was trying his best to ooze sincerity. Probably hoping they'd sound-bite just this part. "All I can say is that I'm here now."

"Yeah. You said. I get that you're here now. I just don't particularly care," I said flatly. "I hope you enjoy Scotland. And if you and Dusty decide you want to play happy family, that's fine, but I don't plan to participate in that."

"I know I screwed up," he said, "and I don't expect you to—"

"Don't. Expect. Anything," I said, as clearly as I could. "Because that's what you'll get from me. Nothing. Exactly what I've gotten from you."

"Well— All right, then." Cash tried to smile again, but I was sure even the cameras could see how forced it was.

"Yes. All right, then," Jamie said firmly as he stepped even closer, placing a comforting hand on my shoulder.

"Come on, Jamie." I grabbed his hand. "Let's just—let's just go."

I probably should have tried to come up with a crushing exit line, but wordplay has never been my strong suit. So instead I left. Luckily, Cash didn't follow us—only a cameraman did. Good. One less cameraman lurking around Dusty. I decided to just do what everyone kept telling me to do and ignore him.

"Do you think there's even a remote possibility that he's sincere?" Jamie asked as he followed me down the hall. I decided to head for the sitting room—it might not have been as private as the library, but at this time of day, there was bound to be a cheese plate.

"No," I said decisively. "Why did he show up *now*, you know? It's too convenient. He just wants the exposure—the publicity."

Jamie nodded, his brow creased. "I had forgotten that fame via reality television was a desirable occurrence to some."

"To many. And to one Cash Keller in particular, I think."

I'd like to believe I wasn't the biological offspring of a fame-whore, but given the rest of my family, it made sense. At least Dusty was honest about it, though. And Mom's job in front of the camera was actually, you know, a *job*.

Jamie squeezed my hand. Whatever his agenda, Cash Keller was right about one thing—he was here now. And there was nothing I could do about that.

CHAPTER NINETEEN

"Pull!"

I covered my ears against the explosion of gunshots and shattering clay. A clay pigeon shoot would not have been my first choice of activity to spice up the Wednesday before the wedding, but it was already abundantly clear that TRC and I didn't agree on anything.

"They shouldn't have given us guns." I shook my head. "This seems like a horrible idea."

"At least the quails are safe," Jamie said. "The only casualties here are ceramic."

"For *now*. This will not end well, mark my words," I said ominously.

"In your FACE, Kirby!" Heaven cheered. She slammed her gun down on the ground and commenced an incredibly elaborate victory dance that incorporated the Sprinkler, the Tootsie Roll, and the Worm.

"Not fair!" Kirby whined. "Not fair at all! You're at a better angle! The sun's in my eyes!"

"Oh, waa, waa, waa." Heaven was now back up on her feet and rubbing her eyes exaggeratedly. "Should Mary Poppins come pick you up for your nap, you big baby?"

"Mary Poppins doesn't make babies take naps!" Kit Kirby threw his gun to the ground angrily. "She takes them on magical adventures."

"Winners get magical adventures. Big baby losers get naps." Heaven started moonwalking back and forth in front of Kit Kirby. "And I only see one big baby loser here."

"Not fair!" he whined. "Not fair! I want a rematch."

"You can have your rematch after I finish my victory dance, fool." Heaven was now doing a very realistic shopping-cart move.

"That'll be in approximately twelve and a half minutes." I mimed checking my invisible watch.

"Any takers?" Kit addressed the line of shooters. "Who wants to shoot against an honest man in a fair match?"

Heaven rolled her eyes exaggeratedly as she cartwheeled past him.

"Don't let him shoot against Dusty," I warned. "He'll never stop sulking. She's lethal."

"You're joking," Jamie said.

"I'm totally serious. In high school she dated a couple guys who were big into hunting and one whose dad was a cop, and she is a total killer. She can probably outshoot anyone here."

"Anyone? Hardly. Not Ronan," Jamie scoffed. "He's a rather good shot."

"Even Ronan," I said confidently. "She can *easily* outshoot Ronan, I bet. You want to make this interesting?"

"Are you asking me to place a wager?"

"Heck yes. Loser makes the winner a snack. And it has to be delicious."

"I accept that wager." He stuck out his hand, and I shook it. "We have an accord. I very much look forward to your delicious snack."

"Don't count your crumpets before they're toasted, buster."

"Sorry?"

"You heard me. Hey, Dusty!" I shouted. "You wanna win a bet for me?"

"You say somethin' about winnin', Dilly?"

Say what you will about Dusty, there was nothing she loved more than winning. Well, except for her fiancé—maybe. She disentangled herself from Ronan's embrace, grinning through her smudged lipstick. Personally, I wouldn't have made out with anyone in front of my mom . . . or future mother-in-law . . . or long-lost father . . . but Dusty apparently had no problem with it. The three adults were bundled up under a tree behind the line of shooters, drinking coffee out of thermoses and making awkward small talk. I was sure I wasn't the only one who'd noticed that Mom had positioned herself as far away from Cash as possible.

I also wouldn't have ever worn pink Hunter boots and a pink plaid coat, so there was a lot Dusty did that I didn't understand.

"Who are you supposed to be, Foxhunt Barbie?" I asked as she and Ronan joined us.

"Dressin' for the hunt is tradition!" she chirped in a baby

voice, widening her eyes. "Which you would know if you ever bothered to get outta that damn hoodie!" Playfully she pulled my hood up, leaning in close as I tried to swat her away. "I'm playin' nice, Dylan," she whispered, little louder than a breath. "Givin' 'em exactly what they want. The dumber I look, the less reasons Pamela'll have to go sniffin' around for more plotlines. Dumb makes for good television."

I was sort of impressed, in spite of myself. The idea of giving Pamela what she wanted was anathema to my very being, but even I could understand that there were more important things at play here than foiling TRC. Or trying not to look like an idiot on TV.

"All right, baby sister," Dusty said loudly. "What am I winning this time?"

"Shooting contest. I bet Jamie that you could out-shoot Ronan."

"Is that all? Easy pickin's!" she crowed. "You ready to lose, baby?"

"Are you sure you should be doing this?" Ronan asked carefully, placing a comforting hand on her back.

"I'm fine, sweets." Dusty laughed it off. "I'm not made of glass. I'm not gonna break, I swear."

I froze—was shooting a gun bad for the baby? In areas unrelated to alcohol, I had no idea what a pregnant lady could or couldn't do. But Dusty didn't seem in the least bit concerned, and presumably, she knew what she was doing.

"I think you're just scared." Dusty poked Ronan in the chest. "Scared that you're gonna get your ass whooped by a girl."

"Ronan's not scared of anything!" Kit said loyally. "He once wrestled an earless seal!"

"Why would you wrestle a seal?" I asked.

"It wasna a wrestle so much as a cuddle," Ronan clarified.

"An *earless* seal?" Heaven asked.

"They lack external ears, but they can still hear," Jamie said.

"Why do you know that?" I shook my head in disbelief.

"This is not the first time I've heard the tale of Ronan and the Earless Seal," he replied.

"Well now, seems like I'm hearin' a lot of chattin', and not a lot of shootin'." Dusty tapped her foot impatiently. "Why don't you quit stallin' and march that cute butt right on up here to the pigeon-launchin' shooter thing."

"Ooo, she knows the technical terms, Ronan," Kit said sarcastically. "Perhaps you should be scairt."

"Oh man, this is going to be so great." I rubbed my hands together gleefully as Dusty stepped forward, raising the gun to her shoulder and checking the sights. "He has no idea what he's in for. No idea."

"Much to my surprise, she does look somewhat . . . lethal," Jamie said.

"Can't back out now, snack boy," I cackled. "You agreed to that bet."

"I would never renege on a gentleman's agreement," he said, horrified.

"You boys may be gentlemen," Dusty said, "but I'm about to shoot like a lady. You ready, baby?"

"I willna take it easy on ye, Dusty," Ronan said seriously.

"If you dare take it easy on me, I'll shoot you," she threatened. "I wanna know I whooped your ass fair and square."

"We shall see whose ass is whooped, madam!" Kit proclaimed. "Shooters, don your earmuffs!"

Dusty put on Heaven's ear-protection things, careful not to smush her hair, while Ronan, much less carefully, grabbed Kit's and jammed them on his head.

"Pull!" Dusty shouted suddenly, and the first clay flew into the air. Seconds later, it exploded. As did the next. And the next. And the one after that. Dusty eviscerated five clays; then Ronan shot, then Dusty again. To be honest, it was pretty boring—just yelling and explosions. But what was not boring *at all* was watching Jamie's and Kit's expressions of shock as Dusty shot. Round after round, as each clay exploded, Kit's jaw dropped lower and lower.

"Bloody unbelievable." Kit shook his head in disbelief. "This is bloody unbelievable! How is— How can she— She's wearing far too much makeup to be good at sports."

"Sexist!" Heaven scolded.

"I'll never understand American girls. I swear," he muttered. "They dinna make any sense. Supermodels with shotguns."

Ronan was good, but he was no match for Dusty. He got nearly all of his, but not quite. Of the twenty-five clays that were launched, Dusty didn't miss a single shot.

"Wooo-eeee!" From underneath the tree, Cash emitted an earsplitting whistle. "Helluva shot, baby girl! That's my baby girl, y'all! She's a killer!"

"Thanks, Daddy!" Dusty chirped.

Barf. I couldn't decide which was worse—if Dusty was completely fine with the reappearance of Cash Keller, or if she was just pretending for the cameras. Either way, from looking at them, you'd never know they hadn't seen each other in sixteen years.

"Brilliant shooting, darling." Ronan folded Dusty up in his arms and kissed the top of her head. "You canna let me win just once?"

"Never." She grinned.

"Not even wi' my masculine pride at stake?"

"Especially not then."

"And that's why I love you."

They started making out again, and the rest of us discreetly turned away.

"Well, Dylan," Jamie said, "I honestly must say I did not see that one coming. That was . . . not what I expected from Dusty."

"Don't judge a book by its pink cover," I said smugly. "Now pony up."

"What, now?" he asked, bewildered. "I don't happen to have a delicious snack on my person."

"Who's got a snack?" Heaven asked.

"Those are the terms of the bet. Since Dusty won, Jamie has to make me a delicious snack," I explained.

"Way to aim low, dude." Heaven shook her head. "You should have bet him a car or something."

"He doesn't have a car. And neither do I."

"Wouldn't have been your problem." She shrugged. "He just would have had to come up with one. Somehow."

"Not everyone shares your cavalier attitude toward grand theft auto," I said.

"I *borrowed* Kit's car." Heaven glared at me. "Borrowed it. With every intention of returning it."

"Only in the face of forcible coercion," Kit said grumpily.

"I wouldna been surprised if ye'd been halfway back to the States if I hadna arrived in time, ye wee besom."

"Anyway," I said to Jamie, interrupting them. "Is there somewhere in the castle we can make a snack?"

"The kitchens shouldn't be too busy at the moment," Jamie mused. "It's ages until dinner. Hopefully, they shan't be bothered if we mess around a bit in there."

"Time for a snack now, is it? Och, I wouldna say nay to a bite of summat." Kit patted his belly genially. "Feeling a wee bit peckish, myself."

"No," Heaven said firmly. "We've got stuff to do. And I need you at fighting weight."

She poked his tummy, and he squealed like the Pillsbury Doughboy. Weird. What "stuff" could Heaven and Kit possibly be doing? And I didn't even want to think about how Kit's weight could possibly factor into it.

"Oi, away from there!" he commanded. "I've got a decent manly shape, thank you very much! And no matter what I eat, it willna make much of a difference to my shape in three days' time. So I dinna see any reason why I canna have a wee sweetie."

"No sweeties!" Heaven barked. "We've gotta practice and you know it."

"She's verra cruel, this one." Kit jerked his thumb at Heaven, then turned to face her. "Your mum got it all wrong when she named you Heaven. Beelzebub would have been much more appropriate."

"Hilarious. March. Back to the castle. Now. Go."

Heaven gave him a decided shove in the back, and he started slowly moving toward Dunyvaig, sighing heavily.

"Hey, Heaven." I grabbed her arm. "What exactly are you doing with Kit?"

"Can't tell you."

"Can't or won't?" I narrowed my eyes.

"It's a *secret,* Dylan," she said, like she was talking to a child.

"You're not, um . . . I mean you're not . . . uh . . . are you?"

"Am I what? Oh, ew!" Suddenly, realization dawned. "God, Dylan, ew, no! He's old! Like super old!"

"I'm sorry!" I said desperately. "I just had to ask!"

"Well, you asked, and now you know, so we never have to contemplate that horrific possibility again." She made a barf face. "Ugh, you've blinded my mind's eye. Thanks for that." She shook her head, and followed Kit up to the castle.

"To the kitchens, then?" Jamie held out his arm, and I took it.

CHAPTER TWENTY

As we started to walk, I heard Mom's on-camera laugh—it was totally fake—the kind she did when a guest on the show attempted a joke. A frown creased my brow.

"I'm worried about Mom," I said quietly. "The whole Cash Keller thing. It's weird for *me*; I can't even imagine how weird it is for her. And I have no problem ignoring him and being rude, but she's so I-am-an-adult-and-a-polite-Southern-lady-and-I-would-rather-die-than-be-rude-even-to-the-asshole-who-abandoned-me-and-my-daughters."

"Southern women and British citizens have a lot more in common than I'd known," Jamie said thoughtfully. "Death before rudeness. And also shockingly lethal hunting skills, apparently."

"Yeah." I laughed, but I ended up chewing my lip with worry. Oh. Crap. Cameraman Mike's footfalls in the snow were so quiet that I hadn't realized he'd been following us. I probably shouldn't have aired Mom's dirty laundry like that. Oh well. It was too late now. All the Leigh family laundry was swinging out in the open for anyone to see. A little colorful commentary from me wasn't going to change anything about that.

"She's strong, your mum," Jamie said softly. "She'll be fine. She handled Ronan's mum without flinching, and Florence is the most terrifying human of my acquaintance."

"That's true. She's tough. And you didn't even see her take down the basketball coach."

"Sorry?"

"On Mom's show. She interviewed this Ole Miss basketball coach who'd come under fire for questionable coaching methods, and she took him *out*. Her show's supposed to be, like, fluffy morning stuff—you know, like, how to make an egg-white frittata, or cost-saving tips for holiday shopping, or whatever. But then this guy made her *mad*. The clip went viral for, like, a hot second."

"So your entire family's famous, then."

"Except for me."

"Thank goodness," he said warmly, and grabbed my hand.

We walked back to the castle in companionable silence, our clasped hands swinging between us. Well, silence except for anytime Cameraman Mike hit a particularly squeaky patch of snow. It really was a lot easier to pretend the camera wasn't there when I couldn't see it. And at least I was providing some romance for Pamela and her stupid B story.

"So what should I be expecting, snack-wise?" I asked as we entered the relative warmth of Dunyvaig's front hall. "Are you a good cook?"

"My cooking expertise falls quite squarely under the domain

of toast," Jamie answered, and led me down the hall and into the formal dining room.

"I said a *delicious* snack. No way am I settling for dry toast."

"I may have a few tricks up my sleeve." Jamie paused in front of one of Dunyvaig's infinite bookshelves. "Good God," he exclaimed with shock, "is that *Florence* in her *knickers*?"

"What the—"

I turned to look. Jamie grabbed my arm, and we disappeared into the wall.

We were plunged into darkness. I reached my arm out but felt nothing. What had just happened?

"Secret door in the bookshelf," Jamie explained as he flicked on the lights, illuminating a sparse yellow room with a leather chair and a small side table covered in, of all improbable things, an assortment of Archie Comics. "There's a lever in one of the volumes."

"Now that just seems excessive." Who needed a bookshelf door that led to a tiny Archie Comics reading room? This space was the size of a good closet.

"I thought it was a rather clever way to evade the cameras."

"Seriously? The point-and-look? Are we in a cartoon?"

"It worked, didn't it?" he said proudly. "I pointed. He looked. And we disappeared."

"Yeah. We shouldn't— We're not supposed to run away from the cameras."

"You're unhappy?" He seemed surprised. Understandable. "I thought you'd prefer to have a moment unrecorded."

"I would. I definitely would. Pamela just had a, uh, chat with me about not running away from the cameras anymore. And you know that she's—"

"Somewhat terrifying," he finished for me. "You didn't run away from the cameras; I abducted you. And neither of us ran at all; we merely took a shortcut the camera crew was, unfortunately for them, not privy to. And I will happily explain all of this to Pamela during our next encounter. Or perhaps Cameraman Mike will be so embarrassed he lost us that he shan't mention it at all."

"Perhaps," I agreed, but I was still worried. Of course I didn't want Pamela to sue my mom for contract violation, but selfishly, I wanted to be alone with Jamie, without the cameras. Well, at this point, the damage had been done. There probably wasn't much to be gained by popping back out of the bookcase, I reasoned. Selfishly.

"Shall we?" As I'd been thinking, Jamie had pulled up a trapdoor in the floor.

"You've got to be kidding me," I muttered. "It's a secret door that leads to a trapdoor? Like I said. Excessive. Did the Murrays get a two-for-one discount on weird castle architecture or something?"

"When you've got a castle, you might as well lean into it, Dylan."

I followed Jamie down the trapdoor, waiting for him at the bottom of the stairs as he shut the door over our heads and grabbed another flashlight. Was it part of the staff's duties to leave flashlights at every trapdoor in this castle? Replace the batteries, too?

Jamie, flashlight in hand, led the way down the tunnel, turned decisively right at a fork, and only a few minutes later, we arrived at a set of stairs where yet another flashlight was waiting.

At the top of the stairs, Jamie pushed, and the trapdoor easily swung open above his head. He stepped up, and I joined him, looking around as he closed the door and replaced the small woven rug that covered it. We'd arrived in the kitchen, but it was unlike any kitchen I'd ever seen before. For one thing, it was nearly as big as the ballroom. Gleaming copper pots and pans hung along every available wall space, glinting in the light that shone down from windows in the lofty arched ceiling. In the center of the room there were six enormous tables with gleaming stainless-steel surfaces and wooden legs. Built into cavernous alcoves along the side of the room were shelving units displaying every kind of bowl and cooking utensil imaginable, and several restaurant-style ovens and stovetops, like a larger, shinier, cleaner version of the diner back home. And then I saw the fridges. So many fridges. Like a whole *wall* of fridges, all taller than Jamie and such brilliant stainless steel I could see the rest of the room reflected in them.

"Impressive, isn't it?"

"I think it's bigger than my house," I marveled.

"Here, please. Take a seat."

He pulled a stool out from under one of the tables, and I clambered onto it.

"Do you have a plan?" I asked as he walked purposefully over to a squat stand-alone freezer. "It seems like you know where you're going."

"There was something," he said as he began rummaging through the freezer, "that I thought—I'd hoped—at one point to be able to—aha!" He triumphantly pulled a Ziploc bag containing weird brown lumps out of the freezer and laid it on the table in front of me like a cat presenting a dead mouse to its owner.

"What's that?" I asked. "They look like frozen poop logs."

"It's chocolate, Dylan!" he exclaimed. "Honestly, you're insane. They're Mars bars. I couldn't find Reese's Peanut Butter Cups in Dunkeld, but I think these will be better for frying. The original, isn't that what you said?"

"Wait, what? You mean the deep-fried candy bars? Like we talked about the first day we met? I can't believe you even remember that."

"Of course I remember." He seemed surprised that I was surprised. "I've been memorizing you from the instant I saw you, Dylan. I don't want to forget a thing. Not a word, not a look, not a moment. I want to remember all of you."

I felt like I'd never really understood the word "bittersweet" before, except for when it applied to chocolate. But that was all I could think of now. Hearing Jamie say that he was memorizing me caused this swell of happiness, but it was poisoned by the knowledge that he was memorizing me because we had to say good-bye. I didn't want to just be one of Jamie's memories, but I knew that was the best I could get. I was resigned to never seeing him again, but I couldn't bear the idea of him never even thinking of me again—because I knew I'd never be able to stop thinking about him.

"Don't forget me," I whispered, horrified to feel the prickle of tears in my eyes. "Promise. Promise you won't forget."

"I couldn't. I swear it. I couldn't."

He leaned down to kiss me where I sat, and we collided so forcefully our teeth knocked together. I clung to his back like

I was drowning, and we stayed there in one long, slow kiss, until I broke away, embarrassed by the taste of salt that had trickled down with my tears.

"So, what?" I swiped my eyes with my sleeves. "You've just been holding on to these candy bars in hopes you'd have a chance to lure me down here and deep-fry them?"

"Precisely. I picked them up from the newsagent while you were sleeping in the van before we left Tilly's."

"That first day? Wow. Weirdo," I teased.

"I cannot play it cool, Dylan," he said wryly. "I am not cool."

"Cool is overrated." I shrugged. "Are you sure you can do this? Deep-frying looks kind of tricky. All that boiling oil . . ."

"How dare you doubt me! One of the production people let me google how to do this on her smartphone. I am perfectly capable. Watch and learn."

He poured oil into an enormous pot and set it on the stove to heat, thermometer clipped to the inside rim to check the temperature. Then he began banging around the room, opening cupboards, pulling out bowls and flour and utensils. With great concentration, he whisked together the flour and salt and some baking powder. Then he was off to the fridge, returning with milk and some more oil. That was whisked in a separate bowl, then they were all stirred together.

"Careful, Jamie," I cautioned as he leaned in to read the thermometer. I could see the oil shimmer with heat.

"Perfect," he said. Using tongs, he dipped a candy bar into the batter until it was completely coated and then carefully lowered it into the oil. It bubbled and sizzled. We watched the Mars bar bob with bated breath, like witches standing over a cauldron. A few minutes later, Jamie pulled it out with a slotted spoon and set it to rest on a paper towel.

"It's beautiful," I said. Well, as beautiful as a greasy lump of piping-hot dough could possibly be.

"Try it! Try it!" he urged, grinning, as he picked the fried candy bar up with his tongs and held it out to me. "Take a bite."

"Baah!" I exclaimed as I bit off a morsel of molten chocolate. "Hot! Hot! So hot!"

"Sorry, sorry!" Belatedly, he began frantically blowing on the Mars bar.

"'S'okay." I swallowed noisily. "Let's try it again."

Gingerly, I took a bite. There was a slight crunch from the outside of the batter, then the doughy fatty deliciousness, and within, pure melted chocolate. It was so good I giggled involuntarily, like a demented candy gremlin.

"Is it good?" he asked anxiously.

"It's perfect," I said.

CHAPTER TWENTY-ONE

"Ouch!" I yelped.

"Stay still, dearie." The grandmotherly type who was currently stabbing me mumbled through a mouthful of pins. For someone who was only as tall as my elbows and looked exactly like Mrs. Claus, she was surprisingly scary. "Dinna move a muscle. And stand up straight, if ye please."

I pulled myself up to stand as straight as I could, imagining that string coming out of the top of my head like Heaven always talked about. I couldn't believe we were at the final dress fitting. Pretty soon there would be no more wandering through the castle, no more meals comprised of unknown foodstuffs, and no more filming the occasional confessional with Pamela and Cameraman Mike—which honestly hadn't ended up being that bad. Mostly, I just had to recount everything Jamie and I did in really specific detail. Pamela did make me say, "Scotland is the perfect place to fall in love!" about fifteen times before it finally stopped sounding sarcastic because of some agreement TRC had made with VisitScotland.com. #ScotSpirit. She had me say that a lot, too.

But now, after a couple weeks of aimlessness, our last few days at Dunyvaig were speeding toward the wedding like an out-of-control train. How could the rehearsal dinner be tomorrow? At least nothing bad had happened since Jamie and I had disappeared through the secret door. Well, nothing bad had happened *yet*. Maybe Pamela was busy drafting her contract-violation lawsuit. Goose bumps broke out along my exposed arms.

"You couldn't have sprung for long sleeves, Dusty?" I asked as the seamstress maneuvered my arm above my head, pinning around my waist. "It's *December.*"

"You're gonna be inside, dummy," Dusty said dismissively. "And that thing's made outta velvet. If it had long sleeves, you'd be sweatin' like a hog by the time we hit the first dance."

"You sweat and you know it." Heaven pointed her champagne flute of sparkling nonalcoholic grape juice at me. "She's just lookin' out for you. Good call on the sleeves, Dusty."

"Thank you, Heaven."

I rolled my eyes as they clinked glasses. The two of them were sitting on the couch in silk bathrobes—Dusty's white one bedazzled with *Bride* on the back, Heaven's pink with *Anne Marie*—and they looked entirely too chummy for my taste. Since Heaven only had brothers, she could never truly understand what a pain in the ass a big sister was. Mom sat across from them in an overstuffed armchair, thankfully not in another stupid bathrobe, but in a typically tasteful cashmere sweater set and slacks combo.

I wondered if this room had been where the lady of the manor got her clothes made back in the day. We were tucked away somewhere on the second floor, but this room was big—much bigger than my bedroom. A three-way mirror in front of a little raised dais, just like in the store at home where Dusty got all her pageant dresses, dominated the room. There were armoires all around, too, but when I'd poked inside, everything was empty. Not where Florence kept her wardrobe, then.

Oh God. Florence. When Dusty moved in here with Ronan, would Florence still be living here, too? Probably. Where else would she go? This was technically her home. I shuddered at the thought. No matter how big Dunyvaig was, I wouldn't want to share a house—or even a castle—with *that*.

"You look lovely, Dylan," Mom said encouragingly. "Isn't it nice to be out of jeans?"

"Not particularly," I replied. It was a beautiful dress, made of a deep blue velvet so dark it was almost navy, but the boning in the fitted waist was digging into my ribs, and the sweetheart neckline left me itching to pull it up every couple seconds lest my flat chest be exposed to the world. Never mind the million tiny buttons marching up the back that had taken forever to do or the tartan sash tied in an absurdly enormous butt bow. At least the dress was shortish and poufy—tea length, Dusty had called it—so there was no way I could trip over it. One stress factor removed from walking down the aisle.

"Don't sass me on the dress, Dilly!" Dusty warned. "I gave you the flats, didn't I? Hmm? What more do you want?"

"I thought we were wearing flats so the bridesmaids wouldn't be a thousand feet taller than Kit Kirby," I said.

"Flats are not gonna help that one itty bit." Heaven shook her head.

"Well?" the seamstress asked, stepping away from me. "What do ye think?"

"Good," Dusty said decisively. "She's done."

"Lovely," Mom agreed.

Heaven shot me a thumbs-up and took a swig of sparkling grape juice.

"Time for the bride, then!" the seamstress chirped. "Down ye go, dearie, and I'll help ye with the buttons."

I hopped off the platform, and the seamstress's pudgy yet nimble fingers made relatively quick work of the buttons. I went back behind the folding screen where I'd stashed my clothes and wriggled out of the dress, my ribs singing in relief. There may have been a pink silk bathrobe with a rhinestone *Dylan*—or worse, *Dilly*—lurking around here somewhere, but if there was, I had no intention of finding it. So I just pulled my jeans and hoodie back on.

Dusty left her champagne flute on the table and stood as I returned, stretching her arms ostentatiously above her head.

"I'm so excited!" Heaven squealed.

An outside observer might think *she* was the maid of honor. I felt sort of bad for not being all squealy and gooey, but hopefully Dusty understood that all this wedding stuff just wasn't really my thing. Besides, it's not like we'd ever been the kind of sisters who were squealy and gooey before. Dusty was so much older than me—for much of my childhood she'd been like a glamorous babysitter, and then once I hit middle school and all of its attendant tortures, she was a constant reminder of all the ways I wasn't enough—all the ways I wasn't Dusty. No perfect hair or perfect smile or constant stream of adoring boyfriends. Just me.

"Have you seen the dress yet, Dyl?" Heaven asked, the exact same thrill in her voice as when we watched the brides at Kleinfeld finally say yes to the dress. This was like every wedding show we'd ever watched come to life.

"I, um, I think I saw a picture," I said lamely.

"The pictures don't do it justice," Dusty said as she disappeared behind the screen. "Prepare for your minds to be blown, y'all."

The seamstress removed an enormous white garment bag from one of the armoires and handed it to Dusty, who disappeared with it.

"You need help, honey?" Mom asked.

"Naw, I got it." All I could see above the screen were long tan arms and an enormous pouf of white tulle. "I'll shimmy it on down, then one of y'all can zip me up."

A few moments later, she emerged. The dress had the same sweetheart neckline as mine, made of a rich cream silk that glowed against her skin. The full, poufy skirt fell all the way to the floor, and the bell shape made Dusty look more like she was gliding than walking. Dusty was beautiful—I knew that; I had lived with that fact for every day of my life—but I had never seen her look like this before.

"Now, it's not the full effect," Dusty said as she crossed to the dais, "because I haven't zipped it, and there'll be a big ol' sash with a huge-ass butt bow made out of the clan tartan, just like all y'all have, but this way you get the picture."

"Dusty," Mom said mistily, dabbing at her eyes.

"Wow," Heaven said, awestruck.

"I've got the sash right here!" the seamstress chirped, waving a banner of Dunleavy plaid. "I'll zip ye up right quick, dearie, then we'll add the bow."

"All right, then, Mrs. McGregor, let's get zippin'!" Dusty grinned. "Now, y'all, don't be shocked, but I decided not to wear a veil," she said seriously, like she was expecting us all to gasp. "I'm gonna wear white heather in my hair. And maybe a thistle. Unless it looks too spiky. But the groomsmen are gonna have thistle and heather in their li'l boutonnieres, and it'll be so Scottish everyone'll just die."

"Ooo, it's a wee bit snug, dearie," Mrs. McGregor clucked from behind Dusty as she attempted to pull the sides of the dress together. "Takin' a bit of a minute to try to get it together."

"Uh-oh," Heaven mouthed as we exchanged glances.

"Havena been keeping a careful watch on yer figure, mmm?"

"I'm—I'm sorry," Dusty stammered. "All the rich food over here, and there's no gym, so I haven't been workin' out. I can suck it in, I think. Just yank that zipper up and then we'll get to buttonin'."

"That's quite all right, dearie. Ye willna be my first bride to get carried away with the cake tasting. Or perhaps . . ." She assessed Dusty critically. "It isna so much the cake that's the problem as it is the bun, if ye ken my meaning."

"Mrs. McGregor!" Dusty yelped. A violent scarlet blush, almost rashlike in its intensity, broke out across her neck. "I don't know what you think you're on about, but I'd appreciate it greatly if you shut your damn piehole."

I froze in my seat, unable to move a muscle, but felt the room spinning around me. We had been so close to making it to the wedding without anyone knowing—only two days away. I felt beads of sweat pop out on my forehead as a sick feeling settled deep in my belly.

"A bun?" Heaven asked. "Like a bun . . . in the oven?"

Dusty clamped her lips together firmly, turning slowly red to white. I couldn't look at Heaven, couldn't look at Mom, couldn't look anywhere but at Dusty.

"Dusty . . . are you pregnant?" Mom asked faintly.

"Holy flamin' hot Cheetos," Heaven whispered.

Dusty moaned, covered her face in her hands, and sank to the floor, her skirts billowing up around her.

"Why don't you give us a minute, Mrs. McGregor," Mom said smoothly, like absolutely nothing had happened. "We can finish the fitting at another time."

"Not a problem, not a problem at all." Mrs. McGregor rapidly began packing up her pins and assorted supplies.

"And I'm sure we can count on your discretion, Mrs. McGregor," Mom added. She was all politeness, but I could hear the steel behind her words.

"Not a peep. Dinna fear." In a wave of flustered "dearies," Mrs. McGregor bustled out the door, shutting it firmly behind her.

"Dusty," Mom said warmly, her voice suffused with love. "You're having a *baby*."

I watched Dusty look up at Mom.

"I'm sorry, Mama," she whispered. "Are you mad?"

"Mad? Oh, honey." Mom smiled deeply, her eyes crinkling with delight. "I am just . . . so . . . happy!"

She laughed, then Dusty laughed, too, a strange spluttery

laugh-cry. Mom crossed the room and plopped down on the dais next to Dusty, folding her up in her arms.

"I'm gonna be a meemaw!" Mom said proudly as the two of them rocked back and forth. I couldn't tell if they were laughing or crying—maybe both.

"So much for keeping it a secret." Dusty wiped her eyes, the mascara coming off in black streaks on her hands.

"It's okay," Heaven said earnestly. "I won't tell anyone, Dusty, I promise."

"Doesn't matter," she replied. "It's too late."

"What's too late?" I asked.

Dusty raised her arm and pointed. I turned to look over my shoulder at the cameraman. Right. I had forgotten he was there.

"Secret's out," Dusty said grimly. "I'm sure you'll take this back to Pamela before I even get out of the dress," she addressed the cameraman, who said nothing. "And I can't *wait* to hear what America has to say about this one. No little baby deserves the kind of hate that's gonna get thrown my way."

"Hate? Come on, Dusty. Have a little faith. People like you," I said firmly. "That's what Pamela keeps saying, right? That America's on your side or whatever."

"On my side? You are hilarious, Dylan," she said, with no trace of hilarity whatsoever. The giddiness of a moment earlier had been replaced with grim despair. "For every sweet old lady that writes into the *People* mailbag wishing me and Ronan a fairy-tale ending, there are ten DieDustyDie blogs."

I snorted. DieDustyDie? Come on.

"It's a real thing, Dyl. Google it," she said seriously, and for the first time I noticed how tired she looked. There were dark shadows under her eyes that even her brightening concealer couldn't cover up. "DieDustyDie is a hashtag. There's a Twitter trend created solely for the purpose of hating me."

"But it doesn't matter," I insisted. "Who cares what these people think? About the baby, or about you, or about anything? Their opinions don't matter. They don't *know* you."

"But they think they do!" she cried, and rose to her feet. Mom leaned forward as if to stop her, somehow, and then thought better of it. "You can't understand what it's like. To have people you've never met think they know you." She started pacing the room frantically, the bottom of her wedding dress dragging on the floor. "It's hard. It is so damn hard. I had no idea how hard it would be. And it's not just those awful trolls on the Internet! It's the nice ones. The ones who are so *invested*. How can they care so much? It's killing me, everyone's opinions. The weight of it. It's crushin' me."

"Then why are you doing this?"

"I have to." She sighed. "I am grateful to TRC every damn day of my life for bringing Ronan into it. But I sure as hell wish I'd read those contracts a little bit closer before I signed." She looked directly at the camera. "I know y'all won't put that part in."

"Dusty." Mom rose up to stand and opened her arms. "Come here, baby."

Dusty collapsed into Mom's arms, her back shaking with the force of her silent sobs. Despite the fact that she was wearing a half-open wedding dress, she looked like a little kid. Mom rubbed her back soothingly, up and down, up and down.

"Maybe we should go," Heaven whispered.

I nodded in agreement, and we slipped out the door as Dusty cried quietly in Mom's arms.

"Holy poop," Heaven said as we shut the door to the fitting room behind us. "Holy flying poop balls."

"You wanna put some pants on?" I asked, gesturing to the robe.

"I don't even remember where I put my pants. Let's get out of here. I need some Cheetos. They have Cheetos in this country?"

"Heck if I know."

"Thank God this damn castle is so big. I need a minute before we run into another camera." Heaven placed a hand on her chest. "I think I've got angina. Like my nana."

"You do not have angina." I picked her up underneath her elbows and started dragging her down the hallway.

"This is too many plot twists. Too many. I can't handle this many dramatic revelations on one episode of *Prince in Disguise*."

"You'd like it if you were watching it on TV."

"Yeah. Exactly. Safe on my TV. Not living it. Or living next to it. This isn't even happening to me and I'm freaking out! Are you freaking out? You don't seem like you're freaking out. Why aren't you freaking out?"

"I'm freaking out on the inside."

By some miracle of castle navigation we'd ended up at my bedroom, and I shoved Heaven inside and closed the door behind us.

"You're gonna be an aunt, Dylan," Heaven marveled. "Aunt Dylan. Wow."

"I know." I grinned. "Aunt Dylan."

"You are definitely not freaking out." Heaven flopped onto

my bed, hand still pressed dramatically to her chest. "Wait a minute." She propped herself up on her elbows. "Did you *know*? Is that why you're not freaking out?"

"Um . . ."

"You knew! I can't believe you knew, and you didn't tell me!"

"I couldn't, Heaven, I promised—"

"No, Dylan, stop—I'm not mad. I'm *impressed*," she clarified. "I'm not sure I could have kept a secret that big."

"I had to," I said simply. "And now *we* have to try to keep Ronan's mom from finding out before the wedding."

"Oh hell no." Heaven's eyes widened. "Don't fear, tiny baby," she said grimly. "Aunt Heaven is on the case."

If Pamela got wind of this—as I knew she would, since it was on camera—I wasn't sure there was any way we could keep it from getting out before the wedding. But Aunt Dylan and Aunt Heaven were sure going to try their damn best. I'd seen Dusty fake-cry a lot, but I'd never seen her cry like that. And maybe we didn't always get along very well, but at the end of the day, she was my sister. And this baby was going to be family, just like Dusty.

And I would do whatever I could to protect them.

CHAPTER TWENTY-TWO

The chapel at Dunyvaig was its own building, detached from the castle but nearby on the grounds. The walls were stone, and the ceiling high and arched. It looked exactly like King Arthur could have married Guinevere in here. Dusty, Ronan, and the priest stood in the circular apse at the front, bathed in the light of three tall windows with points on top—castle windows, I'd always thought of them as. I wondered if they had a real name. Jamie would know. He was probably some kind of medieval architecture genius.

The last of the late-afternoon sun fell across the pew in a burst of color. Filtered through the stained glass window at my side, it looked like a small rainbow arcing through the church. I smiled, squinting at the glass angels, not really sure why they were wrestling a bunch of naked babies, but enjoying the color nonetheless.

"Yo, is that priest old enough to, uh, priest?" Heaven asked. "He looks like a rejected Weasley."

Come to think of it, the priest did look rather young. I'd been distracted at first by the enormous red beard, bright as a new penny, that obscured most of his face. But the bits I could see looked surprisingly youthful.

"He went to school with Kit and Ronan," Jamie explained. "They were in the same year at Eton, played rugby together for ages. That was before he became Father Mackenzie, of course."

"I was expecting a tiny old guy, like from *The Little Mermaid*," Heaven said. "Are we getting started soon? I need to find the *loo*," she said exaggeratedly.

"Loo's up front, just past the vestry," Jamie directed her.

Heaven sidled out of the pew and scampered up the aisle, careful not to disturb Dusty and Ronan in the front.

"Is snogging in the vestry the type of activity that condemns one to the fiery pit, you think?" Jamie whispered once she'd gone.

"Obviously. Didn't you read Dante's *Inferno*? There's a whole circle reserved for vestry snoggers."

Jamie snorted and hastily covered it up with a cough. Kit whipped his head back to look at us suspiciously, then returned to whatever it was he was reading so intently. I had a feeling it wasn't a hymnal.

Jamie's fingers inched closer to where my hand rested on the bench, and the knuckles of his pinky bumped mine. Slowly, our fingers laced together. I shifted closer, pressing the length of my thigh against his. Not in a we're-about-to-snog-in-the-vestry way, just enjoying the feel of him—so warm and solid and real. And *here*.

"I can't believe the wedding is tomorrow," Jamie murmured.

"Me neither," I said fervently. We were in the church, doing the rehearsal, and I still couldn't quite wrap my brain around it—or the fact that I'd be on a plane back to Tupelo first thing Monday morning.

"Don't go," he said suddenly. "I know you're going. Obviously. I'm not insane. And you mustn't say anything back. I simply had to say it out loud, at least once. As if I'd chased you to the airport in the final scene of a film."

"I—"

"You mustn't say anything back, Dylan, remember?" he shushed me.

I sat there quietly, holding his hand. I had a feeling that when I got back to Tupelo, none of this would seem real. I would miss Jamie a lot, but with the same ache of sadness that I'd felt when I'd never gotten my Hogwarts letter. That peculiar grief that comes from missing something that you knew you couldn't have. The end was approaching, and its inexorable pull was palpable.

"Groomsmen up at the front, if ye please!" Father Mackenzie called out. "Ladies, ye can take your places toward the back and get ready to walk."

"That's my cue, then." Jamie squeezed my hand one last time and stood. I pulled up my knees and let him sidle past me, not ready to get up quite yet. When Jamie was halfway down the aisle, Kit sprang up out of his seat and slung an arm around Jamie's neck, maneuvering him into a headlock and dragging him up to the front like he was wrestling his little brother. One admonishing look from Father Mackenzie, however, and Jamie was released. I grinned as he attempted to pat his disheveled hair back into place.

"Oh, wow, Dilly." I hadn't noticed Dusty standing at the end of my pew, watching me. "You really fell hard, didn't you?"

"Shut up," I said genially as I slid to the end of the pew.

"You *really* like him," she marveled.

I chose to ignore her.

"What are you gonna do?" She kept chattering at me as I walked up the aisle to the back of the church. "Long distance? No, that's crazy, you're so young. Are you ever gonna see him again? How could you, though? Oh hell. Hmm . . . I bet if you told Pamela about it, TRC would buy you a buncha plane tickets so they could film you dating long distance."

"No!" I exclaimed, appalled. Quickly, I glanced around. There were of course camera crews there, but hopefully none of them thought this was an important enough idea to mention to Pamela. They looked pretty bored. Over my dead body would TRC produce a long-distance-dating special about Jamie and me. I'd rather never talk to him again.

"Don't you have more important things to worry about than my dating life?" I asked meaningfully.

"I do not," Dusty said crisply, glancing at the cameras. "So far there have been no unexpected developments with the . . . wedding plans."

So Pamela was just sitting on the baby bomb, then. On the one hand, I was glad Ronan's mom didn't know yet, but on the other hand, the idea that Pamela could detonate this at any minute was extremely unsettling. I hoped she was invested enough in this fairy-tale wedding to not derail the actual ceremony with an extremely dramatic objection.

"What'd I miss?" Heaven appeared in the back of the church, returned from the loo.

"Dylan's in love, and it is not gonna end well." Dusty shook her head.

"Dusty, *stop!*" I said in the most vicious low voice I could muster up.

"Didn't miss anything, then." Heaven sighed.

"This is your wedding, right?" I asked shrilly. "Can we just focus on that?"

"All right, Juliet, we can deal with you later." Dusty shrugged. A casual observer would never know she was trying to hide a secret baby from her future mother-in-law. How was she so calm? So *normal*? Dusty must have been a master of compartmentalization. "Mama, where are the practice bouquets?"

Why we needed to practice holding a bouquet was beyond me. But Mom produced a cardboard box of wildflower nosegays tied with tartan ribbons and handed one to each of us.

"So, uh, when does Anne Marie's flight get in?" Heaven asked, twirling her bouquet.

"Five a.m. tomorrow. You'll have plenty of time to get her up to speed."

Heaven went down the aisle first; then I followed, Dusty scolding me the entire way down for walking too fast. As Father Mackenzie maneuvered me into position, Jamie leaned his head out of line to wink at me from behind Ronan and Kit. Kit made exaggerated kissy faces, then stopped suddenly with an unpleasant "Oof!" of distress. Unless I was very much mistaken, Jamie had just elbowed him unceremoniously in the kidneys.

"And here is where the bride's da will walk her down the aisle," Father Mackenzie said grandly, gesturing to Dusty.

I snorted and rolled my eyes, waiting for Dusty to correct

him. But instead of saying anything, she stood stock-still at the back of the nave, mouth opening and closing like a fish.

"I'm verra sorry." Father Mackenzie frowned, clearly unable to read the room. "Did I say aught amiss?"

I waited for Dusty to speak up. Mom was going to walk her down the aisle. She *had* to. I glanced over at Mom perched on the edge of a pew. She stared studiously down at her hands folded in her lap. Cash sprang up out of his seat and jogged down the aisle like he was on his way to accept an award.

"You got it, Padre!" He shot Father Mackenzie a thumbs-up. "Right back here, yeah?"

"Hold this." I smacked my rehearsal bouquet into Heaven.

"Dylan," Heaven warned, "I'm not sure you want to get involved in this."

"I'm already involved. This is my *family*."

I marched down the aisle with absolutely no idea what I was going to say, only the absolute conviction that I had to get down there. Hopefully, I'd figure out what to do when I got there. And hopefully the thing I decided to do wouldn't be to murder my sister, because that was the only satisfactory action I could think of at the moment. I completely ignored Cash and faced Dusty, watching her blue eyes widen in surprise then narrow into slits when she caught the look on my face.

"What. Are. You. Doing?" I hissed.

"Rehearsing my damn wedding," Dusty hissed back. "Which is what you're supposed to be doing right now, in case you forgot. You get lost?"

She grabbed my arm and yanked me into the corner. I was surprised nothing was dislocated in the process.

"Be right back, Daddy!" Dusty trilled.

"He is not your daddy," I whispered furiously. "He doesn't deserve that name. He's your biological father. That's it."

Heaven's dad had this painted wooden sign that said ANYONE CAN BE A FATHER, BUT IT TAKES SOMEONE SPECIAL TO BE A DADDY hung up over his computer. I was tempted to get one for Cash Keller. And break it over his head.

"You don't understand, Dylan. You have no memories of him. He was . . . he was *fun*," she said, deciding on the word, "when he was around."

"Yeah. Exactly. When he was around."

"One time," she said in a weird, dreamy voice, "he came and got me out of school. I thought something bad had happened to Meemaw when they called me into the principal's office, but Daddy just said there was an emergency. And the emergency was that we desperately needed to go to the zoo." She grinned. "We went to the zoo and saw all the animals, and I ate so much ice cream I barfed in a trash can."

"That was really responsible of him," I said snidely. "You're lucky you're not diabetic."

"Honestly, Dylan. Give him a chance. He showed up, didn't he?"

"Yeah, he showed up. Sixteen years too late." I heard her, but I couldn't understand what she was saying.

"He's still part of who I am," she insisted. "That makes him part of today."

"Well, he shouldn't be. Mom is—"

Mom was gone. The pew she'd been sitting in was empty. She must have slipped out another door—maybe there was one at the front of the chapel, behind the altar.

"Gone, apparently," I finished. "Is that what you wanted? I hope you're happy."

"Of course that's not what I wanted, I— Oh, hell."

"You know what? I think I'm done rehearsing for today. Walk after Anne Marie. Stand next to Anne Marie. I think I've got it."

"Don't be a baby, Dilly—"

"I'm not being a baby," I said, remarkably calm, given the circumstances. "I'm going to find Mom."

I walked past Cash Keller like he didn't exist. The blast of cold air when I opened the door hit me like a slap in the face. I breathed deeply, shut the door behind the cameraman who'd followed me, and crunched my way through the frozen snow back to Dunyvaig.

"Did you get assigned to me, or something?" I asked Cameraman Mike as he crunched beside me. Obviously, he chose not to respond. "I'm sorry. What did you do, draw the short straw?"

He said nothing, like a ghost in a gray hoodie and puffy vest.

Where would Mom go if she was upset? To wherever there was coffee. So I headed straight for the Dunyvaig kitchens, the only place I could think of that would have coffee at the ready.

I spotted her immediately, sitting alone at a long table, blond bob bowed over hands wrapped around a coffee mug. She looked up at the sound of footfalls on the stairs.

"Dylan!" Mom exclaimed, clearly surprised. "What are you doing here?"

"Dusty's being a butthead." I pulled out the stool next to her and sat down, plunking my elbows on the table. Cameraman

Mike settled in to the side, giving us more space than I would have thought. Huh. A surprising gesture of humanity.

Mom chuckled into her coffee.

"You shouldn't fight with your sister. Especially not on her big day."

"It's not her big day. Not yet. And I can fight with her if she's being a butthead," I said grumpily. "Aren't you *mad*?"

"I'm not mad, Dyl," she said simply. "It's her wedding. She has every right to do what she wants."

"But what she wants is *wrong*," I insisted. "How can she be so nice to Cash? How could she let him be part of the wedding? How can she even stand to talk to him? How . . . I just . . . I just don't understand her."

I fell quiet, watching Mom's knuckles as they flexed around the chipped blue mug.

"You girls are so different," she said meditatively, breaking the silence.

"Yeah, I know." I rolled my eyes. "I've heard that often enough."

"You are," she insisted. "Dusty, she's a little like me. And a lot like your daddy, bless her heart. She *needs* people. Needs 'em to like her. But you—"

"I'm a cave-dwelling troll who needs no one?" I supplied.

"You are nothing like a troll," she scolded. "And you know I hate it when you put yourself down like that, so stop." I avoided eye contact, but I could feel her gaze boring into me. Somehow, I always remembered all the times Mom made disparaging remarks about my outfits, but I never remembered all the times she wouldn't let me say mean things about myself.

"You like doing things your own way. Going your own way. Being alone doesn't scare you."

"That's just because most people are really annoying."

"That's exactly what I mean!" Mom laughed. "Most of us care way too much about what the annoying people think. But not you, tough cookie."

"Then why is being around the cameras so hard for me?" I asked in a small voice.

"I think it's hard for everyone." Mom squeezed my hand. "The rest of us are just better at faking it."

"But you work with cameras every day."

"I sure do. In a studio, where everything is controlled, where I've got a team of people working hard to make me look my best, where I get to clock out at the end of the day, wipe off my makeup, and pull on those sweatpants with the holes in them."

I laughed. I'd forgotten about Mom's one really, truly disgusting item of clothing—a pair of Ole Miss sweatpants she reserved for relaxing in only after really long shoots. Maybe we weren't quite as different as I'd always thought.

"It's weird, being filmed all the time," she whispered, punctuating it with an exaggerated wink at Cameraman Mike. "Trust me. I'm trying my best to make it look normal, but it sure doesn't feel normal."

"No kidding."

"But you can handle it. You're strong, Dylan."

"I don't know about that," I muttered, embarrassed.

"I do," she said simply. "Which is why I know you'll make your own choice about Cash. Because you know your own mind. You always have. And that's all that matters. What *you* do. Not what does Dusty does."

"He's not my family." Finally, I felt like I'd figured out how I felt. "He may be my father, but he's not my family. You're my family, Mom. You, and me, and Dusty. Even if she is a butthead."

"Unfortunately, being a butthead may be hereditary," she said ruefully. "That's not all Dusty's fault."

"Are *you* okay, Mom?" I asked. "Because of the, uh, supreme butthead's reappearance? It's gotta be weird."

"Weird doesn't even begin to describe it," she said wryly. "If it were up to me, quite frankly, I'd rather not have seen him again. Ever. And to have him come back for *this*, when it seems so obvious he just wanted to be part of the show—"

"Yes! Thank you!" I cut her off, too eager to have someone agree with me. "I hate that he showed up now. It's so . . . so . . . ."

"It's tacky," Mom said distastefully. "Tacky" was the word of judgment Mom reserved for behavior she considered the lowest of the low. "But it seems to mean something to Dusty that he's here. So I suppose I'm glad he's here, then."

"I hadn't thought about it like that," I said. Just because *I* thought it was awful and gross and, you know, *tacky* that he was here didn't mean that Dusty wasn't getting something real out of it. I knew I'd never be able to understand it. But at the very least I could try to be happy for Dusty.

"I just hope he doesn't ruin this for her, somehow. He's got a real knack for screwing up the big moments." She smiled sadly at me. "Good thing he was outta the picture before he could forget any of your birthday parties."

"I'm glad he was out of the picture, too." I reached out and took her hand, somehow too self-conscious to say all the things I wanted to. Like how amazing Mom had done without him.

How lucky I felt to have been raised by her. I just held her hand and hoped she could feel how much I loved her.

"Everything's fine, Dyl. I promise. Just have *fun* at the wedding tomorrow, okay? I plan on having a damn good time, no matter what Cash Keller chooses to do. And it's gonna be one hell of a party. You know there's gonna be cake. So enjoy it."

"Okay." I grinned back. "I love you, Mom."

"Love you, too, sweet girl."

She took a piece of hair that had fallen across my face and tucked it behind my ear, like she had a thousand times since I was little. She pulled me into a hug, and we sat together, in the warmth of the kitchens, safe from the cold outside.

CHAPTER TWENTY-THREE

This rehearsal dinner was a damn minefield. My father was still here, Mom and I were avoiding him, he was presumably walking Dusty down the aisle, and I was kind of avoiding Dusty. Oh, and Dusty was, of course, pregnant. But to the best of my knowledge, she remained *secretly* pregnant. I was sure the cameramen had told Pamela. I mean, how could they not? This was definitely "the most dramatic season ever" material—even if there had only been one season of *Prince in Disguise* so far. But Pamela hadn't done anything with it yet. Not even a hint of anything remotely baby-related. I probably should have been more terrified because something was definitely coming, but I was too relieved that nothing had happened yet to really let that terror sink in. I was still pretty pissed at Dusty, too, but not pissed enough that I had any intention of outing her little bundle of joy in front of the assembled company.

Tilly had really outdone herself. The Atholl Arms looked

like it had been decorated by a legion of drunk elves. I doubted that even the North Pole looked this Christmasy on December 23. Greenery, twinkling lights, and plaid bows adorned every available surface. The mistletoe hanging from the ceiling kept getting caught in my hair. Real candles cast a soft light over the room. It seemed inevitable that something in the overstuffed pub would catch fire, but nothing had yet.

"I'm terribly sorry," Jamie announced as he found me tucked into a corner, hiding behind a large velvet wing chair featuring a throw pillow embroidered with a Cavalier King Charles spaniel. I'm not sure what, exactly, I thought I was hiding from. Cameraman Mike had been practically glued to my elbow the entire evening. I'd seen a lot of him recently—I was now positive he'd been officially assigned to me. He must have gotten some pretty good footage on our date to have been promoted from the breakfast beat. I decided not to think about *how* good.

Jamie extended empty hands, palms up. "I thought it was too hot for chocolate, so I tried to get fizzy drinks, but the crush at the bar was absolutely mad. I couldn't even get close."

"I think Dusty and Ronan invited all of Dunkeld and Birnam. And Dusty's whole sorority. And Ronan's rugby team."

"And probably the entire population of Scotland as well."

"Seriously. I can't even see anyone I know."

"Neither can I." He scanned the crowd, until his eyes caught on something—or someone. A jolt of recognition crossed his face, and he went suddenly pale. Even paler than usual.

"Darling!" A tall woman in an impressively large fur coat was waving her arms vigorously. "Darling, over here!"

"Oh bloody hell," Jamie cursed fervently under his breath.

"Who's that?"

"My mum."

"Your mum," I marveled. Now that I knew, of course, it seemed obvious. The height, the pallor, the black hair—I just hadn't expected to see her here. Jamie had only mentioned his parents once, and I'd promptly forgotten that they existed. Or that they might be coming here for the wedding.

"Darling!" She kept waving. "Gillecroids! Gillecroids, darling! Over here!"

"What?" I heard her, but she wasn't making sense. "What is she calling you? Guh-something? What's that?"

"My name."

"Your name is Jamie," I said, stating the obvious.

"No, it's not. It's Gillecroids Edmund Alexander James."

"Guh-what?" I stammered. "What are you even saying? Is that even a word? Is that even a name? Can you spell it?"

"*G-I-L-L-E-C-R-O-I-D-S*," he spelled slowly.

"Huh." I chewed it over. "Gillecroids. What kind of name is that?"

"Gaelic. It means servant of Christ."

"Gaelic? So then you *are* Scottish?" I poked him in the chest. "What was with all the pretensions of Englishness? I feel like I don't know you at all now," I teased.

"My mum is Scottish. But my dad's English. I grew up in England." Weirdly, Jamie had started sweating. Visible drops stood out on his forehead. It was warm in here, but not that warm.

"Cool. Well, Gillecroids is sort of weird, but you didn't have to hide it. You could have told me your real name, Eugene," I joked.

"Eugene?"

"Eugene Fitzherbert? *Tangled*? For someone who knows all the words to a song from *Frozen*, the rest of your Disney knowledge is shockingly lacking."

An older guy in a sharp gray suit appeared at Jamie's mom's side, holding two flutes of champagne.

"Is that your dad?" I asked. Jamie nodded. "Should we go say hi, then?"

Why was Jamie just standing there like he was glued to the floor as his mom waved maniacally? I started to push my way through the crowd toward his parents.

"Dylan, wait!"

His grip was too tight on my arm, and he was still sweating profusely. I'd never seen anyone have a panic attack before, but I might have been witnessing one.

"Oh." Realization dawned as a wave of mortification washed over me. Of course. He was embarrassed. "I get it. You don't want them to meet me." With some difficulty, I disentangled myself from his viselike grip. "That's cool, Jamie. I'll go find Heaven."

"No!" He emitted a strangled cry, his eyes wild. "It's not that, it's not that at all— It's just— Oh, hell." He awkwardly mopped some of the sweat off his brow with the back of his sleeve. "I should have told you. Should have told you ages ago. This is the worst possible way for you to find out."

"Told me what?" I demanded, searching his eyes for answers I couldn't find. "Find out what?"

"Gillecroids!"

Well, it was a moot point anyhow—Jamie's parents had made their way over to us. Cameraman Mike maneuvered himself into a better position behind us. He must have been thrilled—Pamela would surely be able to spin this meet-the-parents moment into something unbearably awkward. Or more likely, I'd make it unbearably awkward by just being myself.

"Oh, darling!" Jamie's mom enveloped him in a furry hug. "Are you frozen to the bone? I forgot how cold and ghastly it was up here! It's practically Siberia!"

If Jamie's mom was Scottish, I could barely hear it in her voice. She had the same cut-glass accent Jamie did, with only the faintest hint of a burr around her Rs.

"I'm sure the boy's plenty warm. You packed him enough sweaters, Margaret." There was a good-natured teasing in Jamie's father's voice. The man looked like a movie villain—like a business executive who would try to buy up a small town or something—but he sounded nice enough. He also had the shiniest shoes I'd ever seen.

"Have you been eating enough, Gillecroids?" Jamie's mom held him at arm's length, as if assessing him for signs of starvation. "You're thin as a rail! A stiff breeze would knock you over!"

"Please call me Jamie, Mum," he muttered, blushing.

"Oh, what a lot of tosh," she said dismissively. "Jamie is a plain name. Gillecroids is *special*. Like you, darling." She tousled his hair affectionately.

"Mum," Jamie croaked, red as a beet.

From the very brief picture Jamie had painted for me, these were not the parents I'd been expecting. I suppose all he'd said was that they traveled a lot, but I'd drawn conclusions about distant, frosty mothers and cold, absent fathers. Clearly I'd been wrong.

"Well, hello." Jamie's mom's eyes lit on me for the first time. "Who's this, Gillecroids?"

I smiled awkwardly at Jamie's parents.

"Mum, Dad, this is Dylan," he introduced me.

"Why, darling, she's lovely!" Jamie's mom said emphatically. "So tall! A real, proper-sized girl. And those cheekbones! She's like a Roman statue!"

"Thanks," I stammered. "Um. Hi."

"Aha!" she crowed. "I thought I spotted American dental work!" She raised her glass in a toast to dentistry.

"She's not a horse, Margaret." Jamie's dad sighed. "Please refrain from examining her teeth."

"I wasn't examining her teeth!" she protested. "I merely happened to notice they were lovely and remarked upon them. You are American, yes?"

"Yes."

"Bride's side, then?" She jumped right in before I had a chance to say anything else.

"Yeah. I'm Dusty's sister."

"Of course you are." I was so surprised that she *wasn't* surprised that my mouth fell open a little bit. Had dyeing my hair and putting on a little bit of makeup really made that much of a difference? This was the first time I could remember that someone hadn't said "Really?" after I'd said I was Dusty's sister. "The two tallest, loveliest girls in the room! That dress is charming. Girls these days all dress like slappers. So nice to meet a modest young lady with class."

Jamie had groaned slightly at "slappers." I made a mental note to find out exactly what that meant, but I had a pretty good idea from the context.

"It's nice to meet you, too, Mrs. . . ." I trailed off awkwardly, realizing I *still* didn't know Jamie's last name.

Jamie's mom turned toward him and raised an eyebrow. He pressed his lips together firmly as if answering an unspoken question.

"Call me Margaret," she said warmly, after a brief pause. "This is James." She indicated her husband with a nod of her head.

"James, who is incapable of introducing himself, apparently," he said.

"I'm simply better at it, darling." She gesticulated wildly toward the ceiling with her glass. "So, are you two . . . involved?"

"Mum!" Jamie croaked. He seemed to be unable to do anything but say "Mum!" and turn red.

"I knew it! Finally!" Margaret cried triumphantly. "Do you know he's *never* brought a girl home before?"

"I can't imagine why, with this kind of response!" Jamie hissed. "Checking her teeth and eyeing her height like she was a . . . a . . . broodmare for the purchasing!"

I made a face at Jamie. He shrugged helplessly.

"I'm being welcoming, darling!" Margaret said, offended. "It's called a *compliment*. A phenomenon you might wish to become better acquainted with if you intend to keep a precious treasure like the lovely Dylan."

Margaret's many votes of confidence were flattering, but confusing. So far all I'd done was be tall, have straight teeth, and say a half dozen words. I wasn't exactly setting the room on fire.

"Mum, please," Jamie said in a strangled voice. "Just. Be. Normal."

"This obsession with normalcy is tedious, Gillecroids." Margaret exhaled forcefully through her nose.

"Let's not mortify the boy, please," Jamie's dad said. "It would be a shame for him to die of humiliation at such a tender young age. He's barely reached his potential."

Jamie's mom was unlike anyone I'd ever met before, the kind of person I didn't think was real, like Auntie Mame. She needed one of those long cigarette holders and a pair of opera gloves.

"Well, then," Jamie said. "This was just . . . excellent . . . all around. Mum and Dad, thank you, as always, for being horrifyingly embarrassing. But I'm afraid at the moment Dylan and I are urgently needed in another room. Far away from here."

"Gillecroids—"

"Let them go, Margaret," Jamie's dad said gently, placing a restraining hand on her arm. "We're not the Spanish Inquisition."

"Nobody expects the Spanish Inquisition," Jamie and his dad said in unison. I goggled at the two of them.

"Right." Jamie exhaled an enormous sigh of relief and grinned hugely. He finally looked back to normal. "Thanks, Dad. See you later, all right?"

"Your Royal Highness!"

I heard a voice that was unmistakably Florence's, but it couldn't have been her—she sounded happy. And yet, it *was* her. Florence barreled her way into our little corner of the pub, almost unrecognizable because of the wide grin splitting her face. I'd never seen her smile before. Somehow, it did nothing to make her look friendlier.

Whatever had improved Florence's mood had drastically deteriorated Jamie's. He'd gone all weird and white again. I poked him experimentally in the arm, but he didn't react.

"Your Royal Highness," Florence simpered with delight, arriving in our little group in a cloud of lavender water.

Your Royal Highness?! Excuse me, *what*?! I shot Jamie a hard look that he studiously ignored.

"We are absolutely honored that you've joined us this evening. What a delight." She was making googly eyes at Jamie's dad. It had been bizarre watching Florence treat Jamie so nicely these past couple weeks, but that was nothing compared to the way she was sucking up to his father. "And you've brought your lovely duchess as well."

Duchess. Your Highness. What. Was. Happening.

"How's it hanging, Florence?" Jamie's mom swallowed the rest of her drink noisily. Florence made a little moue of distaste, then immediately turned her attention back to Jamie's dad.

"Thank you so much for inviting us," Jamie's dad said politely. "Congratulations on the wedding. You must be terribly pleased."

"It is . . . what it is," Florence said crisply. Even though I was mad at Dusty, she didn't deserve that. A tiny rage-fire started kindling itself deep within my belly. "My, my, my." Her eyes landed on me, standing perhaps slightly closer to Jamie than was normal. "You Leigh girls certainly don't waste any time."

I could feel the insult beneath her words—or maybe in her words—but I had no comeback at the ready. Florence was scary. And Jamie was no help. He was as stiff and cold as if I'd bumped into a wax figure at Madame Tussauds.

"Careful, Your Highness." Florence smiled coldly at Jamie's dad. "Or you'll end up with a gangly American duchess in sweatpants."

"I *adore* sweatpants!" Jamie's mom interjected, brandishing her glass threateningly at Florence like it was a weapon.

Gangly American . . . duchess? Florence throwing shade was the least of my problems. Was Jamie a duke? A prince? A king? What was he? Florence had called his dad a Royal Highness. And his mom was a duchess. Which made him, what, a pre-duke? Also a Royal Highness?! I didn't know enough about hereditary titles to know what any of this meant, but I knew enough to know that Jamie was *royal*. Even more royal than Ronan. I felt extremely confused, and wrong-footed, and stupid—did everyone else know except for me? Had they known the whole time?

"Excuse us, please," Jamie's dad said smoothly. "Lovely to see you again, Lady Dunleavy. Looking forward to the wedding."

He steered Jamie's mom away in a somewhat forceful manner. She was gesticulating wildly and muttering "Sweatpants." Florence sniffed at us once, and left.

"So this is why you didn't tell me your real name," I said woodenly.

"I was going to, Dylan, I swear, I just didn't want to— Damn." He exhaled loudly, hair flopping out of his face. "Can we go somewhere quieter? Please? Just— Here. Come on."

He grabbed my arm and towed me out of the pub, into the lobby, and up the stairs. The cameraman followed us, of course, and I let him, just like I'd promised Pamela I would. This was exactly what Pamela had wanted, right? Drama. Romance. A friggin' *prince in disguise.*

We ended up in a deserted hallway, right in front of a bookcase filled with paperback romance novels. Stupid romance novels. They were probably bursting with princes in disguise. I had an irrational urge to start chucking them at Jamie's head. Well, maybe not so irrational.

"Dylan. Please. Just let me explain. I am so, so—"

"What is it?" I interrupted him. "Your real name. Your *full* name. The title and everything."

"His Royal Highness Prince Gillecroids Edmund Alexander James," he said heavily.

"His Royal Highness," I said faintly. "Prince? Did you say *prince*?! Oh my God. You're a prince in disguise!"

"Absolutely not!" he said emphatically. "That is a construction created solely by this insane television program. I'm not in any sort of disguise."

"Oh God. Is *everyone* on the show a prince in disguise?" I asked hysterically, "Is Kit Kirby the Archbishop of Canterbury?"

"That's not a hereditary title—Kit Kirby's not ordained—not even Church of England, come to think of it—"

"Forget Kit Kirby! You're a *prince*, Jamie."

"I'm hardly a prince, Dylan! Well, technically, I am, I suppose, but—"

"Explain. Now."

"My father is a prince," he said quickly, all in a rush, like he was pulling off a Band-Aid. "Not one of the important ones. A younger son, you know."

"A younger son of who? Queen Elizabeth?!"

Jamie nodded, almost shamefacedly.

"Queen Elizabeth is your *meemaw*?!" I shrieked.

"We really only ever see her on holidays," he mumbled, "and not for very long. Mum hates the Christmas lunch at

Sandringham. She's trying to dodge going on Sunday—it's one of the reasons she was so keen on coming to the wedding. She only really gets on with Harry."

"Harry. You mean *Prince Harry*?!"

"Yes. He's my, er, cousin."

"Cousin?!" I realized I was doing nothing but shrieking the names of various relations, but I couldn't believe any of this. How could Jamie—my Jamie—possibly be a prince?

"I hardly ever see him, either! Honestly, Dylan, I'm a very normal, boring prince. I'm *not* Harry. I'm never in the papers."

"The papers?" I repeated incredulously. "Are you, like, famous?"

"Certainly not. I never do anything. They call me 'His Royal Shyness.'"

"His Royal Shyness." It all clicked into place. "Just like Kit said on the first day I met you! God, I am dumb."

"You are *not* dumb, Dylan, why on earth would you be familiar with British tabloid culture—"

"You're just proving my point. You're famous enough that the tabloids gave you a nickname."

"Just really that one time when I was doing some work with Sentebale."

"And that is . . ." I prompted.

"A charity in Africa founded by, er . . . Harry," he finished lamely. "And Prince Seeiso. Of Lesotho."

"Oh my God." I leaned against the bookshelf, half-afraid I was going to collapse. Jamie was a prince. People took his pictures for newspapers. He had Christmas lunch with the Queen. He was palling around Africa with his *cousin* Prince Harry. And the prince of Lesotho. And who knew how many other royals. The divide between us was so much bigger than just the continents that separated us.

"I am so *stupid*," I said emphatically. I felt seconds away from banging my head against the wall. "Did everyone know except for me? Were you all sitting around laughing, like, 'Oh, ha-ha, you know nothing, Dylan Leigh'?"

"Not at all," he assured me. Except I was in no mood to be assured. "Well, everyone from here knows, but they no longer think of it as anything other than a, uh, job that I didn't apply for. The only person who had ever even brought up my title was Pamela, in her horrid confessionals. Asking how it felt to be prince, whether or not it was hard to *date* as a prince, all these ridiculous, stupid . . . It's not something I'm particularly keen to discuss, unprompted."

"Why didn't you tell me?"

Cameraman Mike circled around us, getting closer to my face. Too close.

"I didn't— I couldn't—"

"Did Pamela put you up to this?" I asked sharply, pulling myself up to my full height, trying to ignore the intrusion of the camera's lens. I wanted to look Jamie in the eyes. "Did she tell you not to tell me? So it would be a big, shocking revelation? A double whammy of princes in disguise? One last big plot twist on *Dusty and Ronan's Royal Happily-Ever-After Hootenanny*?"

"Of course not!"

I couldn't even hear him anymore. I felt like I was drowning in the warm stuffy air. I groped desperately along the shelf, looking for something to hold on to, my fingers scrabbling on the shiny book covers. Had *anything* with Jamie been real? Or had our entire relationship been set up by the show?

"Did Pamela tell you to pretend to like me? To kiss me? To *lie* to me?"

"No! I never lied to you!"

"But you didn't tell me the truth."

"No." He sighed heavily. "I didn't."

We looked at each other warily. This was usually the point in the movie where I threw something at the TV, yelling at the stupid chick-flick heroine who was devastated because her love interest lied about something dumb. But right now it didn't feel dumb.

"Pamela didn't make me do anything. I swear. I swear on my life. This is real. Everything we have, everything we are. It's real. I swear it." He reached for me, but I shrank back against the bookshelf. He dropped his hands despondently. "Do you believe at least that much?"

I took a deep breath and looked at him, really looked.

"Yes," I admitted, grudgingly. Upset as I was, I couldn't imagine Jamie as the type of master manipulator who would engineer an entire romance for TV ratings. He couldn't be that cruel. I knew it. Also he was too weird to not be real. If he had been playing a part, the network would have made him much more generic. And given him more manageable hair and a spray tan.

"It was just . . . so . . . *nice* to meet someone who knew nothing about my family. Who cared nothing for my title. Who knew me only as Jamie. And somehow you *liked* me only as Jamie." He shook his head. "It seemed impossible. Too good to be true. I couldn't tell you who I was. Selfishly, I liked you *not* knowing who I was far too much. And I was terrified the truth would change things between us. That you would feel different, or uncomfortable, or intimidated."

"Intimidated? Because I'm such a classless American hick?"

"No!" he shouted. "It's nothing to do with *you*. It's me. People behave differently around royalty. You saw what Florence was like! Honestly, it's not a big deal, Dylan! I swear it isn't."

"It *is* a big deal!"

"It is absolutely not!" he insisted. "I'm something like sixth in line for the throne."

"Sixth?! *Sixth?!* Normal people aren't in line for the British throne, Jamie! They're in line for, I don't know, a hot dog!"

"It could be worse," Jamie said weakly. "I could be the next Duke of Atholl."

"This is not the time for an Atholl joke!" I said shrilly. "Read the room, Jamie! Or Gillecroids! Or whoever you are!"

"I'm Jamie!" he said desperately. "I'm still Jamie. I'm exactly the same person I've always been."

Was he, though? He'd probably grown up in a castle even bigger than Dunyvaig, riding polo ponies and driving Bentleys and eating caviar with golden spoons or whatever. What would he think if he ever saw my house? The tiny living room, and the bedroom I'd always shared with Dusty? It was probably smaller than his garage.

"Oh no. Dylan. I'm so very sorry."

I felt something hot and wet on my cheeks and realized, to my horror, I was crying. Jamie looked equally horrified. He reached out a hand, and I flinched as he touched my cheek.

"Dylan?"

Mom stood on the stairs below us, resting a hand on the

banister, looking very concerned. And confused. A second cameraman stood behind her. It felt like the cameras were converging on me from every angle. I wish they would all just go away. How had Dusty dealt with this for so many months?

"It's time for the toasts, sweetie," she said gently. "We need you downstairs."

"How many toasts does a wedding need?" I said blearily, wiping my hand across my face.

"We're just gettin' started on that front, I'm afraid." She climbed the last few stairs up to us and placed a comforting hand on my back. "Come on down, Dylan. It's time."

Wordlessly, I let her lead me down the stairs and left Jamie behind.

CHAPTER TWENTY-FOUR

"He's gonna make a grand gesture," Heaven said the next morning as she absentmindedly chewed on her straw.

"No, he's not," I countered. "He would never make a grand gesture at somebody else's wedding. That's way rude."

"Dude. This is the guy who busted out a horse and carriage for your first date. A grand gesture *will* be made."

"Are you *hoping* he makes a grand gesture?" I asked skeptically. "You're the one who was all, like, 'This is ending, let it end, blah, blah, blah, etc., etc.'"

"Well, not hoping, exactly, but—"

"I thought you'd be happy!" I interrupted her. "This is it, right? The story of Dylan's First Kiss now has the tidy ending you wanted. I kissed a guy in a castle. He lied. We never saw each other again, and we're not even Facebook friends. The end."

"He didn't *lie,* exactly—"

"Yes, he did!" I protested. "Why are you defending him? Whose side are you on?"

"Yours! Of course yours!" She chased the last drops of soda around and sucked them up with her straw. "I'm just sayin', technically, he didn't lie."

"Lie of omission is still a lie. Meemaw says it all the time."

"Your meemaw!" Heaven brightened. "Is she here?"

"Meemaw insisted on flying in at the very last minute," Dusty said, eyes closed as a stylish woman in black swabbed eye shadow on her face. "So her feet wouldn't have to be off American soil for a minute longer than necessary. Tried to get her in for the rehearsal dinner, but that woman is stubborn as a mule."

"So it's genetic, then. Y'all bein' crazy, I mean," Heaven said.

Meemaw was crazy. But in the best possible way. Like in the kind of way where she only liked to wear sweatshirts with Tweety Bird on them, which was exactly how I was going to dress when I was old. She was also the only short woman in our family. I harbored a secret terror that she'd once been as tall as the rest of us but had shrunk several feet.

"Can we please no longer discuss Meemaw or Dylan's boy problems? This is supposed to be *my* special day," Dusty whined. "Topics of discussion should be limited to how radiant I am."

I sighed and leaned back on the couch, propping up my feet on Heaven's lap, keeping a careful hold on the top of my bridesmaid's dress. I was mostly ready, except I hadn't zipped up yet. No need for the boning in the waist to crush my ribs before it was absolutely necessary.

Heaven whistled. "Girl, you have big feet."

"This is not new information."

"I swear, y'all could pack for a trip to Hawaii in the bags under my eyes." Anne Marie, Dusty's errant bridesmaid, had arrived before I got up this morning and was currently surveying her face critically in a hand mirror. "I need more concealer. This med school thing is no joke, y'all!" She tapped vigorously under her eyes, like she was trying to wake up. "I feel like I'm doin' an experiment on what happens when you replace all the water in your bloodstream with Diet Coke. I'm gonna be the world's first fully carbonated human being."

Med school aside, she appeared to be the same crayon-eating Anne Marie I had always known. I made a resolution not to get sick anytime in the near future and scooted farther down on the couch.

"Honestly, Dylan?" Heaven said, ignoring Anne Marie. "I can kind of see where Jamie's coming from."

"Excuse me?" I propped myself up on my elbows to get a better look at her.

"It's like . . . you know how much you hate it, at home, when everyone's like, 'You're *Dusty*'s sister? Really? *The* Dusty Rose Leigh? Oh my Lord, that girl is so perfect she poops diamonds!'?"

I snorted, in spite of myself.

"See? You know exactly what I mean," Heaven said smugly. "Now imagine that times a bajillion. That's what Jamie goes through every time he meets someone new. 'Oh, Your Royal Highness, thank you for blessing us with your princeliness!'" she simpered.

"I don't care how royal he is. He should have told me. Up front."

"Should he have, though?" She cocked her head at me like

an inquisitive bird. "Be honest with yourself, Dylan. You would have freaked out."

"Would not."

"Would, too. Well, maybe 'freaked out' is a strong term," she said, reconsidering, "but it would have changed things, and you know it."

"Nooo," I said quietly, but I'm not even sure I believed myself. Maybe it didn't matter so much how I would or wouldn't have reacted; what mattered more was how Jamie felt. Heaven was right—being the younger sister of Miss Mississippi was nothing compared to being the only son of a prince. And in all fairness, I don't think I ever told him my full name, either. Maybe he felt the same way about being a prince that I felt about my middle name being Janis. Which is that I would prefer people not know about it.

"Man." I sighed. "I acted exactly like one of those dumb girls in a romantic comedy, didn't I?"

"*How to Lose a Prince in Ten Days*," Heaven said.

"I cannot believe I'm getting involved in this," Dusty piped up. "But I am. And I can't move 'cause I'm waitin' for my lash glue to dry, so come over here."

Grumbling, I hoisted myself up off the couch, carefully holding my dress against my chest. Dusty waved the makeup girl away for the moment and lay back with her eyes closed, lashes resting against her cheeks. They looked like big plastic bugs, so dark and spiky.

"I would just like to say, on principle, that I am not pleased we are having this discussion today. Today is about *me*. I should be the only thing we are discussing. Today is *my* special day."

I rolled my eyes. Then remembered Dusty couldn't see me.

"Okay, Dusty, I acknowledge your formal complaint. Thanks for indulging me," I added sarcastically.

"Did you not think to ask your big sister for advice? Your big sister who was once in literally this exact same situation?"

"Oh. Um. Yes. I mean, no," I said, honestly, sort of embarrassed by my obtuseness. "I didn't think about it."

Oddly enough, even in the castle, surrounded by cameras, I had sort of forgotten the whole "in disguise" part of the *Prince in Disguise* aspect of Dusty and Ronan's courtship. After all, I did only meet him once when he was still in disguise. For the vast majority of my experience of knowing Ronan, I'd known him as the Right Honorable Lord Whatever. They'd only filmed *Prince in Disguise* for six weeks, after all. Dusty had spent those six weeks thinking she was just on some *Bachelor*-type show, and I'd only seen her during the episode where she brought Ronan home to meet us. Ronan had progressed pretty quickly from "I met the cutest boy!" to "Surprise—I'm engaged to a prince!"

"That is because you are dense as a tree stump, sweet li'l Dilly. Especially when it comes to boys."

I bristled silently in response, but I had no good comeback. Because she was, unfortunately, right.

"I will say this once, clearly, so even you can understand. And then we will go back to today being my special day." Dusty took a deep breath. I leaned in. "It. Does. Not. Matter."

"Excuse me?"

"Did I stutter?" She cracked one eye open. "Oh, good, they're dry." She blinked a few times, fluttering the thickest, darkest lashes I'd ever seen. "You heard me. It doesn't matter, Dilly. Doesn't matter one teeny little bit."

"How does it not matter? He's a *prince*, Dusty," I said almost in a whisper. "A *prince*. That's crazy. Too crazy. I don't know how to talk to a prince!"

"Of course you do, dummy." She rolled her eyes. "You've been doin' nothin' but talkin' to a prince for the past three weeks."

"But I didn't *know* he was a prince!"

"And it doesn't change anythin' now that you do know. It really ain't all that different from when I dated Ricky Lindsay. His daddy was the Mattress King, remember? Over on 178?"

"Being a prince of England is a little bit different than being a mattress prince, Dusty."

"Is it, though? I was so intimidated by how big their house was. Little did I know where I'd be movin' into a couple years later," she said ruefully. "This ain't somethin' Jamie chose. It's just what he's been born into. And maybe it's a bit more rare than bein' a mattress prince, but the idea's the same. Who your daddy is doesn't determine who you are."

I was silent for a minute, thinking about Cash Keller. I was pretty sure that wasn't what she meant, but I thought of him just the same. And how he had nothing to do with who I was.

"And I promise, it ain't that big of a deal," she continued. "You know the monarchy over here is mostly for show, anyway, right? They just welcome dignitaries and dedicate wings of hospitals and watch the Trooping the Colour and stuff. It's pretty much just volunteer work."

"But he lied—"

"Okay, first of all"—she held up one finger for silence as she interrupted me—"Ronan legit, straight-out, full-on lied, gave me a fake last name and a fake hometown and a fake job and everythin'. Lie after lie after lie. But not about anything important."

"No, just about every single aspect of his identity."

"That's not who he *is*, dummy. Your name isn't who you are. And I know you know that and you're just arguin' with me for the sake of arguin' with me because apparently that is what you were put on this earth to do."

"Nuh-uh."

"Put aside your natural tendency to contradict me at every turn and listen." Those were a lot of big words, coming from Dusty. "He just wanted you to like him for who he is, not who his daddy is. And looks like that's exactly what happened."

"Mmrph," I mumbled noncommittally.

"Don't leave it like this, Dyl. Tell him it wasn't cool if you like. But forgive him, and dance with him, and kiss him good-bye. Don't leave mad."

"Anythin' can be repaired, Dylan," Anne Marie said kindly. "Even a brachial plexus injury."

I scowled at the two of them, just on the principle of the thing, but privately, I felt they were right. Even if I didn't know what a brachial plexus was.

"Nothing's changed. He's the same big ol' goofball who likes you," Dusty said. "Crown or no crown. So who cares if he's a prince?"

"Did *you* know he was a prince?" I asked suspiciously.

"Hell no. Ronan didn't mention anything about it, and I've got better things to do with my time than google Ronan's groomsmen. There are too many royals over here to keep track of."

"Even *I* didn't know he was a prince, Dyl," Heaven piped up. "And I have a Royal Wedding mug."

She'd bought it at a tag sale for fifty cents and kept pencils in it, but still. I supposed that showed some interest in the royal family.

"It doesn't matter who knew, anyway." Dusty shrugged. "What matters is that you make things right."

"Oh God." I swallowed noisily. "Does this mean *I* have to make some kind of grand gesture?"

Visions danced through my head, each more horrifying than the last. Me serenading Jamie with a microphone and karaoke machine. Me showing up with a bunch of posters that said *To Me, You Are Perfect.* Me standing outside the castle with a boom box above my head. Dunyvaig had, like, four hundred windows. I would never find Jamie's room.

"No!" Dusty shouted. "Just be *normal*, Dilly."

"Dusty!" Suddenly, Mom burst into the room, so out of breath she was panting, hands on her knees. "I don't know how she did—but she did—and she's— Oh, fudge." Mom looked straight at Dusty. "She knows. And she's coming."

Dusty went white under her foundation. And her spray tan.

"Gird your loins, ladies," she said grimly. "The She-Beast approaches."

"Is this gonna be like the Kappa formal?" Anne Marie sprang to her feet. "Gosh darnit, I took my rings off." She cracked her knuckles menacingly.

Maybe Anne Marie was slightly more interesting than I'd remembered her being.

"What's happening now?" Heaven quietly asked me.

"Um . . . she knows . . . she's coming . . ." I quickly put the pieces together. "Oh no. Florence found out about the baby. And she's on her way."

Heaven's jaw dropped as my stomach did somersaults of distress. I guess I wasn't *surprised*—ever since Mrs. McGregor let news of Dusty's bun in the oven slip, I'd known this was coming—but I thought it was low, even for Pamela, to drop the baby bomb mere hours before the wedding.

Florence strode through the door, nostrils quivering with rage. She was flanked by a gleeful Pamela and a second cameraman, who scooted into the corner, careful to keep out of the shot of the cameraman who was already in there.

"You!" Florence boomed, advancing toward Dusty. There was something clutched in her outstretched hand. Looked like a small white plastic stick. "You . . . you . . . scheming, predatory, manipulative, conniving—"

"Choose your next word carefully, Mommie Dearest." Dusty was wearing nothing but a white silk robe bedazzled with *Bride* on the back, but she still managed to look downright menacing. Maybe it was because she towered over Florence, even in her stockinged feet. "Don't wanna say somethin' you might regret. We're about to be family."

"Only because of your . . . your . . . chicanery!"

Chicanery? This was so awful, but if you closed your eyes and listened it sounded like we were in a Victorian showdown.

"Why don't you stop it with the SAT vocab words and just say it straight out to my face exactly what you're accusin' me of, hmm?" Florence might have been on fire with rage, but Dusty was stone-cold cool. And I was kind of in awe.

"Of . . . *this*!" Florence stuck the white stick up under Dusty's nose. The sleeves of her emerald-green silk blazer fell back to reveal an enormous bangle in the shape of what looked like a badger. It momentarily distracted me from the white stick. "You tricked my son into marrying you! Finally, it all makes sense!"

"Dude, that's a pregnancy test," Heaven whispered.

"How did she get that? Did Lady Florence go Dumpster diving?" I whispered in disbelief.

"But I didn't— How did you— I don't understand." Dusty's brow furrowed in confusion. "I didn't take a pregnancy test here."

Someone coughed discreetly from behind us. I swiveled to look. My money was on Pamela.

"It doesn't matter where it came from," Florence said hurriedly.

Dusty didn't take a pregnancy test here, but Florence had a pregnancy test. I felt like my mind was whirring at a million miles an hour. Pamela had found out about Dusty's pregnancy. And then the show had planted a fake pregnancy test for Florence to find. Or just told Florence Dusty was pregnant and handed her a prop. Whatever had happened, it was seriously messed up.

"What matters is what it proves," Florence insisted. "You're pregnant!"

Dusty's ice-cold resolve had melted. She looked . . . tired. Sighing, she placed a protective hand over her belly and closed her eyes.

"Wait!" I cried, not sure why exactly I was speaking. "Don't do this. Don't do this, okay?" I looked past Florence to Pamela. Florence was awful and a total snob, but I knew who was really behind this. "We all know the production team planted the test. Just drop the story line. Please."

"Dylan," Pamela said icily, all traces of her usual fake smile long gone. "We already had a discussion about cooperating. This is the exact opposite of cooperating. Please don't speak to me and stop looking at the cameras. Return to business as usual."

"Wait. Please," I begged. "If you drop this story line, I'll do something really interesting. I swear. I'll flip over a table. I'll throw my drink at Jamie! No, I'll punch Jamie!" Pamela didn't look nearly as interested as I'd hoped she would. I decided to try a different tactic. "No, never mind. We'll make up. And I'll sneak into his room at night. And you can film it with a night-vision camera like they do on *Bachelor Pad*."

"Good gravy, Dylan!" Mom yelped.

"I'm not saying I'm gonna *do* anything when I'm in the room; I'm just saying I'll *go* in the room! You can edit it in whatever incriminating way you'd like!"

"I'm not sure that's better," Heaven said.

"*I'd* feel better about it."

"I wouldn't," Mom said firmly.

"Thanks for offering to pretend-whore yourself out for me, baby sister," Dusty said, and much to my surprise, she was smiling. "I didn't think you liked me that much."

"I love you, Dusty," I said, embarrassed but needing to say it anyway. "Even when we fight, I'm on your side. Always. You're my family. And so's the baby."

"Don't make me cry, dummy; I'll ruin my makeup," she sniffled, and pulled me in for a hug. I was shocked to feel a small, but noticeable, bump that had definitely not been there before.

"All right, now, y'all, let's calm down." Dusty pulled herself out of the hug, patting away nonexistent mascara stains from under her eyes. "There is absolutely no need for you to engage in any of those reality-show theatrics, Dylan, although I appreciate the offer. I've got this. Pamela." Dusty turned and looked her dead in the eyes. "I'll take it from here."

Then Dusty took a deep breath, turned to Florence, and said, "Yes, I'm pregnant. And we couldn't be happier about it. For the record, I found out I was pregnant after we got engaged, but that doesn't matter. What matters is that I love your son. And he loves me. And that's why we're gettin' married, not because I tricked him or trapped him. You and I both know I ain't after his money, because he doesn't have any. And I don't give a flyin' crap about bein' the next Lady Dunleavy." Florence's nostrils quivered in distaste as I stifled a giggle. "Seriously. You can keep the title, and I'll just be plain old Mrs. Murray. That is fine by me." Dusty took a deep breath. "We are buildin' a family together. A *family*. And that means somethin' to me. So I suggest you get on board. Because I am goin' absolutely nowhere. And I ain't scared of you. 'Cause I'm from Mississippi," Dusty said proudly. "And we Southern girls take crap from nobody. Ya hear?"

I'm not sure who was more surprised when Dusty poked Florence in the chest, Dusty or Florence. Florence looked down at Dusty's French-manicured finger in disbelief, then back up at Dusty with an expression that looked like admiration.

"Do we understand each other?" Dusty asked, flushed.

"I believe we do," Florence said crisply. "And I believe you may do rather well, after all. All appearances to the contrary." She sniffed. "I suppose you'd better finish getting ready. It's terribly bad form to be late to one's own wedding."

And with that, she turned on her sensible heels and left, Pamela and one of the cameramen following her.

"Well, hot damn, baby." Dusty patted her stomach. "This is a moment when I could really use a drink," she said ruefully.

"Wow . . . That was . . . Wow." Heaven shook her head in disbelief. "Dylan, I think your sister might be my hero."

"I think she might be mine, too," I said softly.

Dusty looked up at me, surprised, but then smiled a real, genuine smile. Nothing like her pageant smile.

"I'll drink for you!" Anne Marie volunteered. She raised a glass of mimosa that had materialized seemingly from out of nowhere. "To Mississippi girls!"

"To sisters," I said.

"To babies," Heaven suggested.

"To *my* girls," Mom said.

"To all of that, and all y'all," Dusty said, a note of finality in her voice. "Now drink that mimosa, beautiful."

Anne Marie raised her glass high, as Heaven made little whooping noises. Mom reached out to take one of my hands, and one of Dusty's.

It was funny—I might have been four thousand miles from Tupelo, but right then, I was home.

CHAPTER TWENTY-FIVE

Easy navigation was not one of the advantages of castle living. I had a little map Dusty had drawn for me on a cocktail napkin clutched in one hand and her exhortations not to be late ringing in my ears. Heaven, patron saint of best friends, had thrown a very convincing fake tantrum about not being able to do the Scottish Grand March on camera at the wedding now that Anne Marie had arrived. She'd chucked a champagne flute at the wall in a fit of pretend pique, and I'd slipped out the door in the ensuing chaos, unnoticed by the cameras.

Up a flight of stairs, around a corner, down this hall, one more corner— Wait no, wrong way—back down that hall, one more corner, farther down the hall—and there it was. A door just like mine.

Knock-knock-kna-knock-knock-knock.

"Er, come in!"

I pushed the door open. Jamie was crouched on the floor

in his formal dress kilt, drawing on a poster board with an enormous red Sharpie. I shut the door behind me and walked toward him, toes of my cream ballet flats lining up with the edge of the poster. He looked up and made eye contact with my ankles.

"Is that a . . ." I trailed off as I looked at the red splotch on the poster. "You know what? Never mind. I give up. I have no idea what that's supposed to be."

"It was supposed to be a whole . . . *Beauty and the Beast* . . . thing," he said sheepishly, looking up at me from under a flop of dark hair. "But my rose looked nothing like a rose, and then I became concerned about the implications of Stockholm syndrome, so I attempted to turn the rose into a heart, which resulted in the splotch you see before you. Dylan. Wait. Why are you here? Am I late? Is it time for the wedding? Oh God, is it time for the wedding?"

He scrambled up to his feet, panic in his eyes.

"No! Relax, no!" I grabbed his forearms to steady him. "We've got, like, six minutes. Maybe." Now would have been a great time to have owned a watch. "So don't relax too much."

"Not a moment to lose, then. Dylan, I'm glad you're here. I am so, so—"

"Shh." I placed my index finger in front of his lips. "Save it, okay? I understand why you didn't tell me. And it's okay. I promise."

"Mmrph," he said. I hastily took my finger away.

"And I hope you know this already, but you being a prince isn't like any kind of incentive for me to try to be your friend or your girlfriend or whatever. I have no interest in being a princess."

"You wouldn't be. If we married, I mean. You'd be a duchess, like my mum. Not that we're getting married. Right now. Ha!" His laugh sounded strangled and embarrassed.

"Duchess. Princess. Whatever," I said. "I don't care about being any of those things. I don't *want* any of that. It's kind of a major drawback, honestly."

"That's not any better!" he exclaimed. "That's another reason why I absolutely should not have told you—"

"But that's what I'm saying!" I insisted. "I understand. Why you didn't tell me you were a prince in disguise. Sorry," I interrupted Jamie before he could say anything, seeing the protest rise on his lips. "Prince. Not in disguise. Because if I'm being a hundred percent honest with myself, I probably would have treated you differently. Maybe not in the way you expected—like, I wouldn't have fawned all over you or whatever—but things still would have been different. So I'm glad you didn't tell me right away."

"You are?"

"Yes. Because it meant I got to really know *you*. In exactly the same way you got to know me, the me I really am. Although you should have told me the truth before Florence outed you." I glared at him. "That was not cool. Nobody wants to be scooped by Florence."

"That is an excellent point. And I apologize profusely for that. I should have told you sooner."

"But not too soon."

"Not too soon," he agreed.

"I'm sorry," we both said in unison, in a rush, then smiled at each other. He pulled me into a hug.

"I'm sorry I didn't tell you," he murmured into my hair.

"I'm sorry I overreacted," I mumbled into his shoulder.

"Well, then." He patted my back. "Everyone's terribly sorry. Does that mean things can go back to normal?"

"Yes, please," I said fervently.

"Thank God."

He crushed my mouth with his, so excited to kiss me he nearly knocked the wind out of me. I clung to his arms so I didn't topple over, relaxing into the rightness of Jamie's embrace. Far too soon, we pulled apart.

"If we stand here snogging all day, we really will miss the wedding," he said.

"And then Dusty would murder us."

"And it really *would* be the most dramatic season of *Prince in Disguise* ever." He did a pretty good impression of the voice-over from TRC. "First kisses. Long-lost fathers. A double homicide. This truly was the most dramatic season of *Prince in Disguise* . . . ever." I laughed. "You have to say 'the most dramatic season ever' approximately twice a minute; otherwise no one will believe you that it actually *was* the most dramatic season ever."

"For once, I don't think the drama's in doubt. Now we really do have to go," I said nervously. "I think the wedding's going to start really soon. Like, uncomfortably soon."

"Right. Hang on a moment—just want to toss an extra hanky in my sporran for Ronan. I have a feeling today will be a four-hanky day for everyone's favorite weepy Scotsman."

"What's a sporran?"

"This large furry, purselike item." He gestured to the front of his kilt, where there was, in fact, a dangling furry purse.

"I'm sorry—I can't look at it." I shaded my eyes. "It feels obscene. It's just, like . . . right there."

"Well, look away, then, while I fetch my hanky."

Obediently, I did and noticed the room for the first time. It had the same basic layout of my room, and the same tartan curtains, but there was something different about it. It looked like someone actually lived here. Books cluttered every available surface. A throw blanket printed with a fancy blue lion and a Chelsea Football Club banner lay draped over the end of the plaid bedspread. And in addition to the horse paintings, there were posters tacked up on the walls. I saw Benedict Cumberbatch as Sherlock Holmes, a couple hobbits, and then I snorted as my eyes landed on a somewhat sexy Emma Watson poster, from her post-Hermione days.

"Are you chuckling at my Emma Watson poster?" he asked, affronted. "I'll have you know she's a terrific actress."

"Yeah, she just about acted herself out of her pants there."

"She didn't— I mean, she's not—"

"Relax, Jamie, I'm teasing you. You have, like, a room here. I mean this is *your* room."

He nodded. "Yes."

"Are you and Ronan really old family friends?"

"In a way. We're also second cousins."

"Aha!"

"Damn. I suppose I did outright lie about that, didn't I? Far more ethically murky. I only didn't want you to assume—"

"That you were also a Right Honorable Lord Whatever? When in fact what you are is so much worse?"

"Worse?" he asked, affronted. "Being a prince isn't ghastly as all that."

"It's horrible. That's why America had a revolution. To get away from ghastly princes like you."

"That's quite enough, you ungrateful Yankee. We started your bloody country. Now just try to get away from this ghastly prince. I dare you."

"You'll never catch me!" I shouted, and burst out of the room, laughing as I sprinted down the hall.

"Dylan, you're going entirely the wrong way!"

"I knew that! Hiiii-yaaa!" I screamed as I blew past him and thundered down the hall. "You still can't catch me!"

"Of course I can't, you're quite a bit faster than I am!"

I wasn't entirely sure where I was going, but after a couple turns and long stretches of sprinting down hallways, the staircase appeared. I flew down the stairs, Jamie hot at my heels, and then something tugged on my tartan sash and stopped me in my tracks.

"Hey!" I turned to see Jamie holding on to my sash. "Stupid butt bow," I muttered. "Unsportsmanlike conduct! Unhand me this instant, you blackguard!"

"Blackguard? I'm sorry, have I apprehended Charles Dickens by mistake?"

"Just let go of the damn butt bow."

"There's a better way. A faster way." Jamie grinned and turned from the front door. I ran after him, absolutely no idea where we were going, until all of a sudden Jamie was pushing open a door and we were in the library.

"Oh God, don't tell me: *The Premeditated Trapdoor Returns?*"

"That's what we'll call the television series," Jamie said as he made his way to the center of the room and pushed the rug off the trapdoor. "Once *The Premeditated Trapdoor* has been turned into a film and I've gone Hollywood."

"His Royal Shyness, a sellout?" I shook my head. "I expected more."

"Hush, you." Jamie swung the trapdoor open. "Once more unto the breach, dear friends, once more."

"Why, exactly, are we climbing into a black hole right before the wedding?" I asked as I took the first few steps down into darkness.

"I told you the tunnel system was quite extensive. It's a shortcut, Dylan." The door swung shut behind us, then the flashlight clicked on, casting an arc of light in front of me as I made my way down the stairs. "I'm afraid we haven't time to run across the grounds. And I'd die of mortification if our tardiness delayed the wedding."

"Do you know where you're going?"

"Naturally."

With his free hand, Jamie grabbed one of mine and led me down the tunnel, turning decisively this way and that. I wondered if he'd left bread crumbs down here or something; everything looked exactly the same to me.

"I feel like we just walked in a really big circle," I said as we approached a set of stairs that looked exactly like the one we'd initially descended.

"Your lack of faith appalls me. After you."

I climbed the stairs and pushed on the trapdoor. It didn't move. I pushed harder. Still nothing.

"Jamie," I said, dismayed to feel the first few beads of panic sweat, "we're trapped! We're going to be stuck down here and miss the wedding and *die*."

"These are exactly the sort of dramatics we'll need for *The*

Premeditated Trapdoor Returns!" Jamie said cheerfully. "But for the moment, I'd suggest knocking."

I banged on the ceiling. I heard scuffling noises and scraping, and then the trapdoor was flung open, flooding the tunnel with light.

"Dylan Janis Leigh!" Mom's talons closed around my arm, and she lifted me up out of the darkness. I scrambled to stand. "What on God's green earth are you doing crawling around under the church? Are you half possum, girl? You must have lost your damn mind." Mom banged the trapdoor shut once Jamie was out and covered it back up again with the runner, straightening the corners. I waved good-bye to Jamie as Mom pulled me away from the chapel, down a hallway and into a little room. "Were you trying to give your sister a heart attack?"

"Hey, Dilly!" Dusty did not look like she was having a heart attack. She was sitting in her wedding dress on an armchair, feet up on Anne Marie's lap, as she happily chowed down on a plate of french fries. "Mama, did you find any ranch dressing?"

"No, sweets, I don't think they make that here," Mom cooed, then immediately returned to glaring at me. If anyone was having a heart attack, it was Mom.

"Want a fry, Dilly?" Dusty held her plate out to me. "Everything go okay with Jamie?" she asked in an undertone.

I shot her a thumbs-up as I stuffed a couple fries in my mouth.

"Good," she said smugly. "Well, ladies, should we get this show on the road?"

Mom thrust a bouquet of white roses, thistle, and heather, all bound with blue velvet ribbon, into my hands before taking Dusty's french fries and helping her out of the chair. Dusty's dress fell into its perfect bell shape as she stood. Her hair was simple, and soft—tossed up casually with a crown of white heather. She was beautiful, but completely unfussy. It was the opposite of her Miss Mississippi dress—not a single rhinestone or sequin in sight. It was perfect.

Dusty took her bouquet—an enormous cascade of white roses—from Mom, and smiled at the three of us.

"Well, line up, girls!" she clucked, like she was herding chickens. "Can't keep Ronan waiting up there all day now, can we?"

As the organ music started, I took my place behind Anne Marie, and Mom led us out of the little room. She poked her head around the corner, then nodded at us.

As Anne Marie made her way down the aisle, I took a deep breath, rolled my shoulders back, and imagined that string coming out of the top of my head. Mom adjusted my arms to raise my bouquet a bit higher, then gave me a little shove into the aisle. Heaven, easily visible in the second row in her hot-pink dress, waved.

I saw Father Mackenzie, beaming beatifically down at me and the assembled congregation. Next to him was Ronan, snuffling as his lip wobbled dangerously, but dry-eyed for the moment. There was Kit—was he having a stroke? One of his eyes was twitching uncontrollably. A beat later I realized he wasn't twitching; he was *winking*. Dusty's high school cheerleading squad, sorority sisters, and a handful of pageant princesses from her year with Miss America filled up four spray-tanned, false-lashed, hair-extensioned pews, and he clearly didn't know where to start.

Finally, my eyes came to rest on Jamie, standing tall and

proud in his kilt. His hair was neater than I'd ever seen it before, neater even than when we'd gone on our date, combed back in a thoroughly respectable fashion. How had he fixed it so quickly after scrambling up through the trapdoor? Maybe he had a comb tucked into his sporran, too.

I made it up the aisle and to my spot next to Anne Marie with absolutely nothing calamitous happening, which seemed like the best possible scenario. Well, I did wave in a pretty undignified fashion when I spotted Meemaw in the front row, resplendent in a sequined purple pantsuit, but that was the only appropriate response, given the circumstances.

Then the congregation stood. My breath caught in my throat as I saw Dusty at the back of the church. Not just because she looked beautiful—which she did—but because she was standing in between Mom *and* Cash Keller. I may not have wanted Cash to be part of my life, but if Dusty did, that was her right. I was just glad Mom was part of today, too.

Ronan let out an enormous sob that caused every head in the room to swivel. Tears ran down his face. Wordlessly, Jamie handed him a hanky.

The only thing louder than Ronan's crying was Kit's singing, but somehow, the ceremony was beautiful. It all went by in a blur, until Father Mackenzie pronounced them husband and wife, Ronan kissed Dusty, and the whole church cheered. The organ struck up the recessional, and Ronan and Dusty practically skipped down the aisle, Dusty waving her bouquet around like a trophy. Kit offered me his arm, and we followed them. I looked clear over his head to wave at Meemaw, then Heaven, as we exited the church.

A line of Highlanders in kilts playing bagpipes and drums

stretched all the way back to the castle. Kit hastily maneuvered away from me to walk with Anne Marie, and Jamie moved up to replace him. I certainly wasn't complaining as Jamie tucked his arm around my waist.

"Do you feel Scottish now?" Jamie shouted over the din of the bagpipes.

"I thought bagpipes were supposed to be horrible, but this is actually pretty cool!" I shouted back.

We followed Dusty and Ronan past the line of bagpipers and burst through the doors of Dunyvaig. Staff members waited with trays of champagne and warm mugs of something. Jamie neatly grabbed two mugs and whirled us away from the cold air. He handed me a mug. Mmm. Hot chocolate.

"It's not bad, Dunyvaig, it's really no' bad," Kit said companionably, and loudly. I turned back to see him standing by the fireplace, a cozy arm slung around Anne Marie's waist. He sure worked fast—not that I was surprised. "Terribly small, compared to the Kirby estate in Aberfeldy, but it's verra quaint."

"Wait just one minute—what are *you* in disguise?" Anne Marie asked excitedly. "Where are you the prince of?"

"Erm—I'm nothing in disguise, poppet."

"Oh." Anne Marie frowned, sighed, then said, "Honeybun, why don't you tell me more about this estate of yours."

Jamie rolled his eyes and steered me away from the fireplace.

"Can't wait to hear that best-man speech," Jamie said. "It's going to be absolutely bonkers. That's nice for you, though, isn't it? I hadn't thought of it before. No pressure."

"No pressure?"

"For your speech," he clarified. "Kit's best-man speech is

going to be insane, naturally. No matter what *you* do, maid of honor, it'll be loads better."

"Right." I smiled weakly at him.

Speech.

My speech.

Crap.

CHAPTER TWENTY-SIX

The only advantage of the icy bolt of panic currently gripping my belly was that there was absolutely no room whatsoever for any more dread. So as the bridal party lined up outside the ballroom to prepare for the Scottish Grand March, the idea of dancing into the room while hundreds of people watched didn't faze me in the slightest. Because I didn't have a speech. For my only sister's only wedding. Which made me officially the worst, and a certified grade A idiot.

"So we just march around in a circle? That's all?" Anne Marie asked, clearly a few drinks worse for the wear. Hopefully, nobody's brachial plexus was in need of attendance this evening.

"Stick close to me, lovey, and I'll steer ye in the right direction," Kit purred.

"Ooo, I'll stick *very* close!" Anne Marie tee-hee-hee'd.

Unbelievable. The world's tiniest Casanova was at it again.

"You're very quiet, Dylan." Jamie poked me in the shoulder.

"You're not worried about the Grand March, are you?"

"No. I mean yes. A little. Maybe? It's just marching in a circle, right? Ah-ha-ha-ha!" I laughed a horrible, awkward, strangled fake laugh for no reason at all except that was what my panicking body had decided to produce.

"My God. You *really* hate dancing, don't you?" Jamie's eyes widened.

"I'm going to move to that town from *Footloose* when I get back. No, I'm going to write a letter and ask the president to *Footloose* the whole country," I babbled. "Ah-ha-ha-ha!"

Jamie raised an eyebrow, but wisely chose to say nothing.

The doors to the ballroom finally opened, and it was not what I expected. For once, there wasn't a single plaid anything in sight. Instead, the space had been transformed into a winter wonderland—like the outside had come indoors. The room glittered with snowy whites and sparkling silvers. Actual trees, painted white and silver, lined the room, their spare branches stretching up to the stag mural on the ceiling. It looked exactly like . . .

"Narnia," Jamie said with wonder.

"That is *exactly* what I was thinking," I whispered back.

"I'm half expecting to see Mr. Tumnus come trotting by."

"It makes sense, if you think about it. We've got the lion—Ronan, with his long mane of hair. The witch—"

"Ronan's mum, obviously, yes."

"And Dusty's wardrobe," I concluded, satisfied. "Which, in case you didn't know, is extremely extensive."

Jamie barked out a laugh as the band began playing the first strains of the Grand March. I awkwardly hop-skip-marched into the room on Jamie's arm—technically, as maid of honor,

I think I was supposed to be with best man Kit Kirby, but at this point the only way I could have pried the limpet formerly known as Anne Marie off his arm was with a crowbar, and I was more than fine partnering with Jamie. Before I knew it, it was done.

"You did it!" Heaven was waiting at the edge of the dance floor, holding up a soda with a tiny straw and a slice of lemon. "You survived! You Grand Marched the hell outta this thing."

"Yeah, and now all my troubles are over," I muttered as I gratefully grabbed the soda she proffered.

"So I scoped out our table sitch. Not bad, not so bad." She steered me to a round table half-full of nearly identical teenage redheads. "It's us, Jamie, Kit Kirby—ugh—Anne Marie, and then a bunch of Ronan's cousins, and I cannot understand a single word they are saying. Their accents are so thick you could swim through them. So prepare for a lot of smiling and nodding."

"Heaven." I grabbed her arm and pulled her to a halt in the middle of her monologue. "Ididntwriteaspeech."

"Say what?" She cupped her hand to her ear exaggeratedly.

"I. Didn't. Write. A. Speech."

"Oh hell no." Her face turned stormy. "Dylan. No. *No!* This is like the one thing you had to do, the *one* thing!"

"It's not that big of a deal . . . right?" I asked weakly.

"It is a *huge* deal!" She planted her hands on her hips. "How could you not write a maid-of-honor speech?"

"I just, um, forgot. There's been a lot going on!"

"That's no excuse!"

"I'm sorry, Heaven, I'm so sorry."

"Don't apologize to *me*. Apologize to your damn sister." She closed her eyes and pressed her forefingers against her temples. "Lord. Sit your ass down. I don't have time for you right now."

"You don't have time for me? What are you doing?"

"Stuff, Dylan. I've got stuff to do, too. Now *sit down*."

She pushed me into a chair. I awkwardly nodded and smiled at Ronan's cousins, who said something either very welcoming or completely offensive. I had no idea.

The lights darkened and the room hushed. Jamie found his way to the chair next to me as Heaven flitted off somewhere. A spotlight illuminated the dance floor. Dusty and Ronan stepped into the light, holding hands. And damn if that traditional ceilidh band Florence had mandated didn't play the heck out of "It's Your Love." Tim McGraw and Faith Hill couldn't have done it better. Dusty and Ronan swayed gently in a circle, her head resting on his shoulder. There weren't any fancy steps or anything, but maybe that was part of what made it so nice. Dusty looked so happy, I thought for a minute my heart would burst for her. The song came to an end, and the room erupted into applause, punctuated by a few earsplitting whistles.

"And now," the rugged fellow who'd been singing Tim McGraw's part announced into the microphone, "we have a special presentation from the best man and the maid of honor's best friend."

The what? The what and the who? I swiveled my head all around, trying to find Heaven, probably looking like a demented owl, but she was nowhere to be seen.

The band struck a chord, and the spotlight illuminated the door, where Heaven and Kit stood, arm in arm. They were both wearing kilts and velvet jackets, with knee socks and black shoes that laced up their legs. As the fiddle kicked into gear, they skipped into the room. My jaw dropped open. Jamie reached over and helpfully tapped it back up into place.

I didn't know enough about Scottish dancing to know *what* this was—I only knew that it involved very intricate footwork, very straight legs, and a lot of kicks. *How* did they learn this? Heaven had been really cagey about practicing something, and this was clearly the result, but how did she become a professional Scottish dancer in like a week?

"Did you know about this?" I asked Jamie as the crowd cheered.

"I had no idea!" He clapped in amazement. "They're bloody brilliant!"

The band concluded with a strong final chord, as Kit and Heaven bowed to thunderous applause. But just when I thought the dance was over, I heard a guitar from the other side of the room. Every head turned toward the ballroom doors.

A cute blondish guy entered the ballroom playing the guitar, grinning at the crowd as he made his way up to the band on stage. Was that Hunter Hayes? I wasn't sure. Even though Dusty blasted MISS 98 nonstop on the radio whenever she drove me around, I couldn't have picked any of her favorite country singers out of a lineup, certainly not Hunter Hayes. But if TRC really was trying to make this into their own version of *The Bachelor,* it wouldn't have been complete without a private concert from a celebrity musical guest.

Heaven and Kit grabbed their kilts and jackets, pulled, and revealed entirely new outfits underneath as everyone in the crowd lost their minds. This was like Broadway-level production values. Not for the first time, I wondered just how big the budget was for this whole spectacle.

Under his kilt and jacket, Kit had somehow been wearing a gingham button-down shirt with matching shorts that perfectly matched the gingham romper Heaven wore. It looked a little like a picnic had exploded, but in the best possible way. As maybe—Hunter Hayes sang, "Love don't know what distance is," they threw their arms around each other's waists, began spinning, and launched into the type of intricate partner jazz choreography I had never seen outside of *Dancing with the Stars*.

I realized belatedly that I was jumping up and down, waving my napkin above my head. Well, whatever—the only way to respond to something this insane was by being completely insane. As Hunter sang, "But I don't want 'good' and I don't want 'good enough,' I want 'can't sleep, can't breathe without your love,'" Heaven took a running start, Kit caught her, and lifted her above his head. The screaming was deafening.

"He *Dirty Dancing*-ed her!" I screamed, still waving my napkin. "That crazy mofo just pulled a Swayze!"

"I didn't think he had that kind of upper-body strength!" Far too late, I realized Jamie had been dancing along in an incredibly adorable, completely uncoordinated way.

Kit and Heaven cartwheeled toward each other, but as Heaven stood up, Kit landed on his shoulder with a sickening popping sound. The music cut out abruptly as he screeched in pain.

"Call an ambulance!" he wailed. "I'm injured! And on my good side, too!"

"Back up, y'all." Anne Marie pushed her way through the crowd that had already gathered around Kit. "No need for an ambulance. Future MD here." Anne Marie bent down, poking and prodding around Kit's arm. "Nothin's broken, honeybun.

You just dislocated your shoulder. Hold real still." With another popping sound that turned my stomach, Anne Marie wrenched his shoulder back into place. Kit yelped, then pushed himself up to his feet, rolling his shoulder experimentally.

"She bloody fixed it," he marveled. "Right, then. Enjoy your dinners, all!"

Probably not the grand finale Heaven had been hoping for, but it was certainly dramatic. As Kit waved to the crowd, Jamie and I took our seats and happily set to attacking the bread basket. I still didn't have a speech. Which was, admittedly, not great. But at least I had two working shoulders. And a basket of carbs.

Halfway through the salad course, the bandleader called Kit up to the stage. My stomach let out a loud nervous gurgle. No, it would be fine. Just fine.

"Hello there, lovies!" Kit addressed the crowd, his glass of amber liquid sloshing around in his hand. His other arm was in a sling made from a silver pashmina that definitely wasn't his. "I'm Kit Kirby, the best man. When I first met Ronan, I thought, 'That cheeky bugger's got quite a few Legos.'" Titters from the crowd. "We were four, you see. Wee tots. When I first met Dusty, I thought, 'Lucky Ronan. What a looker! Those legs! Legs for days, that girl!'" I could feel the force of Florence glaring at him from here. "But it's not just the legs. There's the whole top half, too!"

I heard a chair push back and saw Ronan up on his feet.

"With all respect, Ronan, all meant with due respect!" Kit protested. "It's a compliment, is all!"

Ronan didn't stop him, but he didn't sit down, either.

"In conclusion, what I've realized is that Dusty and Ronan

are much more than legs or Legos. Together, they are much better than apart. And being around all this love has, as always, inspired me to poetry. Because I'm verra romantic." He winked in Anne Marie's general direction, then decided to hedge his bets, and winked at a few former pageant queens for good measure. He cleared his throat. "There once was a girl from Tupelo—"

"Stop! No." Ronan was almost up to the front, grabbing for Kit's microphone. "No, no. I think you've said more than enough already. Cheers, mate."

"It wasna going to be inappropriate! Well, hardly."

"See?" Jamie said as Ronan firmly steered Kit back to his seat. "I told you, you'll be fine. Just don't compose any naughty limericks."

"Heh," I laughed awkwardly.

The bandleader said something about maid of honor, Dylan, bride's little sister, and speech, but mostly I just heard white noise through a blind panic. I made it up there somehow, carried along on a sea of polite applause.

The microphone stand was way too short, so I pulled the mic out of the clip. I winced at the sharp, high-pitched squeal of feedback.

"Hi, everybody. I'm, um, Dylan. Dusty's sister." My hand shook so badly the microphone vibrated in my hand. "For most of my life when I told people that I was Dusty's sister, they'd say, 'Really?! *You're* Dusty's sister?!' And that was, um, annoying, to say the least." A few laughs from the crowd. "There were a lot of times when I didn't want to be Dusty's little sister. I wanted to be me. Just Dylan. But today, I couldn't wait to introduce myself. Because I've got the coolest big sister in the world."

I took a deep breath.

"The first thing everybody notices about Dusty is that she's beautiful. And she is beautiful, she's, like, stupid beautiful in a way that is unfair to everybody else. But that's actually the least important thing about her."

For the first time, I looked over at Dusty. She was beaming at me.

"She's tough. Like, scary tough, sometimes. She will threaten to decapitate all of someone's Barbies, if that someone is Krystal Hooper and she didn't invite you and your best friend to her birthday party."

Heaven raised a hand up high and waved to the crowd from her seat.

"She'll follow through on that threat, too. She's patient enough that she'll let you watch the same Disney movie a thousand times, but spontaneous enough that she'll give you tiger face paint on a random Thursday afternoon just because she thought you could use a little something special for soccer practice. Dusty is also the only person who's ever made me laugh so hard I peed."

Definitely shouldn't have said that. But all these memories of me and Dusty when we were little were flooding back so quickly I couldn't stop them from pouring out of me.

"She's got a wicked sense of humor. But she's never cruel. She's way more forgiving than I am, for example. Dusty believes in giving second chances. Even to people who don't necessarily deserve them."

My gaze landed on Cash Keller in the crowd, and we locked eyes. Hurriedly, I looked away.

"And maybe most important of all, she's loving. She loves

me, and our mom, and, Ronan, she loves you so much."

With an exhalation worthy of an elephant, Ronan blew his nose into a big white hanky. Jamie had been right to bring spares.

"I know you know that, because I can see how much you love her, too. And I know that you love the real her, not the pageant princess version, because with you Dusty's not afraid to take off her tiara and be silly. And those are the moments when I love my sister the best—when she's really and truly herself. And she is totally herself with you."

Movement caught my eye. It was a cameraman, swooping toward me to get a closer shot, giant black lens trained right on my face.

"And it's hard, to be yourself. It takes bravery. Especially when you know the whole world is watching."

In that moment, I realized how I'd become able to ignore the camera—it wasn't because I didn't notice it anymore. It was because I didn't *care*. I was exactly who I was, camera or no. Pamela, and the camera, and everyone back home in Tupelo could watch if they wanted to. It wouldn't change anything about me, or Jamie, or my family. We knew who we were. And looking at Dusty and Ronan, I knew that she knew who she was when she was with him. I swallowed noisily, hoping to keep the prickle of tears at bay.

"Welcome to the family, Ronan. I am so honored to be your wee sister." With regard to his own tears, Ronan was making no such effort. He wept openly and joyously. Dusty patted his back, grinning at him. "To Ronan and Dusty!" I raised my glass. "But to Dusty, especially. After all, today is her special day."

As people clapped, I made my way back to my seat, relieved to be out of the spotlight. My entrée was waiting for me. I looked at it quizzically.

"Is this a tiny chicken?" I asked.

"They're quails," one of the redheaded cousins answered. "Shot right here at Dunyvaig."

No, not the quails! How could this be?! White-faced, I turned to Jamie, who patted my hand sympathetically and handed me another dinner roll. I couldn't believe I was complicit in quail murder.

"Good night, sweet quails," I whispered.

"And flights of angels sing thee to thy rest," Jamie added.

CHAPTER TWENTY-SEVEN

Pamela the dementor appeared behind my seat, clipboard at the ready, to steal us away for photos. I groaned in dismay as I scooted out of my chair. But not before I stuffed that dinner roll in my mouth.

Chewing contentedly, I took Jamie's hand and obediently followed Pamela, with Anne Marie fussing over Kit's shoulder behind us. Pamela led us to the grand sitting room, where Dusty and Ronan posed in front of the fireplace, a photographer clicking away surrounded by those big professional light reflector things like they had on *America's Next Top Model*. I noticed Meemaw snuggled up in a cozy armchair, chatting with Mom, and barreled over to hug her, nearly startling her out of her seat.

"The photos are going to appear exclusively in *People*," Pamela announced, silencing the room, the note of triumph in her voice unmistakable. "No confirm on the cover yet, but fingers crossed. So we'll do some shots with the families, bridesmaids, groomsmen, then Jamie and Dylan for the sidebar."

"What now?" I said as Jamie asked, far more politely, "Sorry?"

"You two are going to be the surprise hit of the special! The love story absolutely no one saw coming! We're doing a sidebar on you two and how love can blossom in the most unlikely places with the most unusual people. Little bit of an ugly duckling transformation with Dylan, Jamie's journey from geek to chic, the whole thing."

"What? No. I—"

"Sounds great, Pamela, cheers," Jamie interrupted me, a restraining hand on my shoulder. "Just play along," he whispered. "I'm an epic blinker. There's no way they'll find a useable photo. Certainly not something that suggests I am now chic."

So I let Pamela maneuver me around into photos, helping Dusty prop up a pretty loose-limbed Anne Marie in the bridesmaids picture, letting Meemaw pinch my cheeks as Dusty and Mom and I towered over her, and laughing as Kit kept trying to arm wrestle Ronan in the big group pictures.

And honestly, taking pictures with just me and Jamie wasn't that bad. It was . . . kind of nice, actually. As I stood with his hands around my waist, trying to smile in the least deranged way possible, I realized with a thump that we would never go to prom together. So we'd have *People* magazine instead of a yearbook. I smiled, for real this time, hoping for one moment preserved forever where Jamie and I were still close enough to touch.

By the time we made it back to our table, the quails were gone, thankfully replaced by a cheese course to which I had no personal connection. I happily dug in, laughing and chatting with Heaven and Jamie and the nearly unintelligible cousins.

"There you are, darling!" I turned to see Jamie's mom,

resplendent in a silver cocktail dress, her husband at her heels. "Can we switch tables? Pretty, pretty please? I cannot endure Florence any longer. She is simply too horrid for words."

"Sorry, Mum," Jamie replied. "I quite like my table, actually."

"Of course you do, with such a charming companion! You look lovely tonight, Dylan, as always!" She aimed air kisses at each of my cheeks. "Now, tell me. Has my darling, obtuse boy invited you to stay yet? I was thinking the Easter holidays. Bakewell in the spring is charming."

"Mum!" Jamie exclaimed.

"Oh, fine, it'll probably piss rain the whole time. James, let's take them to Majorca!" she cried. "Isn't that a much better idea? You'll want to pack your sunnies, Dylan; it can get quite bright."

"Majorca, Margaret?" Jamie's dad asked. "Really?"

"Yes, really. You know my seasonal affective disorder gets quite bad that time of year. It's a medical issue, darling. We *must* go to Majorca."

"If you insist," Jamie's dad said wearily.

"I do. Ooo, is there brie on that cheese plate? Gillecroids, can Mummy have your brie?"

"Absolutely not," Jamie said stiffly. "Eat your own brie."

"How sharper than a serpent's tooth it is to have a thankless child!" Margaret wailed. "Fine, I suppose one can endure Lady Horrible Dunleavy if one must. For brie." She sighed. "Dylan, someone will courier you the Majorca itinerary. À bientôt, darlings."

With a flurry of air kisses, Jamie's parents were gone.

"Majorca?" I asked. "Did your mom just invite me to Majorca?"

"Please tell me there's a Heaven-shaped space in your suit-case," Heaven said.

"Something could quite possibly be arranged." Jamie took a sip of water, the tips of his ears pink.

"That was very, um, nice of her, but you realize this is, like, not normal, right?" I asked in an undertone.

"Nothing about my family is normal," he said ruefully. "But I do hope you can come to Majorca. It's quite lovely."

"I'll keep that in mind."

The wedding flew by at the speed of light, a happy blur of eating and talking. And as much as it annoyed me to admit it, I didn't even mind that Dusty had totally bogarted Christmas Eve. This was just as much fun—maybe even *more* fun—than our usual routine of microwave hot chocolate and Christmas movies on Lifetime. Before I knew it, Dusty and Ronan were cutting the cake—a multi-tiered Funfetti creation. Somehow Dusty had gotten Funfetti in Scotland. Jamie and the redheaded cousins seemed very concerned and confused when Dusty smashed her piece of cake into Ronan's face. Apparently, that was not a tradition over here. Ronan, for his part, just laughed and started eating globs of frosting out of his beard.

I had two pieces of Funfetti and zero pieces of the fruitcake Florence had insisted on for tradition—gross—and was floating away on a cloud of sugar and joy when Jamie approached me.

"You have frosting in your hair," I said dreamily, pushing a dark lock out of his eyes as I attempted to dislodge bits of frosting.

"Want to get out of here?" he asked.

"Sure." Heaven was in the middle of a dance circle, as per

usual, and I was too full of cake for dancing. Or for more cake. "Where are we going?"

"Someplace new, someplace you've never been before at Dunyvaig. And I've got a surprise, too. Something I'm willing to wager you've never had before." He patted a strange bulge under his jacket.

"I'm game."

Jamie kept one hand tucked over the mysterious something, and placed the other on my lower back as he steered me toward the ballroom doors. But just as we were stepping past the dance floor, Cash Keller appeared in our path, looking particularly Brad Pitt–esque in a tuxedo.

"Can I have this dance, kiddo?" he asked.

"No thank you," I said stiffly. Jamie squeezed my hand.

"Come on, Dylan. Cut me a break. Are you going to punish me forever?"

"I'm not *punishing* you," I said. "I don't *know* you."

"Get to know me."

"You're too late," I said simply. "I don't want to know you." As I said it I realized how true it was. I didn't think he was evil, and maybe there was a chance he hadn't come here just to promote himself, but I also didn't want anything from him. Maybe that didn't make me a good person, because I couldn't forgive him the way Dusty could, and clearly had, but it was my choice, and that was the choice I had made. He wasn't my family. He wasn't anything to me. And that was okay.

"It's just a dance, kiddo."

I was about to leave. But then I saw Dusty looking at us, frozen next to the dance floor with a plate of Funfetti cake in her hands. And I thought about what Mom had said in the kitchen—about how his being here meant something to Dusty. And maybe there was a way I could do something meaningful for Dusty, too.

"Fine," I snapped, as Cash Keller practically recoiled with shock. "But this isn't for you."

I walked over to Dusty as Cash followed, grabbed the cake out of her hands, and put it back on the table.

"What are you doing, Dilly?" she hissed as several cameras converged on the scene, clearly expecting something dramatic to go down.

"You told me that Cash is part of who you are. So you want him to be part of today. And I want to, um, support that." I looked back at Cash, and beyond him to Jamie, waiting patiently by the ballroom doors, Cameraman Mike at his side. "So I told Cash I'd dance with him. But only if you dance with us, too."

"Well, that'll look goofy," she said, but I could tell she was happy.

"All of my dancing is goofy."

And yeah, it probably did look goofy, as Cash twirled me and Dusty around the dance floor. I saw Mom watching and hoped she didn't think I'd betrayed her, somehow, that she knew I was doing it for Dusty. By the way she was smiling, I think she did. And damn if Dusty didn't laugh as Cash reminded her of all the times she'd danced on top of his feet when she was little. I could see now, clearly, that there was something there for her that was worth remembering and holding on to. But that didn't mean there had to be something for me to hold on to. Like Mom said—like everyone had said my whole life—Dusty and I were different. Maybe I'd change my mind about Cash one day, but for today, I knew what I wanted. One dance, for Dusty's sake, and then Cash could go back to his life, and I'd go back to mine.

The song ended, and I gave Dusty a big hug.

"Thanks, Dilly," she whispered into my hair.

"Dylan," I said.

"Dylan," she agreed.

I walked over to Jamie without a backward glance in Cash's direction. At least I could say, honestly, now, that I hoped Dusty had a good time with him. I also hoped absolutely zero mentions of his radio show made it on air. I'm not *that* evolved.

Jamie smiled at me as I joined him in the back of the ballroom, and I thought that might be the thing I would miss most—the way Jamie smiled whenever he saw me. Fervently, I wished Cameraman Mike would disappear so I could have one moment alone with Jamie. But then Jamie walked just behind the camera's lens so he was no longer on-screen, slipped a piece of paper out of his jacket, and unfolded it so Cameraman Mike could read it. Thirty seconds later, Cameraman Mike grinned hugely, nodded once, and turned back to film the dance floor.

"Adventure awaits," Jamie said as he pushed open the ballroom doors and we slipped out, no cameras in sight.

"What the hell was on that paper?" I demanded.

"I had to communicate with him without the camera seeing or hearing anything."

"Yeah, I get that. But what was *on* the paper?"

"Some things are better left unknown."

Maybe he was right. So I followed Jamie up the stairs to where most of the rooms were, up another flight of stairs, then another, then down several long halls and around a few corners, and just when I thought it wasn't possible to walk any farther, we stopped in front of a funny little door with a pointed top. Jamie pulled the door open to reveal a spiral stone staircase.

I thought nothing at Dunyvaig could surprise me anymore—after all, the place was chock-full of trapdoors—but this did. Jamie gestured me in, and I climbed the narrow spiral staircase, up and up and up, until we arrived in a small stone room that bore a striking resemblance to Rapunzel's tower. The only thing in it was a window seat with a plump purple cushion, just big enough for two to sit on.

"What is— How is— What is this place?" I asked.

"How much of an architectural history lesson are you up for?"

"Minimal."

"Well. Dunyvaig was originally a castle—fortress—keep, I suppose, quite long ago back in the fourteenth century. Parts of that building still exist, but the bulk of the estate was built in the Georgian era. An addition far larger than the original building."

"So this is part of the medieval castle?"

"Not at all. This was actually built during the Gothic craze of the nineteenth century. That Lord Dunleavy was terribly eccentric. History lesson now over, I swear."

Jamie pulled a bottle of Veuve Clicquot out of his jacket. I gasped.

"This is *very* Humphrey Bogart of you."

"Almost uncomfortably suave, aren't I?" He waggled his eyebrows. "Maybe Pamela was right and I went from geek to chic after all. Regardless, although I usually don't go in for illegal activity, this seemed like the kind of night where it might be necessary to break the rules, just this once."

I covered my eyes and ducked as the champagne cork ricocheted off the wall, the bubbles fizzing over the side of the bottle.

"Damn. I should have brought glasses. Stuck two champagne flutes in my pockets. That really would have put me over the edge into Bogart territory."

"That's okay. I'm not fancy."

"Cheers, then."

He held out the bottle, and I took a swig, the bubbles fizzing on my tongue. It was like nothing I'd ever tasted before—sweet and not sweet all at the same time. I handed the bottle back to Jamie and settled down on the window seat, drawing my knees up under me as I looked out over the grounds in the moonlight. It had stopped snowing, but everything I could see was blanketed in white. It must have been far later than I thought. There was a lightness to the night sky that suggested morning wasn't far away. Jamie sat down next to me on the window seat, resting the champagne at his feet.

"What happens now, Jamie?"

"We keep taking illegal sips of this very expensive champagne and watch the sun rise."

"You know what I mean."

"Ah, well, tomorrow, before we leave for Sandringham, I get your e-mail address. And find you on Facebook. Do you have Skype?" I shook my head. "And then I'll talk you through how to get Skype. Or you can simply google it when you get home. It's not terribly difficult. And it won't be the same. It can't ever be the same. But I can't not talk to you. There will always be things I want to tell you. There is so much more I want to know about your life in Tupelo. I want to hear all about your adventures with Heaven. And anytime you eat something that should never be deep-fried but is unexpectedly delicious."

He grinned, laughter dancing in those startling blue eyes, and I felt an ache deep in my chest, so painful it took my breath away for a moment.

"And if one day," he said seriously, "you e-mail me to say you've a date with a Jayden or a Jackson or a Taylor or some other ghastly American boy, that's all right, too." I punched his arm. It seemed like the only logical response. "I'll probably hide in the bathroom and cry like the big girl's blouse I am, but I'd be happy for you. I'd be insanely jealous in a way that would make Heathcliff look relaxed, but I'd be happy—because I want you to be happy. And this—we—are not, er, viable for the moment. So don't, erm, wait for me. If you were thinking on it. And maybe you weren't. I lost the thread of this speech a bit, didn't I? Damn. I'd written out note cards and everything."

"It was a good speech, Jamie." I squeezed his hand.

"Well. Thank you. And perhaps—perhaps I could come visit?"

"Are you kidding? That would be amazing. You would really come visit?"

"Absolutely. And perhaps you could come visit me as well?"

"According to your mom, I'll be there in April anyway. Or in Majorca."

"Ah, yes, Majorca. No matter where we are, I won't let her torture you, I promise," he said firmly.

"Your mom doesn't *torture* me. It's kind of nice, actually."

"Nice? Her insanity is *nice*?" Jamie asked in disbelief.

"I like her. And I'd love to come visit, but it's probably really expensive, right? I'm not sure . . ."

"You wouldn't have to worry about that, I would—"

"Oh God." I cut him off. "Don't tell me you have a private plane."

"Er, well . . . there are *some* perks to being a prince," he said sheepishly. "Might as well take advantage, hey?"

"I liked you better when you were a peasant," I said.

"I liked you always." He reached out and tucked a strand of hair behind my ears, his hand coming to rest on my cheek.

"I'm not ready to go," I whispered.

"I'll never be ready for you to leave."

Sighing, I maneuvered my way under his arm, snuggling in close to him with my head resting on his shoulder. He stroked my hair gently, like he was afraid I might break. I closed my eyes.

"I could love you, you know," he said softly.

"I know," I replied. "I could love you, too."

The first few rays of sunlight broke over the leafless gray branches of the woods. Orange pierced the gloom, illuminating the sky.

"Happy Christmas, Dylan," Jamie said.

"Happy Christmas, Jamie."

Together, we watched the sun rise.

ACKNOWLEDGMENTS

This book would not exist without the wedding invitation that started it all. Thank you, Becky and Callum, for inviting me to your fairy-tale Scottish wedding. Thank you also to the groomsman who never picked me up at the train station. Those forty-five minutes I spent at the Dunkeld & Birnam station clearly gave me a lot to think about. This book combines so many of my greatest loves—the UK, royalty, pageant queens, and romantic reality television—and I am so grateful to everyone who helped me bring it into the world.

Molly Ker Hawn, thank you for being the greatest agent any author could ask for, and thank you for still representing me even after you saw me for the royals-obsessed American I truly am. I feel so lucky to be part of the Bent Agency family. Your UK authentication help truly went above and beyond the call of duty. Someday I hope we can wear fancy hats at a royal wedding together. And that meat thermometer really did change my life.

Big thanks to everyone at Hyperion and especially to Kieran Viola—it is an honor to be your mini-me. Working with you has been a dream come true—better than anything even Disney could come up with. Your edits are so wonderful somebody should publish *them*. Thank you for making this book so much better than it was, for always seeing the true selves of my characters, and for bringing out the best in them on the page. You are a fairy godmother and an editor in one, which is, in my opinion, the best kind of fairy godmother.

Thank you to Max, my Prince Charming, who always makes me feel like the smartest princess in all the land. I'm so glad our wedding wasn't televised! Dad, sorry I wrote another terrible father—I promise you it isn't personal. Mom, thank you for being just as awesome as Dylan's mom, but for never criticizing my outfits. Finally, thank you to my sister, Ali. A sister *is* a special friend, and I am so #completelyblessed that you are mine. Let's get matching bracelets.

Turn the page for a sneak peek at
Stephanie Kate Strohm's newest romantic read,

Chapter One

Henry

The girl across the aisle was staring at him.

At first, Henry had thought it was an accident. Maybe she'd just looked his way randomly, or maybe he'd imagined it, but it wasn't an accident, and he hadn't imagined it. She was definitely staring at him. Well, maybe *at* him wasn't totally right, but definitely *near* him. Her eyes were fixed somewhere around his hands, which were holding the latest issue of *Lucky Peach* magazine. It was weird.

She hadn't been staring when he'd gotten on the plane. She'd been sitting there first, which made sense, because Henry had been one of the last people in boarding group four to file in. He'd decided that, yes, the mini Oreos *and* the Teddy Grahams were *both* good snack choices, so he'd circled back around to Hudson News to get the Grahams, too, and had almost missed his boarding group.

Henry hadn't noticed the girl because she was pretty—even though she was. At first he'd just seen a white girl around his age sitting across the aisle from him, but when he looked again, he'd noticed her crazy-big brown eyes and the thick toffee-colored braid resting on one shoulder. It was the exact same color as the peanut butter toffee Henry had gotten once at the Wicker Park Farmers Market and had never been able to find again. But he'd noticed her because she was just sitting. Calmly. Patiently. Like she was waiting for something. Not on her phone or on an iPad or flipping through a magazine like almost everyone else he'd passed, but just sitting there. She was still sitting, but now she was staring at him. Well, near him.

Henry tried to wedge himself farther into the aisle, trying to get away from the people next to him. Yes, his elbow had been bumped by the flight attendants twice already, but a bruised elbow was vastly preferable to what was going on next to him in 22A and 22B.

"We're on our honeymoon!" 22A and 22B had announced proudly, Mrs. 22B waving a giant diamond inches from Henry's nostrils. They had then proceeded to practically merge into one person, giggling and kissing, and now Henry was the unwilling third wheel in their relationship.

Man. Eight hours was a long flight no matter what the circumstances, but being stuck next to 22A and 22B was truly cruel and unusual. It wasn't the longest flight Henry had been on—that had been when his family had gone on vacation to Hawaii, and that had *also* been an excruciating trip. His little sister, Alice, had won "Halfway to Hawaii" and wouldn't stop gloating about the bag of chocolate-covered macadamia nuts she'd been awarded as a prize for correctly guessing the exact time their flight hit the halfway point. She hadn't let Henry eat any of them, and she'd eventually left them in the back seat of their rental car, where they fused into one giant melted nutty chocolate blob. Mom threw the bag out. On the flight back to Chicago, when Henry had fallen asleep on the plane, Alice had drawn purple zoo animals all over his arms. In marker.

But in eight hours, he'd presumably be purple marker–free— unless 22A and 22B had other tricks up their sleeves besides surviving without oxygen—and he'd be in Paris. *Paris.* Henry still couldn't believe he was really going to Paris. And not just going to Paris on vacation, but to study there. To live there. To *cook* there. For the next nine months, Henry wouldn't be just another random Chicago junior. He'd be a chef-in-training at the École Denis Laurent, the most prestigious cooking program for high school students on the planet. It still sounded unreal when he thought about it, like some place that couldn't possibly exist, but it *was* real, and he was going. Henry couldn't wait to trade the brown rice and *bulgogi* he served at his parents' restaurant for *boeuf bourguignon* and *béchamel.* There wasn't anything wrong with bulgogi—he was just ready for something different.

Henry wouldn't miss standing behind the register all weekend, every weekend, but he'd miss the kitchen. His earliest memories were of sitting on the counter, swinging his legs. "Taste," Dad would say, and Henry would open his mouth, for a meltingly rich mouthful of pork belly, or the sweet tang of pickled carrots, or the salty brine of a still-raw shrimp. It was Dad who taught Henry to eat, and then to cook. Because you have to know how to eat before you can know how to cook.

So Dad was the first person Henry told about the program in Paris, when he'd discovered that Chef Laurent took twenty high school juniors to live and train at his cooking school every year. Henry had pulled up the website excitedly, heart hammering in his chest like he'd found a lottery ticket on the sidewalk. And in a way, he kind of had. The website was full of the accolades of graduates of the program, graduates who had James Beard nominations and featured spots at the Food & Wine Classic in Aspen and well-reviewed restaurants that Henry recognized by name alone, the kind of places you'd have to book a reservation a year in advance. The kind of place that Henry dreamed of running someday. The kind of place Henry *could* run, once his year at the École guaranteed him a stage—kind of like an internship—in any kitchen he wanted and ensured his future. Henry could still feel Dad's hand on his shoulder, almost an electric current running between them as they checked out the website together.

Dad loved Chef Laurent. Maybe even more than Henry did. "The only person on the Food Network who's still cooking," he'd say proudly, like Chef Laurent was his other son. Henry and Dad watched a lot of Food Network. Mom had no patience for it. "The last thing I'd ever want to watch is other people cooking," she liked to say, shaking her head in disbelief. "Don't we see enough of that every day?"

Mom liked crime procedurals. Henry didn't understand how watching people get chopped up and stashed in boxes was more relaxing that watching Chef Laurent sweat some onions in his bright French farmhouse kitchen, but sometimes Henry felt like there was a lot he didn't understand about his mom.

"You don't have to go, you know." That's what she'd said. What she'd chosen to say after Henry had tried to hug Alice— she'd acquiesced half-heartedly—as his family stood on the sidewalk by the departures drop-off at O'Hare Airport, when they were supposed to be saying good-bye. Like Henry was just going to turn around and get back in the car. Like this wasn't everything he'd ever wanted.

She'd tried to backpedal, to say that even if he did go, it could just be a thing he did that looked great for college. That he didn't have to be a chef. She didn't want Henry "trapped in a restaurant for the rest of his life"—her words, not his. Henry didn't understand how someone who had knowingly married a chef could take such a dim view of running a restaurant, but as Mom liked to say, you didn't run a restaurant, it ran you. Mom wanted Henry to do something, anything, that didn't involve chopping vegetables. Henry was pretty sure Mom would prefer he cultivate a career cleaning up toxic waste—provided he had a degree from a four-year college. And preferably if he wore a suit while doing so.

This wasn't the first time they'd had this fight, and it wouldn't be the last. He knew it would come back over and over, like the refrain in that awful cello piece Alice wouldn't stop practicing. What would it take, he wondered, to get Mom on board? The École hadn't been enough. A stage at Alinea? A James Beard Award? A Food Network show of his own? Cookbooks with his face on them and kitchen utensils with his name on them and a fast casual restaurant in O'Hare? Whatever it was, he'd do it. And then she'd see.

Henry flipped to the next page in his magazine, and the girl gasped, loud enough that he heard her over the drone of the engine and the sucking noises of 22A and 22B. He looked up, and they made eye contact, and the girl blushed the exact same color as the end-of-season raspberries he'd bought from Mick Klug Farms at the farmers' market the Sunday before he left. Why was everything about this girl making him think about food? He must not have bought enough plane snacks.

"I'm so sorry," she said, although her voice was so quiet, it was more of a whisper. "Oh my gosh. I'm so sorry."

Henry stifled a laugh at "oh my gosh." He couldn't remember the last time he'd heard someone say "gosh."

"It's okay," he said.

"No. No it's not. Oh my gosh."

"Seriously. No worries."

"I was reading over your shoulder, and that was rude, and creepy, probably, and I definitely shouldn't have been. I really am sorry."

"It's fine. Really. Stop apologizing."

"Sorry," she said again. "I mean—not sorry. Sorry. Argh!" she exclaimed. "Saying sorry for saying sorry is like that snake eating its tail. You can't get out of it. It's linguistic quicksand."

They looked at each other, and Henry was struck again by her eyes—the exact color of tempered chocolate. Perfectly tempered chocolate. Again with the food? What was *wrong* with him? He must have been hungry. Too hungry. He reached into the open bag of mini Oreos in his seatback pocket, grabbed a fistful, and shoved them in his mouth.

Mistake. He started chewing madly, but the Oreo mass seemed unconquerable. The girl probably thought he was crazy. Why couldn't he swallow these Oreos? How were there so many of them? Henry chewed in panic as he contemplated the girl. What should he do now? He should offer her some. Right? Definitely. It was only the polite thing to do. Otherwise, he was being rude *and* gross.

He held the bag out across the aisle. He smiled, then realized there was almost no way his teeth *weren't* decorated by a fine coat of Oreo crumbs and quickly closed his lips. Henry was leering like the Grinch with chipmunk cheeks full of Oreos, and he had never felt more stupid. But he must not have looked entirely deranged, because, tentatively, the girl reached her hand in, and took out exactly three mini Oreos. Like a normal person.

Finally, Henry swallowed and cast about desperately for a new conversation topic. He jammed the Oreos back into his seat pocket—fat chance of him eating those again anytime soon—and looked down at his magazine. His magazine! That was a thing they could talk about.

"Wow." Henry whistled. "That's quite a cake. I would have gasped too."

Henry had never seen a person literally light up before, but that's what this girl did. And now *he* was staring. Which he definitely needed to stop immediately. So Henry looked down at his magazine again. It *was* quite a cake. Three layers of cake interspersed with layers of jam and frosting—no, not frosting, lemon cheesecake, according to the caption—and topped with pickled strawberry icing and a ring of what looked like crumbled cookies. The sides were exposed so they could see every delicious layer.

"It—it's Christina Tosi, isn't it?" she said shyly. "The exposed sides of the cake. That's her thing. And the milk crumbs on top. I recognize them, from the *Momofuku Milk Bar* cookbook."

Henry looked closer—she was right. They weren't cookies.

"Milk crumbs?" he asked, trying to imagine what a milk crumb could be.

"They're made with milk powder and white chocolate. Really good. You're not supposed to eat them on their own, I don't think, they mostly go in or on other things, but they're so good I always save a few to snack on. What flavor's the cake?"

"Strawberry lemon." Henry was staring at her again. He'd never seen someone's face look like that when talking about pastry before. Not even his dad when he talked about the cinnamon buns at Ann Sather.

"Mmm. Strawberry lemon. That sounds good. That one's not in the cookbook. I've only made the apple pie cake and the birthday cake, of course. I make that one every year for Owen's birthday. My brother," she clarified. "Although . . ." She chewed her lip distractedly. "I'm not sure what he's gonna do this year. His birthday's in November. Maybe Mom will make him the Funfetti cake. You know, from the mix. Like I did. Before I knew about Christina Tosi."

She went back to chewing on her lip. Henry hadn't known that someone chewing on her lip could be quite so distracting.

"You can have it," he blurted out.

"What?" she asked.

"The magazine. You can have my magazine." Henry held it out across the aisle eagerly. Too eagerly.

"Oh, no, I couldn't—"

"Please—"

"No, I can't—"

"Take it." He shook it at her insistently. It was suddenly incredibly, vitally important that the girl take his magazine. "Take it. Please take it."

"I—I— When you're done reading it," she said firmly. "It's *Lucky Peach*, right? I've never seen a paper copy before. I've only read it online."

Henry nodded and put the magazine back on his tray table,

wondering how he could possibly read it knowing she would have it after him. What if he left a sweat print? What if there were chocolate stains on the earlier pages? Had he *drooled* into his magazine, somehow? Who knew what horrors he'd left behind, lurking within those innocent pages? Was there an embarrassing way to read a magazine? Probably. And he'd probably been doing it the whole time.

"I just have one question—sorry."

Henry looked up, and the girl smiled at him apologetically. Henry smiled back, probably in a lame way. Why was everything he did so *lame*?

"Just one question before I let you finish reading. Sorry. I mean, I'm not sorry." She cleared her throat and shook her head. "I'm just curious. Does it say if she used an offset spatula to ice the top layer? Ateco, I'm assuming? Did it say what size the blade is?"

And that was the moment Henry started to worry that he might have fallen in love.

Chapter Two

Rosie

Rosie couldn't remember the last time she'd talked to a boy she didn't know. She'd known every guy in her class since kindergarten, or earlier. And sure, it wasn't like East Liberty was so small that Rosie recognized every single person who browsed next to her in the aisles at Walmart, but she recognized a lot of them. Rosie couldn't run an errand or grab a pop somewhere or even walk down to the mailbox without being stopped for a "How's your mom?" or a "When's that brother of yours gonna stop playing soccer and start kicking for the football team?" Didn't matter which brother. They were convinced that any one of Rosie's four brothers was the missing piece that would guarantee East Liberty's long-awaited championship win. Even Owen, and he was still years away from high school.

Maybe that's why Rosie was so nervous, talking to this boy. Maybe that was why she'd apologized so many times. And said *gosh* way too many times, just like her nana. Rosie was never nervous talking to any of the boys at school, not even when Brady Gill had asked her to homecoming last year, and he was a year older. But she'd known him because he played soccer with Cole and Ricky, her older brothers, and there was nothing particularly exciting or nerve-wracking about talking to him. The boys at school were taller than they'd been in kindergarten, sure, and some of them had developed muscles they definitely hadn't had when they were five, but other than that? They were pretty much the same.

But this boy was a surprise. The *Lucky Peach* magazine was intriguing, of course, but Rosie also found herself fascinated by *him*. He was so hot she almost couldn't look directly at him, but found herself staring at the most random things, like the short-trimmed dark hairs at the nape of his neck as he bent over to read. And the straight line of his forearms when he pushed up his sleeves. And his long, tapered fingers with cut-short nails, crisscrossed by faded burns and the scarred mementoes of cuts long gone. Not unlike her fingers, actually.

His hands. The magazine. Rosie realized with a sudden jolt, a jolt that inexplicably caused her pulse to speed up and a distinctly uncomfortable, clammy feeling to start at her temples and spread toward her neck, that this boy was almost definitely heading to Paris for Chef Laurent's École. He had to be, right? She'd only seen hands like that on the guys who worked at Cracker Barrel with Mom. They were chef's hands.

The man sitting next to Rosie shifted as the baby in his arms stirred in his sleep. The baby, all fat rosy cheeks and a soft blond crown of hair, drooled prolifically onto his dad's collar. Rosie thought, with a pang, of Owen, her youngest brother. Most of her earliest memories were of Owen as a baby, how fascinated she'd been by this chubby pink creature with his endless supplies of drool. Not unlike this baby.

The parents had apologized, profusely, as they'd filed into the seats next to Rosie, diaper bags and sippy cups swinging from every available appendage. "You're stuck with us!" the mom had chorused, as the dad announced, formally, "Congratulations. You've officially lost the airplane lottery. An international flight with an eleven-month-old." Rosie had waved off their apologies. She'd been babysitting for so long, she was pretty sure there was nothing this baby could do that would bother her. Honestly, she was *glad* to be sitting next to the baby. He'd distracted her.

Before the family had arrived, Rosie had been sitting in her seat almost paralyzed with fear. Not so much because she thought the plane would crash—not really—but because she just didn't know *what* would happen, what it would feel like when the plane took off, how *she* would feel, hurtling through the air thousands and thousands of feet into the sky. And it was that not knowing that Rosie hated. That was why she loved baking. Baking was all knowing. If you followed the recipe, you got exactly what you intended. An apple pie never surprisingly turned into lemon meringue halfway through the baking process.

Maybe it was that not knowing that had sent Rosie's stomach into a tailspin of anxiety on the five-hour drive to the airport in Chicago. What did she know about France, really? Aside from the food? Appallingly little. Maybe that was why she was having such a hard time imagining it, or believing that this was really happening, that she'd really be living in another country in a matter of hours. When she tried to picture herself in Paris, alone, all she could conjure up was a mental image of herself walking down foggy cobblestone alleyways, wearing a beret, even though Rosie was pretty sure she didn't have the kind of head shape to pull off hats.

It was funny—for almost as long as she could remember, Rosie had been desperate to get out of East Liberty. Desperate to be somewhere that things were different—somewhere that people didn't know everything about her. Or think that they knew everything about her.

But when it was actually time to go, it was a lot harder to leave than she'd thought it would be. Rosie had thought she'd be racing into the airport terminal, tearing straight toward an adventure that smelled like butter and sugar. But Rosie hadn't raced anywhere. Hugging Cole, then Ricky, then Reed, then Owen, and then Mom good-bye, she'd swallowed back the uncomfortable prickling of tears against the back of her throat. No crying. Not today. This was everything Rosie wanted.

When her mother had first told her about the École, Rosie had been lying on her stomach in bed, watching old clips of Chef Laurent's first TV show, *Laurent du Jour*, on YouTube. Mom had knocked on her bedroom door, and Rosie hadn't even looked up when she came in, hadn't looked up until her mother had dropped a packet of papers right next to her.

"Chef Laurent, Rosie," Mom had said.

Her mom knew all about Rosie's Chef Laurent obsession. Well, *Rosie* wouldn't call it an obsession—but everyone else did. She did own all of his cookbooks and read his blog religiously and watched all of his shows—the ones currently on the air and the ones she could only find online. So maybe she was a little obsessed. Which didn't even really make sense, because he wasn't even a pastry chef, like Rosie wanted to be. But there was something about him, the way he casually tossed off jokes in the kitchen as easily as he flipped a crêpe, something that made Rosie feel warm and safe, like she was sitting right there at the table with him, about to tuck into a perfect roast chicken or a *salade Lyonnaise*. But the idea that she could *actually* be in the same kitchen as Chef Laurent was something she didn't even know how to process.

Rosie had read the application six times right then, with her mom next to her, squeezing her hand excitedly. She'd read it again when she woke up in the morning. When she came home from school. Every night before she went to sleep. She read it so many times that she had all the questions memorized. Had all her theoretical answers memorized. She could have taken a quiz on it, could have recited that application as a dramatic monologue. But she hadn't applied. For weeks, she hadn't applied.

Rosie was more of a pastry chef than a chef, she argued with herself. They probably wouldn't want someone who was primarily interested in baking, since the program was mostly cooking. But Rosie *did* cook, all the time, and just because she wanted to be a pastry chef one day didn't mean she didn't want to learn how to cook from *Chef Laurent*, in *Paris*.

The idea of being so far away both terrified and thrilled her. But at least it made her feel *something*.

"You miss one hundred percent of the shots you don't take."

Wayne Gretzky had said it first. But Cole said it all the time. And Dad had said it, too. Rosie heard it, then, in Dad's voice, as she sat in front of her computer in her darkened bedroom, staring at the application the night before it was due. And

Rosie knew that she had taken very few shots in the sixteen years she'd been on this planet. And then she thought of Mom, finding the application, printing it out, probably hoping that Rosie would do something besides sit in her room, reading cookbooks and watching old cooking shows on YouTube. And Rosie wanted to do more than that, too. Almost as if Rosie's fingers were moving of their own accord, she filled out the application with the answers she'd had memorized for months, and she clicked SUBMIT.

The baby stirred in his sleep, bringing Rosie back to the plane. He fluttered his hand like a small pink starfish, opened his eyes briefly, looked at her, then closed them again, heavy.

Rosie was having a hard time imagining life without her brothers. What would it be like? Not to be "one of the Radeke kids" or "the Radeke girl," but just to be Rosie? Her teachers at the École wouldn't call her Cole's sister or Ricky's sister. They'd just call her Rosie. This was uncharted territory, and Rosie was surprised to find herself feeling less excited and more unmoored by the prospect than she thought she'd be.

Hoping to ground herself, Rosie closed her eyes and thought of butter, the way other people probably pictured relaxing tropical idylls. Her favorite thing in the world was creaming butter and sugar, watching the way two disparate ingredients came together to form something new. She could picture it in her mind, back in the kitchen at home: the soft pale yellow of the butter, the old wooden spoon, and the cracked brown mixing bowl. Butter was magic. The starting point for cookies and cake and pie and muffins and everything good.

"I'm finished."

Rosie had been so lost in her thoughts she'd stopped staring at the boy and was almost surprised to see him there, holding the magazine across the aisle.

"I'm Rosie," she blurted out.

"Henry." He grinned. "Not, you know, finished."

"Ha." She'd spoken the word—*ha*—instead of actually laughing.

"Please, spare me the pity laugh."

"It wasn't a pity laugh. It was just . . . strange." *Just strange?!* What a weird thing to say. *She* was *just strange.*

"Do you, um, do you still want it?" The magazine sagged a bit in his hand.

"Yes. Please."

She placed it carefully on her tray table, and then the lights went out, plunging the cabin into a soft darkness that Rosie guessed meant it was time to sleep.

"Crap," Henry muttered. "I guess you can, uh, turn the light on."

Rosie pressed the button above her head with the little light bulb icon. A beam of light that could have been used as a highway flare illuminated her seat. Embarrassed, she turned it off again.

"That's okay," Rosie said quickly. It seemed rude to have her light on, even if the family next to her had been sleeping since the flight attendants had announced they'd reached cruising altitude.

"They have the lights there for a reason. It's *your* light. You can turn it on."

"I should probably sleep anyway," Rosie said, hoping Henry didn't hear any reluctance in her voice. "Here." She slid the magazine off her tray table. "You can have it back."

"Nah. Don't worry about it." Henry pressed a button, and his seat reclined. He stretched, his arms almost grazing the call button for the flight attendant. "Keep it. I read it already."

"I can't keep it." Rosie shook her head firmly.

"It's a gift. From one member of row twenty-two to another."

"I can't take a gift from you. I don't know you."

"Sure you do. I'm Henry."

He smiled, and Rosie felt an unfamiliar, swoony feeling, almost like when she flipped through the glossy pages of a brand-new cookbook, but better. He was even cuter when he smiled, and at that moment, Rosie would have done anything to keep him smiling—at *her*.

"I'm going to return this," Rosie said, but she tucked it into her seatback pocket all the same. "Once I've read it. Tomorrow morning. Or whenever they turn the lights on. I'm reading it, and then I'm giving it back to you."

"Boy, Christmas must be really rough in your house. Did you give Santa a hard time like this, too?"

"Santa's not real."

"NO." Henry catapulted his chair up to its full upright position, jaw open and eyes full of betrayal. "SANTA'S NOT REAL?!"

"Shhh!" Rosie admonished him, but she found, again, that she was smiling. She couldn't even remember the last time she'd smiled quite so much in such a short time. "You'll wake up the baby."

"Yeah, that baby's really about to lose it."

Rosie looked over. Baby and Dad were passed out with matching expressions, jaws hanging open as their heads lolled.

"And who's gonna traumatize that baby more?" Henry asked.

"Me, waking him up? Or you, telling him Santa's not real?"

"I don't think he's verbal."

"When his first words are 'Santa's not real,' you're really going to feel like a terrible human being."

"I'm going to sleep now," Rosie announced. Reaching down, she grabbed the small pillow—what an odd texture the pillowcase had—and pulled a fleece blanket and a sleep mask out of a plastic bag. "And then in the morning I'm reading your magazine, and then I'm giving it back to you."

"Oh you are, are you?" Henry wadded up his own pillow by his neck. "How will you even find me? What if I disappear into the streets of Paris and you never see me again? Kind of thwarts your magazine plans, huh?"

"Well, Henry," Rosie said, "I think I'll be able to find you. I'm going the same place you are."